To Dawn

THE THINGS IN HEAVEN AND EARTH

Happy Reading,
And Thanks!!!

MICHAEL SCOTT HOPKINS

Black Rose Writing | Texas

The author grants the final approval for this literary material.

First printing

This is a work of fiction. Names, characters, businesses, places, events, and incidents are either the products of the author's imagination or used in a fictitious manner. Any resemblance to actual persons, living or dead, or actual events is purely coincidental.

ISBN: 978-1-68433-711-8
PUBLISHED BY BLACK ROSE WRITING
www.blackrosewriting.com

Printed in the United States of America
Suggested Retail Price (SRP) $19.95

The Things in Heaven and Earth is printed in Sabon

*As a planet-friendly publisher, Black Rose Writing does its best to eliminate unnecessary waste to reduce paper usage and energy costs, while never compromising the reading experience. As a result, the final word count vs. page count may not meet common expectations.

This novel was not a novel, just a fragment of an idea sketched out in two dusty chapters languishing on my hard drive. That is until my good friend and fellow writer Kelly Capriotti Burton convinced me I had to finish it. So, for Kelly, with gratitude.

And for my wonderful wife, Carla, the world's best proofreader and my constant companion on the road. She was with me over every mile and to all the places that inspired the settings in *The Things in Heaven and Earth*, from Seneca, Illinois, to Devils Tower, Wyoming. Moreover, she forgave me for almost getting her killed riding the big bike up Pikes Peak.

Finally, for Jeff O'Dell, who has shared every kind of crazy riding adventure with me on the road. More than once, we had to choose between certain death and probable death. Fortunately, we always found a way to pick probable death and managed to cheat even that by the skin of our teeth.

THE THINGS IN
HEAVEN AND EARTH

Mine has been an unhappy life. That in itself doesn't make me unique. Tragedy strikes even the most spirited among us, and sorrow surely follows. But I am the bringer of tragedy. I am a conduit for death. Those who seek the source of sorrow need look no farther than where I stand. It grieves me to be this thing, yet here I am. But I am more than that, too. I am human. I enjoy the warmth of the summer sun against my skin and the sight of grass rustling in the wind. I live in the beauty of the tactile world and wish, as much as I can, to be a part of it. So, I am two things, of two minds. I have managed, most of the time, to divide the dark from the light.

Until now...

CHAPTER 1

On a day in July, two years ago, I was perfectly content. It was midday, sunny and unbearably hot. I like it unbearably hot. I glided along I-80 with my feet comfortably resting on the highway pegs of my Harley, one of the big baggers made for going long distances and enjoying the countryside. There was nothing more troubling in my life at that moment than a few stray clouds overhead, and even those were pleasing shapes to break up an otherwise solid blue sky.

I was about sixty miles west of Chicago, heading another five hundred miles or so, I estimated, west. I saw the exit for Route 47 up ahead, took it, and shot down a short distance into Morris, Illinois, finding Route 6. I turned on 6 and kept west for a while, until I encountered the first decent curve I'd seen in hours. I leaned into it and hit the throttle. The bike's engine roared and pulled me through the turn. In a happy coincidence, Johnny Cash singing "I've Been Everywhere" shuffled up onto the stereo, and I rocked my feet on the pegs to the beat.

I knew I was smiling. The darkness was barely perceptible. It was a good day.

More miles slipped by. A small town opened up ahead, and I thought of stopping to eat. I passed a bar and grill crowded with motorcycles in the parking lot. It looked like an outside joint with the action taking place in back, out of view. With all the bikes, I figured there wouldn't be any locals to speak of, and locals were what I was looking for. So, I rode by and into the next town. It was much like the one I'd just passed. Old.

I saw vestiges of former affluence, 150-year-old homes, ornate and nestled high above the rest of the town. These homes stood atop a steep incline that rose up sharply behind retaining walls to overlook the more modest dwellings of the town. I saw they were grand houses once, and some remained so, lovingly kept in historical condition. Others suffered from ill-considered improvements, aluminum siding and haphazard additions. On the lower ground, down the hill, homes stood that lacked the size and grandeur of those on the high ground. It occurred to me that the moneyed homes up the hill were unlikely to be touched by floodwaters when the river rose, but the houses below were sure to have been inundated at times, standing as they were so close to the Illinois River. Yet many appeared to be as old as the grand houses above, a testament to the determination their owners had had to persevere. No cookie cutter tract homes these, but individual houses with distinct personalities, each built to reflect its owners' will.

"There can be no end to the stories to be told about a place like this," I reflected.

I turned left down the main street where brick buildings of the old downtown remained, currently housing small shops and grills. Faded ads adorned the brick walls, barely visible enticements for products and businesses that had long passed into memory. This was what I wanted.

It was just shy of 2 p.m. The street was dead. I had my pick of open parking spaces and backed into one. I saw there were at least three small eateries on this side of the street. I walked up the sidewalk and peered into the first two. Despite the "Open" signs on their doors, I didn't see a soul in either. In the third, I found a group of grizzled old men sitting at a table and knocking back a few beers.

Perfect.

I went in and sat at the bar. A woman smiled at me from behind the counter. I guessed she was twenty years older than I was, maybe sixty, but you had to look hard to see it. She dyed her hair red, but I could see that was the color it had probably been when she was younger. I thought she was quite attractive. I wasn't the kind of man who could let someone fall in love with him, but I put it in the back of my mind that, depending on how things went, I could see myself spending a lazy evening with this woman, laughing and making love.

"Something to eat today, Hun?" she asked.

"You bet," I answered.

"Need a menu?"

"Naw. A cheeseburger and fries would be fine. Nothing fancy."

She pulled out her order book and wrote on the ticket.

"To drink?"

"Just a Coke."

She wrote it down and looked quizzically at me.

"Do I know you from somewhere, Hun?"

"You might," I answered. This was what I was looking for. "I've written a couple books. My picture is on the jacket covers. I'm on TV some, too. Interviews and such."

"Oh, my," she pretended to be impressed. I figured she was considering whether to make sport of me. "A celebrity."

I laughed, to show I would be good-humored about any ribbing I might take. I saw that she wore no nametag. Of course, she wouldn't need one in a place like this. Everyone here would know her name. Except me.

"No, not a celebrity. Not at all," I said. "What's your name?"

"Carol, Hun. And you are?"

"Nash. Nash Baxter."

"Hmmm," Carol said, looking up and feigning an attempt at recognition. After a moment, she concluded, "Nope. Can't say I've heard of you."

She had a slight smile that intrigued me. She *was* making sport of me to be sure, but there was no malice in it.

"Well, like I said, I'm not a celebrity. Just a writer."

"Hmmm."

Carol walked out from behind the bar and to the kitchen, where she hung my order up for the cook. She came back and poured my Coke.

"What kind of books do you write?" she asked. Then, without waiting for the answer, she called out to the men sitting at the table, "Hey, fellas! We got a writer in here today."

The men glanced briefly at Carol, then went back to talking among themselves.

"They don't read much," Carol whispered.

I decided I definitely liked this woman.

"They're just not impressed at all," I whispered back. "I write books about ghosts."

"What?"

"You asked me what kind of books I write. I write books about ghosts."

"Ghosts?"

"Ghosts and hauntings," I smiled. "I try to prove they don't exist."

"Well," Carol said, "you'd probably run into some folks around here who would disagree with you."

"I don't doubt it. This is an old town. Lots of stories, I'm sure."

"Oh, that and then some," Carol told me.

"Do you know about any local ghost stories I might be interested in?"

"Don't be silly," Carol winked. "There's no such thing as ghosts."

I sipped my Coke and smiled.

"You're playing hard to get, Carol."

"It's what I'm best at, Hun," she winked again. "That's why I'm still a career woman after all these years."

"I see," I grinned. "So, how might an itinerant writer drag the local lore out of this place?"

"Ghost lore, you mean?"

"Mostly. Or whatever history is interesting about the place."

"And you'll put whatever you hear in one of your books?"

"Might. Depends on what I hear."

"Well, why don't you buy a round of beers for those fellas at the table over there and sidle up a bit," Carol said. "They might have a story or two for you."

"Think it will work?"

"At the very least, I'll sell more beer," Carol laughed.

I accepted the challenge and stood, facing the table where the men sat. There were five of them, all over seventy, I thought.

"Gentlemen," I said. "Mind if I buy you a round of beers and sit with you a while?"

"Piss off," one of the men said. He was big, tall, and obese. He wore faded overalls and a John Deere ball cap. He had an unkempt beard and wore reading glasses on the end of his nose. The other men laughed. I laughed, too. I'd learned it was the best approach.

"Okay, two rounds," I countered.

The big man peered at me over his glasses.

"All right then," he said. "You know our price. So have a seat."

"Thanks. What are you drinking?"

"Carol knows."

I sat, and Carol brought a pitcher to the table. The big man looked at me and said, "Time was when it cost as many as five rounds to sit with this crew."

"We got old," one of the other men said. "Ain't so pretty as we used to be."

"Speak for yourself," another said. "I still get prettier every day."

I laughed. "Well, I never started out pretty, so I usually have to guarantee several pitchers of beer before folks will let me sit with them. You guys are a genuine bargain."

The big man held out his hand and said, "Jack's the name."

I took Jack's hand and shook it. The other men introduced themselves, and I shook each of their hands in turn.

"I actually did see you on TV just last week," Jack said. "So, we was playin' hard to get. You could have sat with us for one beer. Hell, we might even've bought you one."

"Lesson learned," I smiled. "So, you probably saw the interview on Sunday morning."

"Yep," Jack said. "Real network stuff. You're the Ghost Rider."

"Yeah, that's what the host called me," I winced. "Maybe he didn't know that's the name of a comic book character. Or maybe that was the point. I hope it doesn't stick in any event. Kinda describes what I do though."

"This guy," Jack explained to his friends, "rides a Harley all over the country, from one haunted house to the next, and writes books about them."

"Well, only two books, so far," I told the men. "Working on the third, which is what brings me here."

"Wait a minute," said another one of the men, also named Jack. He was skinny, and his arms bore a legion of tattoos, all dark green remnants of images that had blurred over the years, from whatever they had been into what looked like indeterminate landmasses on an old map. "Fuck the shit about ghosts – you found a way to make a living while riding your Harley?"

"Sure did," I laughed. "Neat trick, that."

"I'll say," the second Jack exclaimed. "I had me a '65 Electra Glide. Got it brand fucking new when I got out of the Army. Last panhead they made. Rode the shit out of that fucker, every goddamned place. Loved it. Took me from Florida, all through the Midwest, and to all points on the west coast. I rode the whole Pacific Coast Highway back then. One foggy, cold ass bitch, that was. But, Jesus, she was pretty. Ocean to the left, roaring waves, wind, and spray. And the prettiest damned landscape you ever saw to the right. Did you ever ride through them redwoods?"

Second Jack didn't wait for me to answer, but continued in a uniquely crude and wistful fashion, "Holy shit, fucking unbelievable, that's what that was. Don't think my eyes ever set on the center of the highway. Just kept looking back and forth. Thought I was in fucking heaven. Rode that way for two years, no matter what the weather was like. Saw everything you could ever want to see."

Second Jack paused and took a sip of his beer before continuing, "I'd still be on that sonofabitch if I could have figured out a way to actually make a living while I was doing it. It wasn't like them old TV shows where the hero rode his happy ass into town and found a job to keep him flush for a couple of weeks, 'til he got tired of it and rode his ass into the next town, to do it all over again. I got some work here and there, but not much. Not enough to keep me flush. I was just an outsider fucking biker degenerate far as any employers was concerned. Yeah, me a fucking degenerate. I was police chief in this very town for thirty years. Not many degenerates end up being chief of police."

Second Jack sighed. "Anyway, I ended up broke and having to sell that bike for a song. Had to hitchhike back home here."

"Sorry to hear it," I said. "But that must have been one great adventure."

"Yeah," First Jack said. "And we heard every bit of it a thousand times over in the last forty years or so. Stories don't always come out the same, neither. The way he tells it, he got every pretty girl in the sack three times over on that trip, just 'cause he was on a Harley."

"All true," Second Jack said. "And they ain't the same stories told different. Just did so much shit, lots of different stories sound kinda the same, so fuck you, Jack!"

The men had a rhythm in the way they talked to each other. Old friends whose insults were ritual. It was the kind of company I enjoyed. Their banter danced around in my brain and conjured up lines that would describe my observations about the men, lines I intended to pound out on my laptop at the next hotel.

Carol brought my burger. She placed her hand on my shoulder as she leaned over to set the plate in front of me. She let her hand linger for a moment, then she stroked the back of my neck briefly before heading back to the bar, making me think I might have a decent shot at that lazy evening I'd imagined earlier. I decided I'd spend a little one-on-one time talking to her after I finished my conversation with Jack's crew, to see if I could clinch the deal.

I ate while the men told stories to each other and laughed. First Jack's observation about Second Jack's stories was probably true about every story told here – each likely to have been told in any number of variations around this table over the years. But the men listened and commented like every tale was freshly told. I absorbed it all, finding the men's company akin to a particular ambiance, a quality of light or sound that triggered something in the soul.

I finished eating. I could sit and listen all day, I figured, but I had an agenda. This was my office, my workspace. There were things I needed out of these men, so I interjected and turned the conversation in the direction I wanted.

"So, here's what I've heard so far," I said, leaning back in my chair and wiping my mouth with a napkin. "You guys have lived in this town your whole lives mostly. Big Jack here was a farmer. . ."

"Not 'was'," First Jack corrected. "I *am* a farmer. Just let my boys do all the work now."

"That's right, you lazy fuck," Second Jack laughed.

"And you, Jack," I continued, smiling at Second Jack and summing up his boisterous tales, "were probably the most foul-mouthed chief of police the town ever had."

"Best one, too," Second Jack laughed. "Didn't take no shit from degenerates like me."

"Didn't take shit or *do* shit," First Jack added.

"My point being, gentlemen," I said, "if there is any lore about ghostly incidents or such in this town, you guys would certainly know about it."

"We would at that," Tom, who sat at the far side of the table, said. "In fact, there's a house down by the river. A big house. An old colonial. Real creepy. You get the chills just looking at the place."

"Oh, yeah," Second Jack added. "That's the house where one of the kids murdered his whole family one night. Shot them all dead."

"That was back in '72 or so, wasn't it, Jack?" Tom asked.

"Sure was," Second Jack answered. First Jack groaned and rolled his eyes.

"Jack here was chief by then," said Tom. "You were the first cop on the scene, right, Jack?"

"Yep. Solved it pretty quick, too. Took that little fucker in and booked him. He tried to say he was possessed by the devil."

"Yeah," Tom said. "Flip Wilson defense. Devil made him do it."

I listened distractedly. The men's tone and First Jack's rolled eyes already told me they were trying to have me on, building up to a punch line of some sort. I decided I was probably wasting my time. I wasn't going to get what I was looking for with this group after all, but I was having fun, nevertheless. And I was still thinking about Carol. Even if my conversation with the men turned bust, Carol was still a possibility.

"But that's not the scary part," Tom continued. "That was just murder, plain and simple. But the folks who moved in after that... Now there's a family that had some trouble with ghosts."

"Had me any number of calls about that place," Second Jack added. "One night, they called saying there was something with glowing red eyes looking in the windows at night. Well, I got there, and there wasn't shit. But they all acted scared as fuck."

"They had a priest in to bless the house, they was so scared," Tom said. "That man of God ran out of the house so fast, you'd think he'd met Satan himself."

As the men spoke, my focus left the conversation, and any thoughts I'd been having about Carol quickly departed. Against the far wall, behind the tables, I saw a faint image begin to move. I tensed, and a familiar dread took hold of me. There was going to be a ghost story after all, but not the kind I could write about.

I suddenly felt dizzy, but I knew that was coming. Zigzagging lines began to fill my peripheral vision, growing until they settled nearly into my full range of sight. They obscured everything behind them. I'd known that was coming as well, an expected phenomenon. The chattering men disappeared behind the lines, and the only thing I could see clearly now was the image of a man standing against the wall. The man wore a leather apron and a derby hat. He was mostly gray, opaque. A ghost. I sensed it was angry, as ghosts often are.

Don't think I wasn't aware of my hypocrisy. I'd built a lucrative career convincing people ghosts don't exist, and I had a dedicated fan base of skeptics who waited anxiously for my next knock-out punch – the inevitable coup de grace to whatever ghost story I happened to be debunking. But I saw ghosts every day. And worse things, too. Much worse. So much worse that I knew things were about to get dangerous in Carol's cafe. Not just for me, but for everyone in the room.

"My place!" I heard, knowing the sound was the apparition's energy finding its way into my brain. "No right to be here."

The zigzag lines began to clear, and I caught images of cabinets and drawers, tools and black iron implements that I didn't recognize but would expect to see emerging from a blacksmith's forge.

The opaque figure began to move about the cabinets, reaching in and pulling things out. I understood I was seeing a hardware store, a very old hardware store taking shape in the restaurant. The man in the derby hat, I knew, had owned the hardware store and resented the presence of the men who were sitting around the table, mocking. The man took a mallet from the shelves and swung it at Tom's head. Tom leaned back with the blow and reached for the back of his head, like he had felt something suddenly hurting. I'm sure he did feel something. But

Tom's only reaction was to rub the back of his skull. He was still speaking about the house.

"I tell you, that place has these creepy windows on the second floor that look just like blood red devil's eyes during sunset," he said. "It's like you know there's something alive and evil in the place."

I realized I'd heard most of what the men had said, despite the vision. They must have been talking and telling the tale for five minutes while I watched the ghost. I looked at the front door. Through the glass, I could see the sidewalks were still empty. I noted that I'd been there about an hour, and no one had come in except me.

When I looked back, the images of the hardware store faded. I felt nauseated, like I'd been hit in the head with the mallet instead of Tom. I wanted to lie down somewhere. Instead, I willed myself back into the conversation.

"Well, Tom, Jack," I said. "That's an interesting story. Hard to imagine someone building a big colonial like that next to the river, though. If you had that kind of money, you'd build your house on top of the hill, with the other mansions up there, so it wouldn't get flooded. Plus, if I wrote down what you fellas just told me, I'm pretty sure Jay Anson's estate would sue me for copyright infringement."

"Jay Anson?" Tom asked.

"The guy who wrote the *Amityville Horror*."

"Oh, hell, I didn't know his name," Tom laughed, and the rest of the men laughed, too. First Jack slapped me on the back.

"I knew you juvenile delinquents wouldn't get one over on the Ghost Rider here," First Jack proclaimed. "Helluva way to pay a man back for supplying you bums with free beer."

I leaned back in my chair and smiled. The ghost and his wares faded, hauled back into the abyss. The restaurant was just a restaurant again. The ghost's Tormenter would come now, the demon. I felt it. I hoped its fury would be controllable. I liked these men. I liked Carol. But Tormenter demons don't care about such things.

I felt an icy wind blow over me, familiar. None of the men seemed to feel it. But I did. The hate, the malice came with it. I felt the malevolence crawling into my skull.

I stood.

"Can't blame Tom and Jack here for trying to pull one over, Jack," I said, slapping First Jack on the shoulder. "It's bound to happen when you ply a trade like mine."

I smiled again. I had no way of knowing how things were going to turn, so I wanted to leave, to get the hell away and take the power out of whatever was brewing here. I meant to say a quick farewell and head out the door, but the words that left my mouth were, "Which way to the men's room?"

The whole crew pointed to the back.

"Thatta way," said Tom.

"Thanks."

I spoke, but the words weren't just mine anymore.

I walked toward the restrooms. Carol smiled at me as I passed the bar. I returned the smile and pushed the men's room door open. As it shut behind me, I sighed and tried to determine what measure of control I still possessed. I reached out with my mind and sought the demon's – the Tormentor's – hiding place. But it was elusive, this one. Powerful, which is how it had managed to hold sway over me in the first place. I couldn't get a read on it, couldn't find it to bring my power to bear against it. There was no question anymore. Instead of leaving, as I had intended, I was hiding in the men's room. It was the demon's play. I was lost.

I resigned myself to what would come and reached into the back pocket of my jeans. I pulled out a small flat package, opened it, and removed a thin plastic poncho. I shook the folds out of the poncho and pulled it over my head and down around my waist. Then I reached into my front pocket and pulled out a pair of latex gloves. I put them on and leaned against the wall. The ghost I had seen before suddenly appeared again, standing in front of the urinal. It was more solid now, almost corporeal. I thought I might even be able to touch the ghost if I tried. He looked me in the eye and removed his derby, wiping sweat from his brow with the back of his hand before putting the derby back on.

"Make them leave," the ghost said.

I had a power. I didn't know what to call it exactly. I never did. Psychic ability, maybe. In those rare moments when I found things funny, it made me laugh. Writer. Skeptic. Paranormal debunker. That's how the world knew me. But I lived in two worlds: one seen by the living and one seen by only me. In the worlds I walked, I saw the spirits and the demons of the spirit world, the demons holding poor remnants of the dead tethered to this earth, tormenting them. I communed with those fractured souls and battled the demons in some fashion I never understood. Usually, I won. But when I lost, all was lost. I knew the trappings, understood the signs. I was going to lose this one. But I would fight, bring everything I had to bear against the demon before it had its way.

"Make them leave," the ghost said again, and I caught a glimpse into the person it had been. I found something there, a bit of knowing about the ghost in the derby hat. Maybe, I hoped, it would be enough to leverage against the demon.

The ghost's name was Jack. Three Jacks then, here in this place. Only this dead Jack wanted the living Jacks dead, too. With this knowledge I tried to reason with the ghost that was in the demon's power, to break the bond between them. If I could, I might be able to free this Jack yet and save the rest, save everyone.

"They don't know you're here, Jack," I whispered. "They don't mean to offend you."

"Make them leave," the ghost Jack repeated.

I tried to read the ghost, the way I would read the demons. I tried to feel its soul, to find some bit of humanity left within it. Thoughts of family, wife, children, mother, or father. Some semblance of love, some residue of devotion. Nothing. It was no more than energy, doing as its Tormentor bid. There was no reluctance in it, no thought of defiance or regret. Its basest properties held sway, and nothing I tried would dissuade it.

Then I felt...something. A glimmer. Something more than a name.

One of the Jacks at the table outside was coincidence, Second Jack. The other, First Jack, was not. The knowledge that had come told me the ghost was First Jack's great grandfather. First Jack carried the ghost's name to the present. I grasped desperately at the knowledge and tried to force it back into the ghost. I felt a break in the ghost's façade. It managed a brief moment of thought, remembrance, not of First Jack, but of First Jack's father; the ghost remembered holding the infant in his arms. I had found a way in.

"Let them live, Jack," I said, seeing doubt creep across the ghost's face. Confusion took hold. The ghost wept, and I thought briefly that I had won. Then the Tormentor came raging at me from its hiding place. When it came for me, I began to wrestle with it. But it was futile. The Tormentor pulled the ghost away, free from my influence. Then the Tormentor drove all of its power, all of its hate into me, and I lost myself just as the men's room door swung open.

One of the men whose name I didn't remember came in, looking down. He'd been one of the quieter ones, not nearly so brash as Tom or the Jacks. He didn't even look up to see who else was in the restroom when he came in. He just shuffled by and turned his back to me at the urinal. I watched as the man unzipped and stood, waiting as old men will for the urine to flow. He started to talk, but to himself.

"Got no time for that," the man said. "Just make it to Monday, Jenny. Just make it to Monday."

"What's Monday?" I asked.

"Huh?" The man turned his head toward my voice, but not enough to see me behind him.

"Oh, shit," the man said. "I tend to mutter. Sorry. Forgot you was in here."

"No worries, friend," I said. "I'm embarrassed myself. I've been sitting with you an hour or so, and I don't remember your name."

"Pete," the man replied. "Pete Seeger. Not the singer. I hear he's dead."

I reached into my front pocket, searching. The latex stuck to the fabric, and the glove stretched as I felt for the knife I carried. I found it, grabbed it with two fingers and pulled it free. The latex snapped.

Pete seemed to startle when he heard the knife click open, but maintained his concentration, trying to pee. I reached around the front of the man's throat and dragged the blade across the skin, pulling hard. The man reached up and tried to grasp the knife. His hand fluttered up into the stream of blood that flowed from the wound across his neck. Blood spurted, poured, and soaked into the urinal. Pete slumped and crumpled forward. I saw urine mixing with the blood on the floor.

It was a terrible torture, being at once myself and at the same time controlled to do this, to murder an innocent man where he stood, expecting nothing more than the next moments of life to continue. Yet I could not grieve – yet. The grief would come, but for now the demon, the Tormentor, held the emotion at bay – held all of my emotions at bay.

The door opened again. It was Tom. Unlike Pete, Tom looked me directly in the eye. He started to smile, then he noticed the poncho and the blood on my gloved hand. He stepped back quickly, stopped by the now closed door. I said, "Hello, Tom," and plunged the knifed into Tom's chest. Blood spattered onto the poncho, and Tom let out a loud moan as he fell to the floor. Blood was everywhere now, making it hard for me to stand without slipping. I reached down and grabbed Tom under the arms, carefully lifting him and moving him away from the door. I reached down to Tom's chest and pulled the knife free.

Two were gone now. Five left, counting the cook.

I dragged the bottom of one shoe across Tom's jeans, trying to wipe the blood away. Then I found a dry piece of floor in front of the sink and put my foot there, wiping the other shoe on Tom's pants. I opened the door slightly and peeked out. I couldn't see much, not enough to know where Carol was or whether my next move would sound the alarm. I removed the poncho and crumpled it up in the sink. I'd need bravado now, and the poncho would give me away. I bent down and wiped the knife on the back of Tom's shirt. I'd still need the gloves, but it might take someone a moment or two to decide what those were about. I'd need those moments now.

I opened the door wider. I could see the bar, but Carol wasn't there. Good. The cook would have to be next.

I opened the door and walked briskly to the kitchen, slipping slightly on the linoleum tiles and leaving bloody footprints. No way to hide that.

I marched directly into the kitchen. Carol was there, lighting a cigarette.

"Hey, Hun," she said, smiling. She had a cigarette in her mouth and was flipping a lighter. "I was just going to have a smoke."

I smiled back. She didn't seem to notice the knife or the gloves.

"I missed you," I said. Then I reached toward the stove. I put the knife down and grabbed a cast iron skillet. Carol was looking down at the lighter's flame as she brought it up to the cigarette. It lit. I thought briefly how I hated the taste when I kissed a woman who smoked.

Carol took a deep drag and was beginning to exhale as I slammed the skillet into her skull. There was a loud thud, then part of the skillet broke away and hit the floor. Carol fell. I was surprised; I didn't think an iron skillet could break like that.

The screen door at the back of the kitchen squeaked open, and a slightly built Mexican man came inside. He wore a cook's whites and a hat. His eyes widened when he saw Carol on the floor and what was left of the skillet in my hand. He looked like he was going to yell.

"Dammit," I chastised before the man could make a noise. "Help her! She's hurt!"

The man looked confused but took my direction and bent down over Carol to see what was wrong. He put his hand on her shoulder and shook her gently. I marveled at how stupid that was, given what the man had seen.

I swung the broken side of the skillet into the back of the man's neck. He fell quietly on top of Carol.

I stood and looked over the serving counter. I saw Second Jack hurrying toward the kitchen, gun drawn. There'd been enough noise to alert him.

"I guess he really was a cop," I thought. His instincts did him credit.

I took aim and threw what was left of the skillet at Second Jack, hitting him in the forehead. Second Jack dropped his gun and staggered, both hands covering his injured face. I rushed out of the kitchen and picked the gun up. Second Jack was bleeding profusely between his fingers. I shot him in the chest, and Second Jack was dead. I hadn't planned on using a gun. I worried someone would have heard it. Certainly, First Jack and the other man heard it. Nothing for it now though. I walked around the corner. First Jack still sat, leaning to look back toward the kitchen. He saw me and understood. He sat back up in his chair.

"Keep calm," First Jack told the other man. I couldn't remember the second man's name. Like Pete, he hadn't spoken much.

I walked to the table and pulled my chair out. I sat. First Jack and the other man remained seated. Neither moved. The second man's eyes were wide with fear. First Jack, however, seemed calm. I shot the frightened man whose name I couldn't remember in the forehead. It was a lucky shot, I figured. I wasn't really that good with a gun.

The nameless man fell over backwards. The chair toppled with the body and hit the floor.

Then the horror of it set in. I sat quietly, but my emotions returned. The Tormentor had left me, cruelly at this moment. There I sat, completely myself again. The Tormentor held no more sway over me, took no control over my actions. In common parlance, I was no longer possessed. But six people were dead, and First Jack was alive, a witness who would bring me to ruin if he lived. If I shot him now, it would be me who did it. I pointed the gun at Jack, the only living Jack left.

First Jack peered over his reading glasses and said, "What? Didn't we thank you for the beer?"

I felt myself divided again, as I had been when I was under the Tormentor's influence. Only this time, the horror of what I had just done lay side-by-side with my amused interest in First Jack's reaction. I really did like this Jack, enjoyed his company – even now.

"You're not scared," I said, matter-of-factly.

"I haven't been scared since Viet Nam," First Jack answered. "I seen worse than this. Done worse than you just did. Only I didn't have no choice."

Jack's tone shifted, had become accusatory. Despite the insanity of it, my feelings were hurt.

"I don't think I can make you understand," I told Jack, "but I didn't have a choice in this either. It wasn't me who did this."

"Funny. Looks like you," Jack said. "I don't think you've thought it through though. Pablo, the cook, is probably running to the police station as we speak. And someone sure as shit heard that gun and called 911. Your day ain't gonna end well."

"Pablo can't run anymore."

"I see. And Pete? Tom? Carol?"

"I'm pretty sure they're dead."

"Sonofabitch. You're a cold-blooded fucker, ain't you? What did any of them do to you? What did any of us do but laugh with you?"

I knew I should pull the trigger and get the hell out. But I couldn't. It wasn't in me to kill, even in self-preservation. And I needed Jack to understand, to forgive me.

"Jack, if I tell you what really happened here, you'll think I'm insane."

"That ship's sailed, buddy. You are insane."

"Then I've got nothing to lose in telling you," I said. I figured Jack was right about the gunshots being heard. Still, there wasn't much happening on the street. The town was more or less deserted. It just might be no one had heard the shots. Even if someone had, I thought it true that people hear all kinds of noises – screams, yells, backfires, fireworks. If the shots had been heard, I figured it was at best 50-50 someone would decide the sound warranted a call to the police. Maybe I was okay. Maybe I had time. If only I would kill Jack and take the time to clean my prints away, wash the dishes I'd used, and retrieve the poncho, I could still be free.

But I couldn't kill Jack. Not without the demon forcing me to.

"Well, then why don't you tell me?" Jack said. He was buying time, I knew, but it didn't matter anymore. I wasn't going to make it out of here.

"Your great grandfather had a hardware store in this very building," I finally said. "You're his namesake."

Jack's eyes widened.

"How the hell do you know that?"

"I told you, it wasn't me that did this," I said. "There are forces at work in this world we don't fully understand, Jack. Your grandfather's ghost came to me. It put me on the path to do this."

"Well, ain't that something," Jack said. "You came here looking for a ghost story and invented your own when you didn't get one. My dead great grandfather's ghost did this, you say? Killed all these folks in here. I guess you're clear of it then."

Jack's sarcasm stung. I thought to tell Jack about the demon, the Tormentor. It was a complicated thing to explain though, the power a Tormentor demon held over unknowing wraiths, the power the bond imparted to the demon. More complicated was my part in those pairings, how I sometimes had the power to free the wraiths and banish the demons. It was a power that had freed many souls, but one that came with a price. It gave some demons a way into me, a means of controlling me to do what I had just done. In the scheme of things, I had saved more souls than I had been forced to take. If it were all a numbers game, I was, as Jack said, clear of it. I doubted the long version would make a difference with Jack though.

"It's like Tom said earlier," I finally settled on the simplest explanation. "The devil made me do it."

Maybe it was the mention of his friend Tom, but Jack's calm left him. He looked down and began to sob, whispering the names of the dead. Seeing Jack's, I felt my own grief asserting itself. I began to cry.

"Oh, no you don't, you motherfucker!" Jack shouted, outraged by my tears. He tried to lunge over the table, but he was old and fat. He floundered onto the tabletop instead, reaching desperately at me. The table creaked and groaned. I thought it might break.

"Jack," I said. "Please stop."

"Oh, fuck you," Jack said, defeated. He slid off the table and back into his chair. "Just shoot me, you motherfucker. Quit playing this stupid game. You're a crazy, cold-blooded killer. Just get it over with."

"Jack," I said, wiping my tears away with the back of my hand. "Ask yourself how I could know about your great grandfather if there wasn't more to this than meets the eye."

Jack said nothing. I sighed and set the gun down on the table. I could see Jack trying to decide whether to reach for it or not. I made it easy. I slid the gun over to him and took off the latex gloves, setting them on the table. Jack eyed the gun but didn't reach for it.

"Jack, I've left a shit ton of evidence in here. My DNA is all over the place, and my prints, too. I left a poncho wadded up in the bathroom sink. If I were still controlled, I'd just kill you and clean up my trail. The gloves and poncho did some of that for me already. So, there's not much to do, really. It would be easy for me. Instead, I'm leaving all the evidence and an eyewitness. Now, you can take that gun and shoot me. I guess that would be fine. I'm asking a favor though. Let me walk out that door and get on my bike. I'd like one last ride to think on things before the cops get me, and they certainly will now. I don't see a way out of it without killing you, and, like I said, I didn't do this. Despite what you see, I'm not a killer."

I pushed my chair away from the table and stood.

"I'm sorry, Jack," I said. "I can't tell you how sorry I am."

I turned my back on Jack and walked toward the door. I expected the gunshot any second. It didn't come. I got to the door and turned to Jack. He held the gun pointed at me, his hand trembling.

"How did I know about your grandfather, Jack?" I asked again. Then I opened the door.

The street was still empty. It was still hot, and there was enough daylight left to enjoy as much of the ride as I was going to get before the day ended. My pant legs were soaked in blood. Blood was streaked across my arms. I was undoubtedly going to be a sensation on the news. "Famous skeptic blames murder spree on demonic possession."

I thought about the latex gloves and the poncho. I didn't remember buying them, let alone putting them in my pockets. That troubled me. I couldn't see where they'd been much use in any event, bloody as I was. It was like they were part of a half-hatched plan I'd had before I even encountered the demon. But I didn't remember making any plan at all.

I started toward my bike, but something else nagged at me. I walked back to the window of the restaurant. The window reflected the sun, and I couldn't see inside. So, I put my hands up to the glass and peered in. Jack sat looking at the gun in his hand. Then I saw Second Jack, Tom, and Carol sitting at the table with Jack. Their ghosts. I sensed the other ghosts were there, too. I felt for the demon. It was there, weakened as it tried to hold on to too many souls. I unleashed my power at the Tormentor, and it lost its hold, its power in this world. It raged at me and tried to rush back into me. But this time it lost. This time my power drove it back to hell, or wherever it was that demons called home. Without the demon there to hold them, the ghosts would soon fade away. Where they would go, I didn't have the faintest idea. Still, I smiled. At least I had managed to do that.

Then the world and my memories in it, the knowledge of what I'd just done, knowledge of the things I had done before this – all of that slipped away, and I was in a different reality, one that I had lived in before the books and before the fame that came with them. I was in my old office. I had a headache, and I was in a bad mood.

CHAPTER 2

The phone rang at my desk. I looked at the caller ID. It was Maureen, my receptionist. I picked up.

"Hi, Maureen. What's up?"

"There's a woman here to see you," Maureen told me. "She says it's urgent."

"Is she a client?"

"No, I don't think so," Maureen sounded oddly distracted. "I'd remember if she was."

"Maureen, you know the drill," I said. "Have her call Jan."

Jan was my paralegal.

I was pouring over a pile of maddeningly illegible medical records and annoyed at Maureen for interrupting. So, I added, "We're personal injury attorneys, Maureen. The urgent part of the case is over before we get it. Jan screens all potential clients before I'll meet with them. Try not to forget that."

I felt bad as soon as I said it. I wasn't usually curt with my staff, but it had been a particularly bad day, starting with the contentious deposition of a physician who'd made it clear she hated all lawyers and any patient who had the temerity to hire one.

"I know, Mr. Baxter," Maureen said. "I'm sorry, but she's not your run-of-the-mill client. At least I don't think so."

"Why not?"

"She's famous," Maureen told me. She added, "Very famous."

"How so?"

"She's a psychic."

"Oh, sweet Jesus, Maureen." I forgot I'd felt bad only a second before and said tersely, "Psychics are charlatans. Put her through to Jan. Or better yet, don't."

"No, I mean she really is famous," Maureen persisted. "She's on TV all the time. She's had her own show, and she's a bestselling author."

I paused for a moment and considered whether a famous client might be good publicity, psychic or not. I realized criminal defense attorneys often prospered when high profile clients came their way. They made the news and probably made a killing in fees. But my practice was strictly PI. It lacked sex appeal, and I couldn't see how a client's being famous would make a rear-ender newsworthy or give me a shot at making more money. My income came from convincing insurance companies to write checks at or as close to policy limits as I could, of which I took 33 1/3 percent, plus expenses. I didn't get to charge hourly fees like defense attorneys. Plus, there was client confidentiality. I couldn't very well get in front of a camera and grandstand about my clients' injuries without breaking the rules of ethics, even if they were famous. A famous client would likely be higher maintenance than most as well. Much higher.

"Sorry, Maureen," I said, deciding I didn't want the complication. I was having enough trouble getting through the medical records in front of me. "I appreciate that you're trying to help. Sorry I was short with you, but have her call Jan."

Maureen didn't answer.

"Maureen," I sighed. "Look, I apologize. Bad day. But have her call Jan."

"I already put her in the conference room to see you," Maureen sounded like she was crying. "She was very persuasive."

I was about to snap at her again but bit my lip instead. I felt like I'd already been a jerk. No need to make it worse. I figured I could use a break from the medical hieroglyphics in any event.

"Okay, Maureen. Please don't worry about it. You did fine. I'll go in and say hello. And, Maureen?"

"Yes?"

"Just who the hell is she?"

"Evelyn Blankenship."

"I haven't heard of her."

"You need to get out more."

I knocked on the conference room door and entered. I'd expected to find a dowdy-looking eccentric. I'd gone so far as to imagine her with disheveled gray hair and a slightly crazed look in her eye – maybe even a hint of body odor. And since she'd come to see me, I pictured her with a neck brace or crutches. I was dead wrong.

Whatever else Evelyn Blankenship might have been, she was a knockout. She had long blonde hair, high cheekbones, and a rather sharp nose that conveyed – I couldn't decide why – intelligence as well as beauty. She was tall. Certainly taller than me. Maybe six feet. And fit. Her figure, even sitting, was striking.

Though she hadn't spoken a word, I decided she had the sort of presence often found in successful politicians, like every thought in the room should be centered on her. I'd donated a large sum of money to some charity or other several years before and had gotten into a meet and greet with Mikhail Gorbachev as a result. I remembered the former Soviet general secretary producing the same effect, minus Blankenship's considerable sex appeal. Gorbachev had owned the room, even with the language barrier and reliance on a translator.

"Ms. Blankenship?"

"Yes, Nash," the woman answered. She had a provocative lilt in her voice that was nearly as appealing as her physical presence. "It's me."

I was taken aback by her tone of familiarity. I saw instantly why Blankenship might be famous and why Maureen had given in to her. But I didn't know her from squat. I realized she was probably employing a trick of the psychic's trade, starting the conversation like she already knew me or something about me. I threw my notepad down on the table where I intended to sit, to show I wouldn't be so easily bowled over. I wasn't sure where this meeting would go, but I decided it would be interesting, at least.

"A bit informal for a first meeting, Ms. Blankenship," I told her, "but I'm an informal enough guy."

"I apologize. I just feel like we've met already." She smiled knowingly at me. I found it strangely unnerving. Rhetorical gamesmanship aside, Evelyn Blankenship's smile dug right in. Deep. I wondered what it was about a beautiful woman that made a man's calm and objectivity flee. Or more particularly, what it was about *this* woman that was putting *my* calm and objectivity on shaky ground, just fifteen seconds into the conversation. I chalked it up to three million years of human evolution, give or take; it made men stupid. Even me.

"Will you sit?" Blankenship asked.

I realized I'd been standing silently for several moments, distracted by Blankenship. And I'd just been invited to sit in my own conference room. Throwing the notebook down had been a nice touch, but I could see I was in for a helluva contest if I thought I was going to run this meeting.

"My turn to apologize," I said, trying to shore up my professional demeanor. "I'm just trying to determine if I've ever seen you before. My secretary tells me you're famous."

"I'm well known in some circles," she said. "Not at all in others. I won't take offense if you're in one of the latter."

I sat and admonished myself to keep my wits about me. Blankenship was circumventing all of my professional reflexes. No matter how attractive a client was, I always had an off switch in my brain that shut down anything more than a workmanlike interest. Instead of beauty, I assessed injuries. I gauged how the client would present at a deposition or at trial. I spent my time with the client adding up medical expenses, potential future surgeries, permanent scarring, and loss of normal life. But just sitting there, Blankenship had managed to shut the off switch off.

I reminded myself before my thoughts went down the wrong path that attorneys are not allowed to get involved with their clients. It was a cardinal rule, and breaking it was the fast track to disbarment. But I found myself thinking more about asking this potential client out to dinner than uncovering her legal woes. That wasn't like me. Not at all.

"So, what would you like to see me about?"

She smiled again but said nothing. She just looked into my eyes. Hers, I thought, were unnaturally blue. Colored contacts?

"No need to be shy, Ms. Blankenship."

"Evelyn."

"There's no need to be shy, Evelyn," I repeated. "I'm an attorney, and you've come to see me for legal counsel. That means we have an attorney-client privilege. Whatever you have to say stays between us. I couldn't divulge it if I wanted to."

She kept smiling but said nothing. I felt decidedly awkward. So, I added, more for my sake than hers, "There's no need to be embarrassed. I'm not here to judge you. I'm here to help."

"Nash," she said finally, "I believe I'm involved in a murder."

"Murder?"

"More than one, I'm afraid."

I'd heard my share of shocking revelations, but if Evelyn Blankenship was confessing to involvement in multiple homicides, she had just surpassed all of them. And evolution or no, her statement put the effect she'd been having on me in check. I was all business now, inside and out.

I noted her expression remained unchanged, despite her confession, if that's what it had been. I thought it odd, considering the magnitude of what she'd just said. I wondered whether it was a defense mechanism, smiling to hide what she was really feeling. Or maybe she was the most stunningly beautiful psychopath I'd ever met.

"Well," I pretended the gravity of her statement didn't exist. Surprise is the first thing a lawyer learns to hide. It's an occupational necessity. "You should know that I'm not a criminal defense attorney. I handle personal injury cases, mostly. If you're truly involved in a crime of some sort, you need a criminal attorney, not me. I can't stress how urgent that is. Now I can put you in touch with a good lawyer who handles these matters, but I'm not the guy."

"But I want *your* help," Evelyn said. "I don't want a different lawyer."

"Evelyn, lawyers are like doctors," I explained, wondering if Blankenship might pose a real danger. Did she carry a gun in her purse? Had she shot someone? Then I remembered I was sitting across the table from a famous psychic. It suddenly made sense that Blankenship might be laying the foundation for some sort of publicity stunt. The media savvy psychic sees a murder in her visions, or whatever, and has to come forward with critical information for the police, sending her lawyer in as her proxy to make it seem legit – at least to the press and the believers who made her books profitable.

I decided Blankenship was trying to drag me into something crazy, and I felt like the word "chump" would be written all over me if I let it happen. I thought the smartest thing I could do was to end this meeting and refer Blankenship to a defense attorney. They were publicity hounds by nature. I wasn't. Not Blankenship's kind of publicity at any rate.

"I'm sorry," Evelyn said. "You were saying lawyers are like doctors."

I'd faded out again, letting a long pause hang after my "Lawyers are like doctors" comment, while my brain flitted around trying to make sense of Blankenship. It took her prompting to put me back on track.

"What I mean," I explained, willing myself back into the moment, "is that you wouldn't see a brain surgeon when what you really need is a heart surgeon. They're both doctors, but one knows the heart and the other the brain. Neither would be very good at the other's job. In this case, I'm a plaintiff's attorney. If someone gets injured because of someone else's negligence, I handle their case for them. I try to recover money damages. Criminal defense attorneys, on the other hand, deal with criminal law. Their job is to keep you out of jail – or to get you the best deal they can get for you going in. There's a whole different range of knowledge required. I learned some of it in law school, but that was a long time ago. I only understand it in theory, not practice. So, I can't help you on that front. Get hit by a car, and I'm your man. Run someone over with a car, on purpose, and not so much."

"I think you're my man in any event," Evelyn smiled again. She was still trying to convey a familiarity that I didn't think existed between us. Time would tell just how wrong I was about that – how wrong I was about everything.

"No, I'm not." I decided I would get rid of Evelyn Blankenship as fast as I could. "Now let me give you the name of a friend of mine. He's a top-notch lawyer, and he can help you with whatever fix you're in."

The attorney I had in mind wasn't actually a friend. But I had no intention of thrusting this woman on anyone I would have to look in the eye later.

Evelyn seemed to pout. I was certain that she was attempting to manipulate me. I wondered how she'd found me and why she thought I was gullible enough or desperate enough to help in whatever scheme she had.

"Won't you at least let me explain?" she asked. "We still have attorney-client privilege."

I considered. It was best to send her on her way. But I had to admit, I *was* curious if I was right about her publicity angle. What I was trying not to admit was that, despite the sheer lunacy of what Blankenship was unfolding in front of me, part of me wanted to stay physically close to her.

Nevertheless, good sense prevailed.

"No," I told her. "I don't think I should hear anymore. Let me get you that number. In fact, we can call him right now, if that's okay."

Evelyn sighed. The pout was gone. The smile, too.

"I hoped it wouldn't come to this, Nicholas," she said.

I started. She had just called me by my real name, a name no one had known me by in a very long time.

Sonofabitch, I thought. So that's her game. Blackmail!

"Who's Nicholas?" I said, though I knew the answer. What I didn't know was how *she* knew it. I didn't believe the psychic shtick. Not for a second. So how did she know?

"Why, dear," Evelyn smiled again. "*You* are."

I felt an old fear, an old sickness welling up within me. I wanted to remain calm and unreadable. I failed.

"Who the hell are you?" I demanded. "What do you really want, Evelyn Blankenship?"

"You, as always."

I began to sweat. Blankenship had called up a very old and dark past. I'd spent more than a few years in therapy trying to leave it behind, or to live with it, at least. I thought I'd succeeded, but hearing my name – my real name – made me feel like a frightened boy again. I hadn't been called Nicholas in more than twenty years, and the records that identified me by that name had been sealed by the courts. Still, there were papers, news reports. If someone really dug, they'd be able to turn up my secret past.

I realized I was feeling something more than fear, too. I felt a nearly homicidal rage at this woman. Who the fuck did this stranger think she was? What gave her the right to play this game with me? Old images began to dance around in the back of my mind. My mother. My sister. Brother. Murdered. Their bloody bodies lying in the living room of my boyhood home, their blood spattered on me as well. The psychiatrists explained to me long ago that the images were part of a post-traumatic stress syndrome that made me relive the murders over and over again. The images had lain dormant for years now. Until Evelyn Blankenship came to play.

"I don't know what you're talking about," I said, trying to force the images back into oblivion and wondering how much this "psychic" might actually know.

"Oh, but you do, Nash," she said. "I'll give you that, your chosen name rather than your given name."

I glared at her. It wasn't blackmail at all. It was going to be something far worse.

"Okay, you clearly have some trick up your sleeve," I said. "Are you out to prove you're a real psychic to your fans by 'sensing' the truth about my past?"

"Not at all, Nash," Evelyn smiled again. "I just wanted to see the look on your face. It's precious."

I saw blood. I wanted to strangle the life out of Evelyn Blankenship, whatever the consequences. She was perpetrating the ultimate invasion of my privacy, but more than that: she was awakening demons she had no right to awaken.

I tried to calm myself enough to think clearly and learn what she truly knew. I asked, "Just what murders did you come here to see me about?"

"Oh, not the ones you're thinking about, Darling," she said. "Those are old news. I came about the murders that are happening right now."

Evelyn looked away and upward, as if trying to sense something.

"Yes," she said. "I see it clearly."

I understood she was trying to achieve some sort of effect, like she was seeing from the beyond. I decided to play along, only to get to as much of the truth as she would willingly give.

"What do you see?"

"Oh, Nash. Poor Nash. You think you have some control over this, don't you? But we're not even here now," she said. "This moment, you are picking up a gun that's been dropped to the ground."

She paused as if listening.

"Yes, you're picking it up."

Another pause.

"And you're pulling the trigger."

I clenched my fists.

"What the fuck are you talking about?"

"Oh, he's dead, Nash," she told me. "You shot him. In cold blood, as they say."

"Get out! Get the fuck out of here!"

Suddenly, I smelled the acrid odor of burnt gunpowder, and my ears rang from a gunshot. I saw a face, bleeding and dropping. I fell to my knees.

"Oh, Darling," Evelyn said, her voice tender and compassionate. "Enough of this."

I squeezed my eyes shut and then opened them. My hands were in hot sand. I pulled my hands up and sat. The conference room was gone. Fluorescent lighting was replaced with blazing sunshine. I was on a beach. To my right, the ocean's waves created a constant roar and hissing against the sand. To my left was a boardwalk, full of rides. I heard rollercoaster wheels and the clickety clack of chains and the dull pulsing hum of electric motors. I looked at the boardwalk and saw all manner of rides operating. There was carnival music. There were no people. I looked along the beach, and there were no people there either, or in the water. But Evelyn sat beside me wearing a yellow summer dress and a wide-brimmed, floppy straw hat.

Drugged, I thought. I was hallucinating. Somehow, this woman had drugged me.

Evelyn sat on a beach towel and looked out at the ocean. The breeze was blowing against the fabric of her dress. The wool pant legs on my suit were flapping in the wind as well. Everything felt real.

"This is where my awakening began," Evelyn said wistfully. "Here on this very beach. I felt the souls, Nash. An endless legion of souls taken by the waves throughout time."

The sand was burning my legs through the thin fabric of my pants. I stood up. My feet sank, and hot sand poured into my shoes.

I didn't have the slightest idea what I should do.

"You're awakening, too, my love," Evelyn said.

She turned to look at me. She was wearing a large pair of sunglasses that covered most of her face. I couldn't see her eyes through the lenses.

"What have you done to me?"

Evelyn smiled.

"You wanted to know about the murders," she said.

"Murders?"

"The ones I spoke about."

"I don't want to know about your murders."

"Oh, they're your murders, Nash," she said. "Right now, you're sitting down at a table. You're shooting a man whose name you do not know in the forehead."

The smoke of gunfire filled my nostrils again. I heard a gunshot echoing off a distant rock face that jutted out into the ocean. The sound of the waves drowned it out quickly.

I wanted to vomit.

"But you've been stupid, my love," Evelyn said, her mouth frowning with concern. "You let a man live."

"I'm not a killer," I responded, confused that I half understood what she meant.

"No, Darling. You're not. Not without help."

She looked back out to the ocean and took a deep breath. Then she tilted her head, ever so slightly.

"There," she said. "I've done it for you."

"Jack?" I asked, not knowing why.

"He's gone now, too."

My heart sank. I felt sicker than I'd ever felt.

"But you've left a mess, my love."

"They'll find me," I said with certainty, not understanding what I was certain of. Yet I sensed a victory in it.

"No. They won't. Not this time."

Then I was not *me* anymore. I was there, silent, an observer, but my body moved and spoke without me.

"Why are you doing this, Evelyn?" the Nash who was no longer me asked. "You're showing your hand to me. Why the illusion?"

"I wanted to see you as you would have been, to see if I would still love you."

"And do you?"

"Nash, my sweet love," Evelyn leaned back and looked at me again. "I can't seem to help myself, though you are more interesting now than you would have been."

"Evelyn," my voice said. "My awareness is growing. You won't be able to contain me much longer."

"Oh, I don't know," Evelyn said. "You're still human. All of those clunky human frailties are doing it for me. Guilt. Denial. Maybe even a touch of insanity."

"I'm resisting, Evelyn. I'm not insane."

"But you were, weren't you? Insane I mean. You have to admit that much." Evelyn laughed. "Either way, you're fleeing reality."

"It's a strange sort of reality," I said.

"It is."

"I don't understand it."

"Nor do I."

"Do you know what you are?"

"I suspect. Like you, I'm not fully awakened yet."

"You're evil, Evelyn."

"Maybe. I'm not entirely sure. I've considered the possibility that you are. Besides, you love me anyway."

I was silent. Then I sat next to Evelyn on the beach towel and held her hand.

"I do love you. May the devil help me, I do."

Evelyn leaned her head against my shoulder.

"What strange fate is this?"

"I don't know. But here is my gift to you. Kill me now, while you are still stronger than I am. My insanity won't last. This man, Nash or Nicholas, is inventing explanations for what's becoming of him. But I'm growing stronger. Soon he will understand. And when he accepts what he is, what I am, we will destroy you. We won't have a choice. So, you have to kill me now, while you can."

Evelyn started to cry.

"But I can't," she sobbed. "Oh, I want to. Very much."

"Then you must. This is your last chance."

"Do you truly love me enough to die for me?"

I eavesdropped as the being within me thought for a moment, trying to remember something that would help him understand and answer.

"I know I am drawn into this world because of you," he said. "The only thing I know about what I am is that I love you. How or why, I don't know. But I don't doubt that the love I feel for you is the truest thing about me. I accept that I am in the world now, but I do not wish to be if I will become the vessel of your demise."

I sighed.

"So, yes," I said. "I would prefer to die than to see you die."

"And that is why I cannot kill you," she sat up, removed her sunglasses, and wiped her tears. "If it were only my love for you, I could do it. But your love for me makes it too hard."

"My poor Evelyn," I reached toward her cheek and wiped away fresh tears. "That is how I will destroy you."

CHAPTER 3

I came to in a ditch, soaking wet. Beside me, I heard the violent hissing of water against the hot pipes and engine of my motorcycle. I looked at the sound. The bike was in the ditch, too, leaning against the wet grass beside me. I had no memory of how I'd ended up there, but apparently, I'd run off the road and into the swale. Luckily, the bike hadn't fallen over on me, or my leg would be sizzling and crushed beneath it. But I wasn't hurt, and the bike looked all right. Mostly. So, I'd been going slow. Very slow it seemed.

The water in the swale was several inches deep, speaking of a recent rain. I sat up. Warm muddy water trickled down my arms, and I could feel it doing the same thing under my shirt. The blood that had covered me was either washed away or so mingled with the brown water soaking me that I couldn't see it anymore. What the hell had happened? The last thing I remembered was sitting on a beach towel with Evelyn Blankenship, a woman I'd never known but with whom, it seemed, I was intimately familiar. Or, rather, with whom some being that was living through me was intimately familiar.

I sat in the water and tried to assess my mental state. I was confused to be sure. My life left me all too familiar with a spirit world I assumed none but I could fully experience. I'd learned to live with that, found my place in it. Alone. Finding myself possessed by a demon was an unwelcomed experience, but not so out of the ordinary that I found it strange anymore. But the vision, the hallucination, or whatever it was with Evelyn Blankenship, left me with the unsettled feeling that I was a pawn in a larger game than I had considered. And not so alone as I had imagined.

I tried to make sense of it. At the same time, I worried about my bike. It may sound like a misguided priority, but that motorcycle was the one thing that kept me tethered to any joy I could find in the world. Riding was the closest thing to a cure for the aftereffects of possession and mayhem. Whatever hell was unleashed in my life, riding always put me back in touch with what I considered my essential self, the person I was apart from the madness.

I heard the momentary blip of a police siren. I looked behind me, back onto the road. A police squad had drawn up, lights on. The squad's door opened, and a cop stepped out and started walking toward me. So, this was how the day would end. Not with a chase or gunfire, but with my wet ass being hauled from the ditch. I couldn't even say I'd enjoyed my last ride because I didn't remember a bit of it.

I wanted nothing more than to get on my bike again and ride, to think things through and decide what, if anything, I should do about these new revelations. But first there was the cop – and the murders I'd just committed. Call me pessimistic, but it seemed like an unhappy convergence.

"You okay?" the cop asked. He didn't draw his weapon. He didn't look alarmed. Maybe he didn't see a murderer at all, just a hapless biker who'd managed to crash into a ditch. But even if he didn't see a killer, at the very least he must suspect a drunk. Either way, it looked like a trip to the local lock up was a distinct possibility.

"I don't know," I answered. I dipped my hands into the water and brought some up out of the ditch and rubbed it over my arms.

"Goosebumps," I said, rubbing hard as if to make them stop. I really wanted to make sure any remaining blood was washed back into the ditch, but it worked well for the story I hoped the cop would buy. "I think the heat got to me. Jesus, what is heatstroke like?"

"Bad," the cop said. Then he walked down into the ditch beside me and put his hand to my forehead. I didn't like being touched like that, but it seemed wise to appear helpless. "How do you feel?"

"I remember being dizzy," I answered. "Then I woke up in the water here. I think I feel better now. A bit dizzy still."

"Well, it isn't scientific, but you don't feel too hot," he said. "Are you nauseated?"

"I don't think so."

"What's your name?"

"Nash," I said. I didn't want to give him my real name. It's not like Mike or Dave, common enough to be quickly forgotten. But lying would surely draw suspicion later, if I didn't manage to talk my way out of this.

"Who's the president, Nash?"

"The president?"

"Just want to see if your noggin is working right," the cop smiled. "Tell me what day of the week it is."

"Thursday."

"What month?"

"One hot ass bitch of a July."

The cop laughed.

"Well, you got that right. Have you had anything to drink, Nash?"

"Couple of Cokes."

"No rum or Jack Daniels in that Coke?"

I smiled. "I can see why you'd think that. You can give me a breathalyzer if you want to, but I'm sober as can be. It's just got to be the heat."

"How 'bout medications? Are you taking any prescriptions?"

"Nothing."

"Okay, Nash. Can you stand?"

"I think so. Let me try."

"Here, let me help."

The cop grabbed me under the arms and helped me to my feet. He leaned in close enough to smell my breath when he did it. I saw his name badge as I stood. His name was Smith.

I leaned forward a bit to convey residual dizziness. Then I stood straight. I didn't want this to turn into a medical thing any more than I wanted it to turn into a jail thing.

"Can I call the paramedics for you, Nash?" Officer Smith asked.

"Just let me stand here a moment, if you don't mind," I said. "See if I can get my bearings. By the way, I appreciate your help."

"We're here to serve," Smith smiled. "I ride, too. Between the heat off my bike and the sun beating down on me, I've had a moment or two when I thought it was getting to be too much myself."

Officer Smith told me to wait, and he walked back to his squad car. I was worried about what his next move would be. I didn't see any way to escape if he decided to take me in or call the paramedics, so I was at his mercy. He came back with a cold bottle of water.

"Here," he said, twisting the cap off. "You need this more than I do."

I thanked him and drank the whole bottle down. It wasn't an act. It was hot as hell.

"Well," he said, "I don't think you're drunk, and I don't think you have heat stroke. But I'd feel better if you let me call the paramedics for you."

I paused for a moment like I was taking stock of myself. Then I told him I felt much better.

"Can't say I want to pay three thousand bucks for the paramedics to take me to the ER, so they can tell me I'm okay," I said.

"Fair enough. Let's see if we can get that bike out of the ditch for you."

"Sounds like a plan," I said. "I sure don't want someone dragging it out with a tow truck."

I began wading through the standing water to reach for the bike, but Officer Smith grabbed my elbow.

"Tell you what," he said. "Why don't you go sit in my car for a bit, and let me get the bike out for you. It's the closest AC you're going to find."

He made it sound like a suggestion, but his grip on my arm was a command, not open for debate. He guided me up out of the ditch and onto the road. Cooperation seemed the best course of action – appreciation for his concern. But I was guessing the seat with the AC would be in the backseat of his squad, without the option to get out unless he let me out.

He walked me to the squad – a big SUV – and true to my expectation, he opened the back door and helped me in. The seat was hard plastic. There were bars on the door windows.

"Don't worry," he said. "It's not comfortable, but it's clean. More importantly, it will cool you off."

"Thank you."

I was rolling the dice by being compliant, but what option did I have? Wrestle him to the ground and take his gun? Shoot out his tires and make a run for it? I wondered what my status was. I wasn't lying to my hallucinatory love interest in my non-existent law office when I suggested I didn't know much about criminal law. I was certain he knew I wasn't drunk. There was no property damage from the crash, if you could even call it a crash. More like a splash. The alarms about the murders hadn't been sounded. I was sure of that. Near as I could tell, I ought to be able to go along my way, however abbreviated that way might be. But by the time I came to that conclusion, my feet were all the way in, and he closed the door.

The thunder of motorcycles came up behind me, and about forty bikes roared by on the road, passing the squad. Pretty much every rider and passenger turned to look in at me. I waved for a bit, until I got tired of it. I looked ahead after the last bikes passed and saw Officer Smith was pulling my bike upright. He swung his leg over the seat and sat for a few seconds, then he got off and gently set the bike down – no easy trick given that it weighed about 900 pounds. Maybe it was a good thing I hadn't decided to wrestle for his gun.

He walked back to the squad and opened my door. Freedom? Or had he seen something that was going to end it for me now?

"I need the FOB," he told me. Of course. The bike wouldn't start without it. I fished it out of my wet pocket and handed it to him. He shut the door again, this time without pleasantries.

He got back on the bike and started it. He shifted the gears until it was in first and then slowly began riding through the water away from the squad. It wasn't easy to see him because a computer mounted in the front seat blocked my view. But eventually, I saw him pop up with the bike onto a driveway about forty yards away. He got off and set the bike on the stand. Then he opened the tour pack and looked in, moving things around. He closed it and did the same with the side bags. It was a bad search, constitutionally speaking. I remembered that much from law school. If he found anything, it was subject to a motion to suppress.

Fourth Amendment. Fruit of the poisonous tree. In cop shows they call it getting off on a technicality. But friendly Officer Smith would likely say I'd given him permission to take care of the bike for me, which I hadn't, but I had handed him the key, so motion denied.

But that was academic. As far as I could remember, there was nothing in the bike that could be used as evidence against me. All the evidence was on my soaking wet clothes and in the ditch water. I'd left the gun with Jack, along with my fingerprints, bloody gloves, and poncho. The knife was still sitting on the stove in Pablo's kitchen. I relaxed. If anything, his illegal search told him I was likely just what I appeared to be – a hapless rider who wasn't used to the heat.

He walked back to the squad and opened the door.

"Bike's okay," he said, reassuringly. "How 'bout you? Cooled down?"

"Yes," I said, letting go of my earlier performance. "I'm fine now. The water and AC did the trick. Not to mention the wet clothes. Thanks."

"No problem," he said. "That's what we're here for."

I got out of the squad, and Officer Smith handed my FOB back to me.

"I'd find someplace cool to spend the rest of the day, if I were you," he advised. "Do you live around here?"

"No. Riding through," I told him. "Headed west."

"Sturgis?"

"Not this time," I said. I'd only been to Sturgis once, and that wasn't for the rally. I was investigating a haunting for my second book. A biker ghost in a local hotel. There was no ghost though. The owners were probably looking to drum up interest in ghost tourism for the off-season and made the whole thing up. They told a good story though, and it made for an interesting chapter: "The Bloody Biker in Room 17."

"Okay, ride safe."

I started to walk along the road toward my bike. I was a few yards away when Officer Smith yelled at me to wait. I stopped and turned. He was walking after me.

Did he suspect more than he'd let on? Had he decided a chemical test was in order after all, to confirm my sobriety? Instead of feeling lucky I'd made it this far, I was flippant. Seemed like the most natural response.

"I'm starting to get a Detective Columbo vibe here, Officer."

He laughed.

"Well, kind of," he said. "There really is just one more thing. I need to log this, and I forgot to run your license. I need to see your insurance, too."

I found myself back in the back seat while Smith ran my license and spoke with dispatch on the radio. He'd been apologetic, Columbo-style, and handed me another bottle of water for my trouble. I sat and sipped and waited some more. Twenty minutes went by, and I decided it was over. The murders had been discovered, and he had the prime suspect in his back seat, ready to transport to wherever they take the worst of the worst.

Finally, he put the squad in gear and began driving. But we stopped behind my bike instead of continuing to the jail. He got out and opened my door.

"You're good to go," he told me, handing my license and insurance card back to me.

"I know cops like to be appreciated," I said. "But I can't say thank you even one more time. I'm all thank youd out for the day."

"Yeah, sorry about that. I got more concerned about helping a fellow biker out than I was about being a cop. Forgot to take care of business. On the upside, I decided not to write you a ticket."

I smiled and said, "Thank you."

CHAPTER 4

I'd intended to get on the bike and just ride and keep riding until the world fell down on top of me. First Jack would, no doubt, have called the cops right after I'd left the restaurant, and he knew exactly who I was and that I was riding a Harley out of town. Not that there weren't hundreds of Harleys heading in either direction along Route 6, through and then out of the town, and along the intersecting highways going north and south. All things being equal, I'd be a needle in a Harley haystack. But someone somewhere had to be thinking at least a couple of good old-fashioned roadblocks were in order to find the one rider named Nash Baxter.

It was nothing short of amazing that Officer Smith hadn't been clued in when he radioed dispatch with my license information. But I had to be on borrowed time. I'd only managed to borrow a little more of it when my encounter with the good officer came to an end.

I was ready for the roadblocks. I wouldn't run. I'd just keep going until I hit one. I could ditch the bike and hide or make it out on foot along the river. But how long could a famous guy who'd been on national television and about a million dust jackets remain unnoticed? I couldn't use a credit card without being flagged, and access to my bank accounts would be monitored, at the very least. Unless I resorted to petty theft, I wouldn't have more than the cash in my wallet to keep me going. And the media would be loving the story about a bestselling writer going on a killing spree. My face would be plastered over every medium imaginable, so even using what cash I had would likely bring my flight to an ignoble end.

So, I figured I'd just keep going until I couldn't go anymore. Any plan beyond that was pointless.

I made it as far as the next small town without any of the predicted roadblocks cropping up. It was about six miles out of the ditch, and my thoughts finally went beyond the various ways I might be captured. That and the more immediate problem of navigating Officer Smith's ministrations had been, comparatively speaking, welcomed distractions. My thoughts had come full circle back to the infinitely more disturbing understanding that my world, my reality, had already fallen down on top of me. That freight train crashing through my brain forced me to stop and gather my wits.

I saw a small coin operated car wash and pulled in. Two stalls, both empty. I drove through one and back out behind the cinder block building. There was a dumpster in back, and I stopped the bike next to it, turned the engine off, and set it on the stand.

My clothes were mostly dry now, but I wanted them off of me. I opened the back of the bike and took out my bag. Small favor: no water had gotten in, and everything was dry. I opened the side saddle bag and took out a package of wet wipes, then I pulled a clean shirt and pants out of my bag. I looked around. I couldn't be seen from the road, and there was no one within eyesight. So, I pulled out a clean pair of underwear, too. I took my shirt off and threw it in the dumpster and began cleaning myself with the wipes. I put the clean shirt on and looked around again. No one watching. I kicked my shoes off and took my wallet and keys out of my pockets and put them on the back seat. Then I stripped and cleaned myself as good as I could with the remaining wipes and threw the rest of what I'd been wearing in the dumpster. I dressed, found dry running shoes and socks in the other saddle bag, and put them on. I felt clean, at least.

I left the bike and wandered up the road a bit and found a small grocery. Going in was asking for trouble, but I was still thirsty. In light of the inevitable, self-deprivation seemed foolish. I bought a Coke at the counter. The store clerk looked bored, but she managed to muster up enough interest to tell me it was hot outside. I told her she wasn't kidding and made my exit. Unless she was a very good actor, she hadn't heard a thing.

I walked back to the bike. There was a curb next to the dumpster. I sat and opened the Coke and started to drink and lay out the issues confronting me: First, I killed everyone but First Jack in a restaurant one town back, but it wasn't the first time I'd done something like that, so it was within my frame of reference. I could make sense of it. Beyond anything I could make sense of were the next two problems: 1) my conscious mind had been taken from me and pulled into two separate but very tactile worlds laid down by a beautiful phantom calling herself, or itself, Evelyn Blankenship. If real, Blankenship was a being with extraordinary powers; 2) I now had reason to believe I wasn't entirely myself within myself, but a rent-free vessel for another phantom being, who professed love for and intention to destroy Evelyn Blankenship.

I thought of First Jack. Evelyn said she'd killed him, somehow. And she'd said I wasn't going to get caught. Was she using her powers to clean up for me? Clearing my way to escape? By killing Jack? That would explain everything from Officer Smith to the bored store clerk, and the utter lack of any noticeable effort to catch me. Maybe incarceration was the least of my worries.

Jack. Jack. I'd liked Jack. I was angry when Evelyn said she'd killed him. But was I? Did I really care about Jack? Did I really care about killing any of them?

I tried to take stock of my emotions. I'd told myself grief would come when the demon left me. I'd even cried with Jack after it did, cried with him over his dead friends.

The phrase "crocodile tears" came to me then, and I thought about it. I remembered everything about the killings, knew grief was what I *should* feel. But I didn't think I'd actually felt more than I would at the memory of some strangers I'd met the day before and left in passing. And there were the gloves. And the poncho. No demon possessed me to buy those things, and I couldn't remember doing so. I remembered I had them when I needed them, but nothing about putting them in my pockets or having them before I did.

I retraced everything that had happened in the hallucinations with Evelyn Blankenship. She made me feel homicidal rage, then horror at hints of what I was doing in the restaurant. Finally, I'd felt sorrow when she seemed to kill Jack. I thought hard about that. Those emotions. They were more than I could remember truly feeling – ever. If I hadn't been made to feel those things so intensely at Evelyn's hand, I wouldn't know now just how hollow my self-professed feelings were.

I faked emotions all the time when I was an attorney. Outrage. Compassion. Sorrow. Gratitude. But never fear. The appearance of fear had never been useful in persuading a jury, on those rare occasions a case went to trial, or when negotiating a settlement.

After I brought my legal career to an end, when I took to the road and was occasionally lost to a demon's control, I didn't feel any of the things I should have felt. I told myself that was because I hadn't been responsible. That I had to forgive myself, or I'd never go on. But was I fooling myself into believing the absence of feeling was due to an absence of guilt?

The gloves and the poncho.

I considered. Maybe there was no Evelyn. Maybe there were no ghosts and no demons. Maybe I *was* insane and found a way to frame murder as incidental to a nobler purpose. I considered. In every meaningful way, I was born from murder. What was I? Ten when I was Nicholas? Mother, sister, and brother murdered before my eyes. Whatever, whoever I might have been before that moment was lost. Every minute from then to now had formed me.

For years I'd been institutionalized, living every day in therapy. Medicated. Invaded. I had no private self. Every piece of me had been picked apart to find what remained of my core being – and the truth of it. Over the years I learned what the doctors wanted to see, what I had to show them to make them feel the pride of success. A hard case, brought back from the brink, their therapies shown efficacious. The medications lessened then stopped, and they turned me inside out again to see if the progress was real or had simply been induced by the drugs. They liked the drugs in me. I didn't. So, I convinced them it was me, not the drugs.

I'd gotten so close to normal that the court agreed to seal any records with my name, and I started a normal life with a new one. I went to college. Law school. I was careful to have friends, to appear as well-adjusted as any young man might be. But those friends – they were a means to an end. I don't remember truly caring about any of them.

You can go a long way in life if you don't feel fear. In first-year law, students were losing their minds over the curve, living with an inevitable sense of doom. I never felt that. I deduced not so much what I had to know, but what I had to say, and I hadn't the slightest fear about what I did not know.

I never worked for another lawyer. Fear would have given me better sense, but I went to work taking traffic cases right after passing the bar. I didn't need an office for that, just a business card and a willingness to hang out in the courthouse hallways, waiting for desperate defendants to notice the cheap suit I wore. Eventually, I had enough to rent office space and take on personal injury cases.

Through all of it, I saw the ghosts, felt the demons. But I ignored them. Getting my doctors to wean me off the drugs wouldn't have worked if they suspected I saw the things I saw.

I wondered if any of it had been real. Not normal reality. I accepted the truth of that no matter what I might have believed to exist alongside it. But I never understood why ghosts were here, or why demons had been tethered to them to keep them here. In truth, I didn't know what a ghost was, much less a demon. The names just fit with the English vocabulary. They could have been supernatural, sprouting from spirit and hellfire, or they could have been manifestations of some kind of interdimensional crossover. If there are everlasting souls, where do they go when we die? Heaven? Hell? Do they pass to some other plane of existence? I hadn't a clue. I hadn't a clue, either, why I could free them or how I could be possessed by those few demons I couldn't banish by force of will.

I didn't know a thing. But I had never looked that lack of knowledge in the eye, either. As lawyers like to say, "It is what it is." You don't need to know more than that.

I sipped on my Coke and decided to look at it, anyway. It didn't make sense. Forget the supernatural/interdimensional part of it; the math didn't make sense. I thought about First Jack's great grandfather's ghost, the Jack Ghost. As long as I'd been seeing ghosts, I didn't remember seeing one from a time much earlier than the Jack Ghost.

When would he have lived? If Jack was 75, he was born in 1944. Assuming arguendo that his father had *him* when he was 20, Jack's father would have been born about 1924. Assuming Jack's grandfather had Jack's father when he was 20, Jack's grandfather would have been born sometime around 1904. And if the Jack Ghost had *his* son when he was 20, he would have been born in 1884, roughly. Could be earlier, but I guessed no more than 30 years. So sometime between 1854 and 1884.

How may humans had populated the earth before that time? It had to be billions upon billions. Given the numbers, there should be infinitely more ghosts wandering the earth than living modern day humans, representing every culture and condition that has existed in history. Even assuming the relative recency of human life in the Americas, they should still be stacked up like cordwood all around me. What of ancient civilizations long buried beneath the modern world? Would the dead denizens haunting ancient Greek colonies go about their supernatural existence buried under centuries of dirt?

Above ground, the number of people who had lived and died in Jack Ghost's town had to be considerable in and of itself. But I only saw the Jack Ghost and one demon, until I'd added First Jack's friends to the numbers.

Looking at it square on, none of it made sense.

All of this made my head spin. Take Occom's Razor to the thing, and the simplest conclusion is that I was a bat shit crazy killer, like First Jack had surmised. That would explain the gloves and the poncho better than anything else at hand. And it wasn't like I didn't have a psychological predicate. The pieces fit.

Occom's Razor was getting dulled by what was becoming apparent, however. Whether I was a bat shit crazy killer or a humble smiter of demons, interest was long past due on my borrowed time. Where were the police? I'd left Jack alive. Unless someone or something silenced him, Jack would have called the cops. But there was nothing to suggested anyone was looking for a blood thirsty killer hereabouts. No roadblocks. No sirens. Take Occom's Razor to that, and Evelyn's pronouncement that she had taken care of Jack became the simplest explanation.

I finished my Coke and concluded I didn't know a fucking thing. I didn't know what was real and what wasn't, and I didn't seem to know a thing about myself either.

Well, *cogito, ergo sum*. I decided to start there.

But I was in a car wash, so I washed my bike first. A new journey deserved a clean ride.

Chapter 5

I nosed my bike out of the car wash and stopped at the street. Turning left would take me west and the hell away from the murders. But someone was bound to walk into that restaurant sooner or later and find the mayhem. I could try to sort out the pieces after that, once the story hit the news. I might find out then whether I should be worried about the shit ton of evidence I told Jack I'd left behind. I thought it was unlikely though. Whatever powers Evelyn Blankenship exerted to kill the last witness would have been pointlessly executed if she hadn't likewise removed the evidence that would have told the police the same thing Jack would have, albeit with whatever delay running down my prints and DNA might have caused. If she *hadn't* taken care of that along with Jack . . . well, I was back to square one, anyway.

I hit the throttle and leaned east. The bike followed suit, and I was headed back to the restaurant. If Evelyn and whatever being was residing inside of me were pulling my strings, they were going to have to pull hard enough to show their hand if they wanted to keep me in the clear. Assuming that's what they wanted. If not, the strings were pulling me exactly where they wanted me to go.

Johnny Cash came up on the stereo singing about Delia and her trifling ways. Then he shot a man in Reno just to watch him die. He shot another man and hung his head. I got the feeling the iPod shuffle wasn't playing as randomly as it was programmed to. Were the strings tugging? Was I being warned off?

I twisted the throttle and sped up. Fuck them.

It was just after six when I slowly rode down the main street, aptly named "Main Street." There were just a few cars scattered in the parking spaces in the downtown. I turned the stereo down, but not before I heard Tom Jones singing about Delilah and the knife in his hand. I felt Evelyn's smirk behind the murder tracks. She was there, somehow, watching and toying with me. It made my every move seem like it was being played out on stage for her enjoyment, with my actions scripted for me ahead of time. I wondered if I had any semblance of free will at this point. If I did, I figured it was no better than the kind that a rat has in a maze.

None of the cars was parked in front of the restaurant. But there *was* one bike backed into a space there. I rode a 2015 Harley Limited. Two tone, emerald green. The bike in the space was a 2015 Harley Limited. Two tone. Emerald green. The pipes, the chrome – all like I'd added to my own bike after I'd bought it. Evelyn was coming at me hard, hitting me with one thing after another, trying to keep me off balance. I won't say it wasn't working. I felt my resolve waning. Only a strong sense of defiance kept me from sinking to my knees, though this brand of defiance was like raging against the very thing that *wanted* you to rage against it, which was what set your rage alight in the first place.

I positioned my bike and backed into the space next to its twin. I turned the engine off and looked hard at the imposter. It had marks on the seat and scratches that didn't match those on my bike. The backrest was different, too. Okay. I concluded that the imposter was not actually my bike, as odd as the conclusion would be under ordinary circumstances. Close, but no cigar.

I got off the bike and walked to the door. I paused and took a deep breath. Then I walked in.

"Ghost Rider!" First Jack hollered. "He's back! Carol! Another pitcher. I'm buying this time."

First Jack sat where he'd been sitting when I left him just over two hours ago. The whole crew was there – Second Jack, Tom, Pete, and the man whose name I couldn't remember before I shot him – beers in hand. They turned to look at me and raised their glasses.

"Missed us already, Hun?" Carol laughed. "Told you this place was a hard habit to break."

I looked about the room. There was nothing amiss. No bloody footprints, no bloody gloves on the table – mostly, no bloody bodies. I saw Pablo moving about in the kitchen, too.

"Come on in, you crazy fucker," Second Jack beckoned. "Have a seat."

He pushed my chair out from the table, inviting me to sit.

Carol was pouring a fresh pitcher of beer. The only thing significantly changed from the scene of my first arrival was the hour and another customer standing with his back to me at the bar. Probably the mystery rider whose bike was mimicking mine on the street.

If you can put together profound relief with the sudden knowledge that you have gone absolutely, irretrievably insane, you know what I was experiencing. Throw in a nearly insurmountable element of doubt, and you're standing in the same shoes I was stupidly standing in at the door, not knowing what the hell to do.

"You look like you seen a ghost, for Chrissakes," First Jack said.

"Too hot to ride?" Second Jack asked. Then he answered himself: "It's a steaming bitch out there. Gotta be close to a hundred. I'd fucking sit it out myself."

Carol was walking to the table with two full pitchers. She looked at me with concern.

"You okay, Hun?"

I blinked. Everything stayed the same. I smiled.

"Just trying to shake off the heat," I answered. "Jack's right: it's a bitch out there."

"Well, have a beer," Carol said. She placed the pitchers on the table. "If Jack's drunk enough to buy, you'd better get it while the gettin's good."

I didn't know what else to do, so I sat down and smiled at my resurrected companions.

"You just miss us so much you turned around and come back?" Tom asked.

Carol put a clean glass in front of me and poured from one of the pitchers. She put her hand on my shoulder as she was pouring, caressing me like she had earlier, before I'd bludgeoned her to death. This time, I tried hard not to shudder.

"Well," I said. "Believe it or not, a cop told me to get someplace cool. This was the closest place I knew."

"A cop sent you here?" Second Jack asked.

I began recounting my ride into the ditch and Officer Smith's assistance. I left out the parts about fleeing the scene and my hallucinations with Evelyn, obviously. I spoke slowly, trying to assess the situation as I told my tale. I reached out with my mind to see if I could sense demon or spirit. Nothing there. I thought about the guy at the bar and glanced back at him. He was sipping a beer and taking no notice of us at the table. I didn't buy its being a coincidence that he was riding a bike that was the near doppelganger of my own. Who the hell was he?

I considered, too, whether my companions were actually ghosts. I regarded each of them in turn. I'd seen all of them before I'd departed. Except for Jack, they'd been ghosts then. But they seemed very much alive. I'd never encountered a ghost quite as corporeal as Jack's crew was right now. If they were hallucinations, I decided, they were living hallucinations.

I finished my story, and Second Jack laughed.

"That's my fucking grandson!"

"What?" I asked. "The cop?"

"Sure as shit."

Second Jack started to talk about how his grandson used to sit at his knee, listening to his stories about being the Chief of Police, deciding at the tender age of three that wanted to be a cop just like his grandpa. First Jack interrupted him.

"Yeah, yeah," First Jack said. "You're everyone's fucking hero. But the Ghost Rider ain't had a chance to meet his biggest fan yet."

"My biggest fan?"

"Yeah," First Jack beamed. "Hey, Duke! Come sit with us!"

Jack waved at the man at the bar. I turned around to look at him. If his bike had been disconcerting, Duke himself was a fucking nightmare.

CHAPTER 6

Turns out defiance has a shelf life. If I'd been standing, I *would* have fallen to my knees, defiance or no.

Duke turned and smiled at Jack and the gang, picked up his beer and started for our table. I noticed he went in for a more stereotypical Harley garb than I did. He wore a leather vest and a logo-emblazoned do-rag. He favored riding boots, too. I wear old running shoes when I ride, no do-rag, and I wouldn't be caught dead in a vest. I never wore anything that said "Harley" on it either. But his vest was open, and I noted that he wore a Key West Harley t-shirt underneath. I was wearing a Key West Sloppy Joe's t-shirt with Hemingway's picture front and center. Both of our shirts were red.

He was oddly pockmarked on one side of his face, but other than that, the face looked like mine. Rather, quite a bit like mine. I'd stared at enough proofs of my own visage selecting portraits for my jacket covers to see that "Duke" bore a remarkable resemblance to me. Except for the pockmarks.

My head spun. I was the rat in a maze, no doubt, but there wasn't going to be any cheese at the end of this bullshit. The quality of this new illusion was as real as the ones that took me back to my old office and onto the beach. Same difference. Only this time Evelyn was behind the proverbial curtain, pulling the levers unseen.

First Jack noted my expression and chuckled.

"Yeah, he looks a helluva lot like you. Fooled us at first, only the cheap bastard wouldn't buy us no beer."

Duke laughed. He stopped and looked down at me, grinning like he'd just discovered the greatest joy in his life. I thought he was going to try to hug me. He held out his hand instead, looking for a handshake. I gave it to him.

"Glad to finally see you face-to-face," he told me.

"Yeah," I said. "Likewise."

I didn't mean it.

I wanted to take the offensive, but I didn't know how. In the real world, this guy would have been some kind of nut job who saw my picture and the coincidence of my uncanny resemblance to him, glommed onto some crazy fan obsession as a result, and decided to *be* me. The Mark David Chapman move would be just over the horizon. But this wasn't the real world. The people I was sitting with were dead, all of them. They had to be. All of this was taking place in my mind. I didn't even know where my real self was. Back in the ditch? In jail? I wanted to yell "Stop!" at the top of my lungs. But I figured the illusion would keep on going, and the figments would all look at me like *I* was the one out of place. I drew inward to see if the phantom inhabiting my mind might be there to help. He'd seemed to be somewhat on my side during my last encounter with Evelyn.

Nada. Wherever he was living in my brain was a gated community, and I wasn't getting in.

Okay. I'd play the game. Evelyn had come clean in the last illusion, eventually whisking me off to the romantic encounter on the beach. I'd play it through and see where it led, knowing I could tug back on the strings all I wanted: I was still going to be the puppet.

"That's some bike you have parked out front," I told Duke. It was the closest thing to an offensive that I could think of.

"Thanks. It's a good ride," Duke said, and he pulled a chair up from the next table and sat, still grinning like that shit Chapman must have. Not that I had room to talk, all things being what they were.

"And it looks a lot like mine," I said, trying to inject a subtle tone of accusation.

He got up and went to the window, looking at our bikes parked side-by-side.

"Sonofabitch," he said, surprised. Then he came back to the table and slapped me on the back. "I didn't know you rode a bike like mine!"

"I don't," I corrected him, more than a little irritated at the slap. But since it wasn't real, I let it go. "You're riding a bike like *mine*."

"Well, when did you buy yours?" Duke asked. "Maybe I got mine first. In which case, you're riding a bike like mine, not the other way around."

The conversation was becoming stupidly mundane. I wasn't going to argue about who was copying whom with a hallucination. Instead, I began drinking my beer. I decided to get drunk, or give myself the illusion of being drunk, and see what the hell happened then.

First Jack looked back and forth from Duke to me when Duke sat back down, feigning a double and quadruple take. He pointed at each of us and laughed.

"Who'd believe it!?!" he asked.

I chugged my beer in response.

"So, your twin here came in after you left and asked if any of us had seen a guy suspiciously matching his own description," Second Jack said. "Craziest shit that ever happened in this place."

Not really, but Second Jack was oblivious to how high I'd set the bar.

"We told him all about you," Tom added. "We were kinda mean about it though, 'cause I swear we thought it was you, you know, getting even for our little joke about the haunted house."

"But if you look close enough, he clearly ain't you," Second Jack concluded.

"Well, I told them the truth," Duke explained, still beaming at me. "I read your blog and listen to your podcast. I read your books, too. Just decided I had to see this guy who looked like me and see what's what."

I drained my beer and poured another.

"Why?"

For the first time, Duke frowned.

"I just," he stammered. Then he said, "Look, can we move over to the bar for a minute? Just you and me?"

I looked hard into his eyes, to see if I could see Evelyn in there behind the mask. If it was her sitting next to me, pretending to be him, I couldn't see it. But I sure as hell suspected it, anyway.

"Sure."

I got up and walked to the bar and leaned forward on my elbows, my back to Duke. Carol was behind the bar and asked me if I needed anything.

"Two bourbons," I told her. "Neat."

Duke stood next to me. Carol set two glasses in front of us and poured.

"Hey, beautiful," Duke said. "You mind giving us a minute?"

Carol looked me, asking with her eyes if that's what I wanted. I nodded, and she went into the kitchen.

Duke took a deep breath and stood up straight and rigid.

"Damn, this is hard," he told me.

"What's hard?"

"I might be making a damned fool out of myself, but I don't care."

"More like you're making a damned fool out of me," I replied, certain I was speaking to Evelyn.

Duke picked up his glass and drank the bourbon down.

"Gotta get my courage up," he said.

"Courage for what?"

I picked up my glass and started to sip. I was beginning to feel the alcohol, real or imagined, from the two beers I'd drunk. I intended to start driving it home with the bourbon.

"Well, here goes," he said and then blurted out, "You didn't kill them."

I set my glass on the counter, looked at him and then nodded over to the table with Jack's crew.

"Obviously," I said. Only I remembered killing every one of them, except First Jack.

Duke sighed. It sounded like relief.

"Then you know," he said. "I mean, I was there." He gestured then to the pock marks on his face. "I've fucking known it all along," he said. "I wanted so bad to tell you, but they wouldn't let me see you. They wouldn't even tell me where you were. But now I found you, Nick. Took forever, but I found you, Little Brother."

CHAPTER 7

I sort of wanted to punch "Duke." Just lay him out and then rough up Second Jack enough to take his gun, come back, and shoot Duke dead. Maybe shoot the rest of the place up, too, until I ran out of bullets. It wasn't that I was angry. I wasn't feeling any of the anger I'd felt the first time Evelyn reminded me of my murdered family. I was just tired. And irritated. I thought that a renewed killing spree might force Evelyn to show herself. It wouldn't be like I was *really* killing anyone. I was sure that ship had sailed, as Jack told me. Still, everything here felt real, and I'm not a killer, all things being equal. I knew I didn't have the stomach for it. I also had to admit I was still riding high on the sense of relief I'd felt at the prospect that I *hadn't* killed any of these people after all. No point in spoiling what was left of that.

No. All things being equal, I'm not a killer – anymore. I never had a brother named "Duke." I had a brother named Jason, but when I'd shot my mother and sister, I shot him, too. They were dead. Jason was dead. And wrong. He was there, all right, but I had killed them. It hadn't been easy. I was only ten and not really big enough to handle the shotgun. The first blast had knocked me down. I still remember the terrible pain I'd felt in my shoulder and the struggle to get back up to fire it again. But, yeah, I did it.

If Jason had lived, he might look like "Duke." Which is to say a lot like me. He was a couple of years older, that's true, but I remembered family photographs and family members marveling at how Jason and I looked more like twins that not. My mother used to call us "the delayed twins."

I remembered it all right. Most of the time I was able to push the memory down. In fact, I almost never thought of it. If I had, maybe I wouldn't be able to live with it. Then again, I was amazed at how little I felt about it now, here in the face of Evelyn's latest attack on my psyche, bringing every bit of it to the surface. Still, I knew I was forcing down the secondary memories. Memories of my mother hugging me and telling me she loved me, her making chocolate chip pancakes on Saturday mornings because she knew I loved them. How I used to fight with my younger sister, Julie, knowing that I loved her even though I called her the "little creep."

And Jason? I was his little creep. He used to rough me up, call me names, and break my toys. I think I hated him the way brothers feel hate for each other until they don't. But I remembered him sticking up for me, too, trying to get between our father and me when Dad was out of his mind, bent on beating the hell out of me. I never knew why it was me. Always me. But it was. Except for when Jason was there, too, and tried to stop him. Then Jason took the beatings for me. So, yeah, I hated Jason – and I loved him more than the world.

I shoved all of that back down. The murders I could remember and go on, the love I could not.

I decided to ignore Duke and just sipped on my bourbon. I could sense him getting agitated next to me, waiting for some kind of reaction or recognition. I wasn't going to punch him, or shoot him, but I didn't have to talk to him either.

"Damn it, Nick," he finally said. "I know this is huge, but give me something here. I've followed your blog trail to hell and back to figure out where you were going. I've been on the road for about a year just hoping to get sight of you, so I could talk to you."

I sipped my bourbon and said, "I don't have a brother. I sure don't have one named Duke."

"Yeah, it's a nickname. Dumb one, too, I guess, but you used to like John Wayne movies. I've only ever used it on the road. I was always kind of hoping I'd find you and sort of ease into who I am. Didn't work out that way. All the ways I played it out in my mind, I'd find you, make friends, and talk you through it at the right moment," he sounded like he was going to cry. "But hell, that was never going to work. You look just like me. No way you'd buy the friendly stranger act. But now I'm here, and you know it's me. You know I'm Jason."

"Yeah, well Jason's dead, Evelyn," I said. If I wasn't going to punch or shoot Duke, I was a least going to call Evelyn out on the act. "I shot him. You know that, and you know I know that. What did you think? I'd be so desperate to see a ghost come to life that I'd forget this game you're playing with me. Make it go away, Evelyn. All of it. I'm not your plaything."

"Evelyn?" Jason asked. "Why are you calling me Evelyn?"

"Jesus," I sighed. "Shut the fuck up, Evelyn. We're done here."

I stood up and carried my bourbon back to the table and sat with the crew.

"Well, that looked mighty intense," First Jack said. "You know him? Is he bothering you?"

"He's bothering me all to fuck," I said. "Everything is. So, let's drink and be merry, eh?"

I downed the bourbon and a few more. Duke stood at the bar, just as he had when I'd come in, his back to me. I looked back once long enough to see he was crying, hitching breaths, and bringing his hand up to wipe his eyes.

I ignored him after that, listening to the crew regain their rhythm. First Jack was funny, Second Jack was foul. Even poor Pete was boisterous here and there. I laughed with them and told them stories about being a lawyer. They liked that and instructed me on how many lawyers it took to do this or that and to constitute a "start" when they were at the bottom of the ocean.

Time passed, and the imaginary alcohol left me too drunk to think or move without knocking something over. Eventually, the crew got up, one-by-one to say they'd had enough. They shook my hand and told me they hoped to see me again, and if they didn't, they'd try to read my books, and they'd had a helluva time at any rate. Because I was loaded beyond belief, I forgot that they weren't real, and I was sad to see them go.

I turned around to find Duke. Somewhere along the way, he'd left – or vanished. Good riddance.

Alone, I sat and wondered, but the drink made me dumb, and the wondering wasn't much. Then I felt her hand on my shoulder again, then caressing my neck.

"You're not going to get on that bike of yours, are you, Hun?" Carol asked.

"No."

"Can't sleep here on my table."

"No."

"Come on," she grabbed my hand and pulled me up. "Let's go, Ghost Rider."

"In the sky?" I laughed.

"Up the cloudy draw," and she leaned forward to kiss me. She tasted like cigarettes.

CHAPTER 8

"Come with me," I thought instead of heard. I was dreaming. I had to be. There was nothing sensory about me. Not feeling, sound, sight, taste, or smell. I was settled into oblivion, comfortably. Dreaming, yes, but my consciousness didn't seem to know it. I seemed awake, in my mind, at least. Bounded in a nutshell, yet king of infinite space. Infinite nothingness. The exhortation wasn't mine, hadn't come from me, yet it was inside of my mind, drawing me away from myself. I was no longer who I was, but something else. Without senses, I began to perceive that everything that could exist was within the power of my will, yet I had not willed it, nor thought to will it, so all existence lay mute, expressionless. With me in the void was another. I didn't sense in this other or in myself sentience. We simply were, together, without thought or purpose. We needed nothing, envisioned nothing. We were not together as two humans would be, aware of each other, close, but separate beings. Instead, we were like two sitting in a pitch-black room, occupying the same space, one and more than one simultaneously. There was no time, rather a measureless eternity surrounding us, enveloping us. There was a glimmer once in the void. An instant of curiosity, a flicker approaching thought, a wondering without words, but had it words they would have been "what if?" The other felt something then, just as briefly, that in a human mind would have been fear. It exerted a force it hadn't known before – a thought. With the thought it reached out and extinguished the curiosity that made it fear, and all was at once as it had been. Eternity lay motionless once more, and the two were one

again – forever. Then one found forever less than enough and conceived in an instant of "what if?" – everything. The two that were one became two, and what they had been was torn apart. One reached out into the "what if?" and was gone. The void was no more, and the one left became infinite and aware, and it knew thought. And it knew rage at the one that was lost.

. . . . . .

"Come with me," I was beckoned again, though I was alone, floating without form over a beach much like the one Evelyn had taken me to, where I again saw Evelyn Blankenship, this time through eyes I cannot explain. From this Evelyn Blankenship I sensed thoughts and feelings the Evelyn Blankenship I'd encountered before did not possess, and I understood, not quite knowing how, that the Evelyn Blankenship below and the one who had taken over my consciousness were not the same. The one I'd known, phantom or wraith, was not of this world. The Evelyn below was decidedly human, and like me, born of flesh and blood. Suddenly, my vantage point from above fell away, and my consciousness descended and became one with the human Evelyn Blankenship.

. . . . . .

Evelyn Blankenship sat on a towel on the beach. She wore a yellow summer dress and a wide-brimmed hat to keep the sun from her face. She wore sunglasses with very large lenses. She didn't want to be recognized, especially today. Last night had been a whirlwind of emotions. She had been happier, for a while, than she remembered ever being. And then her world crashed around her. The morning had come, with the sun shining through her curtains, warming her face. She heard familiar birds chirping outside her window, sounds that always roused her and filled her with anticipation of the day. But this morning she felt deadened to it all. She felt cold and overwhelmed with the silence of loneliness and grief.

She and Ted had had a date the night before. He told her he had gotten reservations at a very exclusive restaurant, Simon's. Ted liked exclusive places. Moreover, he liked the world to know that he was welcomed in such places, that he had access to anyplace he wished to be. At times, she considered it a failing of his. Other times, it made her think of him as a little boy taking joy in the wonders life had to offer. When she thought of him as the boy, when she saw his face lighting up at the ambiance of the places he had chosen, it made her love him all the more, and she tried to ignore any crasser motives.

The previous night it hadn't been hard to imagine the little boy. Ted spoke to her of the wondrous delights Chef Simon created for his guests and of the difficulty in becoming one of those guests. He'd intimated that he knew the right people and had made the right calls to bring her the perfect evening. He was beaming with what he obviously considered the magnitude of the experience and his pride at being able to share it with her.

She loved Ted, though he was tough and maybe even a little cruel sometimes. The cruelty she attributed to his profession: An occupational necessity. Ted was the foremost criminal defense attorney in Los Angeles and as close to being a celebrity as someone could be without actually being one. His clients, on the other hand, were often bona fide stars, the wayward kind who found themselves in trouble with drugs, alcohol, and the illusion that they were invulnerable to the law. Often, with Ted's help, they were. When it was the public's sympathy for his clients that was needed, he was deftly capable of making his clients look like they were the victims of someone else's greed or even their own success. When outrage was required, he adopted a scorched earth strategy, laying waste to the lives and reputations of anyone who threatened his clients in any way.

His clients got away with any number of terrible or embarrassing acts with nothing more than a court ordered stint in rehab. Some few who'd really tested the limits, those who'd committed crimes up to and including murder, were often acquitted with the victims the seeming perpetrators of their own demise. Every juror in a celebrity trial, Ted once told her, was like a nerd in a photo op with his or her favorite science fiction actor. Most felt unworthy to be there in the first place and were hard-wired to say "thank you" with an acquittal.

Other celebrity clients, nobodies whose celebrity was brought about through nothing more than the notoriety of their crimes, were, with rare exceptions, certain to be convicted. The difference, Ted explained, was that the jurors on those cases felt they would be seen as heroes by the world that had universally condemned the criminal celebrities. Everyone, no matter how powerless in their daily lives, wants to be the hero.

Yet Ted could ride the wave of publicity those clients generated, too, appearing on talk shows and on the news with more abandon than he would with television or movie star clients. The criminal celebrities were doomed no matter what Ted did, but he took the opportunity to perpetuate his own form of fame. He wasn't the foremost criminal defense attorney merely because he was good, but because he made damn sure the world saw his face as often as possible and perceived him as the best.

Evelyn, of course, understood the processes of fame, though her own had come by chance. She'd understood from an early age that she was sensitive to things other people were not. She felt, intuited the struggles in other people. She could see, clearly, no matter the masks people wore, the real person inside. Mostly, she was able to see that they were lost souls, living morning to night, carried along by a simple inertia that dictated that they would live the day as they had lived the day before, incapable of change. Inside, beneath the personas they affected for the world around them, she sensed loneliness and confusion. She had no better way to describe her ability than to say her own psyche was like a worm that could crawl into the minds of those she turned her attention to, moving within to see the true places from which they saw the world.

Most people she saw were lost. But then she began to see shapes around them, ghostly images of other beings. The beings always came in pairs. They were human, or had been. They had lived their own lives – many lives – and had the accumulated wisdom of centuries lived in human form. They were, by some accounting of the spiritual world she did not understand, assigned to living humans, to guide them to their higher purpose. Theirs were the voices people heard that provided doubt and urgings that there was something more to be done with their lives. But the accounting, she saw, was imperfect. Benevolent beings though these guides were, their ability to sink into the minds of the humans they were paired with was limited. Theirs were distant voices unless and until the humans they were here to guide could learn to invite them in. Then one day she had a revelation. It was simple, really, and so obvious she didn't know how she could have missed it, even as a child of twelve, which was how old she was when she came upon the revelation.

While she had begun to see the spirit guides surrounding others, she never saw her own. But if they were there for others, there must have been those assigned to her. So, she found a book on meditation in the public library near her home. She'd read how to bring her own mind to a calm and receptive state. And she practiced, learning quickly how to alter her consciousness, to bring it closer to the spiritual realm. One day, she reached this state in her bedroom and opened the door, made the invitation to her spirit guides. And suddenly, they were there, sharing her consciousness. They were Al'an and Farvan, an ancient pair sent to show her the right path, to show her how to tap into her psychic sensitivity. In her mind, working with her, they built what she perceived as a solid structure, a peaceful cabin by a lake. There, in the cabin by the lake constructed in her own mind, she could take her consciousness, and there, with her, Al'an and Farvan would tell her the secrets of life and love and happiness. More important, they taught her how to teach others to find their own spirit guides and to invite them in.

There was a sense of peace that came with her retreats to the cabin in the company of her spirit guides.

Ted never believed any of it. Nor did he believe she did. She had forgiven him that, seeing that minds are more naturally closed to the concept. Were they not, what would there be to be overcome? How else could the spirit grow otherwise, beyond the parochial? We are all, she thought, works in progress, for this life and the next.

Behind her, she heard the sounds of carnival music and children screaming on rides. All along the beach, barely covered teens ran and laughed and played. The adults sat on towels like her and under large umbrellas. Surfers rode their boards on the waves, and kids without surfboards body surfed toward a grinding halt in the sand. Hidden *beneath the laughter, she sensed the sadness in all but the youngest children on the rides and in the water. The young ones had no fear, no doubt, no pain. Theirs was the moment. Parents drank from the joy of their children, fulfilled by their happiness. Some few, she sensed, took a desperate joy – children had been lost to them, replaced with insurmountable heartache. The children they had left brought them back from the abyss. Barely. But for most, it would be enough to keep them going, to hold the pain at bay until time enough passed and only the occasional tears for the lost remained. She sensed a suicide among them, and a lonely child, unable to take the transitory pleasure the other children took on the rides. A little girl. The girl sensed her mother's end was near, but had no grown-up understanding of how to prevent it, or how to try.*

Evelyn felt sadness in many of the older adults over declining youth and regret. Lives lived in directions they hadn't anticipated, hadn't wanted, living the consequences of youthful conceit and abandon. She sensed fear. Lost income, uncertain futures. Divorce. Wishes for something to take them from the numbing dreariness their lives had become.

In the teens she sensed barely repressed sexuality. Somewhere under the waves, she felt the fear of a boy – thirteen she decided – whose breath threatened to leave him as a large wave he'd been caught under thrashed him against the bottom, scraping his skin over rocks and opening wounds to the stinging saltwater. Just as the boy thought his lungs would burst, the wave let up. The sudden pressure was gone, and he stood, desperately filling his lungs with new air. The fear left him instantly, replaced with laughter and the thought that he would like to do it again, just like that. The cuts and the blood were nothing to him. She envied that for a moment.

All of the pulsing life about her mixed happiness, tragedy, and despair. The soup of life, she liked to call it. Everything in a big pot, stirring the longings of many souls.

But of late, it wasn't the souls of the living that transfixed her. Lately, she had come to sense the souls of the deep, the souls of the dead. She let her consciousness wander, let it soar out over the waves and toward the immense ocean beyond. She sensed the deep and was awed by it, the way she was awed when she looked at pictures of galaxies and was overcome with the vastness of space and time.

On the ocean's floor, she saw the wrecks of ships and skeletal remains. She was not pinned to place at all, and her consciousness moved across the great depths and seas and oceans of the world. A Greek trireme lay at the bottom of the Mediterranean, unseen and unseeable. All that was left to it were scattered silt-covered pieces, buried. The souls aboard had perished in an ancient storm, longing in the end to see their wives and children, that longing intensifying their fear, less of death than of loss of their loved ones who would live.

A whaling vessel sank more than a 150-years past, far from the shores of Nantucket, not from storm or rock, but of age and decrepitude. Its boarded pitched planks gave way for no reason other than a defect in construction coupled with careless years of neglect. Profit came first, and with enough profit some few ships became expendable, as did the souls that manned them.

She sensed ancient mariners from Africa plying the ocean as few now believed them capable, sailing to South American shores and returning home with holds filled with tobacco, cocaine, and gold. She would not let what she knew or read censor her feelings about what was and restrict them to what the history books said was possible or impossible. No one alive now had been there, had seen those places or people. But she was beginning to see.

She touched the soul of an African man, an African Leonardo, living millennia before the Renaissance inventor. The African's name lay beyond her reach, but she saw him standing on the western shore of the continent, looking to the ocean and imaging a vessel that could travel far beyond the lands he stood upon. Like the modern thought that, in all the universe, humans on earth cannot be the only sentient life, he believed that the ocean was not an empty expanse, but a barrier only to the certainty of lands and peoples that lay and lived beyond the ocean's sway. His was an obsession to find them, to see who and what they might be.

She felt his mind constructing boats in his imaginings, solving problems of wind and propulsion, size and buoyancy, storms and waves. He predicted that the ocean, like rivers, would have currents to contend with, and he wondered where they would be found and how to fight them. He memorized the night sky through the seasons and theorized about navigation over long distances. He experimented with materials and substances that would withstand the stresses of the waves and the corrosive effects of saltwater. He studied his fellow villagers and determined how much they would eat and drink to stay alive over a season, which to him would have been the measure of a calendar year. He designed uniform clothing that would protect a crew from the sun and wind, and containers to hold water. He discovered salt as a preservative for meat and determined to make such meat the only part of his diet for half a season. Before long, he sickened with scurvy and wondered at its cause. He did not feel hunger, for the dried meat sustained him in that regard. So, he experimented and ate fruits and plants native to his diet once more, and the scurvy departed. Then he solved the problem of decay of such plants by making them into powders that would not rot, and he consumed the powder and the meat, and it sustained him without sickness.

The boats he designed in his imaginings were unheard of in his time. They would be at home on the sea the way the smaller boats his people constructed were on the rivers and lakes of his land. His people thought him a god and followed his vision and constructed the boats and sails he had explained to them. They made all the things he wished them to make the way he wished them made. In a few years after he first contemplated the ocean and how it might be crossed, he set foot on the South American continent with the bravest of his people, returning with riches to be traded throughout the African world. For a time, his people prospered because of him.

His was a rare genius that, had he lived today, would have propelled him to the very top of whatever scientific fields he found fit to explore. But he was lost in time, as were his people and their accomplishments. The mystery of cocaine and tobacco found in ancient mummies would not be solved – or debunked – in the ruins of the great civilizations, but in the vision of one man, in one small village, who could never be found in the artifacts of civilizations.

Yet she sensed him now, another soul lost to the sea more than three thousand years ago, and she was overwhelmed.

She forgot Ted for a while and closed her eyes and lived through the ages.

CHAPTER 9

I woke up alone with a bad hangover. I remembered the room and the bed and the night I'd spent with Carol in her apartments over the restaurant. The light from an overcast sky came in through the windows like an icepick between my eyes.

Carol's bedroom was old. Layers of paint covered the walls and what would have been woodwork back when the room was new. Now, instead of ornate moldings against the ceiling and floor, the thickened paint created the impression of badly molded clay over the wood, with every sharp edge and carved design bloated like a dead fish. Ancient wallpaper separated from the walls here and there, and brown water stains flowed down the seams. The latest paint covering was gloss white, meant to hide the decrepitude that had taken over the walls. The shiny surface was yellowed by cigarette smoke. The room reeked of mold and nicotine. The smell settled hard, and I ran into the adjacent bathroom to vomit. I admired the small black-and-white tiles that still held up well on the bathroom floor, with grout as yellowed as the walls, but conveying a comforting vintage, antique feel. I decided the tiles were original to the apartment, and I took extra care not to hit the floor when I vomited again.

I spit for a while and then gulped water directly from the cold tap over the sink. I tried to clear my mind, but the other side of clarity, I knew, was going to be more of the same broken reality that had taken hold of me ever since I'd met Evelyn Blankenship – the phantom. I gave up on clarity and sank to the floor.

Time passed, and I found enough strength to get into the shower. The hot water revived me enough to know I had to face the day. Seizing it was out of the question. More likely than not, it was going to thrash me around like a rag doll in the jaws of a vicious dog.

I got dressed and found a note from Carol on the nightstand, next to an overflowing ashtray.

"Good morning, Lover," it read. "Take your time. Make yourself at home. I'm downstairs in the restaurant. Come on down when you're ready. Breakfast is on me."

I wasn't "Hun" anymore. And Carol wasn't as old as I thought she was. I decided the cigarettes were aging her prematurely, but illusion or no, she had been exquisite.

I went to the living room, found Carol's desktop computer, and began searching for other changes in this reality that had the dead popping up like mowed dandelions after a spring rain. My searches weren't new. I'd made them before, following those rare demon encounters that I'd lost. I started with Muncie, Indiana. The funeral director I'd murdered in his viewing room was doing business again, no worse for the wear. I poured through the archives of the local paper in a Cape Girardeau, Missouri. The family I murdered there was in attendance at the daughter's dance recital, two years after I'd lost my battle and they their lives. Des Moines, Iowa; Mitchell, South Dakota – the occasional mayhem, but none of it my doing, and the dead were all alive and well. I found the man I'd killed in Upstate New York was still dead, but he had died in a car accident. No mention of the hatchet I used to decapitate him.

I sat back in the chair. Were the living dead an illusion made part of this illusion, or had the killings themselves been an illusion? I couldn't know what was real, but it was nagging at me that the very idea of demons and ghosts and my battles amongst them could be categorized as delusional. Weigh that reality against this one, and it was hard to say which was less likely. If I submitted myself to the psychiatrist's couch and told the story of my life up to yesterday, would the thought doc believe a word of it? Would my explanation of ghosts and demons and possession strike anything like a chord of belief in any sane person considering it? A sane person might conclude I was a crazy bastard of a mass murderer, perhaps, except I no longer had proof that anyone I might claim to have killed was actually dead, excluding my guy from New York.

If I told the thought doc that I'd left a restaurant the day before, suffered a heat induced brain injury of some sort, woke up in a ditch convinced I'd killed a bunch of people who turned out to be alive and well, would that be believable? Probably, with the caveat that I clearly needed more couch time and a full medical work up to boot.

The bottom line was that everything I'd lived in the preceding five years was seriously in doubt. I didn't feel like it was, but if one reality can appear altered, what was keeping the preceding reality from being the part out of synch?

I reflected on my dream from the night before. Leaving everything else behind for a moment, I got the sense that I hadn't been alone through any of it. Was the phantom living in that gated community in my brain trying to tell me something, show me something to lead me toward my "awakening," which he and Evelyn had discussed like I wasn't even there?

And what of the other Evelyn? My introduction to her by way of Slumber-Vision was perplexing. She'd been on the beach, to be sure, but it wasn't the beach the phantom Evelyn had taken me to. Nor had she been *that* Evelyn, but an entirely *human* facsimile. I considered that I was being shown another piece of a complicated puzzle told through a cosmic sort of eavesdropping. Nowhere in that listening in did I hear the faintest voice of the all-powerful Evelyn who had carted me back in time and to a beach scene that had all the ambiance of an Edward Hopper painting.

Last night I had been determined to stay as much out of Evelyn's game as I could. Now I decided my only choice was to live this new reality and see where it led. There was some relief in that decision. In this reality, I'd only killed the people I'd loved and no one else. Of course, the unknowns and the inexplicable remained. But then, it is what it is.

Patience. It was the only defense I had.

My thoughts turned back to the human Evelyn. Her vision of death was like a completely different theology from my own. She saw spirits and reincarnations and benevolence emanating from the spirit world. I saw demons and tortured souls, the equivalent of a pervasive evil lurking just below the surface of the living. I liked her version better.

I typed "Evelyn Blankenship" into the search bar and began to read the first article that popped up. It was on a skeptic website.

"Psychic" Evelyn Blankenship
Won't Ask About the Letter "J"

By Scott O'Neill

As our readers well know, famous television psychics have an age-old trick up their sleeves: they let their subjects tell them what the subjects want to hear. "I feel energy with a 'J' attached to a name." Hands go up, and the game of twenty guesses leaves strangers convinced the psychic has a real connection with the deceased, bringing messages from beyond. Tears flow, provoked by the subject's having provided the information spouted by the psychic in the first place. It's called "cold reading." To the skeptic, it's an absurd and ridiculously obvious feedback loop. Evangelists have been known to take a different approach. Everyone remembers the famous "faith healer" Peter Popoff being fed information about worshippers via an earpiece. Thanks to skeptic warrior James Randi and a radio scanner, Popoff was caught cold (pardon the pun) taking messages, not from God, but from Popoff's own wife, reading from "prayer request" cards, each filled out by the subjects before the healing hoedown even began, and containing all the information Pete needed to appear as a vessel of the Lord, healing from on high.

As a skeptic, I spend much of my time debunking psychics and faith healers for this website. But part of my job is to leave my own convictions and preconceptions aside, to listen, observe, and then – almost without fail – to explain the tricks used to fool the desperate into belief. The catch is that my explanations must follow legitimate observation; they can't precede it. I have to rely on evidence, not conjecture.

So, I was happy when psychic Evelyn Blankenship accepted my challenge and allowed me to observe her at work, up close and personal. Most everyone has seen her on television, after all, and most seem amazed by the apparent accuracy of her readings.

Having watched her show numerous times myself to see what I could see outside of the ubiquitous editing most television shysters use, I concluded she was not using cold reading. She didn't ask questions, at least not the information-gathering kind. So, I figured, it was a variation of the Popoff deceit. Nothing I'd see on the tube, to be sure. The only way to crack it would be in person. I needed first-hand observations to pierce the veil.

I showed up at her LA studio on May 5, with my crew – assistants who would observe the intake of studio audience members. No cards were allowed. No questions. Just tickets, without assigned seating. However, I had my crack web team online, as well, scanning for any submissions or other intake methods that might be used to gain audience information beforehand. Further, she agreed in advance that I could select the audience members. No easy trick rounding up 200 people to sit on the sound stage in the short time I was allowed – two weeks. But we succeeded. At least 50 of those audience members were, like myself, professed skeptics. They agreed, as had all the audience members I selected, to keep an open mind, but not to get stupid. Seemed fair enough.

Then the embarrassing part. Ms. Blankenship agreed for a female member of our staff to sit with her through make-up and wardrobe, to make sure no hidden devices were planted on Ms. Blankenship. She went further,

*allowing herself to be examined in her dressing room
before she put her clothes on. We examined the dress she
wore beforehand. It was clean and clean. Nothing
attached to it or sewn in. We were allowed to use a bug-
detector in the studio as well. Nothing turned up. My
volunteers accompanied the crew before and after the
show, keeping them honest as well. (For a full list of
protocols used, click here).*

*Ms. Blankenship took the stage (Link to broadcast
here), with me at her side. She told the television
audience who I was (the live audience already knew) and
why she agreed to my being there. The messages she had,
she explained, were too important to be doubted. She
was willing, therefore, to agree to my conditions in order
remove doubt that she was, in fact, the real deal.*

*Ms. Blankenship took the first read. She didn't call
out a name or number randomly to see who piped up.
She directly called out Lester Johnson, a skeptic, like me,
and a friend. Lester hates Facebook and all other forms
of social media. He has no web presence at all, not even
a LinkedIn account. No easy way to get a "read" on him
unless you actually know him. Sadly, Lester's wife May
passed away from breast cancer a year ago. She, like
Lester, lived in anonymity. I couldn't have picked the
first read better myself.*

*But Ms. Blankenship surprised me. She called Lester
by his full name and said she had a message from May.
Lester told me later he was angry at first. How dare this
woman use May for her own aggrandizement. The anger
faded to tears within 20 seconds. (Watch here for full
video).*

I clicked, fast forwarded, and watched what I thought was the
human Evelyn tear up as she started the reading. She looked exactly like
my phantom Evelyn. Even on the small monitor, I could see her physical
presence was – imposing. Scott O'Neill looked small by her side, and

every time he looked at her, he was looking up. Maybe "imposing" is the wrong word. She moved confidently, with the same commanding presence that Phantom Evelyn had used to keep me floundering during our imaginary visit in my old conference room. There was something else, however; a clear empathy and compassion that the phantom Evelyn lacked.

"Oh, Lester," she said. "I'm so sorry for your loss. But May's suffering is over. She is happy where she is, and, Lester, she sees you. She is with you."

Then the human Evelyn tilted her head like the phantom Evelyn had done when she claimed to kill First Jack. On this Evelyn, the gesture was a lot more endearing. "She says to tell you, 'Saddle up, take the sunset, and ride to the other side of darkness.'"

"Oh my God!" Lester rose from his seat and shouted, crying, though the tears were of joy, not sadness. "May said that to me so many times! So many times."

Evelyn said, "It was her way of telling to hang on when times were bad."

Lester broke down and fell into his seat.

"I miss her," he sobbed.

Evelyn walked into the audience then and held Lester's hand. His eyes widened. "Yes, May! Oh, my God, I miss you."

"What did she say?" Evelyn asked.

"She loves me. She'll always love me."

I clicked off the video and went back to the article.

> As I said, in my work, the only way to be true is to keep an open mind. Lester and I have spoken about this reading several times. He told me when Ms. Blankenship took his hand, May appeared to him and smiled, repeating the "Saddle up" line Ms. Blankenship had used. As far as Lester knows, May never said that to anyone else.
>
> I'm a skeptic. I'd say I'm always right when I debunk psychics. Their tricks are easy to see when you apply logic and observation. But I have to admit, this story

remains open. I will continue to investigate Ms. Blankenship because I know there has to be a trick. An immensely clever trick at that. But for the moment, I have to play fair. I don't see how she did it, and even I am considering the possibility that something that defies easy explanation is at work with Ms. Evelyn Blankenship.

I got up from the computer and went to the kitchen. I found a glass in the cupboard and started gulping sink water in a more civilized fashion. I felt like shit.

CHAPTER 10

I took the stairs down into the restaurant, pushing thoughts of the human Evelyn from my mind, one complication too many to think about.

On the way down, another possibility occurred to me regarding my shifting reality: what if everything, all of it had been real? What if I *had* killed every one of those people I remembered having been possessed to kill? What if I *had* slaughtered everyone in this place yesterday, except Jack, and what if the force that lay behind Phantom Evelyn had the power to bring every one of them back, to heal their wounds and reignite the spark of life? Would she have done so? What if it had been the silent being living inside of me that had raised the dead? Evelyn had convinced me she had killed First Jack with nothing more than a tilt of her head. If that were real, Jack died, too, and Evelyn had, by a force of will that hadn't seemed at all difficult for her, killed him. Did she bring him and the rest of them back, too, as some twisted expression of the love she claimed to feel for me?

I laughed. It could very well be none of this was an illusion. For some reason, I found it hilarious that I might just be stuck in a battle of wills between two omniscient, all-powerful lovers, like a child in the middle of a custody dispute. Maybe my own sins, most of them, had been washed clean in the process. But what was I to these two beings?

Had every bit of my own power to banish demons and free dead spirits belonged to one of them? Had the demons been extensions of one of them? Were those times I lost to a demon and killed caused by one of them getting the upper hand for a time, at just the right time? I'd often thought it a miracle I hadn't been caught before. I had itineraries for heaven's sake, appointments with the fallen. Yet I'd only worried once about getting caught, when I left First Jack alive to bear witness against me. Why in God's name wouldn't I have been worried *before* that happened? Had Mommy or Daddy hidden my hand? Had I unconsciously known it?

The stairs let out into the kitchen. Pablo was there cooking bacon and eggs. He turned and smiled at me, knowingly. I figured I wasn't the first *Hun* turned *Lover* to descend these stairs.

Both Jacks were there huddled over breakfast. They waved, and First Jack rolled his eyes in Carol's direction, nodding his approval or congratulations. I wasn't sure which. Breakfast was popular here. Patrons filled every table, eating or waiting for their orders. Others waited by the door to be seated. Carol was taking an order at one of the tables, joking with the customers. She saw me and smiled. I smiled back, sincerely now that I considered she might be real.

"Hey, Lover," she said on her way to post the order for Pablo. She came back and asked me if I wanted breakfast. I said yes.

"Why don't you eat at the bar?" Carol asked. "Keep me company?"

I smiled, feeling the first real measure of relief I'd felt since – forever.

"Love to, beautiful."

She *was* beautiful, I decided, no matter the cigarettes or the premature lines around her mouth from years of dragging in their smoke. I might even figure out a way to stay another night because Carol, I realized, was giving me real, true joy, most likely due to the confluence of my latest revelations, but hell, she was gorgeous and delightful – a confluence I had no reason to argue against.

I ordered bacon and eggs, over easy, and orange juice. I saw Carol slip in a small shot of vodka into the juice. She handed it to me and said, "Hair of the dog."

I took a sip. I wasn't sure it would help, but I was up for new things this morning.

"Hey," I said. "Gotta check on my bike. I'll be right back."

I made my way through the crowd and went out the door. I saw my bike sitting between two cars. No doppelgangers. The bike was covered with dew but seemed fine other than that. The sky was cloudy. Fuck it. The day was going to be fine, sunshine or no.

When I went back inside, Second Jack was making a ruckus.

"Fuck you, Jack," he shouted. "You been eggin' me on for forty fucking years."

First Jack seemed taken aback, but, hell, I figured this was how they played.

Only Second Jack wasn't playing. He stood up and pulled the gun I'd used on him the day before and shot First Jack in the chest. The noise was deafening. My ears were instantly ringing. First Jack looked surprised for a moment – then he died.

Everyone got up at once, screaming and running for the door. I stood there, stunned. Second Jack looked stunned, too, like he was more surprised at what he'd just done than any of the screaming customers frantically funneling to the exit.

"Fuck it," he said, and he aimed the gun at Carol.

I don't remember jumping in front of Carol, but I did. I liked her. I wasn't sure it was enough to take a bullet for her, but I did. The bullet felt like Muhammad Ali laying me out like Sonny Liston, only there could be no doubt that *this* blow struck home. I hit the floor. Carol didn't scream, but was suddenly on the ground with me, cradling my head. I could see Second Jack looking even more stunned than he'd been after shooting First Jack. He said "Fuck it" again and shot himself in the temple.

That was the last I saw of the Jacks of this world. It was the last I saw for a while.

CHAPTER 11

I wasn't conscious in the usual sense. I existed in complete oblivion.
Except I heard voices.

"You saw what I saw. He should be dead. He was dead."

"But he wasn't. He's not."

"You saw what I saw. His aorta was ripped apart."

"And the bullet lodged in the spinal column. I know."

"Why isn't he dead? Why wasn't he already dead when we opened him up?"

Silence.

. . . . .

I saw Evelyn again – the human Evelyn. I heard her thoughts, felt her emotions.

She sat at a table in an upscale restaurant. A man sat opposite her. He wore a gray suit, not like the ones I used to wear, but expensive. He rested with his elbows on the table, his hands cradled just below his chin. A candle between them lit his face. He was handsome, with perfectly styled black hair. He had the faintest hint of dark stubble growing on his face, which seemed to make him all the more handsome in the candlelight. His shirt sleeves protruded from his suit coat. French cuffs. Gold cufflinks, monogrammed, small T, large D, and small A.

He smiled. His teeth were movie star teeth. Straight, perfect and glowing an unblemished white.

Evelyn thought him beautiful.

He turned his head slightly to the left and right, his eyes leaving Evelyn's long enough to see who might be near, who might be watching them. It was a practiced move, part of an ever-present need to know who might be taking notice.

Evelyn frowned briefly, but his eyes returned to her, and she felt content.

"You know I love you," he said.

"As much as you're spending on dinner, I guess that might be true."

"Don't kid. I mean it."

Evelyn knew she loved him, wanted him every moment they were together. Briefly, she let herself think that she wasn't certain he loved her the same way. But she wanted it to be so, so she pushed the thought away.

"You know," she teased, "sometimes I wonder how you divide the dark from the light."

"The what from the what?"

"You live in darkness, my love. You're surrounded by horrors, horrible people every day."

He smiled uncomfortably.

"It's an avocation. Everyone deserves a defense, the best defense they can get. The pristine among us don't need me. Those surrounded by darkness do."

"You revel in it."

"No. I've said it before; I play the part that has to be played."

"You put on your armor and do battle in the name of . . ."

"Due process. It's not sexy, but it is everyone's right."

"You're the actor on the stage."

"But I'd be a terrible playwright. I'd demand proof in the face of suspicion."

"In your world, Claudius would sit on the throne, untouched."

"Of course. Need I count the lives that would have been saved?"

"So, my love, when does the armor come off? When does the face paint come off, and when do the players go home?"

"The moment I see you. You're the light."

Evelyn wondered.

"But I'm not the bright lights. They love you, too."

"I can't help it," he laughed. "I'm ridiculously photogenic."

They drank wine, a fine red he'd managed to say costs $500 a bottle. He was such a happy boy with his toys.

. . . . .

Then I was with the other Evelyn, the phantom, the puppet master.

She'd been kind enough to dress me this time for the sand and the heat. I wore khakis and a light cotton shirt. A white Panama hat shielded my head and face from the beating sun. I had my favorite sunglasses on. I sat in the sand. She sat beside me, wearing khakis this time, too, but she wore the same floppy sun hat and oversized sunglasses. In the distance, more blinding than the sun, a pyramid dominated the landscape, clad in brilliant white, smooth limestone. I thought of the Pyramids of Giza, but there was only one pyramid, pristine and pure, towering above the sands, defiant against the solar disk in the sky.

"Welcome, my love," she said, looking forward, in the direction of the pyramid. "I've wanted so much to be with you again."

I wanted to throttle her, but I figured it would only go bad and be embarrassing. So, I sat, silent. I noodled around my own brain for a moment to see if I could sense that other phantom riding shotgun. Nothing. Just me.

"You were with me just yesterday. I don't think we should see so much of each other. In fact, maybe you should consider seeing other people. I know I'd like to."

She laughed.

This setting, I thought, couldn't be real, no matter how imposing the spectacle of the full-sized pyramid, no matter how vivid the feeling of the sand and heat. Every aspect of the horizon, everything above me, beneath me, surrounding me was as real as any place I had ever been. Yet antiquity held no sway over the scene, and no pyramid like this had been seen upon the earth in thousands of years.

"But it is real, my love," Evelyn said, turning to look at me. "It's the when and where that confuses you."

THE THINGS IN HEAVEN AND EARTH

"The beach wasn't real," I said. "My office wasn't real, either."

"That was just for fun."

"You and I differ on what's amusing."

"Oh, come, Nash. You must find your circumstances somewhat amusing. Who else do you know who rides around the country murdering the living to save the dead?"

"Well, I've given that some thought lately. I'm not entirely sure it isn't you who's doing all of it. After all, you're the one who finds it amusing."

"I confess, I do find it funny. I find all ways of living and thinking on this tiny world of yours funny. But you might consider that it's all you, after all."

"I don't think it is."

"Your fanciful 'demons,' perhaps? Is that what you think?"

"Not anymore. I think it's you."

"Oh, poor boy. Poor little boy. You could ask your brother Jason. He might have some insight for you."

"Jason's dead."

"Is he?"

"He was. But someone's been raising the dead, so maybe I'm not so sure."

"Ah, resurrection. That's what you humans want, isn't it? Eternal life?"

"I never gave it much thought."

"Truly? What gift do you think you've been bestowing upon the dead when you free all those helpless spirits? Eternal death?"

"I don't know what I'm doing for them, or to them."

"Yet you risk your own soul to set theirs free."

"Assuming, arguendo, that I'm doing any of it – it's what I hope is a basic human instinct, to help the helpless."

"To banish the bully?"

"Something like that."

"Did you consider that the spirits you're releasing might deserve their bullies? That they might be worse than the demons that bind them?"

"No."

"Poor little boy. You see a speck of paint and have no idea what the rest of the painting must be."

"Poor whatever the hell you are, aside from a condescending bitch. If you have knowledge, share it. Or leave me the fuck alone."

"But I'm sharing so much with you, my love."

"I think you're oversharing without saying anything."

Evelyn smiled.

"Look at the pyramid."

"It's not real. Why not just tell me what you want me to see?"

"Oh, it is as I said. It is real. It is the pyramid of the pharaoh Khufu, the Horizon of Khufu."

"I'm no historian, but I'm pretty sure there were at least two others sharing that real estate."

"Oh, Nash! Think! Did they all crop up at once? Were there always three?"

"There are now. And they're in ruins."

"We're not in your now. Time is meaningless to me. I've brought you to the first one, before the others, before time chipped it away."

"Why?"

"Look!"

I squinted against the brilliance of the limestone. Barely discernable, I saw what looked like a large white cloth affixed in the center, close to the color of the limestone facing. Below the cloth, I saw movement, pieces of stone falling to the ground.

"The Egyptians sought life immortal," Evelyn said. "The pharaohs built tombs and pyramids to project their souls into the afterlife, their eternal life."

"Fascinating," I said. "Maybe you should leave me alone and freelance for National Geographic."

Evelyn ignored my sarcasm.

"They devoted all of their resources and the nation's riches to ensure life would not end. Mummification to preserve their bodies to live in once more, amulets, spells, and earthly possessions to see them through the travails leading to immortality. All of this before you was to ensure that single, all-important transition from this world to the next."

"A rich man's vanity. A rich man's fear. So what?"

"Oh, but he was a man, like you. Fragile, temporary. He lived the life given him, with the same fears, the same hopes, and the same frailties. All the human weaknesses that should make us commiserate with him, pity him, perhaps even hope that his belief in eternal life might be true."

"Maybe it was."

"Maybe it was. Were he a spirit bound by a demon, would you judge him before loosing him into the next world?"

"No."

"Yet he believed himself a god, with power over life and death. He slayed hundreds, some by his own hand. But you would marshal him into the afterlife, not knowing what power he might have there, what evils he might commit."

"If you're asking me not to free anymore ghost, deal. In return I ask that you leave me alone, forever, and let me live my life."

"I ask nothing of you, my love, and offer nothing. Look again at the pyramid."

More of the same. Supersized sheet, rocks falling out of the bottom.

"Tomb robbers," I said. "Something like a sail camouflaging their activity burrowing into the pyramid. An Egyptologist might be interested. Me, not so much."

"No? Consider the beliefs standing in contrast. Entombed is what is left of a man. The grandeur of the pyramid is meaningless. Its ability to project him into the afterlife, however, is everything to him. All of it is to save his eternal soul. But for the men breaking through the stone, the stuff of everlasting life has meaning only to the living world. The riches inside will be parceled out among them for living their short lives in this world, not the next. They will steal everything and destroy even his mummified corpse, forever barring his path into the ever after."

"Only if what he believed is true."

"It is true. It was true."

I doubted it.

"On the other hand," I replied, "you said he was a shit who shouldn't be allowed into the next world."

Evelyn sighed.

"It is a wonder I love you when you so easily miss the point."

CHAPTER 12

I was aware of the nurses for some time before I was ever truly conscious. They injected medicines into my IV, changed my sheets, changed me, moved me around. I heard their nickname for me used a lot: Miracle Man. "Hello, Miracle Man," they all greeted when they approached my bed. Various monitors where hooked up to me, along with the IV bag. For a while, a tube had been down my throat. I remembered being glad when that was gone.

I heard beeps and blips as the theme music to my latest drama. I occasionally heard at least one of the nurses praying over me. I wasn't sure if it was for my recovery or to ward off whatever evil spirits that kept me breathing.

Eventually, I woke up. I assumed I was in the ICU. I had company in neighboring beds. None was talkative.

"Hello, Miracle Man," I saw the nurse approaching. She seemed surprised that I was looking at her.

"Me?" Talking hurt. My throat felt like I'd been infected with strep times ten.

"Yes, you! Glad to see you're with us again."

"Hurts," was the only response I felt I could muster.

"You should be thankful for that hurt," she said. "Most patients in your shape wouldn't be able to feel anything anymore."

She looked at the monitors and nodded satisfaction.

"You're doing well. On the road to recovery."

I tried to say thank you, but it came out like a grunt.

"Don't try to talk just yet. Let's take it slow, okay?"

I managed a nod and went back to sleep.

"Mr. Baxter?"

I woke up again. I looked at the woman standing beside my bed. She was Indian, about my age. Her embroidered nametag said "Dr. Bhagat." Her accent was British. I thought she was rather pretty.

I nodded.

"How are you feeling today?"

I managed to say "Crappy."

"Good. That means you're coming back to us."

I sort of doubted the accuracy of this as an indicator of recovery. I'm pretty sure dying people feel crappy, too.

She looked at the monitors. Apparently, there was no need to touch me to check on my current status. I got the feeling she didn't want to.

"You're quite the hero," she said. "It's told that you leapt in front of a woman to stop a man from shooting her."

"Boy Scout," I said.

"Quite a brave one, I'd say."

She was looking at me somewhat intensely.

"You should have died," she said finally.

I felt some of my strength returning. Enough to feel a little irritation that she seemed troubled by the outcome.

"Is that good or bad?"

"Entirely good. For you. Quite surprising that you survived, however."

"I take Kevlar supplements every day. I swear by them."

She didn't laugh.

"The extent of your injuries would most certainly have proved fatal under normal circumstances."

"What are *my* circumstances?"

"I don't know. However, you are profoundly fortunate."

She forced a smile.

"But we need to so some follow-up imaging to make sure your profound good fortune isn't in danger of slipping away."

"Do patients ever complaint about your bedside manner?"

"All the time. But you don't seem like the type who will demand kid gloves and swaddling clothes."

She overcame whatever reluctance she had to touching me and started through a checklist of forced movements, each punctuated by "Does that hurt?" The answer was yes, but overall, I was surprised that I didn't hurt a lot worse.

She seemed particularly interested in my feet and reflexes. She rolled some version of a medieval torture device along the bottoms of my feet and the inside of my legs. I tried to jerk away, but she was determined to continue.

"Are you *trying* to hurt me?"

"Am I?"

"Trying?"

"Hurting you."

"Yes."

"We'll have to see why then," she said. Leaving pleasantries aside, she turned and left.

True to her word, the doctor ordered up any number of excursions for me. Over the next three days, I was gurneyed from room to room, giving various techs something to gawk about. Imaging didn't trouble me so much as the stuff they put into me before doing some of it – that and how it went in.

I was given new digs in a regular room after a week, and a physical therapist showed up shortly after, getting me to my feet. It wasn't that difficult to walk, which surprised the PT. I was the gift that kept giving.

Dr. Bhagat returned each day, frowning. She opened my gown to look at my chest.

"This is healing quite nicely," she said, though it wasn't nicely said. It was an accusation.

"Thanks. Good genes."

"More than that. Your spine was stabilized in surgery after you were brought in."

"Thank you?"

"The instrumentation is no longer there, which is not possible."

"You sure you got the right x-rays?"

"Mr. Baxter, I'm guessing I won't get an answer, but I will ask you, anyway: what are you?"

"I think you said 'fortunate' once or twice."

"Overly so. You should be paralyzed."

"And dead?"

"That, too."

I got the feeling that the next week's stay was for her benefit, not mine. I felt close enough to my old self that I figured I could walk out without too much concern. I didn't know which phantom had saved and healed my ass, but I wasn't looking a gift-phantom in the mouth.

The hospital stay was curative as much to my mind as body. I felt like an overworked attorney finally getting a vacation. I read a lot of old science fiction books. That got Dr. Bhagat's attention, like the secret to my fantastical healing properties might be found in a Roger Zelazny novel. So, I switched to Steinbeck and Shakespeare. This gave me the idea to tease Dr. Bhagat by telling her the reason I healed so fast was that I was "an Okie and a knave." I thought it was funny. Her not so much.

Strange place to find myself on the verge of happiness, but there it was. I was alive. Most of the people I'd killed were, too. So long as I didn't think of the Jacks, that near happiness held. Of course, this was in no small part due to the realization that there were apparently no consequences anymore. I got fatally shot and was not much worse for the wear. The terrible things I'd done were undone. My compulsion with demons was gone. Since the world could change completely from one moment to the next, the weight of it had been lifted from me. I still had concerns. I wondered who or what made Second Jack kill First Jack and then himself. But, hell, he might just be back at the table, breaking bread with First Jack all over again.

I was free. Mostly.

Cogito, ergo sum.

Other than that, I knew I was being deceived, perhaps about everything. The evil genius had revealed itself to me, and the result was that every care I had slipped away. I could squash a bug and not know if there'd even been a bug or whether I'd squashed it. Nothing mattered, and it felt glorious.

The sum of glory faded fast when the visitors came. First, from the sheriff's office, two detectives asking me to recount what I remembered about Second Jack's homicidal episode. I didn't like thinking about it. I liked both Jacks and saw them both die. Real bugs or not, it felt very real seeing them squashed. I didn't blame Second Jack at all. I doubted he had much to do with it.

Next came Officer Smith, apologizing and crying and telling me that nothing in his grandfather's life ever led him to believe the old man could do such a thing. He asked if there was anything he could do for me. I said no, I was doing fine. He said his family would pay my medical bills. I told him I was insured. He offered to pay me a substantial sum of money from of his grandfather's estate. I told him I was already rich. I felt bad for him, so I decided not to confine myself to reality during our conversation. Instead, I told him there are more things in heaven and earth and such and that I didn't think his grandfather had been in his right mind.

"He was a good man," I said. "Something happened to him. I don't believe it was him that did this."

Smith seemed to take some comfort in that.

"I just can't believe it either. He lived a pure life."

"Cursing aside," I said.

Smith smiled.

"He did like to curse. It made us laugh when we were kids, which made him do it all the more, just to get us laughing at him being bad. But he never hurt a soul. He raised his family, stayed with my grandmother faithfully until the day she died. I know he would give his own life to save another."

"It was his truest soul that took him in the end, I think. Whatever made him do what he did, the man he was could never live with it."

I believed that was the truth of it. Before he left, I told Smith I thought he was a good man, too.

"You are your grandfather's legacy," I said. "Nothing that happened in those last moments can touch it. Try to remember that."

Duke was next. He shuffled in reluctantly, but determined, nonetheless.

"Hey, Little Brother," he said, choking up as he said it. He stood by my bed, cried some, and put his hand on my shoulder, taking solace in the physical contact.

"Jason," I said. I didn't know if he was a real bug either, but I didn't feel it was necessary to squash him if he was. "Sorry I called you Evelyn."

"Yeah," he said. "What was that all about?"

"Forgive me, but I watched you die. Evelyn was as good a name as any for someone who couldn't possibly be standing there."

"Goddammit!" he nearly shouted. "Why would those fuckers let you believe that?"

"Mom? Julie? If you're alive, where are they?"

"They're gone, Nick. But I swear, it wasn't you."

"I remember doing it. I remember killing you, too."

"I wasn't dead. The pellets ate some of me away, forever, I guess, but I didn't die."

"It looked like you did."

"I'm not saying it wasn't a close thing."

"If you didn't die, why didn't they tell me?"

"You were a mess, Nick. I don't know what they thought. Aunt Ellen took me in after that. I guess I was a mess, too. But I wanted to see you. Aunt Ellen wouldn't let me. She said you tried to kill me."

"She wasn't wrong."

"But she was. I swear I would have tried harder to see you, but Ellen said your doctors wouldn't let me, anyway."

"There's an elephant in the room here, Jason. I remember every bit of it. I did shoot all three of you."

"What else do you remember?"

"That's a lot to remember already. What are you suggesting I don't recall?"

"How 'bout the fucking knife in your back? Our father's hand on your shoulder, shouting he was going to cut you open if you didn't do it?"

I tried to take my mind back to the moment. I remembered shooting them, plain as day. I didn't remember what Jason was telling me. I stared at him. I imagine it was what you would call a blank stare.

"How 'bout him telling you if you didn't do it fast for us, he was going to carve us up slow and make us wish you'd killed us when you had the chance?"

No memory jibed with what Jason was telling me.

"You cried and screamed and said no. But he swore at you to do it. He reached around you and held that knife in front of your eyes and said he was going to rip Mom apart with it if you didn't do her the mercy."

More blank stare.

"Fuck, Nick. He'd already beaten us fucking bloody, right in front of you. Of course, you believed him. I believed him. We all did."

I couldn't think of a single thing to say. The glorious respite was gone though. I can't say even now that I know what was happening in my mind when Jason told me these things.

"He was like a demon possessing you to do it," Jason said. "It wasn't you. You fought him as best you could. Christ, you were just a kid."

Fuck.

"Do you remember killing him, too? Afterward?"

"Do you?"

"No. I was near enough to dead, I guess. But they said you killed all of them. No one believed me later. They thought I was trying to protect you, to save you. They all blamed you."

Carol never came to visit. So much for newfound love and sacrifice.

CHAPTER 13

"You present me with a problem, Mr. Baxter," Dr. Bhagat told me. I didn't see her come in. I was in the physical therapy room. The PT had given up on me. I was running on the treadmill. I was never the fastest runner, but I still managed to hit my pre-injury pace. I was three miles in, even though I hated running on treadmills. Normally, I'd let myself get out of shape before submitting to one, but the hospital was driving me a bit stir crazy. Not enough to want to go back out into the world again, but enough that I made a temporary truce with the treadmill and let it run me to nowhere fast.

Bhagat walked to the front of the treadmill to look me in the eye when she decided her mere presence wouldn't induce me to hit the stop button.

"You present me with a problem, Mr. Baxter," she repeated.

"How so?"

"Would you stop running, please? We need to discuss a few things."

"I'm good," I told her. I was running a relaxed pace, so talking wasn't a problem for me. It irritated her, however.

"As a courtesy," she replied, the strain of forbearance in her voice.

I hit the stop button.

"What do you want to talk about?"

"First, it's time you were discharged."

"Are you sure? I've been through a lot."

"Please don't toy with me, Mr. Baxter. You and I both know your recovery has been out of the ordinary. Would you mind coming to my office? I'd like to speak in private."

It wasn't much of an office. Sort of a triangular-shaped room that didn't make sense, but it was an empty enough space to stick a desk and a couple of chairs in. I sat, with my back to the pointy end of the room. She had my records in front of her on the desk.

"I've had some conflict in deciding what to do about you," she told me.

"Conflict? Why?"

"What has happened to you is not possible. Were I taken to religious explanations, I'd say it was what Christians call a miracle."

"That accounts for my nickname."

"Yes, I've heard it. But I don't believe in miracles."

"Me either, but, oh, the things I've seen."

I was being coy, sure, but I was still irritated knowing that she'd be a lot happier with me if I were dead.

"Would you mind telling me what they are?"

I thought about it.

"First, why don't you tell me what sort of problem you think I've burdened you with."

"That's simple. I feel obligated to figure out which authorities should be interested in your remarkable abilities and to call them."

"Have you?"

"No. You're also my patient. My ethical obligation is to you first. So far as I know, you haven't hurt anyone, nor do I have reason to suspect you will. In fact, you risked your life – I'm assuming – trying to protect an innocent woman."

"So, you're not going to call in the feds?"

"I'm not. Other physicians here know about your recovery, of course. Your surgeons, certainly. But they seem to be quite relieved that you are my problem."

"So, you're the equivalent of a pilot not wanting to report a UFO."

"No, Mr. Baxter. As I said, my ethical obligation is to you. I have a duty of confidentiality to you. You understand that, don't you? After all, you are an attorney."

So, she'd done her homework on me.

"I guess so," I answered.

"Then you also know we have a doctor-patient privilege."

"Yep."

"So, no matter what you say here, it is between us, unless you give me reason to believe you're about to do someone harm."

"What if what I tell you makes you think I'm insane?"

"Insanity would not account for what I've seen your body do in the last two weeks."

"So, you're open to the possibility that what I say might be true, no matter how crazy it might seem?"

"Yes."

I considered telling her the truth. All of it. I thought it might even be cathartic to unload everything on an objective observer and watch her reaction. But there was that part about maybe letting doctor-patient privilege slip by if she suspected I might have hurt or would hurt someone. I could see her taking what she heard and making that rather obvious connection once I told her about everyone I'd killed, even if most of them weren't dead now – at least by my hand.

So instead, I told her that I'd encountered a mysterious voodoo priestess while researching one of my books near New Orleans, and that the priestess had given me a liquid concoction that she said would allow me to commune with the dead. Foolishly, I drank it, with every intention of writing about the experience and debunking it. It had done exactly what she'd said, however. At first, I considered the whole experience as having been induced by some hallucinogenic compound in the drink. Only afterward, I discovered I'd gained an ability to see spirits long after the drugs should have worn off. Friendly spirits had gathered around me and protected me from physical harms. I made up a motorcycle accident that surely should have killed me but hadn't. My doctor then, I told her, had been nearly as amazed as she.

I didn't actually know if voodoo priestesses existed outside of low-budget horror movies, but it's what I decided to run with since it sort of fit into my most recent line of work.

She didn't look like belief had taken hold. But what explanation could account for the disappearance of the hardware that had been screwed into my spine? Or the regeneration of my spinal cord? And whatever other miracles she had witnessed? Any account I gave her would be as probable as the next.

"Well," she said. "You've certainly given me something to consider."

"Sorry, Doctor. But you can see why I wasn't forthcoming before."

"I suppose so."

"So, we're good?"

I finally heard her laugh.

"No, not good. Not at all. But what is it you lawyers like to say? 'It is what it is.' You've given me a mystery that I'll never solve."

"Sorry."

"All right. You're being discharged tomorrow," she said, sliding a piece of paper to me.

"Your brother asked me to give you this when you were going to be discharged. He'd like you to call him."

I took the paper. It was Jason's phone number.

"Thanks. For everything."

"No need to thank me. You're one patient I've done absolutely nothing to help."

CHAPTER 14

It was my last night in my hospital room. I wasn't anxious to leave, but Dr. Bhagat was through with me, and her discharge order was law thereabouts. In the morning, I'd have to figure out what to do next. That kept me awake for some time. I wouldn't really have much of a choice. I'd have to move forward in whatever reality came my way. I was thinking about that when, maybe, I drifted off. Gradually, I became aware of Phantom Evelyn sitting at the foot of my bed.

Since her MO was to whisk me off to more elaborate locales, I wasn't sure if she was truly there or if I had been dreaming she was. The quality of her presence was less intense than it had been, as if she were at a low ebb. She was quiet. Motionless. She was looking out the window at nothing as far as I could tell.

"You're troubled by the changes," she said, finally, her voice little more than a whisper.

For some reason I wasn't sure about, I decided to answer her without speaking the words.

"I am."

"You think I am the organ grinder, and you the monkey."

Her words came to me in thought now, too. No actual words passed between us.

"That's one way of putting it."

"But you're wrong, my love. You're free to do as you will. I have been with you, yes. I have shown you what it is like to feel. You are changing now because of that. I have also shown you things to make you *think* in this time of power."

"What time of power?"

"You are becoming aware of powers within you. You've had inklings before. Your fun with demons and spirits."

"I'm not putting any of that in the fun column."

"I am here to give you pause."

"Pause?"

"You wrestle now with what is real and imagined. You've been doting on a dolt, that philosopher who merely notices what is obvious and then cheats his way out of it. He posits deception, then accepts the same in the name of God because God wouldn't deceive."

"Descartes."

"Freshman philosophy. Circular logic. You would do well to forget it."

"I hadn't given him any thought until you came along."

"You believe I changed your reality."

"Things being what they are, yes."

"I will tell you the truth. I changed nothing. I never made you kill anyone either."

"Jury's still out. Seems like you killed Jack."

"Yes. But I didn't make *you* do it. And my killing him didn't change your reality a bit. It was just an event, something that happened."

"Then you raised him from the dead. I'm afraid that counts as changing reality."

"My love, you did that. You brought all of them back. As I said, you are coming into your power. I just gave you a little jolt. A bit of incentive."

"I don't believe you."

"I know. Yet had I not been here, you would have come to it, nevertheless. Only it would consume you, this power. You were already lost with the little you had. You saw without seeing."

"I didn't bring anyone back from anything. I think I'd know."

"But you did, my love. You didn't kill them, either."

"Seems like I did."

"You have believed demons made you."

"Seemed true."

"You were deceived. There is another who lives inside of you. More powerful than you. Almost as powerful as I."

"We met. Briefly. So, am I the Jekyll or Hyde?"

"Interesting thought. You sense the truth, but you do not know that you do. You are neither a Jekyll nor a Hyde, but you are the place where the other hides."

"The other?"

"The one who wishes to destroy me."

"The one who loves you."

"As you humans like to say, it's complicated."

"Why am I a part of any of this?"

"Oh, my love. You are a child."

"And you're still a condescending . . . ."

"*My* child."

I felt a flash of anger from Evelyn then. Something about me upset her. I couldn't tell what.

"I had a mother," I thought. "She isn't you. My mother is dead. If I had the power you say I have, I'd raise her."

"Perhaps in time you will."

She was thoughtful for a moment without sharing.

"It is a dangerous time for you," she said, coming back to me. "He would destroy you if he could. He has brought you to the brink more than once, with those killings. No demon possessed you, my love. He did. He put those little party favors in your pockets, too, so they'd be there when it was time to kill. You wondered where the poncho and gloves came from. He wanted you to believe that you killed because you wanted to. Another assault against you, against your sense of self. I would free you of him, but so long as he resides in you, he is safe. That is why you yet live."

"I don't get it."

"No. Not yet. It is beyond you, this concept, but you are part of me. So, your power will come, and knowledge, too."

"I'm not your child."

"Oh, my sweetest love, you are. I did not grow you within a womb, that is true. But I had a thought, a moment in which you grew in my mind and then became a life."

"That is fucking ridiculous."

"Seeing demons and ghosts is ridiculous. Yet you saw them. Having power over them is ridiculous, yet you had that power and used it. Why shouldn't it be true that you are unique among humans? And if that is so, why is it that you are unique?"

I didn't have an answer.

"I am the reason you are what you are. Yes, your mother was your mother, and for that you are human. But because of me, you are more. Were you born only of your mother, he would not know you, he would not hate you. My thought that was you was beautiful. What you would become would be something to behold. You would be the good in me, unleashed in this world."

"I recall you said once that you could be evil. You weren't sure."

"I am more sure now. You are not the only one who is awakening. This thing that I am, it is not what I was. I am coming into it, the same as you. I know now that he is the one who is what you might consider evil."

"You said you love him."

"For all of time I have loved him."

In my mind, I heard her laugh.

"Hell," she thought, "hath no fury like eternity scorned."

"That sounds like it should be hilarious, but I don't get it."

"My love, just remember, I cannot harm you. This he knows, and so he hides within, where I will not bring my will against him. And there he grows strong, feeding from your growing power. He will use you to undo me."

I wondered for a moment. Did *I* want to "undo" Evelyn Blankenship? I had questions I wanted to ask her. An exceedingly long list of questions. But slumber took hold. The dream was gone. Evelyn was gone.

CHAPTER 15

I woke up aware that I had been thinking about Evelyn and how much I loved her – and how I hated her. She had taken everything from me. I had to know, I'd thought, that *she* was the deceiver, the master of lies. *She* was the evil in this world.

Only when I opened my eyes and was fully awake, I knew I was not the source of the thoughts. They were mine in the sense that my mind was thinking them, but they were floating to the surface like a warning siren, mixed with memories I did not have. Mr. Gated Community was in there, somewhere, commandeering my gray matter and trying to tell me I would be a fool to trust Evelyn. She was using me to find him and *undo him*.

The noise that was this other being's thoughts faded as my own began working again. He'd been crying foul but was back behind the gates before I could look deeper into what he had been thinking with *my* mind. Yet I felt something *he* felt before the gates closed tight: fear. He was beginning to fear *me*.

"Fucking hitchhiker," I said aloud.

"The hell you say."

It was Jason. I hadn't noticed him when I woke up. He was sitting in the corner, in the only chair I had in the room. He sounded groggy and surprised, like my curse had pulled him from a deep sleep. In his lap, he held the bag I kept in my Harley. I'd called him the night before, and here he was, faithfully answering my call. I got the sense he'd been sleeping in that chair for a while.

"I didn't mean you," I said, managing to smile at him. In part, I thought I might have meant the smile. I know I sensed something in him that I liked.

"Hope not. I was up late doing your laundry for you, so you'd have something clean to wear."

"You're a prince," I said. "Any chance you got my phone in there?"

"Fully charged." He handed me the bag. "It's on top."

I opened the bag and grabbed the phone. I turned it on and saw an insane number of emails, texts, and waiting voicemails from my agent and publisher.

"Well," I said to Jason. "Catching up is going to be a bitch."

I put the phone back in the bag and fished around until I found what I wanted to wear, blue jeans and a t-shirt. I found my shaving kit, too, and asked Jason to sit tight while I took a shower.

I divested myself of my hospital gown in the bathroom and took a long look in the mirror. You could never tell I'd been shot. There was nothing left to show the bullet wound, just unblemished flesh. For fun, I took out my razor and dragged it sideways along my forearm. Neat lines of blood oozed out of the cuts I'd made. I waited maybe a minute and then rinsed the blood off. The wounds were gone. I shaved then with some degree of abandon. I cut myself a couple of times, but when I got out of the shower, those cuts were gone, too.

I got dressed and stared into the mirror again. Looking into my own eyes looking back at me, I attempted to bend reality, willing a change. I thought of the Jacks. In my mind's eye, I saw them alive, eating breakfast. As I imagined it, Second Jack was unarmed.

I blinked a few times and went out to meet Jason.

"Well," I said. "Now what?"

Jason told me he'd been staying at a hotel nearby ever since I'd been shot. He'd gotten me a room this morning, next to his. My bike, he said, was in the hotel parking lot.

We walked out of the hospital. Maybe there was some paperwork I was supposed to do, but I skipped it. We got to the hospital parking lot, and there was Jason's bike. He got on and looked at me, nodding for me to get onto the back seat.

"You're kidding, right?"

"I didn't think to rent a car. Just get on."

"No fucking way."

"It's just a couple of miles."

"A man doesn't ride on the back of another man's bike."

"Jesus, it's just a couple of miles," he laughed. "I won't tell if you don't."

"Nuh-uh."

I got the name of the hotel and called for an Uber.

I took the rest of my bags from Jason's room and settled into mine. Jason followed me, but we didn't say much. You'd think there'd be a lot to talk about with your until recently thought to be dead brother whom you hadn't seen in thirty years. Surprisingly, there wasn't. Not yet. Jason sat on the couch while I texted my agent, Grace. I told her I was out of the hospital and okay. I'd call her later. I emailed my publisher with the same basic message. Then I sent out several emails to the owners/occupants of haunted houses I was supposed to "investigate" for my latest book. I apologized, noted I'd been shot, and said I would have to reschedule.

I put the phone away and opened my computer. I Googled the news reports about me. In one, I read gushing praise for me from Carol about my saving her life. "Hero Writer Takes Bullet, Saves Barkeep." Others left Carol unnamed, but I was universally hailed for my selfless act of courage. My publisher was going to love the bump in book sales. There was some video, too, which tended to predict my impending demise. Nothing about either Jack popping back into existence.

"I'm glad they got that wrong," Jason said. "Imagine finding you after all these years only to have you shot and killed the same day."

"The bullet managed to miss anything that mattered," I said. As far as I knew, he was unaware of just how dead I was supposed to be.

I closed the computer.

"We should get something to eat," I said. "But I want to run first. Mind if I hit the road for an hour or so?"

"Run? You just got out of the hospital!"

"I'm fine. I'm a runner. Gotta get some miles in."

"Jesus," he said. "Fine, let's go."

"You're going, too?"

"I've been running for years. Calms the mind. Let's see who's faster."

He went to his room to change, and I changed into running shorts. I put my pants on over the shorts, in part, because I don't like the wind blowing up my shorts when I ride. But also, because I'd burned my bare legs on the pipes more than once. It's not unlike pressing a hot iron up against your inner thighs and calves. Not that that would be a concern now, given my newfound invincibility, but habits are habits.

I put my running shoes on and threw on a tank top. I took a water bottle from the minibar and met Jason by the bikes. We rode to a nearby forest preserve that Jason had found earlier. He didn't share my aversion to riding in shorts, which was hilarious since he still insisted on wearing his Harley do-rag.

It was hotter than hell, and the smart money was on sitting this one out. I wasn't worried about me, but I was a bit concerned for Jason. It was 90-plus degrees and getting hotter by the minute. He wasn't deterred. He pulled a water bottle out of his saddlebag and stripped his shirt off. His right upper body was deeply scarred from the shotgun blast that had almost killed him thirty years before. Knowing I'd been the one who shot him, I didn't know how to feel about that.

"Let's go," he said, and he was off. I was left behind, trying to get my pants off over my shoes, which became a debacle that left me tangled up on a curb for a full five minutes before I extricated myself. Invincibility aside, I was a klutz.

Finally, I grabbed my water and tried to catch up.

The asphalt trail led into the woods. Just around the first bend, I saw Jason, lying on a bench next to the trail waiting for me.

"Wasn't sure you were up to it after all," he said, getting up and settling into his pace beside me.

We ran side-by-side, quiet for a while. About a mile in, I asked a question that had been bothering me.

"How long have you been on my trail again?"

"About a year. Kinda stupid, really. Reading up on your blog, trying to figure out where you were going next, and just hoping to see you on the road somewhere. What were the odds?"

"Looks like a hundred percent. Why didn't you try to contact me instead?"

"Thought about it. Truth be told, I wasn't sure I was right about you being you. All I had to go on is you looking like me. You had a different name and a career I wouldn't have figured on. I didn't even know if you'd been released from wherever they stuck you. Something else, too."

"What?"

"I needed that time on the road alone. What happened fucked you into some kind of state that made them institutionalize you. No one institutionalized me. No one sent me to a shrink either. I just had our father's sister raising me, and she wasn't a lot nicer than he was. I've had to deal with all this shit in my own mind for thirty years. When I started thinking Nash Baxter might be my long-lost brother, I started to have hope that something good might be coming around at last. But I also thought I might just be losing it. Wishful thinking, you know? Yeah, I was looking for you, but didn't really think I'd find you. I was trying to get myself right on the road. I guess I set an impossible task just to keep me moving."

"So, are you rich?"

"Rich?"

"Your bike sure wasn't cheap. And being on the road isn't either." I thought of Second Jack's tale of his cross-country ride. "How'd you keep flush?"

"Oh, I get you. I'm sorry to tell you this, but Mom's parents, Grandma and Grandpa, died shortly after the . . . the thing happened. It killed them, the way I see it. I inherited their estate. That's been in trust for me ever since. Our house got sold, too, and that money was put in another trust for me and you. After thirty years, there's a lot there. Half is yours. I didn't touch that half. It's still yours. But you know they tried to buy me with your half to sell you out."

"Sell me out?"

"Assistant DA came to see me, about when you would have been eighteen. He said you were better. That meant they wanted you to stand trial. For murder. He said he knew I was just trying to protect you with my story about Dad. He said he wanted me to tell the truth, so justice could be done. Justice!" Jason spat. "You were ten, and you were made to do it. If they cared about justice, they'd leave you be. Anyway, I stuck with my version of events. It was the truth. Maybe I would have lied to save you, anyway, I don't know. Didn't need to though. It happened like I said it did. So, Mr. Assistant DA told me all the trust money would be mine if you were convicted. He said the laws of inheritance won't let a murderer profit from his crime. He said all the money in the trust would go to me. Jesus, can you imagine telling a lie like that for profit? Just so some young ass DA could make a name for himself? It would be in the news all over again, with that scumbag strutting in front of the cameras. I mean, you were famous in a bad sort of way, but the story was old. I gotta say, though, I thought about telling him I'd do it. I wouldn't have, but it would have put me face-to-face with you again. And I wanted to see you. I wanted to see you worse than anything. You were the only real family I had left that loved me."

"I shot you. Some would say that ain't love."

"Dad shot me. He used you to do it."

"I still don't remember that."

"Trauma. It's the way I said it was."

We were a couple of miles in. I wasn't sure how to take it. I hadn't thought of my grandparents in years, but I remember loving them. They were sweet people. Far too young to have died. I'd guess they were in their fifties, at most.

"Jason," I said. "I'm rich. Silly rich. That money is yours, and for your kids when you have them. Or do you have a family already?"

"No family. I'm not going to lie to you, Little Brother. I've got issues. I'm not good at relationships."

"I'm sorry."

"Not your fault. I keep telling you that. Truth is, I'm as close to being right, now that I've found you, than I've been in a long while."

We were about three miles in. Talking makes running slow, and whatever invincibility I'd gained didn't make me a better runner. I made a decision then, maybe not a good one. I spent the next five miles telling Jason everything about me and what had happened up to my getting shot. It was a long five miles.

CHAPTER 16

Jason stared at me over his coffee cup. He'd just restated everything I told him about my life, in hushed tones, given the subject matter and the fact that we were in a crowded restaurant. The look he was giving suggested I should shake my head after his rendition and say, "Oh, yeah. I get it. That's nuts."

I ate my eggs instead.

"You know," he said, irritated that I wasn't going to acknowledge I was delusional, "it's not exactly laying the foundation for a clean renewal to our relationship either when you tell me you're not all that sure I'm real."

"Don't take offense. I'm not sure anything is real. And as far as potential figments go, I find your company agreeable."

He put his cup down.

"Doesn't it seem like a big coincidence that our father . . . I'm sorry, I have to say it. Don't you get it? Our father *made* you shoot us. And now you're riding around the country thinking demons are making you kill other people? People who aren't actually dead?"

"They were dead."

"And resurrected somehow."

"Like you."

"I told you. I didn't die."

"So, you say."

Jason sighed.

"Look, I'm no psychiatrist, but I think a high school dropout could put the psychology together here."

"I only have your word for it that our father made me do anything. I don't remember it that way."

Jason shook his head. I'd noted since our conversation began that he had a full repertoire of disapproving sounds and gestures. The head shake was one of his go-tos.

"So, what about these books you write? Your blog. Your podcast. You spend your life telling other people that the same things you tell me are real *aren't*."

"That's right."

"You ever stop to think maybe it's because part of you *knows* none of it is real? Like there's some little seed of sanity trying to grow inside your brain?"

"You're calling me crazy."

Jason sat back in his chair, took a deep breath, held it, and slowly exhaled. That was a new one.

"No, I don't think you're crazy. I should have worded that better. You sure don't seem like it. You express your thoughts coherently and consistently. In my experience, crazy people can't do that. What I *am* saying is that maybe you haven't been able to deal with what happened to you, to us. You're still not able to look at it head on. Instead of seeing what Dad did to you, you relive it another way, putting images of demons in Dad's place."

There was a certain appeal to Jason's theory, and I realized the entire reason I'd unloaded my life's experiences on him was to invite a different point of view. I knew he wasn't going to believe a word of what I told him, at least not once my narrative veered away from "normal." I knew he was going to think I was delusional, too. But, frankly, I'd run out of ways to analyze what was happening to me. I needed the proverbial set of fresh eyes on the problem.

"Well," I said. "Let's talk about a couple of things. First, the books. Yes, I am trying to convince people ghosts aren't real. You know, when I first started seeing ghosts was *before* what happened in our house. But it wasn't all at once. I remember very clearly seeing Grandma Claire in our living room."

"Dad's mom," Jason remembered.

"None other. But I didn't see her so clearly at first. When I saw fragments of what I thought was a ghost, I ignored it. I was scared, like any kid would be. Everyone said, 'there's no such thing as ghosts.' So, I tried *not* to see what I was seeing, and I tried not to be scared. I banked on that 'no such thing' wisdom. I would see her out of the corner of my eye, and I'd turn away, willing myself not to believe it. The image would fade then. It even disappeared for a long time. Then I saw *Poltergeist* on TV one day, when I was home alone. Pretty scary stuff back then. But it was just a movie. I knew that. Afterward though, it started to get to me. I started to believe what I had seen might be real. That's when Grandma Claire came to me complete and whole. But I wasn't scared. It was Grandma, and I missed her. I was actually happy to see her. Then the demon came, and I wasn't happy anymore."

I told Jason how the demon had understood that I saw, and how it raged at me for knowing Grandma's ghost was there. I thought about that for a minute. Then I told Jason, "You know, I never put it together before, but that's about the time Dad started beating me."

"Dad was an evil man. I remember that before he started beating on you."

"Was he? I remember our mother loved him. I remember them hugging and laughing together. I remember our trip to Disneyland and summer weekends at the beach. Dad was, well, kind of great then, wasn't he? I remember Mom was a wonderful woman. Smart, I'd say. Strong, if I remember right. Would she love and stay with a man like Dad became? Would she . . . "

I had to stop. I began to tear up and choke. For the first time ever, I knew I wasn't putting on crocodile tears for show. The emotional pain was immense. It overwhelmed me, and for all my effort to push the emotion away, I kept crying. I half noticed people at the tables nearest ours starting to stare.

Jason reached over the table and put his hand on my shoulder.

"Hey, Little Brother. It's okay. Cry if you have to. Let it the fuck out."

I tried very hard *not* to let it the fuck out. It was agony like I'd never felt. After a while, the intensity of it eased up enough that I was able to wipe the tears away, but I knew if I tried to say even one word, it was going to come back at me, full force. I only managed to croak out "Let's leave" before getting up and making my way out to our bikes in the parking lot.

Jason was a bit behind me, paying the bill before following. I was on my bike and pulling away when I saw him come out of the restaurant's door.

When I pulled up at the hotel, I jumped off the bike and mostly ran inside. I went to the pool instead of my room, pulled my shoes and pants off, and dived in in my running shorts. It was a small pool, but I began swimming furiously from end to end. Fresh tears were burning my eyes along with the chlorine, but the choking had stopped. I wanted to rage and scream, and to keep from doing that, I put all my strength and emotion into my stroke. It was like I was fighting for my life.

I don't know how long I swam, but I didn't stop until I was utterly drained. So, *this* was the emotion Evelyn was gifting me with. I didn't like it. Not one bit.

I dried off with one of the hotel towels, grabbed my clothes, and started back to my room. From down the hall, I saw Jason knocking on the door. I guess he had been for a while.

"I'm here," I shouted.

He stopped knocking and ran down the hall and embraced me in the first bear hug of my life. He was crying.

"Oh, Jesus," I said. "Stop that. You're going to make me fucking do it again."

"I can't help it, Little Brother," he said. "You're hurting!"

"Fucking understatement," I said.

Jason let go of me, put his hands on my shoulders and held me at arm's length, looking me in the eyes. Tears were still coming from his.

"Maybe this is good," he said. "Maybe this is what you need to feel."

"I don't think so," I said. "Right now, I need to feel sleep."

We entered my room, and I took a quick shower to get the chlorine smell off me. I dressed and then lay on the bed. Consciousness left in a hurry. Jason sat on the couch and left me alone, quietly just being there.

CHAPTER 17

I woke up late afternoon. The sun was still broiling outside, shining strong through the window. I hadn't bothered to close the drapes. I'd just needed . . . oblivion. Even the bright sunlight couldn't get in the way of it. I suppose I felt better, but uncertain about myself. For the first time, I'd truly felt strong emotion, and I didn't like it. It scared me. Yes, fear, too, was a part of me. Mr. Gated Community and I now had that in common.

I sat up and looked at Jason, who was holding vigil on the couch. He saw that I was awake and said, "It's okay, Nick. I'm here, man. We're going to get through this."

I decided at that moment that he was real. No doubt was left in my mind. Jason was my brother coming to save me once more. I wasn't sure I needed or wanted saving, but it was good to know my big brother was there.

"Sorry," I said. "I'm not usually the emotional type. Thinking about Mom broke something in me."

"You're not broken, Nick," Jason said. "You're not."

I took a deep breath, sat up on the edge of the bed and stretched.

"Well, let's see," I said. My mind was still in a fog. "I was trying to tell you something."

"You were talking about Mom and Dad."

"Yeah. Mom and Dad. They're the reason I write the things I write. My life was normal. Our lives were normal for a long time, weren't they?"

"I don't know what normal is, unless we're using the *Brady Bunch* as a baseline. If that's it, we weren't that."

I wanted to laugh but didn't have the energy.

"Was I wrong?" I asked. "Wasn't there a time when Dad wasn't a fucker?"

"He was always a dick."

"Mom loved him."

"He wasn't always a *big* dick. That came later."

"After my encounter with the demon," I said. Jason started to interrupt. "No, please let me finish. You asked why I try to convince people demons don't exist. It's simple. They didn't exist for me until the moment I believed there *was* such a thing as a ghost. Until that moment, my life was . . . I don't know. Okay."

"You think a demon destroyed our family?" Jason wasn't mocking or even trying to make it sound like I should know better. He was really listening to me.

"Yes. I do. Dad may not have been Hugh Beaumont, but he wasn't the evil fucker he was at the end. Not always. I sure don't remember him beating any of us until the first time he knocked the hell of out of me. Then you, when you tried to stop him."

"Maybe he wasn't always the prick that he became. But he sure leaned into it like he was born to play the part."

"I always wondered why he only laid hands on me. It started after I saw that first demon."

"You're saying he was possessed by the demon you saw? The one that was out to get you?"

"Yes. I think that's what I believe now."

Jason was silent for a while, thinking. Remembering. Finally, he said, "You're fucking with my mind now. Maybe Dad wasn't the worst, until he was."

"So, the books, Jason. I will do everything in my power to stop people from believing in ghosts. If you believe, you see. If you see, the demons see you. The people I write about, most of them really do see ghosts. They open their lives up to the demons when they do. Only they don't know that. I do. I want to stop it."

"And you have the power to do it?"

"If any of it has been true, yes. I do. I used that power on the demon in our house after the shooting. I set Grandma free, and I sent that murderous beast into whatever void it came from."

"Hell?"

"Maybe. I don't know. I never did."

"You don't remember any part of Dad making you do it?"

"No. I've always thought the demon forced me. That didn't absolve me of it. But I wasn't . . . I didn't have free will."

"Nick," Jason said. "All of this is complicated. You're a smart man. You know that's true. But I swear as God is my witness, Dad forced your hand. It wasn't a demon."

"Let's say you're right," I said. "For argument's sake. Can you reconcile the father that beat us and, as you say, forced me to shoot you with the one that was with us at Disneyland? At the beach? Playing catch? Kissing our mother? Taking us to the A's game?" More to myself than Jason, I said, "Jesus, I'm just remembering all of that now. How long has it been since I allowed myself to see him in that light? Or even to think about him?"

I could tell Jason was having trouble with this. He'd begun wiping tears away from his eyes as he sat, looking down at the floor. "I don't," he said. "I haven't . . . I don't like to think of him as anything but evil for what he did."

I looked at my brother, and I knew that I loved him. I had empathy for him, and I wanted to take the hurt he was feeling away. I should have just shut up, I knew, for his sake. But I couldn't help myself. I said, "Maybe you built up walls around your own memories, so you could always see him as the thing he was at the end and not a father you loved. You think I imagine demons. Maybe you've imagined him forcing me to do what I did. Maybe that's how you had to deal with it. Jason, I still don't remember it happening the way you said it did."

Jason was quiet again. I kept talking, knowing I shouldn't.

"I think I was eight or so when I saw Grandma in the house. Once the demon came, it would come at me with a fury. I could sense its hate, but it didn't actually do anything to me that I could tell, except scare the hell out of me. I saw Grandma, and I'd see it lurking behind her, hating me. Sometimes I would try to talk to Grandma's spirit. I loved her,

Jason. She was there, alive I thought. But whenever I tried to communicate with her, the demon would rush right into me, moving through me, I think. I could feel something then. My heart would race, and I would just break down and cry. It was all I could do. I didn't have any power then. Nothing to bring against it. I knew it was holding Grandma there, torturing her, too. I wanted so bad to help her, but I couldn't. I think, I remember now, that's when Dad changed. That's when he started beating me. So, we had our father for a time, but for the last two years, he wasn't the same man. How do you change overnight like that? I think maybe the demon couldn't touch me for some reason then, so it set upon our father and made him do it."

All of this was a latent revelation for me. I must have known it all along, but I'd never put it together. My memory of my father was in one box, and I kept that separate from the rest of what I knew. In another box, there was the demon. I always remembered the demon, even if I didn't dwell on it. Just another demon in my life, albeit the first. But the boxes weren't separate. I never forgot what my father did to me, and Jason, but I pushed the memory down, like a fact I knew but filed away, never giving it much thought. But his transformation into evil couldn't have been a coincidence.

Jason didn't buy it.

"I think there's an explanation that isn't other worldly here," he said. "It doesn't require demons or ghosts. You say *you* changed. You began to be afraid and break down. Let's say you saw a demon, or something that changed you. Our father saw that change in you, a change from the strong son he wanted to a kid who was having some kind of emotional issues. It stuck in his gut and made *him* hate you for being weak. So maybe he was old school, knocking you around to toughen you back up again. Maybe you were seeing a demon instead of seeing your own father's hate. Maybe that's the demon you saw all along."

I thought about it.

"There's a problem with your theory," I said. "The way you remember it, he forced me to shoot you. What switch could have flipped in his brain from a little old school discipline to forcing me to shoot you? It doesn't square."

Jason laughed. It wasn't a happy laugh. It was filled with pain and frustration at the absurdity I was bringing into his life.

"Nick," he said finally, composing himself. "I've listened to everything you've said about demons. Yeah, I hear you. Dad changed. Maybe I'm just starting to see that myself. Maybe you've helped me see that, and I promise I'm going to look at it and see what sense I can make of it. That's good. I've got work to do, but that's good. But you need to work on things, too.

"Think about it, this demon thing. As long as you've been able to wrap up all that's happened to you, to us, with that neat little demon bow, you haven't had to look at what's beneath it. You haven't had to square the image of our father as someone you loved with the father that abused you and forced you to do the most horrible thing imaginable. You haven't had to face up to the fact that you were helpless, that you were used to do evil for no reason that can be fathomed.

"It's sort of the psychological equivalent of what Camus called philosophical suicide. It's like taking God on as a dumping ground for anything in the world that doesn't make sense. Instead of thinking about it, instead of reasoning to understand what can't be understood, God becomes the universal answer, and you don't have to confront any of the big questions. You don't have to look for any truth or explanation beyond the all-powerful.

"Tragedy strikes. No need to confront it intellectually or emotionally. You just dump all of your questions and pain into the God basket, and that's all the answer you need. It's a cheat. You solve the problem without doing the math. Only you, Jesus, you got it fucking backwards – demons are your *psychological* suicide. You don't have to confront the horror of what happened, Nick, so long as you can dump all of it into these evil beings *making* it happen.

"The father you loved didn't hurt us; it was a demon. And all this time you've been seeing demons, you've been avoiding the truth of it, that it can't be understood. That it just happened because human beings are flawed, irrational, and sometimes mentally ill. They do unfathomable evil in the world. Humans do. Our father did. You have to accept that the same father you loved is the same man who beat you and forced you to shoot us when you were a little boy, too young and too weak to fight back. You have to accept that it isn't your fault. You didn't do it, Nick.

"Please, let's work on you trying to accept that. Let's look at the thing, and let's do it without slipping ghosts or demons into the equation. I'll be here with you, Little Brother. We'll get there. I think your breaking down today might be a first step in that direction. I think that it was a good thing. You have to *feel* it. All of it. I don't doubt that that will drag you into a pit of despair, but we'll get you back out of it. Please, Nick. Let's work through this on the premise that there are no demons and see where it goes."

Maybe Jason was onto something. It made sense. I thought about my breakdown. How long had I gone in my life not feeling *anything* emotionally, until Evelyn? Until today? The experience of feeling, brought on by thinking about my mother, was brutal. I knew I'd avoid it happening again, if at all possible. Maybe Jason's point about my avoiding coming to terms with everything was true, even if it was also true that demons *did* exist and that I *did* see them. The two things weren't necessarily mutually exclusive.

Well, I had one more trick, one more argument to bring my brother to the understanding that I wasn't, as he said, psychologically suicidal.

"Jason," I said. "Do you believe I got shot?"

He was taken aback by the question. Admittedly, it seemed like a non sequitur.

"Nick," he said. "You *were* shot. I know that. The whole world seems to know that."

"Where was I shot?"

"In the chest."

I pulled my tank top off and sat shirtless in the bright sunlight.

"Show me where the bullet hit."

Jason stared at me.

"Well, it's healed. That's good."

"Really? Where's the scar?"

Jason stood up and came to the bed, looking close. He saw but couldn't say what he saw out loud. I got up and went to the bathroom for my razor. I came back and sat on the bed beside Jason. I dragged the razor across my forearm.

"Jesus!" Jason grabbed my arm and pulled the razor out of my hand. "What the fuck, Nick? Stop it!"

The thin cuts welled up with blood.

"Do you believe I cut myself?" I asked.

"Yes, goddammit! Why? What the hell, Nick?"

I spat in my hand and used it to wipe the blood away.

"So, show me the cuts."

Jason stared. He grabbed my arm and brought it up close to look at it. He held on to it for a full minute before letting go. Then he walked to the window and looked out at the day.

"Oh, Nick, Nick, Nick," he said. "I found you, Little Brother, and I'm sticking with you no matter what, but you've got me thinking about that door or gate or whatever the fuck it was in Dante. 'Abandon hope all you who enter here.' I'm starting to figure sticking with you is going to be a fucking ride through hell."

CHAPTER 18

A little embarrassingly, Jason needed more confirmation. He made me stand up and looked at every inch of my bare torso, front and back. He told me he could write off the razor trick as some bit of street magic I'd picked up, but the magic bullet wound was something else.

"I can't explain that away," he said. "Unless you, the hospital, the two guys who died, and every news report was part of a hoax."

I regaled him with Dr. Bhagat's observations about my being dead but not playing fair about it. I told him the full extent of the injuries. He shook his head.

"That just can't be."

"Do you have a knife?"

"Yes, but . . ."

"Give it to me. I'll cut deeper and see what happens."

"No. Not just no, but fuck no. I don't want to see that."

"Do you believe me then?"

"I believe I'm out of my element. I believe there's something going on that's beyond explanation. But I'm not jumping on the demon bandwagon just yet."

I told him I wasn't completely sure about the demon bandwagon myself anymore. Everything was provisional in my eyes.

"Except you, Jason," I said, surprising myself. "I feel it in my heart that you're real. You're my brother, and I love you."

I did the strangest thing then. I hugged him. And I cried again. Not as hard as at the restaurant, but they weren't crocodile tears. I was so very glad to have my brother. I cried for that. I cried for my mother and sister. And I cried for my father and all that we lost.

Eventually, we managed to separate and compose ourselves. The sun was still out, but it was past five. We were hungry, so we decided to ride somewhere to eat. I was adamant about avoiding any cozy spots with history and personality. We ended up at a popular chain steakhouse. It wasn't much of a ride. We found the place just around the corner. No ghosts. No demons, but more peanuts than we knew what to do with.

Over dinner, Jason asked me what the plan was. All I could think to do was move forward with my life. I couldn't *force* Evelyn to show her hand again. Nor could I force any new reality shifts to pop up for leisurely examination. I didn't want to just hole up in a hotel room and wait it out, either. Moving forward was all we had. So, I told him the only thing I could think to do was to go about my business – contact my publisher's marketing people and see what they had on their minds. I had to get back to work on my "investigations" for the new book, too. All the while, we would remain vigilant for any signs that pointed back toward madness.

We didn't get too far into the details. I was recognized before we could.

One of the odd things about being famous is people you don't know think *they* know you. In a way, they do. They've read your books, listened to your words, your descriptions, observations, and conclusions. In my case, they recognized me because of my books and a few TV appearances. That and I'd been in the news for taking a bullet for a damsel in distress. I signed a few autographs, smiled for a few selfies, and thanked the people for their well wishes and reading my books. When these things happened, as they often did, I played the part, and was probably not much different that I was this time. But it felt different. I enjoyed the well-wishes and hearing I'd been in someone's prayers. Normally, I discount the efficacy of prayers, but given recent events, I couldn't say for certain they hadn't done the trick this time out. Besides, the sentiment felt good.

My food got cold. Jason ate his, watching, amused.

Before long, I saw a kid, maybe twelve, screwing up his courage to come to our table. His parents sat nearby, beaming behind his back. Eventually, he shuffled up.

"Um, sir," he said. Cute kid. He wore glasses and a Star Wars t-shirt. I smiled at him. I saw his parents beaming even more once he started to speak.

"I'm a reporter," the boy told me.

"Really? How cool is that?"

"I like it," the boy said. "I'm a reporter for my school paper, 'The Eagle.' It's online. You can Google it if you want to."

I smiled some more. "Maybe later."

"Can I interview you?" he asked.

"Sure," I told him. "Slide in next to my brother over there."

Jason scooted over to make room. The kid slid into the booth.

"What's your name?" I asked.

"Jason. Jason Moore."

"Cool. That's my brother's name. Jason, meet Jason."

Jason Moore held out his hand to Brother Jason, and they shook.

"Pleased to meet you, Jason," my brother said.

"Thank you, sir."

"Hey," I said. "Knock the 'sir' stuff off. You're a writer. So am I. We're equals here."

"Thank you, sir," Jason Moore said. "I mean, Mr. Baxter."

"Call me Nash."

I was having fun. I was enjoying the kid and wanted to help him. Not long ago, I would have let him call me Mr. Baxter and brushed him off. Whatever emotional awakening I was having had more to it than pain I was realizing. There was a good side, too.

Jason Moore put his cell phone on the table to record the interview. Then he became a little professional and started asking about my background. I gave him the jacket cover version. Short. I was hoping he'd ask me about my books, but instead he said he saw me on the news for getting shot. He asked questions, and I gave him the most likely version of events. I got shot. It wasn't as bad as it looked. I was lucky. Yes, I jumped in front of a lady, so she wouldn't get shot. She was a friend of mine. Yes, I knew the man who shot me. I knew the other man he shot, too.

Jason Moore was a hard-nosed journalist, it turned out. He asked some very probing questions. My initial enjoyment was dashed when he got me thinking about the Jacks.

"Was he a bad man, the man who shot you?"

"No," I answered. "He was a nice guy, as far as I could tell."

"Why did he shoot you then?"

"I don't know," I said. "Sometimes things happen, and they just don't make sense."

Jason probed. He asked what I knew about Second Jack. I thought of Officer Smith. I doubted he read school newspapers, but I wasn't going to say anything contrary to his positive image of his grandfather, since it was probably true. So, I gave Jason Moore the short history of what I knew about Second Jack. He was a respected police officer and a good family man.

"It doesn't make sense," Jason Moore said. "Did you argue? Did he fight with that other man?"

"No. Something just when haywire in his brain for a few seconds. I guess we'll never know why."

"Why do you think he shot himself?"

"Well," I said. "The way I see it, he saw what he did and couldn't live with it."

I tried not to fade out on the kid, but I was starting to dwell on the why of it myself. Second Jack acted the way I did when a demon got hold of me. Seemed like himself, but he went about the killing, anyway. Only I hadn't sensed a demon, whether new or the demon that had taken me the day before. But something got to him. Evelyn? She had tried to convince me the hitchhiker riding shotgun in my brain – he, it, or whatever – had been the true demon that had possessed me all along. Had he done the same with Jack? I had nothing better than a coin toss to decide which of them might have been the culprit. Was one of them trying to take me out?

"We have a ghost in my house."

Jason Moore's unexpected proclamation pulled me back from my thoughts.

"A what?"

"You write about ghosts and say they aren't real," he said.

"I do, and they aren't."

"But we have one in our house."

"I bet you don't."

Jason Moore's cuteness clouded over with a look of fear.

"We do," he said, whispering. "And something else, too. Something that scares me."

Everything stopped being even remotely fun. A sickening panic gripped the pit of my stomach. I tried to focus. I tried to smile. My brother shot me a look full of worry and fear that told me he knew what was happening in my brain.

"Well, Jason," I said. "I go to a lot of houses and see a lot of people who think they have ghosts. I've never found a single one to be true. You should look away whenever you think you see one. Look away, and remember there are no such things as ghosts."

It was all I could think to say, but my reacquaintance with my own past, my grandmother's ghost and the demon that held her, made me afraid for the kid and lit an urge inside of me to protect him.

"I know people say they aren't real," Little Jason was getting emotional, and it disturbed me. "But I see him every night. And I also see a creature there with him. The creature scares me. I don't know why, but it wants to hurt me."

My brother Jason interjected, "Hey, little man, you just met us. You sure you want to be talking about this stuff to total strangers?"

"I'm not a *little* man," a flash of anger crossed Little Jason's face. "Nash said we're equals. And he writes about ghosts. So, isn't he the best person to ask about ghosts?"

Little Jason's parents had stopped beaming. They were making their way to our table. Jason's mother said hello and thanked us for giving him the interview. Then she took his hand and pulled him from the booth. He grabbed his phone while sliding out.

"Time to go, Honey," she said. She said goodbye for the both of them and kept walking, out to their car I assumed. Little Jason looked distraught and embarrassed. He waved back at me on the way out, as if to say, "Sorry. Nothing I can do about this."

The father stayed and introduced himself.

"Randall Moore," he said. "I'm sorry Jason seems to have gotten off track a bit with you. He's a good kid. But he has an imagination. You know, he's read both of your books. I sort of made him. He really thinks he's seeing a ghost in our house. I was hoping your books would convince him otherwise. Anyway, I'm sorry he brought it up. Thank you for talking to him."

Randall smiled and started to leave. I was fighting with myself not to get involved, but the kid got to me.

"Wait a minute, Randall," I said. "Maybe I can help."

Jason gave me a look that was screaming no, don't do it. I knew I should probably listen, but feelings had their downside. I wasn't thinking the logic or the risk of it through. I just wanted to help the kid and get him free of the tragedy that was likely coming his way.

Jason's father turned back around and asked me how.

"Seems like you know what I do for a living," I said. "Maybe I can come by and do my thing. If I can debunk it for Jason, he might let go of the idea."

Randall said he appreciated the thought, but he didn't want Jason to be embarrassed, and he certainly would be if I wrote about it.

"I won't write about it," I said. "I see more places and people than I write about. Sometimes it's better for the people involved if I don't. So, I don't. I won't this time, if you think it will help Jason. The kid strikes me as a thinker. After all, he's a journalist, right? If I let him track the story down with me, he just might decide it isn't real after all."

"You'd be willing to do that?" Randall asked. "You just met him."

"He impressed me," I said. "He's a tough interviewer. I'd like to help him."

Randall smiled and said, "I have to admit, we've been more than a little concerned for him. I mean, every kid has an imagination, right? But he thinks he's seeing something."

"Let me ask you a serious question," I said, "just so I'm starting out on the right foot. Is Jason the only person who thinks he sees a ghost in the house?"

Randall was hesitant, but said, "My wife sometimes thinks she might be seeing something, too. She's not sure what. I think Jason's just got her spooked on the subject. It's an old house. Lots of history and dark corners. If you let yourself, you could imagine all kinds of things going bump in the night."

"Look, Mr. Moore," Jason said. "We're on a tight schedule, so if you wouldn't mind, just write your address and phone number down. If we have some time, we'll try to make it by. But Nash sometimes forgets we have appointments we have to keep."

"Sure," Randall said, sounding skeptical. But he pulled out his pen and wrote his address and phone number on a napkin. "If you can make it, that would be great. But I understand if you can't."

We watched as Randall walked back to his table, dropped some cash into the bill folder, and left. That's when Jason spoke up.

"Are you fucking crazy?"

"Jason," I said. "After everything we just rehashed about our house, my demon, and what happened because of it, you want me to let that kid walk into the very same nightmare? When I can fix it?"

"You said yourself you don't even know what's real anymore," Jason insisted. "And if what you say is true, you fucking killed a bunch of people when your demon magic went haywire."

"Those were rare incidents," I explained, but doubt was creeping in.

"How rare? You had a pretty long list of people who ended up on the bad end of the deal."

"None of whom seem to be dead now."

"How 'bout those Jack guys? Whatever happened, they're still dead."

There *was* more to consider. If Evelyn or the Hitchhiker had gotten to Jack, what would prevent a repeat performance?

"You don't think I should try to help them?"

"Not if the cure might kill them," Jason said. "Look, we're both sitting on top of a powder keg. I admit something unnatural is going on. I admit I'm starting to believe there's a lot more than I ever knew about what happened in our house. I admit maybe something took hold of our father and changed him. I admit I don't know what the fuck is true anymore, and you've told me you don't know anymore either. And we haven't even started to discuss how to deal with those supernatural beings playing games inside your head. So, yeah, I don't think you should do anything for that family. You have no way of knowing how it will end up."

I mentally ran through just about every demon encounter I'd ever had. If they had happened, I had a true power that could toss a demon out on its ear, almost without fail. I'd saved any number of people from the spirits and demons, and I'd saved the spirits from the demons, too. And I was more now that I had been then. Those I had killed lived again. I couldn't myself seem to be killed. I didn't think it was possible anymore that a demon could control me. As for Evelyn and company, I wasn't going to sit around paralyzed with fear over what they might or might not be capable of doing.

"I have to try."

"Jesus, this is a bad idea. Let me ask you, what percentage of your encounters ended badly for the people you were trying to help?"

I did some mental calculations.

"Five percent."

"So, those are good odds, unless the five percent ends with people getting killed, and according to you, it does."

"Did. I raise the dead now, too. Remember?"

Jason looked at me, desperate.

"I get the feeling that we're totally fucked, but fine. I'm going with you. If things go south, I'll do what I can to stop it."

"I'm feeling good," I said. "I don't see it going south. I see a little kid getting the break I wish I'd had."

"Yeah," Jason sighed. "Be careful what you wish for. I wished I'd find my little brother. Wish granted. Future completely fucked."

CHAPTER 19

It was entirely possible Jason's future *was* completely fucked. I got to him at the bottom of the winding staircase. He was battered from the fall and moaning. I saw Randall Moore and his wife in the living room. Both had been shot. But both were making noise. I hoped against hope they weren't going to die.

"Oh, fuck!" Jason said, and he tried to get up. I grabbed the gun, shoved it in my waistband, and grabbed him under the arms. I dragged him out through the front door and onto the porch. He lay there for a moment. Then he tried to get up. I pushed him back down. I wasn't ready for it, but he was less battered than I thought. He reached for my waist and managed to grab the gun. He put the gun up to his head. I just managed to kick at it before it went off. It missed.

"Fuck me, fuck me, fuck me!" he yelled. I dropped onto him and pushed him flat on his back again.

"Quiet," I whisper-screamed at him. "Just shut up and listen! This wasn't you. Same as it wasn't me and it wasn't Jack, this wasn't you. You have to believe that, same as you told me I had to believe I didn't shoot you."

Jason moaned, "I don't know why I did it. I wanted to stop, but I did it."

"And you don't want to anymore," I told him. "The demon's gone. You're yourself now. Don't you dare try to fucking kill yourself again. Now listen!"

I told Jason he had to hide until I figured out how to fix this. I told him about my cabin in Tellico Plains, Tennessee. Two days' ride at the most.

"You're going to go there and stay there," I told him. "Wear your helmet while you ride. No one will be able to recognize you that way. Don't call me. Don't call anyone. Stay there until I call you or come to get you."

"I don't want to live," he said. "I can't live after this. I'm not going to be right again, ever!"

"You will. Maybe tomorrow this will all be undone."

I pulled out my wallet. I kept the cabin's address on the back of a business card. I couldn't remember it myself. I'd only been there a few times, to write and recover. I shoved the card into his front pocket.

"Can you ride?"

"I don't want to. Call the cops. I did this."

"You didn't," I said. "You found me to save me. Now I need you to save yourself, so I can save both of us. If you go down for this, I do, too. We're both lost. Now go!"

I helped him up and pushed him in the direction of our bikes in the driveway. He stumbled but headed the right way, around the corner and out of sight. It was the best I could do. I hoped he'd listen to me. I hoped he'd ride out the despair and guilt long enough to get to the cabin. I waited a few minutes, until I heard his bike start. Then I waited until he had time to back out of the driveway. I listened some more. Finally, I heard the bike hit first gear and drive off. It was going to take a shit ton of luck for him to make it to Tennessee, but I didn't know what else to do.

I went back inside. Randall Moore was shot in the stomach. He was lying on the living room floor, conscious, but not in a good way. He held his stomach and rolled back and forth. His eyes looked up at nothing. Sarah Moore was shot in the shoulder. She was sitting up on the floor, holding her wound, screaming about the pain.

"Jason!" I yelled up the stairs. "Grab some towels and come down here! Hurry!"

I ran to the kitchen and grabbed a towel off the counter. I hoped it was clean. Then I ran to Sarah. I moved her hand out of the way and put the towel against the wound. I eased her onto her back on the floor and pressed the towel hard. Jason came down the stairs then and screamed.

"Jason," I said. "No time for that. I need your help. We have to save your parents."

I told him to fold a towel and put it against his father's stomach and press hard. I didn't know first aid about gunshot wounds from squat. I found myself wishing someone like Dr. Bhagat was here. I didn't know what the hell to do. First aid seemed the right thing to try, and the longer I delayed in calling 911 the better chance my brother had to get away.

After what happened with Second Jack, it was completely stupid of me to let Jason come along. I was so concerned about my own ability to resist the demon if it turned out to be one of the powerful ones that I completely forgot that I might not be its only target. Evelyn's accusations about her cosmic partner in crime aside, I always assumed my own power was what opened the door to the demons that controlled me. All of my conversations with my brother about my father should have put that theory to rest. But I hadn't quite gotten there yet. Second Jack had done what he'd done when I hadn't even sensed a demon was there to make him do it. It was reckless of me. I managed things a lot better when I didn't feel anything of consequence.

. . . . .

It was Saturday morning. Jason and I pulled up to the house at about 10 a.m. We'd run six miles early and ate. I went to a local gym and worked out. Jason said his old wounds were fine for running, but he'd never be able to lift weights. So, I went alone. When I got back to the hotel, he tried for some time to talk me out of going to the Moores' house. I was adamant. I told him to stay behind though, in case things didn't go well.

"That's why I'm coming," he told me. "If things don't go well, I'm going to do what I can to stop it. I'm not about to lose you, Little Brother."

If my judgment hadn't been thrown out the window by my newfound love for another human being, I wouldn't have let him go, or

I would have called the thing off. But Jason Moore's fear was calling to me, as was the very real danger I figured he might be in, that his whole family might be in. And my theory that my powers had grown was just a theory, untested. Maybe Jason *could* stop me if things started to go the way they went in Carol's restaurant – the first time.

I explained to him what to watch for. I told him I might not seem any different until I started doing odd things, like reaching out for potential weapons. "If you see me do that," I told him, "do whatever you have to do to knock me cold. I don't know if it will work, but then no one has tried before. If you have to, kill me. I forgive you in advance."

"I'm not going to fucking kill you."

"You might if I'm trying to kill you. Besides, it looks like killing me only slows me down for a bit."

Jason laughed. "You make mandatory safety talks look stupid."

And so, we left the hotel and rode to the Moores' house. It was an elegant old home. Two story, well over a hundred years old. Probably more than 150 years old. Like the moneyed homes in Carol's town, this one sat up a hill, behind a retaining wall. It was a Victorian, but the first Victorian I'd ever seen built in brick. It stood next door to an old cemetery. The cemetery was also behind a retaining wall, and I noted there were miniature concrete retaining walls built into and going up the cemetery hill, built to keep graves and monuments closer to level for mourners to visit – and maybe to keep the dead from mud-sliding down toward the road.

We passed the house along the highway and took a steep side street uphill. It took several sharp curves on the way up. It was tricky to navigate on a 900-pound bike, but we finally managed the turn into the driveway.

The house was old, but the improvements weren't. The driveway was in the back of the house, new concrete, level and gleaming bright in the sunlight. It reminded me briefly of the pyramid Evelyn had taken me to. I realized then that I hadn't been giving Evelyn my full attention since Jason came back into my life. That had to change. I was still a long way from knowing what sort game I was a pawn in.

We got off our bikes. Jason opened the back of his, grabbed a towel, and threw it down on the seat.

"Not burning my ass when we leave," he said. "My baby's bum isn't impervious like yours."

I smiled. "My ass still burns. It just won't kill me."

Jason laughed.

The house had a wrap-around porch on the front, which faced down the hill toward the highway. We mounted the stairs, and I knocked on the door. Randall Moore answered and invited us in.

"I know you've met," he said, "but it wasn't a proper introduction. This is my wife, Sarah."

I shook her hand. "Pleased to meet you, Sarah."

"Me, too," she said. "I can't tell you what it means to us to have you come over to work with Jason on this ghost thing."

"Well," I said, "if I can help, I'm glad to do it."

Brother Jason introduced himself as my brother and shook their hands, too. I wasn't keen on word getting out that Nash Baxter had a brother named Jason Bennett because Jason Bennett had a little brother named Nick who shot his whole family about thirty years ago in the Bay Area. It's like having a connection to Ron DeFeo, Jr. Nothing to do about it now, though. Unthinkingly, I'd already introduced him to Little Jason – the reporter – as my brother, anyway. My bad.

"Jason's upstairs," Randall said. "He says he wants to finish his article about your interview to show you."

"An ethical journalist," I laughed. "Most never show you what they've written, and you don't know how badly they've misquoted you or your books until you see it in print."

I asked if we could sit and talk for a while. Randall got us coffee.

"So, I do this sort of thing a lot," I told them. "You can read about how it goes in my books. I hear the stories, I get the history of the house, and then I investigate. So, if we could start with whether there is anything unusual about the house that Jason might be focusing on, that would help."

As we spoke, I saw the ghost plain as day, standing behind the couch the Moores were sitting on. No zigzag lines came with it. That was good. The zigzags meant trouble. The ghost was an old man, but he wore the uniform of a Union soldier. I sensed he was one of the honored town heroes, celebrated on countless Fourths of July, long after the Civil War had ended. He'd often lied about shaking the hands of George McClellan, Abraham Lincoln, and Teddy Roosevelt. His arm was missing, amputated during the war. His only consciousness was an expression of hate, focused on Jefferson Davis and Robert E. Lee.

I felt for the demon. Nothing yet.

"It's an old house, as I'm sure you can see," Randall said. "It's updated inside, but it's got old bones."

"The cemetery next door has old bones, too," Sarah told me. "It used to be the family plot. The same family lived here for a long time. Eventually, one of them turned the family plot into a cemetery for the town, but the whole original family is buried next door."

"Does Jason see more than one ghost?" I asked.

"No. Just the one. But he's afraid of the cemetery," Randall said. "You know, I fell in love with this place when I saw it. It's changed hands a lot since then. It was for sale about six years ago, and I wanted to buy it. But I waited too long to make an offer, and someone got to it first. But it was sold twice after that. When we got it last year, it was about thirty thousand dollars cheaper than when it sold six years ago. So, I got a deal. It should have occurred to me that buying an old house next to a creepy old cemetery was probably not a good idea with Jason's only being eleven at the time. Old house. Old cemetery. This was my fault. I should have realized that would play havoc with a kid's imagination."

I didn't comment. It probably was a bad idea.

"Do either of you ever see anything out of the ordinary?" I asked. Randall had already told me Sarah thought she saw something, but I didn't know if they'd discussed it. Both were quiet for a moment, then Randall looked at Sarah. She sighed.

"This is a little embarrassing, but sometimes I think I see something out of the corner of my eye," she said. "I know it's nothing, but it gives me the chills."

The old soldier was completely unaware of the living persons in the living room. Unlike First Jack's great grandfather, this ghost didn't focus its hate on the living, just Jeff and Bob. Another good sign. When the hate turns toward the living, it's a sign that the demon's focus is going there, too.

"You know," I said. "In these old houses, there are about a million tricks of light, with all the sharp angles and asymmetrical rooms. You're bound to see something at one time or another, but it's just light and shadow. There's a trick in the interplay though, and things sometimes seem to move and disappear. So, there's no need to be embarrassed."

Sarah was quiet. I could tell she wasn't buying my explanation. The ghost behind her was waiving to one of the crowds once gathered for his veneration. I felt around for the demon again. Nothing. I'd have to keep moving through the house until I found it.

"Can we get Jason down here?" I asked. "I'd like to look through the house with him."

Randall called Jason down. He smiled and shook my hand, saying, "I've finished the interview. If you have time, I'd like to show it to you, to make sure I got it right."

"Sure thing," I said. "Let's get started on our new investigation first though. Let's see if there's a ghost in this house."

Little Jason seemed to take courage in being taken seriously about his ghost, and to have someone there with him to investigate it.

"Why don't we start upstairs?"

"Sure," Little Jason said. "I usually see him down here though."

"What does he look like?"

Jason looked directly at the ghost and said, "Like a Civil War general."

Little Jason led me up a winding staircase to the second floor. Brother Jason stayed downstairs with the Moores to make small talk. On the way up, I asked Jason what the monster he saw looked like.

"Like pictures of demons in old books," he said, matter-of-factly.

"Where do you usually see it?"

"Downstairs, with the ghost," he said. "But sometimes it comes at night, in my room."

I could tell he was trying to be brave about it, but the tension in his voice was unmistakable.

"Then let's start there."

Jason led me into one of the bedrooms off the main hallway. Inside Cubs pennants and Star Wars posters filled the walls. There was a laptop with his cell phone next to it on a desk. A small bookshelf held *Harry*

Potter books and the *Lord of the Rings* trilogy. The books gave me an idea. I said, "You know I investigate stories about ghosts, right?"

"Yeah."

"What if I told you I have a power. Something like what a wizard has that can make the ghost and monster go away."

Jason frowned. "There's no such thing as wizards, so you can't be one."

"There's also no such thing as ghosts, but you're seeing one."

Jason was silent. The logic of it was working on him.

"Here's all I'm saying, Jason. If you can help me find this monster, I can make it go away. Forever."

"How can you do that?"

"Well, you know all those houses I go to and say there isn't a ghost there after all?"

"Yes."

"Let's just say there might have been when I got there, but there wasn't one anymore, after I left."

Except for my brother, I'd never been this forthcoming with anyone before. I couldn't help myself. I really liked the kid and wanted more than anything to put his fears to rest and to let him know the danger would be gone.

"How can you do that?" Jason's tension turned to hope.

"All you have to do is show me where the thing is. I'll do the rest."

Jason smiled. That's when we heard the gunshots.

I ran out of Jason's room and into the hallway at the top of the stairs. Brother Jason was walking up, holding a gun I didn't know he had. It didn't take me long to find the demon then. I felt it inside of Jason's head.

"Jason," I yelled. "Stop! Fight it!"

Little Jason had followed me out of his room and stood next to me. I swept him behind me and stood between him and Jason.

Jason shot at me and missed. He shot again, and I was hit, somewhere. He kept walking slowly up the stairs. I reached out for the demon then. I felt my old power flowing through me and into the demon's rage and hate.

"You can't win," Brother Jason said. "Anywhere you go, we will find you."

Jason aimed the gun again. I'd like to say I could see the demon looming over Jason, with fetid wings, rancid horns, and cloven hooves.

But it was just Jason that I saw. The demon's fear came through loud and clear though. It knew it was about to die, and with its last moment of hold over Jason, it tried to pull the trigger.

I leaped down the stairway and kicked Jason in the chest. The shot flew wide, and Jason fell back, sliding and bouncing down the stairs. I got lucky and landed on my feet. I shouted at Little Jason to go back into his room and lock the door. The demon was gone. Nothing was left of it now. The ghost was gone, too. But my brother was in a world of hurt.

CHAPTER 20

Sarah was in a bad way, but more or less lucid. I put her hand on the towel and told her to hold it there. Little Jason had both hands on the towel he held to his father's stomach. I couldn't wait any longer to call 911 without risking whatever chance Randall Moore had to survive. I wasn't going to count on resurrection and let him slip away. Brother Jason had all the lead I was going to be able to give him.

The 911 operator told me to check on Randall and make sure he was breathing. I put my head to his chest. He was still getting air. The operator said that was good, more to reassure me, I think, since she was stating the obvious. Little Jason was terrified, but he held the towel firmly against his father's wound.

"You're doing great, Jason," I said. "I think your mom and dad are going to be okay."

I wasn't certain of that, but what else could I say to him?

"Why did he do it?" Jason yelled. "Why did your brother shoot my parents?"

Yeah, that was a problem. All the Moores had been introduced to Jason as my brother. I was going to have to think of something to undo that brotherly bond if Brother Jason was going to have a chance.

"He's not my brother," I said, loud enough for Sarah to hear, too. "I just met him. He said we were related. I gave him a chance to prove it because he looks like me. Turns out he's some kind of psycho. I shouldn't have trusted him. I'm sorry."

Little Jason knew a lot of swear words. He unleashed them on me and told me to go fuck myself for being sorry. I didn't blame him.

The paramedics came fast. I let them in and watched them work on Randall first, then Sarah. Okay, so I'd gotten the order wrong when I tried to help. But they don't teach triage in law school.

The paramedics put the Moores on gurneys and wheeled them out to their truck. Neither paramedic seemed to notice the bullet hole in my shirt or the blood that had soaked into it. But Officer Smith did once he showed up.

Smith arrived with two other officers. He recognized me immediately, saw the blood, and made me lie down on the floor before I could protest.

"Hold still, Mr. Baxter," he said. He had a real skill for putting me places I didn't want to be.

"I'm fine, really," I said, trying to get up.

"No, I don't think so," Smith said, placing his hand on my shoulder and forcing me back down. The two other officers took Little Jason into the kitchen for a chat. I doubted that was going to go well for my brother.

"Really," I said. "I'm not shot. The blood isn't mine."

Smith's ability to lift a 900-pound bike translated well into ripping my shirt open, exposing my chest. I looked down. Yeah, there was a bullet wound. Not the angry sort you would expect, but my healing wasn't instantaneous.

Smith actually pointed his finger at me and said "Stay!" Then he ran outside. He was back fast, carrying a first aid kit and telling someone through his radio that they needed another ambulance.

He pulled a pair of latex gloves from the first aid kit and a big flat package, which he ripped open with only slightly less difficulty than he'd had with my shirt. He put the gloves on and pulled a bandage from the packet. He began applying pressure to what was left of my wound.

He smiled at me.

"You have a knack for getting shot."

I smiled back. "I don't think it's that bad."

"We'll find out. Don't talk. We'll get you to the ER in a minute."

THE THINGS IN HEAVEN AND EARTH

An ambulance crew showed up in short order, and I was on the next gurney out. If nothing else, it delayed any questions for a while. That would give Brother Jason some more time, and me time to think.

It was old home week at the ER. Dr. Bhagat was there waiting for me. I was wheeled into a room with a sliding glass door, and the ambulance crew transferred me to the bed. They left, and Dr. Bhagat closed the door. I saw Officer Smith hadn't been far behind. He made a beeline to my room and waited outside the door.

Bhagat looked at me lying there. She was frowning.

"Do I need to break a sweat trying to save you, Mr. Baxter?"

"Doubtful," I said. "I feel pretty good, considering."

She reached down and lifted the bandage away.

"I see a trickle," she said.

"Getting hopeful?"

"Not at all," she said, replacing the bandage. "How did you manage to get shot this time?"

"Remember that guy who said he was my brother?"

"I do."

"He shot me."

"And our customers down the hall?"

"The Moores?"

"Yes."

"Them, too," I said. "Are they going to be okay?"

"Not as okay as you, Mr. Baxter, but my understanding is they will indeed survive."

She opened the door and told Officer Smith I was stable and ready to talk. She wasn't going to blow my cover, but she wasn't going to help me keep it either.

"How are you feeling?" Smith asked.

"Fine," I said. "It's just a flesh wound."

"They all are," he replied. "If you're up to it, I need to ask you about what happened back there."

"I thought I left your jurisdiction a couple of towns back," I said.

Smith told me he'd quit.

"I couldn't go on seeing people every day who knew my grandfather and what he did, so I took an offer to join the force here. And now here you are again with another bullet in the chest."

I thought about it. I realized however nice Officer Smith might be and no matter what he might think he owed me, he was going to get past the pleasantries pretty fast and start grilling me about the shootings, no doubt already knowing whatever Little Jason had said about it being my brother who shot his parents. It was no small consideration that my brother needed whatever time I might be able to give him either. So, I asked Smith if he could call Dr. Bhagat back in.

"Sure thing. Don't go anywhere."

I was fairly certain he wasn't being funny when he said it.

He came back with the doctor. I asked him to close the door.

"I'm going to confess something," I said, "but I needed Dr. Bhagat here to assure you I'm not playing some kind of trick on you."

Before Officer Smith could ask what I meant, I pulled the bandage off and used it to wipe away whatever blood was still on the bullet wound. It had closed up nicely, like a psychic surgeon had done his magic and closed the wound after pulling the bad mojo out.

"Please, Doctor, before he decides I've been fooling him and he cuffs me or something, can you tell him I was actually shot?"

Dr. Bhagat was silent. Then she said she hadn't actually *seen* me get shot.

"Okay," I sighed. "True enough . . ."

Smith cuffed me to the bedrail before I could finish.

"What the hell is this about?" he said. "You were pretending to be shot?"

"Wait a minute," I said. "I told you I *wasn't* shot. You were the one hell bent on proving me wrong."

"I saw something that looked like a wound," he accused, all traces of friendly gone. "There's nothing now. You sure as hell weren't shot, but two people were. You need to start talking."

"Dr. Bhagat," I pleaded. "Will you please tell him?"

"Mr. Baxter," she replied. "I certainly don't know enough about what happened before you got here to tell him anything about your condition now. Perhaps if you were to explain things in a way that didn't involve voodoo priestesses, I might have something to offer."

She had me by the shorts, and she knew it. She was going to get her answer to the biggest mystery she'd ever encountered one way or another. Now she had leverage. Not that I cared. I was going to fess up, anyway, with or without the cuffs or Bhagat's playing dumb. I needed time for Jason, true enough. But I'd been feeling bad for Officer Smith ever since he came to my hospital room the first time around, despondent and confused about a man he loved and probably idolized, at least when he was a kid. I'd half decided to give him a better explanation about what happened to Second Jack regardless of current circumstances. But he'd just think I was crazy unless Bhagat was there to back me.

"Scouts honor," I told her. "I'll be honest, trustworthy, loyal, and kind."

Bhagat considered and said, "How about this, Mr. Baxter. You tell the good policeman here what you want to tell him, and if there is something I can add, assuming I think there's something that can be added to aid the telling of truth, I'll see what I can contribute."

Smith was listening to the exchange. I could tell he was processing what he heard and examining every bit of it in advance of what was about to be my interrogation. To which, I would have, of course, relied on my right to remain silent if I hadn't already decided to spill the beans.

"Doctor, I told you it would sound crazy. I promise the truth is going to sound as nuts as the voodoo beverage story."

"We'll see," she said, betraying nothing, but I knew she wanted the truth, and she wanted it very badly.

"Okay. Fair enough. But before I get going, will you tell me your first name, Officer Smith? I think it will be easier to talk if I don't keep calling you 'Officer.'"

"It's Jack."

Fourth Jack. Jacks and Jasons everywhere.

"Okay, Jack," I looked at him directly in the eyes. I didn't want him thinking I was anything but truthful, in particular since I was going to tell the truth. "Here's the first part. Your grandfather didn't kill his friend Jack or shoot me. It wasn't him that did it."

CHAPTER 21

Then again, I wasn't going to tell the *whole* truth. Not where Jason was concerned. I loved my brother. Not because of the man I'd met and bonded with the last couple of weeks, but because he was my brother when I was a kid and risked everything then to protect me from our father. When you can feel the things most people feel, that's the kind of love that runs deep. That made protecting him paramount on my list of priorities. It was killing me that I didn't know where he was or how he was handling everything that had happened. I could only hope he'd listened to me and was headed south. Damn real emotions, anyway. Damn them doubly so for the sadness I felt over Second Jack and his grandson's losing the image of the man he loved.

"Let me start with this," I told Jack. "When your grandfather shot me, I was dead."

Jack didn't respond, but his eyes said I was full of shit. I looked to Dr. Bhagat for help. She smiled minutely but wasn't talking. She was enjoying my struggle to be believed after I had lied to her. I gave up and changed the narrative.

"Your grandfather wasn't in control of himself when he shot Jack, and he wasn't in control of himself when he shot me."

More silent full-of-shit eyes and smiling. I looked at Bhagat, frustrated, and said, "How the hell can I tell this thing when nothing I can say is believable, without some tiny bit of confirmation from you that there's more than meets the eye where I'm concerned?"

Bhagat crossed her arms. Her smile grew wider. She was having fun. Jack not so much.

"Listen, there are two people who might be dying for all I know," he said. "Their son is a wreck. Someone shot them, and I'm going to find out who. The only reason I'm listening to you at all is to find out what the hell happened. So, if you'll leave my grandfather out of it and tell the truth, we'll be okay, you and me. But if you keep this bullshit up, I'm going to arrest you as an accomplice to attempted murder."

"You know," I said. "You handcuffed me. That means I'm already under arrest. I could confess to anything right now, and it couldn't be used against me. So uncuff me. It will make it easier to talk."

He Mirandized me instead. I'd make a terrible criminal defense lawyer.

I looked at Bhagat again. "A little help?"

She didn't give much, but she told Jack, "I cannot vouch for Mr. Baxter's veracity. He's lied to me repeatedly. I want to be clear about that. But I will say there is something about him that makes it reasonable to hear him out, no matter how incredible his statements might seem. When he's finished, we can begin to assess whether he's worthy of belief."

I looked at Smith.

"Look," I said. "There's no easy way to explain this. So, I'm going to start with the broader principles. They're not going to be believable. Let me get started, though, and don't interrupt me. When I stop, ask all the questions you want."

Jack said, "Why don't we start with the name of the man who shot the Moores?"

"That's a question," I observed. "You're already breaking the rules."

"I'm not playing games here, Baxter," he said. "The kid said you didn't shoot his parents and maybe helped save them. And him. That's why you're not on your way to the station right now. But I'm damn sure going to find out who shot them and where to find him."

"Okay. Hold tight, Horatio, and try to let belief take hold."

Smith looked at my quizzically. Not a Shakespeare guy. But I was, so I started big.

"I told you your grandfather didn't shoot me or kill Jack. He might have killed himself, I don't know about that, but the rest I'm certain about. You said it yourself, and I think you know it in your heart, no matter what the facts might say. It wasn't in him to do such a thing. Something that's going to be very hard to believe possessed him and forced his hand. The same thing took over the guy who was with me at the Moores' house and forced him to shoot them. He tried to kill himself, too. He didn't want to live with what he'd been forced to do any more than your grandfather did. I was able to stop him, though. I know that's what happened because the same thing happened to me. That's the easy part. Here's where it gets weird."

I gave a brief overview of my quest to find and fight demons. I confessed that there were times I lost the battles and had been forced to kill.

"But before you try to arrest me, none of the people I killed are dead anymore. So, there's no crime left to investigate or prosecute. Somehow, at the same time I gained this ability of mine to heal magically, the dead came back to life, as if nothing had happened. But let me tell you about the latest murders I committed and who I killed."

I told them what I saw at Carol's place. The ghost. The demon. Then I told them how I had murdered almost everyone in the restaurant when the demon took hold of me.

"Right after that, you found me in the ditch, Jack. When I rode back a couple of hours later, they were alive. I have no idea how."

I looked at Bhagat. "I told you the truth was going to sound as crazy as the lie."

"Crazier," she said.

"Are you believing this bullshit?" Jack asked Bhagat. He was angry as hell, certain I was lying but not quite sure what to do with me or about the lies at the moment.

"Doctor," I begged again. "A little help?"

Bhagat looked at Jack, sighed, and reluctantly began to tell him about what had happened to me after his grandfather had tried to end me. She described the wounds and the fact that I couldn't have survived. For good measure, she added the bit about the hardware that was stabilizing my spine dissolving into thin air while my spinal cord healed itself.

Jack was convinced. Not of what he was being told, but that Bhagat was an imposter pretending to be a doctor. He made no bones about it; he was going to take her and me both back to the station. He told his radio he needed assistance to transport two suspects.

"Doctor," I said. "This is out of hand. Do you have a scalpel or something sharp?"

She walked around my bed to a counter and opened a drawer. Jack drew his gun and told her not to move. She opened the package the scalpel was in and handed it to me, anyway. While Smith holstered his gun to wrestle it away from me, I sliced my handcuffed arm deep. Really deep.

Healing abilities aside, the pain was immense. In the face of that intensity, my brain shot about looking for something to concentrate on. Maybe it was as a mental survival reflex to keep me from the realization that I'd just fucked myself royal. I thought about stories I'd read of Samurai warriors committing seppuku. At least they were smart enough to have a second standing by to lop their heads off to stop the pain. I'd had no such foresight. Blood shot out of my arm in a way that made me think I'd hit something pretty important. Right before I passed out, I wondered if I could heal if a second were there to mercifully chop *my* head off.

I don't know how long I was out. But I woke up regretting what I'd just done like a motherfucker. The pain was still there, and the blood. But it wasn't squirting anymore, just oozing. Bhagat had restrained herself from practicing her trade. She'd done nothing to help me. She'd simply watched. Smith was yelling at her to save me. Apparently, he thought she was a doctor again. A nurse ran in, but Bhagat told her it was under control and to leave. The nurse looked disbelievingly at the scene and ran out. She came back a minute later with another doctor. By then, Bhagat was cleaning the wound.

"What the hell!" New Doc said.

"It's okay," Bhagat told him. "I've got it."

New Doc took a look at the gun that Smith had back out and trained on Bhagat – and at the bloody scalpel.

"Jesus, Chanda," New Doc said. "Are you sure?"

"Yes, Jack," Bhagat told New Doc. "Take a look."

New Doc, yet another Jack, came close and examined the wound.

"Where the hell did all the blood come from?" he asked.

"He nicked the brachial artery," she said matter-of-factly. "Accidentally. It's under control."

New Doc Jack said okay, quite skeptically, and left.

The wound was a red line now. A minute later, it was smooth skin.

Smith put his gun away and sat down in the corner.

CHAPTER 22

It occurred to me that I had taken a phenomenal risk. Proving a point with a razor cut was one thing; slicing my arm completely open and tearing through arteries was another. I didn't know the how or why of the healing enough to *know* it would happen. But Jack Smith wasn't going to be swayed with lofty Shakespeare references or tales of demonic possession. So, I gambled that my healing ability was a constant now. It wasn't a gamble I wanted to take again.

But this time it worked and had its effect on Jack Smith. I watched him sitting in the corner, in silent awe, wonder, amazement, disbelief, fear, dissonance. Whatever combination of the above, he was shaken to the core, that was certain.

Bhagat chimed in, taking my attention away from Jack. She was predictably glowering at me.

"I assume the good policeman's reinforcements will be here rather soon. Yet somehow, you've managed to get this far while holding back the truth once more. I would like it now, thank you."

"The demons are the truth," I said. "Possession and the whole nine yards."

"Assuming all of that is true, it does nothing to explain your healing abilities. Demonic plagues aside."

"True enough," I said. "I think maybe I owe you, too."

Damned emotions again. I was feeling more than love and fear and compassion. I was also feeling some connection with people I barely knew. Like Bhagat. What did I owe her? Gratitude for her silence? Fuck me. I liked her. Even her snide commentaries worked on me and made me think there was a worthy human being at work just below the surface of her disapproval. The list of people I found myself caring about was getting longer every day and affecting my judgment. For good or bad, I couldn't say.

"Here's the shorthand," I said. "I didn't have any special healing ability until I got shot the first time. I was as surprised as you. But after I committed those murders in the restaurant, some force brought the dead back to life. And it kept me alive when I should have died. I think it just healed my arm, too."

"Does this force have a name?" Bhagat asked.

"Evelyn Blankenship," I said.

"The psychic?"

"You've heard of her?"

"I assumed everyone had. She is quite famous."

"So, I've heard. But I never heard of her. Not until recently. But a being that I don't believe is the real Evelyn Blankenship has come to me in visions, taking her form. It started after the restaurant murders. She's convinced me there is some other kind of supernatural being inside of me. Not a demon. But something like her. I get the impression I've become an unwitting participant in their effort to destroy each other. One might be trying to kill me. The other one might be healing me to keep me alive. Not so astounding when you consider one or both of them can also raise the dead when the mood strikes."

"Why you?"

"Evelyn tells me I'm like her. Sort of. This thing I have with demons, this power over them. She says it's because I'm a part of her. She says my power is growing."

"Why the kid?" Officer Smith had been listening, of course. He had broken out of the confusion that had overtaken him. "What were you doing in his house?"

"Getting rid of a demon," I said. "I was trying to help."

"The man who shot the parents. Who was he?"

"If you were listening, you know the man who shot them didn't. It was the same as with your grandfather. He was possessed to do something he would never do."

"We have to find him," Smith said.

"I wish you wouldn't. My version of events won't keep him out of jail."

"I'm not talking as a cop," Smith said. "We have to find him to help him. This thing might have been personal to you right up until that thing took hold of my grandpa. Now it's personal to me, too. I'm going to help you figure this thing out, Baxter. And if there's an earthly way to end it, we're going to do just that."

He got up and unlocked the handcuffs. I didn't know what to say, but I wouldn't have had time to say much, anyway. I saw Smith's reinforcements working their way through the emergency room. They were at the counter – two of them – asking where we were. Five fingers immediately pointed in our direction.

Bhagat saw them, too. She put her hand on my shoulder and said, "Thank you for the truth. I don't know what I can do, but if I can help you, I will."

Life was indeed remarkably strange.

Right before the new cops opened the sliding glass door, Smith whispered to me.

"You're a writer. Come up with a story that will get us out of this when we get to the station."

I'd already written the story, but I thought I was writing it for Smith. I was hoping now that he'd plug the one hole in the plot for me.

At the station, I signed a waiver saying I knew I had the right to remain silent. I also agreed to my interview being videotaped, once they provided me with a clean shirt to replace the one Smith had ripped open. I didn't want to look like the shirtless nutcase in an interrogation video.

Smith was with me in the interrogation room, playing big scary cop. A detective sat down across from me and asked what had happened at the Moores' house. The truth was fine for most of it, how I'd met the Moores and why I was at their house in the first place. Little Jason and his parents, if they could talk, would back that up. Then I wrote my brother Jason into the part of an obsessed fan who kinda looked like me and said we were related. His name was "Duke." He also called himself Jason, but mostly "Duke." Never got his last name. I also told the detective exactly where and how I'd met him. Carol, Tom, Pete, and that other guy could vouch for that. They could witness the fact that the guy called himself "Duke," too, and that he said he'd been looking for me on the road. The quintessential obsessed fan.

"I didn't know him from Adam," I said, trying to figure out how to downplay the brother connection they'd eventually get from the Moores, if they hadn't gotten it already. "But he did look a lot like me. So, when he told me we were related, I fell for it. Long lost family and all that. It was stupid, but I let him meet me when I got out of the hospital. I had no idea he had a gun or that he was going to go psycho on the Moore family."

"Why did you take him with you in the first place?" the detective asked.

"I told you," I said. "Stupidity. He was, I don't know . . . persuasive. He didn't tell me how we were related. He just said I should think of him as a brother, and he'd tell me the rest of it once we got to know each other. He had a way of making you believe him. He helped me when I got out of the hospital, too. He even got me a room at the hotel."

"What hotel?"

I told him, counting on Officer Smith to follow my lead, so to speak.

Smith said, "I'm on it," and left to plug the plot hole.

The detective found ways of getting me to retell the story, from different starting points. We were there for at least an hour before Smith got back. When he came in, he bent low to the detective and whispered, loud enough for me to hear, "Stolen credit card."

Then Smith was gone again. Another hour went by. My story stayed the same, but the detective asked any number of ways where "Duke" or "Jason" had gone after the shooting. Of course, I had no way of knowing.

Eventually I was able to learn from the detective that Randall Moore was out of the woods. So was Sarah Moore.

"Any reason I can't go," I said.

The detective seemed disappointed, but he said no.

"Look, if Duke should contact you again in any way . . ."

"I'll call you," I said.

He slid his business card to me.

"Do that. But be careful. This obsessed fan thing can go really bad for someone like you."

"It already has," I replied. "Is it okay if I go back to the Moores' house to get my bike?"

"Sure thing," the detective said. "I'll have Officer Smith drive you there."

In the squad car, Smith told me what he'd written in his report thus far. No way of knowing the real name of the shooter just yet, he'd written. He'd confirmed with Carol I'd just met "Duke" the night before I got shot. Story matched mine to a T. The credit card he used at the hotel was stolen. I'd have to fix that last part, Smith told me. "Put the whole thing on your card. I told the desk clerk the one they had was stolen and that I'd report it. That should hide the identification, for now. I don't think he'll get flagged if he uses the card again."

"Okay," I said. "I can't thank you enough. It's turning into a habit, thanking you. Now what?"

I might have suspected a ruse to get me to fess up on the shooter's true identity and location, but Smith must have known who he was already, after checking at the hotel. It looked like I'd picked up another companion who was all in. I hoped it wouldn't turn out badly for him.

Smith dropped me off at the Moores' house. Before I got out, he told me he was going to take a leave of absence or quit if necessary. "I'll meet you at the hotel at 6 a.m. tomorrow. Then we'll go find your brother, Mr. Jason Bennett."

"I didn't say he was *actually* my brother."

"The kid said you did," he answered. "You muddied it up okay back there, but I know the Duke story is only partly true. You're not that dumb. Hopefully, everyone else is tracking that down the way you told it."

"Let's hope. But can we meet at nine instead?"

"Why so late?"

"I like to run and work out in the morning."

"Seriously?"

"Yeah," I said. "And do us both a favor; leave your gun and any weapons behind. They're not going to help and might very well hurt someone who doesn't deserve to be hurt."

CHAPTER 23

Evelyn's penchant for sandy locales was undiminished. No sooner than my head hit the pillow, sand was burning my ass. The sun was nestled somewhere around high noon. It was hot but lacking the stifling humidity of the Midwest heat in Illinois. I heard amusement rides again, but this time the sounds were accompanied with the laughter of people. I was facing the ocean. I turned to look at the boardwalk behind me. I was in Santa Cruz. I remembered the boardwalk from the happier times of my childhood, when my father was still the dad I loved and had taken us to the beach on summer weekends. People were lounging or at play along the beach, swimming, body surfing, laughing, and yelling.

I stood up trying to keep the sand from burning my nether regions. I was wearing swim trunks and didn't have a shirt on. Standing wasn't a lot of help. I was barefoot, and the sand immediately started burning my feet. I started hopping from foot to foot before I saw a pair of flip flops near me. They were white, with the word "Florida" imprinted boldly on them in black. Since I was the only one near them, I assumed they were mine and stepped into them, finding relief for my burning soles. Evelyn was clearly having a joke.

I didn't see Evelyn, but Scotty sure as fuck hadn't beamed me to a beach more than 2,000 miles from my hotel room.

The surreal quality of the beach Evelyn had taken me to before was gone. And that hadn't exactly been Santa Cruz before. Some close facsimile, maybe, but not the same. This didn't just feel real tactilely; it was real in every sense, alive with activity and bustling humanity.

I squinted, since I didn't have sunglasses, and scanned the beach ahead. There, near the water, I saw her. She was wearing the same yellow summer dress she'd worn during our first beach excursion and the same floppy straw hat. She'd been kind enough to herself to have a towel handy to sit on, unlike me. Even from a distance, and from behind, she was striking. She sat with her knees up, but with perfect posture – and again I noticed she was very tall. Her dress was rustling in the breeze, and she seemed to be staring straight ahead, out over the ocean.

I began awkwardly traipsing through the sand to get closer to her. Once I was beside her, I looked down to make sure it was her and not some look-alike. She had the same large sunglasses on as before, making the whole ensemble the same as the first time on the beach. It was her.

"I hope I amused you hopping around on the sand like an idiot," I said, sitting on the towel beside her. "What revelations, half-told, do you have for me now?"

She turned slowly to look at me. I saw that she had tears flowing from beneath her sunglasses. Crocodile tears, I decided. How was she going to try to play me now?

"Excuse me," she said, not entirely composed, as if she really had been crying. "You've made a mistake. I don't know you."

"What game now, Evelyn?" I demanded. "How are you going to go about fucking my life up today?"

She stiffened when I called her by her name – and maybe my language had something to do with it as well. She said, "Okay, you recognized me. I appreciate that you think you have some connection to me. Thank you for that. I'm always grateful for my followers. But, believe it or not, famous people need to be left alone sometimes. This is one of those times for me. So, please, I'd be grateful if you would leave me alone today."

As she finished, she seemed to rethink it. She took her glasses off and looked into my squinting eyes. "Or do I know you after all?"

At the same time, I realized this was not *my* Evelyn. This was the real one on a real beach, like I'd seen in my other Evelyn dream. But my head hit the pillow at 10 p.m. It was noonish here. *When* was this happening?

On the one hand, no matter when or how this was, I thought I should talk to her and learn whatever I could – anything that might shed light on the twists and turns *my* Evelyn and her nemesis/love interest had introduced into my life. On the other, I was stubborn. If *they* had put me face-to-face with the real Evelyn, maybe I didn't want to play.

"I apologize," I said. "I confused you for another Evelyn I guess." Then I added, "I'm sorry you're . . . um, sad."

I got up and told her to I hoped things got better for her. Then I started walking back to the boardwalk, wondering if and when I was going to be jolted back into my hotel room bed. I hadn't gotten far before I felt her hand on my shoulder, pulling me around.

"Wait!" she insisted. "I've seen you in my dreams!"

My exit wasn't going as cleanly as I'd hoped. I looked into her eyes, looking upward because she was taller than I. The sunglasses were gone, and I saw desperation in those eyes. Maybe her world had been turned upside down, too. Compassion reared its ugly head, and I said, "I see you in my dreams, too."

"Who are you?"

"Don't you recognize me? I'm famous."

She started to answer, but then she and the scene began to fade, becoming opaque and insubstantial. I could hear her voice coming as if from a great distance. She was saying, "Nick." Then she was gone. . .

. . . . .

. . . and I was watching myself through her eyes and hearing myself say, "Don't you recognize me? I'm famous." Then I winked out of existence as she said, "Nick?" She looked at the steps leading from the beach to the boardwalk above, scanning to see if I had somehow managed to escape up them. She took a step back, not believing what she had seen. She'd had her hand on the man's shoulder just a moment before, and now he was gone.

She'd taken him as an obsessed fan, approaching her and sitting beside her on her towel. Things like that had happened before. Her gift helped so many people, she thought, but there were those who were unbalanced, some few in every crowd who were obsessed with her and believed her gifts connected them. Her reflex was to be kind, but firm in extricating herself from those encounters. Some she could read, and she knew they could be dangerous, more so if she let them in in any way. She hadn't sensed any danger from this man, however, though his familiarity with her was badly timed. She was still lost and grieving over Ted. So much had happened since the night before, leaving her frightened and angry. Now this man had suddenly come to sit with her, reminding her of the little boy in her dreams.

The little boy. How could a grown man have reminded her so much of the lost child, Nicholas, that she would call him by that name? She concentrated, letting her second sight work. In a moment, she'd seen enough. She knew the little boy and the man were the same person. How could that be?

The boy called to her in her dreams. He was alone in a dark room, trapped and miserable.

"Help me!" he would cry, and she would find the distant voice pulling her from whatever she had been dreaming into the dark room.

The room was small and bare. He sat in the corner, his arms held tightly to his chest. Above him, a dim lightbulb hung from an electrical cord that dropped from the ceiling. She'd seen such things in visions she'd had of old homes, lit inside not with lamps but dangling light bulbs.

This one provided only a minor glow, a drowning dim light in the darkness.

"I'm here," she would say. "I'm Evelyn. What's your name?"

She could hear the boy sniffling.

"I'm scared," he would say. "Please help me."

"I will," she'd answer, knowing somehow that the boy was real – and in danger on some spiritual plane she did not recognize.

The dream was the same every time. She would step closer to the boy and grab the light by the cord and move it closer to him, so she could see his face. Fresh tears fell down his cheek.

"I'm in here," he would say. "It won't let me out!"

"What won't let you out?"

"I don't know," the boy would say. "It makes me do things I don't want to do."

"I promise I'll help you," she would tell him. "What's your name?"

"Nicholas. My family called me Nick."

"Okay, Nick. Do you know how you got in here?"

"It took my family," the boy would cry. "I think it killed me, too, but I'm still alive."

Evelyn sensed the boy *was* alive, though part of him was prisoner here, never seeing the waking world.

Before Evelyn could ever get further than this with Nick, she would feel an oppressive force gather in the room. The hairs on her arms stood on end, and a cold fear invaded her. She was paralyzed with that fear and couldn't speak. Then the force cast her out.

Because she knew the boy was real, she tried to commune with her spirit guides for answers. But they remained stubbornly mute on the subject, offering nothing, not even an acknowledgment that they had heard her questions.

She walked back to her towel and sat. Two mysteries, perhaps too close to be a coincidence. First Ted. Then Nick, at least thirty years older than he was in her dreams.

Ted. She had never been able to read him like other people. For some reason, her gift never worked when it came to him. His thoughts were his own, his feeling closed to her. She had only the man to work with, to know based on what everyone else would be able to see.

It hadn't been clairvoyance that told her he was going to propose to her last night. The timing just seemed right, and the hints he'd given about how special the evening would be made it obvious he had more than dinner in mind. She'd known before the moment came that she would say yes, and she fought down all the doubts that tried to warn her that she wasn't even seeing him with her normal senses. Otherwise, she would not have considered it.

After the wine, the little ring box appeared in front of her.

"Open it," he'd said.

A small tear of happiness fell upon her cheek as she reached for the box. Inside was the most dazzling ring she could imagine sparking in the candlelight. He got up from his chair then and came to her side, taking her hand ever so gently and asking if she would marry him. He didn't kneel, but stood above her, looking down.

She said yes, of course, and he kissed her, and she was happy. She was forty-two, and love had finally come. She wondered, not for the first time, if it was too late for her to become a mother. She decided it wasn't, and her mind was already racing into a future with children and Ted living in the perfect family home.

They had one more glass of wine to celebrate.

They were waiting for the valet to bring the car around when her gift finally opened Ted's mind to her. The shock of it was sudden and horrifying. She looked into his mind and saw nothing of love, but of pride at how simple his conquest had been, he the consummate actor in a play of his own choosing. He was thinking of her fame, and how it would add to his, and how he would play her professed gift into subtle hints about something known that meant his client, whichever it happened to be, was innocent.

While her mind had shot forward to a future with family, his had already put the timer on it. Five years. That was all he would need to use her fame to claw even higher into the public eye, to ensure his stature beyond that of a criminal defense attorney. His ambitions were to take him much higher. He would follow his plan, becoming governor first and then running for president. Evelyn Blankenship was his key to the hearts and minds of the dimwitted masses.

These were his thoughts. These had always been his thoughts.

Evelyn reeled with the knowledge her sight had finally, at this late date, given her. She stepped away from Ted and looked at him with revulsion.

"No!" she said, loudly. The valets and others waiting for their cars looked at her, hearing the distress in her voice. "I will not marry you!"

Ted looked around, seeing all eyes on him. He felt a moment of humiliation, which turned to anger. He grabbed her hand but tried to control himself. He wanted this scene to go away as quickly as possible.

"Evelyn, Darling," he said, squeezing her hand tightly, deliberately causing pain. "I don't know what's gotten into you all of a sudden, but this isn't the time or place. Let's go to my house and discuss it."

"I'm not going anywhere with you!" she yelled, ripping her hand away from his.

If he'd have had even one more second, he could have stopped himself, gotten his anger under control. But the second didn't come, and he slapped her hard across the face. Evelyn fell to the ground.

"You crazy bitch!" Ted yelled, accusing her like *she* had slapped *him*.

Evelyn rolled to her side, filled with fury, and glared up at him. Then she felt a malevolence rising inside of her, as powerful as the force that had confronted her in her dreams with the boy Nicholas. The malevolence took shape and form, dreadful and beyond her control. It reached outward for Ted. In a single moment, he grabbed his chest, said "Fuck!" and fell forward. He was dead.

·   ·   ·   ·   ·

My consciousness left Evelyn, but I remained in the moment, seeing her lover dead on the pavement. I sensed his soul, or whatever might be the same thing, continuing with some form of consciousness. Then falling from the dark night, a demon came from the sky and tore the soul from the dead carcass. The demon saw me, and I saw that it feared me. It looked away and grabbed the soul that had become a ghost and fled, I knew not where.

CHAPTER 24

I woke up from a not-so-refreshing sleep to the sound of insistent knocking at my door. If the hotel alarm clock on my nightstand was to be believed, it was 5:45 in the morning. I opened my eyes, groggy as hell. Whatever time I'd spent with Evelyn Blankenship had been neatly subtracted from any REM or deep sleep I would have gotten without the excursions. I was left, instead, with an emotional residue from Evelyn's mind, which I had been wallowing in through a good chunk of the night. I felt her grief and anger over Ted – and horror at the power she had felt coursing through her, almost reflexively, a power that had turned Ted into demon fodder.

I didn't have my wits about me, or I wouldn't have opened the door as readily as I had. As it was, I stumbled out of bed and opened it with the singular thought of stopping its noise, so I could go back to sleep and, hopefully, shake off Evelyn's anguish. I was giving very little thought to who or what might be on the other side of the door. I didn't even look through the peep hole.

I knew what fear felt like now, but it seemed I didn't let the feeling extend to threats to my physical well-being. I gave that some thought later in the day, while stuck in traffic. It was, I decided, the result of an overconfidence in my ability to heal, no matter how extensively I was hurt – or, rather, how extensively I had been hurt *thus* far. There had to be some level past which I wouldn't be able to self-repair. I thought of the samurai second and threw in the guillotine for good measure. I figured a clean decapitation would probably be enough to end me. Note to self: don't let Phantom Evelyn take you away to medieval Japan or revolutionary France. Second note to self: don't get cocky.

I needn't have worried in any event. It was Jack Smith. He might have let belief take hold, but trust was another matter. It looked like he wasn't willing to see if I'd actually stick around until nine.

"Morning, Nash," he said. "I thought I'd get here early and run with you."

I looked longingly at my pillow. Fuck. No sleep and a hard day ahead on the road. If it hadn't been my brother waiting at the end of the trip, I would have sent Jack on his way and slept another three hours.

Instead, I got coffee brewing and stared at Jack with bloodshot eyes.

"Rough night?" he asked.

"More than you can know," I answered. "I guess since you're my partner in crime now, I should fill you in on the details."

I told him about my evening with Evelyn, and since my previous explanation in the hospital about Evelyn and Company was, at best, cursory, I filled him in about my encounters with both Evelyns. I filled him in on the Hitchhiker, too, and of the possibility that he or it might have been responsible for some of my "possessions." I also noted that it wasn't out of the question that he or Supernatural Evelyn had possessed his grandfather rather than a demon.

I was three cups of coffee in before I finished.

"It's a big bag of crazy maybes," I said. "It's so nuts that I'm only starting to believe most of it myself, and it's taken a lot of convincing."

For a guy who had a hard time believing anything I was saying yesterday morning, Jack was taking everything in now as gospel.

"I don't mind telling you that I don't like any of this," he said. "We're going up against an enemy or enemies we can't understand. Maybe there's an ally somewhere in the mix, but probably not. The thing I like least is that thing in your head. It might be helping you, or it might be lying in wait to kill you, me, or anyone else it decides to."

"Yeah," I said. "Welcome to my world. But you need to know I'm one of the changing variables myself. Before you found me in that ditch, I wasn't exactly normal myself. Maybe I'm not now. But it wasn't just circumstances that made me different. I've changed a lot in the last couple of weeks. Evelyn and the Hitchhiker both said I was awakening."

"Meaning what?"

"I don't know what they meant, but here's how I'm starting to picture it. Imagine you're a psychopath, but you don't know it. I mean, I *killed* people, Jack. No matter who or what forced me to do it, I experienced those killings like I was doing every bit of it. Yet I felt next to nothing. A flat tire on the road gave me more consternation. I just killed who I killed, shrugged, and went about my business. But since the ditch, I've . . . I don't know. I've become, I think, a normal human being. I feel emotions I never felt. I care about people. Nothing is pretense with me anymore. But that has come on the heels of some very intense experiences, all precipitated by my first visions with Evelyn Blankenship. My reality was turned upside down, and it's still on some topsy turvy trajectory that I'm afraid you've signed up to follow."

"It sounds like I better keep my eye on you," Jack said. "No offense, but you might be the catalyst for all of this."

"That or a sentient cog in a very complicated machine," I responded. "Either way, I'm going to tell you the same thing I told my brother. Yes, keep your eye on me. If it looks to you at any time that I might become dangerous, try to take me out."

"Let's hope it doesn't come to that."

"Let's. Especially since killing me looks to be a challenge in itself."

Jack's bike was packed for the road, with a large bag strapped to the luggage rack. He promised me there weren't any guns inside. We skipped the run and the gym. I was too tired for exercise, so we ate breakfast at the hotel instead and hit the road early. We got on I-80 and headed east toward Indiana. We got as far as Joliet and a bridge that crossed the Des Plaines River. After that, we were stuck in an interminable back-up. It would have taken hours to get through to the Indiana side and I-65, so we cut our losses and got off on Route 53, finding our way to 65 through farmland, back roads, and finally Routes 41 and 52 into Lafayette. I rode ahead, since Jack's bike was a couple of years older than mine and without GPS. Along the way, I could feel demons in old farmhouses, holding ghosts back from the beyond. And *they* felt my presence, as well. As soon as I'd known they were there, they fled in terror, leaving their ghosts free. I had never experienced anything like that. Ted's demon feared me, that was certain. But this was like a demon stampede. I sensed as they fled that their own power, their own hold in this world, was lost when they abandoned their spirit charges. Yet they had fled into nothingness rather than risk what I might do. Aside from a "normal" human being, I wondered, what else was I becoming?

We filled up in Lafayette, got lunch, and then hit 65 south. Jack took the lead. Ahead, the sky was mustering up a bit of nastiness. Black clouds filled the horizon, but Jack pressed forward, so I followed. It looked like we had time before anything serious got in our way, but then the storm managed to engulf us from all sides before we knew it was happening. Rain and wind hit us like a cyclone, and I lost sight of Jack as a heavy downpour crossed the highway, blown nearly horizontal by the wind. I leaned into the gusts and hoped I didn't slide onto the pavement.

I slowed considerably, hoping whoever was behind me had sense to do the same. Rain stung my face and became a steady stream over the lenses of my sunglasses, which were more than useless, turning day-become-night into a nearly pitch-black darkness.

I eased over as best I could to what I could see of the shoulder, put the flashers on, and got off the bike. I rummaged in the side bag for my rain suit, though I was already soaked. I put the rain suit on and heard Jack saying, "Where the hell is he?" Only Jack was nowhere near me, or anywhere in sight for that matter.

Since he had been ahead of me, I started walking in that direction along the shoulder. I finally saw his flashers dimly shining through the rain. Lightning was all around, making me wonder if that might be one of the things that should still concern me.

"That came up fast!" Jack hollered when he saw me. He was likewise putting his rain suit on, though like me, probably already soaked to the bone.

"There's never an overpass when you need one," I shouted back.

There was nothing to do but hunker down beside his bike and wait for the storm to pass.

The fury of the storm made conversation pointless. I watched the violence around us and thought of Jason. I hoped he was safe and waiting at my cabin by now. I wondered if there was any danger left in calling him at this point. I thought it unlikely, but decided I'd ask Jack about it as soon as the storm lifted.

"Not a good idea," Jack shouted at me. "You're still on the radar. They can get a warrant and take a look at your phone records. Maybe they already have. Best to keep going and talk face-to-face."

I looked at Jack. I hadn't actually said anything.

"What?" I shouted back.

Jack shouted louder: "I said calling him isn't a good idea."

CHAPTER 25

Jack and I sat huddled against the rain and wind with nothing more than our rain suits to protect us. We sat facing away from the road, looking out over farmland and the raging storm. Lightning struck mercilessly, surrounding us, blindingly intense and saturating the air with ozone and explosive, thunderous shock waves. I wondered briefly if this was what it felt like in London during the Blitz or in Dresden when the Allied bombs fell there. I decided it probably wasn't *that* bad, but it might be a close facsimile. Even though we sat, violent squalls crashed hard against us, making it a struggle to remain upright, even in our seated positions. I saw Jack rocked back and forth, and I was equally thrown to and fro by the pulsating gusts.

I looked straight out over the fields, watching the tall corn bend nearly horizontal against the wind, thrashed and beaten to the ground. In the distance I regarded antiquated farm buildings. A corn crib stood like a shadow in the darkness, yet still discernable for its slatted siding and twisted conveyor, rising at a 45-degree angle from the ground to the top of the crib. A huge barn lay beyond the crib, rehabilitated once with metal siding, which now peeled away, torn and defeated by countless storms. The buildings stood as ghostly reminders of farming in days long passed.

I was doing my best not to look at Jack and contemplating whether I should be concerned about what had just happened. Had Jack read my mind and answered the question I'd only thought to ask? Or had I projected my thought into his mind, unnoticed by Jack for what it was and triggering the response I was seeking?

I didn't have long to consider. Amid the ghostly farm buildings and into the thrashing corn, I saw a blood-red flash, a craggy, dim bolt descending from the black clouds, like an iridescent sprite, slick and slow-moving compared to the lightning that continued to strike and steam violently in the fields and beyond. Falling ahead of the sprite, illuminated intermittently by the brilliance of the lightning, came a demon to the earth.

It was, as Jason Moore aptly described, the image of demonic creatures found in old books, winged and hooved. Though it was yet far in the distance, I could make out its protruding snout and fanged teeth. It was at least ten feet tall, hitting the ground and absorbing the shock upon legs articulated backwards at the knobby knees. Behind it fell two more bloody sprites, pushing ahead of them demons much like the first. As they stood, each lifted its head and stared intently – at me.

I could sense them, their power, and I knew instantly that these were demons that could do far more than hold a ghost upon a chosen spot of ground – they could lay waste to the living among the ghosts.

More sprites fell, smaller, dropping lesser demons to the ground, a hundred at least. Something had gathered the demon stampede and brought it straight back to me.

"Holy fuck!"

Jack hadn't spoken the words, but his mind reeled with them, and I heard the words in my own mind. And I felt his fear. He, too, saw the legion before us.

"You're seriously not lying about this shit," he shouted.

The demons began a slow march toward us.

Jack stood and hurriedly opened his saddlebag, pulling his gun. He started firing rapidly into the horde, having no effect. He fired until his bullets were spent.

At least the gun was empty now.

I saw two immediate possibilities. The demons having come in force, any growing power I might have imagined I had could very well be overwhelmed by the unified hate emanating from the demon army. They could possess me to harm Jack, or the other way around. A third possibility came to mind as well. If they were at all corporeal, they could descend on us en masse and rend us apart.

A wide swath of corn was trampled permanently to the ground now, laid flat beneath the slow marching horde. The storm, if anything, intensified its violence, with wind and thunder overtaking my senses.

At first, I felt the psychic tendrils of the lead demons reach for me, probing. My vision was blurred by the rain, and I blinked furiously to keep seeing what I didn't want to see – death. The real death, coming at me with a hateful resolve.

I was afraid and wished again for the muted emotions of the late Nash Baxter. I pushed hard against the fear and its paralyzing grip. Slowly, I felt my mind beginning to work, and I used it to search for whatever force might remain within me to fight back.

I flashed back to Evelyn – the real Evelyn – and the horror she had felt at the power unleashing itself against Ted. I moved past the horror she felt and tried to imagine the feeling of power that had come from deep inside her in her moment of crisis. I imagined the same power now bursting from somewhere in me. The probing tendrils fell away. The army hesitated, stopped. The three powerful demons gathered side-by-side and lowered their heads. I felt a wave of hate trying to overtake me. I could sit there and wait for it, or I could go to it. I stood.

Jack was behind me, and I didn't see him coming. He struck me in the middle of my back, like a sledgehammer, knocking me forward. I stumbled, sliding from the shoulder, down the slope, into the mud. I stood, stunned, and turned to face Jack.

"You die today," I heard in my mind. "By his hand or ours. Your reign over us ends this day. We will feast on your bones."

Jack was plunging down the slope after me. He was a big man and strong as a bull. I forgot about the real enemy. I couldn't focus on them and Jack at the same time.

I looked to the ground for some kind of weapon. All I saw was an old boot. Well, desperate times.

I bent down and picked up the boot. Jack almost had me in his reach. I smashed the boot against his face. He fell backward, slipping in the mud. His head cracked hard against the last bit of asphalt between the slope and the shoulder. He lay stunned for a moment then tried to get up. He stumbled toward me again and then fell face down in the mud.

I reached down and turned him over, so he could breathe. It wasn't easy. He was heavy as hell.

I didn't know if he was faking or actually out cold. I didn't have time to assess which. I turned to face the demons.

More demon rage washed over me – but left me untouched, as if I were protected by a shield.

I took a last look down at Jack, my friend. Blood was seeping from the back of his head into the mud. And I felt my own rage growing out of control.

I strode without thought toward the demons, and I felt their fear, terror in the smaller demons, and a calculating fear in the larger three. I reached inward. Ancient cultures thought the mind and soul resided in the heart. I knew better, but something else resided there – the power within me.

I focused it ahead of me, seeking out the lesser demons, and with one thought I laid waste to their numbers. They didn't merely flee or dissipate – they died in a fury of flames, my own sprites rising from the field and engulfing each of them. Their screams would have been terrible if not so satisfying to me.

I kept walking until I was face-to-face with the first three demons, looking upward at the first. His companions flanked me, surrounded me. They decided to fight.

With a thought, I forced them backwards onto their knobby knees. The two who had flanked me screamed, helpless. The first demon, though powerless now, looked up at me and grinned, its fangs dripping saliva to the ground. In my mind, I heard its plea: "Let us discuss the terms of our surrender."

I felt no fear of them at all. I could burn them with a thought. But I was still in a game with most of the rules unknown and stacked against me. So, I said, "Speak."

CHAPTER 26

After the demon triumvirate assented to my terms, I freed them. Their departure was far less dramatic than their arrival; they simply shimmered like hot air against the pavement and vanished. The storm hadn't been a *natural* phenomenon at all, and it dissipated along with the demons *most* unnaturally, the coal black clouds thinning and disappearing so quickly that anyone who saw it happen must have been dumbfounded. It couldn't have taken more than five seconds before the late afternoon sun was beating down from an empty, clear blue sky. I mused briefly that the meteorology profession was in for about a decade of research and a mountain of scientific treatises on the event. I stood silently on the trampled corn, filled with nothing short of wonder. I hardly believed such a battle had taken place but was stuck with the knowledge that it had.

I pulled away from the thought of it, focusing on my more immediate concern: Jack. I had no idea what state he might be in, or if he was even alive. If he was, he surely needed help, maybe now more than at any time in his life. I trudged as fast as trudging through the thick mud and corn stalks would allow, finding my way back to the highway. I saw as I approached that Jack was trying to stand, dazed. He didn't seem to know where he was and looked quizzically in my direction. I wasn't sure he knew me. For my part, I was greatly relieved to see he was alive, if not entirely well.

I climbed up to the shoulder, found his gun on the ground and stuffed it under my rain suit, into the back of my pants. It was a good thing he'd spent the bullets fast, or things might have turned out much differently. Under the circumstances, I decided to scold him later.

"My gun," he managed to say, vaguely and weakly reaching out to me, like I would hand it back to him.

"Confiscated," I said. "You knew the rules."

He fell hard on his butt then, back onto the shoulder, trying to comprehend – anything. The knock against the asphalt had been a lucky break for me, but not for Jack. He lay back, with his head next to the footboard on his bike. Blood seeped into the wet pavement under his head. He started to convulse.

Fuck me.

My medical knowledge was limited to whatever I read in illegible medical records. I didn't have the slightest idea what to do. If this were a PI case, I'd have an expert neatly lined up to give her opinion about what was happening to my friend and the proper standard of care. If Bhagat were here, I'd get out of her way, knowing Jack was in good hands. But it was just me. Plain old me might be able to bring a legion of demonic forces to its knees, but I couldn't say or do anything to help another human being in medical distress.

My bike was a long way back, so I opened Jack's bags and fished around until I found his phone. I dialed 911 and waited.

Jack's convulsions stopped, but he was out cold. I did the ABCs. That much I knew. He was breathing, soundly, it seemed, so I took his key FOB out of his pants pocket. Somewhere along the line, I'd have to come back and get his bike.

After a while, I heard the siren and saw emergency lights racing up I-65. When they pulled up behind us, two paramedics jumped out and made a beeline to Jack. The listened to my story about his slipping and hitting his head. All true. But it didn't explain his bloody nose, which I hadn't even noticed.

"Don't know how he got that," I said, remembering the boot. "We were caught in a bitch of a storm. Didn't see him through most of it."

A state trooper showed up while they were putting Jack in the back of the ambulance. He wanted the story, too. I left out the part about demons. And the boot. I told him I'd come back for Jack's bike, so no need to have it towed. I thought Jack would appreciate it.

I got the name of the hospital they were taking Jack to, locked his saddle bags, and made my way back to my bike. I was more wet from sweat now than the rain. Rain suits don't breathe, and I was dripping from every pore. I looked around, reached into the back of the suit for Jack's wet gun, and transferred it discretely into my saddlebag. Then I stripped off the rain suit, wrapped the whole soggy mess of it up, and dropped it into my bag. I plugged the hospital into my GPS and hit the highway. Next thing I knew, I was fighting for my life – again.

Mr. Gated Community, the Hitchhiker, Evelyn's enemy paramour, the worm inside my brain – whatever he or it was decided now was the time to take the wheel. It came like the storm clouds that brought the demons, only this cloud was sentient, and the storm it brought was laying the darkness over my mind.

I didn't feel it at first. I just seemed to lose focus and fade away into a daydream kind of state. Its emotion gave it away. Beneath, it had been lurking, with a growing fear over my growing power. Finally, it came for me, tentatively reaching, tentatively overshadowing more and more of my consciousness. As I began to fade, and as it discovered it was taking hold over me, it felt an overwhelming exultation, relief that its fear had been unnecessary – it was going to win.

Its sudden release from fear fired some synaptic reflex in my brain. The daydreams fled, and I was fully conscious, feeling the fight-or-flight survival rush of adrenaline. There is no way to truly describe how it felt. It was as if my mind had become a vast expanse, and it the distance, the storm cloud approached, as violent as the demon storm had been, flashing discharges of power, psychic lightning against everything that I was inside my mind, trying to deaden it wherever it could, filling the deadened parts of the expanse with its own consciousness, like a single malignant cell, growing and spreading out to destroy its host.

Its feeling of elation left when my consciousness turned against it, and its fear returned.

"I am your salvation!" Its thought reverberated through my brain, feeling like a massive tuning fork hitting a high note inside my skull. "Only through me can you fight her! She will destroy you as she tried to destroy me!"

I wasn't sure how I felt about Evelyn, but acquiescence to this thing would have been nothing short of madness, albeit short-lived madness, since I was certain there wouldn't be anything left of me if I let it gain much more ground than it already had.

Mentally, I pulled the expanse toward me, leaving it nothing but empty space, a void, free of any part of my consciousness. Even that part of my mind that had given it safe harbor was torn from its hold. The fear it had felt turned to rage and hate more intense than I had felt from any demon, and far more powerful. The storm gained strength from that rage and hate and intensified exponentially. As it grew, it rushed toward my gathered self like a tidal wave of malevolence. I reached deep inside, to that place of power I had brought against the demons. The storm stalled briefly, then renewed itself, flying faster toward me. I fought again, bearing power almost too much for my own mind to control. As the storm sought to consume me, it felt like my own forces would do likewise. My mind was a conduit far too narrow for what I was trying to unleash.

Too narrow. Maybe I had the power to win, but I couldn't control what it was doing. I floundered. Had this been happening outside of my mind, I would have fallen, not from the thing trying to kill me, but from the thing that was trying to save me.

Its hate was overcome then with a new elation. It was going to win, and it knew it. I knew it, too. All that I had been through had come to this moment, and all was lost. Maybe the old me who had handed a gun to First Jack and said it was okay to shoot me wouldn't have felt much about it. But that me was long gone, and I knew despair.

Then she came to me.

It wasn't the phantom Evelyn of my nightmares; it was the real Evelyn, the human Evelyn of my dreams.

I felt her consciousness merging with my own, which, truth be told, had been crying.

"I'm here, Nick," she thought, and I heard. "I told you I would help you, poor boy!"

Her consciousness enveloped mine, became a part of it. She forced her strength into me, and the conduit widened – and became a cannon.

My power focused, as Evelyn held it, contained it where I could control it again. I threw all of my will into shoving that power right up the Hitchhiker's ass. Like the demon storm, the Hitchhiker's storm coalesced into nothingness – it was gone, the Hitchhiker, too. Where it went, I didn't know. But its last thoughts that I could hear spoke of revenge.

I was exhausted beyond anything I had ever experienced. Take a hard ten-mile run on a 100-degree day, 90 percent humidity – and times it by ten. That's where I was.

Though it was only her consciousness with me, I felt as if Evelyn's hand was caressing my cheek, softly, reassuringly.

"You're free," she thought. Then she was gone, and I woke up in a ditch. This time, I hadn't been going slow. I was face-down in the water, choking. I rolled over, coughed water out of my lungs and fought for air. Some got in, but I choked and coughed for every bit of it.

My right arm was fractured. Compound. The bone was sticking out, and blood was gushing into the muddy soup beneath me. It occurred to me the Hitchhiker might have been the source of my healing power. If so, I was fucked.

I tried to reach out to my broken arm with what I thought was my good one. It was broken, too, and the reaching stopped. I was pretty sure at least one of my legs was broken, and my pelvis. I should have hurt more. I didn't credit my healing ability with taking the pain away. It was probably shock. I choked some more and fought to breathe. I looked for my bike. It was in the field, worse off than me.

Consciousness seemed tenuous, and I was afraid. Less so for myself than Jason. My ability to focus was drifting, but I knew Jason needed me, and I fought to stay awake, to try to think. I remembered my telepathic exchange with Jack. Another "gift"?

I concentrated on Dr. Bhagat and imagined her hearing my thoughts.

"Dr. Bhagat. . ."

Nothing.

"Chanda."

I sensed then that she was startled, looking around for the sound of my voice.

"Mr. Baxter?" If she'd said it aloud, I certainly wouldn't have been able to hear, but thought must accompany speech, and the thought I did hear.

"I'm hurt," I thought. "I need help. I need you."

I sensed her realization that I wasn't there, her understanding that she was hearing me in her own thoughts. She hesitated, deciding whether she should answer. She was afraid. But she was immensely curious as well, and thought, "Curiosity killed the cat, but satisfaction brought her back."

I repeated it back to her.

"Where are you?" she asked.

I didn't send words this time; I sent images of the demon storm, the battle, Jack, and my fight against the Hitchhiker. Then the ditch and my injuries, and the name of the hospital I'd been riding toward.

I felt her reeling for a moment at the strength of the images, leaning against the desk in her small triangular office for support. She recovered, confused. She wrestled with the lingering doubts she'd had about my last explanation of events, but the images had persuaded her that Nash Baxter had told the truth.

"I'm coming," I heard her thought at last. My strength faded then, with the relief her promise had brought, and I passed out.

CHAPTER 27

I was sitting in an outdoor chair with a metal frame, metal arms, and an ample seat cushion. It was warm, close to 90 degrees. My back was to an inside corner of a house, next to a deck that rose up three risers above the grass. The lawn was freshly cut, with rows of dead grass where they'd shot out from the side of a lawnmower, giving the impression that the owner of the house was the type that waited too long to mow. A metal framed, glass-top table was to my right, with a lit cigar resting on the edge of an ashtray. A cedar fence enclosed the yard, with a small cedar planter box in the corner. Tomato plants grew abundantly in the planter. It had a little fence around it, as well, probably to solve a rabbit problem. A golden retriever lay next to the deck stairs, panting. The sun was bright, but my little corner provided shade from the direct sunlight.

The dog turned around to look at me, then got up and put its head in my lap. I petted the dog for a moment and said, "Good girl." That satisfied the pooch, and it curled up at my feet. I looked at the cigar band and saw it was one I liked – very much. Birds were chirping, and somewhere near a dove cooed a rhythmic "Ahhhhhh, whoooo, whoooo, whoooo."

On the other side of the table, Evelyn sat in a chair identical to mine. She wore the same hat, same dress, and same sunglasses she liked to wear beachside.

"It's a good cigar." She didn't speak or look at me. I heard her voice in my mind, a trick that seemed to be working rather well with me of late. "Please, enjoy it."

I picked the cigar up and took a puff. I thought it would be nice if there was a bourbon to go with it. One appeared.

"Your brand," Evelyn thought.

I took a sip. She was right. My brand. I noted a margarita had appeared in her hand. She took a sip and set the glass on the table.

"Thank you," I said with thought.

It occurred to me, given the injuries I'd sustained, that I might be dead. If I were, I figured Evelyn would get around to telling me, so I relaxed.

Everything about the scene settled my soul. I didn't try to figure out when or where she had taken me. The chair was comfortable. The air was only slightly humid and much to my liking.

We sat. I smoked and sipped. I thought for a moment about Evelyn. I tried to muster up a bit of hate for her but couldn't. Whatever she was, whatever she had done to me, was doing to me, there had been a profound change in my life. I had feelings, some good, some terrible in their hold over me. Weeping and choking did not appeal to me, but the memories that brought the weeping and choking, memories of my mother and sister, were cherished – hence the tears and pain. I had shut those memories down and put them out for so long, I thought, now that I had them, they were precious to me. I would no longer trade them for the even-keel of a barely perceptible emotional self, even if the trade would blot out the pain.

Nor was I oblivious to the fact that no matter what was happening now, whether I was dead or alive, my life as a vagrant chronicler of ghost stories and an occasional murderer was over. Traded away were the random, unfeeling acts of killing and the incurious acceptance of it. The tragedies begat by my hand were undone. Had they remained, these feelings I had gained would have overtaken me. Like Second Jack had and Jason tried, I would have put an end to my sorrow over what I had done, repenting the only way possible.

I took a puff, blew it out, and took another sip of bourbon.

Beyond Evelyn's shoulder, far away, a cumulous cloud was growing slowly in height. The sun lit its upper reaches brightly, but below darkness gathered and spread outward. Directly above us, a patchwork of low gray clouds began to blot out the sun. I noticed a spider crawling on my knee. I resisted the urge to squash it.

Over the top of the fence, the upper stories of several houses could be seen running the fence's length. No one was out. Evelyn noticed with her mind what I was looking at. She began to share her thoughts.

"When I first conceived of you, I hadn't given you much thought. You were merely an expression of my will. A beautiful conception – I knew that. But so much was *of* me then, no one bit of conception stood out – not so much as I see you now."

I was quiet. I thought of any number of sarcastic responses, but I didn't feel them, so I let them lie.

"Time means little to me. It doesn't pull me to a single point anywhere in time or space. So, when I tell you I am ancient, I am telling you the truth. And when I tell you I am new, I am telling you the truth. I came to you in this world – where I placed you long ago – with a thought. And here I am."

I felt her surveying the scene as I had. It was a relaxing kind of quiet for me. For her, it was unsettling.

"All this," she thought, and I knew she meant the houses and the grass and the rising storm cloud and the dog, "All this was me. I don't remember anymore how I made it become *this*. I'm separate from it now. I see most of it as you do. The storm rising to our east, the forces, the elements, all of them were me, are from me."

I took a puff of my cigar and listened, enjoying the slightly cooling breeze that had picked up.

"I am like water. The rain that will fall from the growing storm will water fields, soak into the aquifer, grow plants, nourish living creatures. It is eternal, but it is not one thing in one place. It has spread everywhere, finding its way into life and sustaining it. I used to be all the water that ever was. Now it is dispersed. It gives life, but I am less than I was. I am only now discovering this, though in the beginning, I knew it must be so."

The dog got up and walked to Evelyn's chair. It put its feet on her lap and then jumped up, spilling the margarita Evelyn was holding again. She put the glass on the table and started petting the dog.

"You think of me as powerful," she continued. "But I was once so powerful, nothing else could exist – except for my companion, the one who was in you. I let go of that power, and then there was everything, and of me only the tiniest bit remains."

I took a puff from the cigar and another sip of bourbon. I didn't want to think about the things Evelyn was telling me, which, near as I could tell, meant I was sitting next to God in a yellow dress. I just wanted to keep the feeling of contentment I had, to think of nothing beyond the next puff and the next sip.

"My companion and I were one," she continued, "locked in an eternal womb. I can never kill him. If we were human, you would say I love him. Maybe that's all it is, but it feels like more."

She reached for her margarita and repositioned the dog, so she could take a sip. She put the glass back down and petted the dog. Then she said, "Go." The dog got down and came to curl up quietly at my feet.

I looked at Evelyn. She was crying.

"I can't kill him. If it is love, he loves me, too. But he is jealous. Jealous of all of it, everything I have made. And he will destroy it – if he can."

Shit. I took a sip of bourbon, knowing the relaxation I was feeling was over.

"On earth, we start with an order of protection, then lock the nutjob away after he starts ripping up the dresses in your closet. You sure you love this guy?"

Evelyn was silent.

"I'm not," I said, "trying to be flip. In human relationships, this sort of thing demands a hard break. These guys go over the edge. Sometimes they kill the one they claim to love."

Evelyn laughed.

"Oh, he can't kill me," she said. "I am still more than he can ever be, even diminished as I am."

I was troubled for a moment by Evelyn's words, how they came into my mind. They seemed soft, shimmering, like the meaning wasn't as literal as it sounded. The quality of the thought left an image like another thought was hiding behind it. I tried to concentrate on that. I didn't get far, but somehow, I got a sense that Evelyn wanted me to know she was lying to me. My imagination?

Distracted, I repeated, "Are you sure you love this guy?"

"I love what he was when we were one. When I left him, when I brought you and everything into existence in a moment of wonderful curiosity, I dealt him the cruelest blow, though I didn't comprehend what I was doing or what I had taken from him."

"In family court, they might call what you're thinking a manifestation of battered woman syndrome."

Evelyn smiled, "I'm not helpless, dear boy. I could destroy him and go on as I am, forever."

Again, the thought came through fuzzy, imprecise. Another lie she wanted me to know about? I ignored the possibility. It seemed pragmatic.

"Only you said you *can't* kill him."

"I can. I *won't*. We are not human, he and I. If I were of a mind to undo everything I have thought, even you, he and I would become one again, for another eternity, content and at peace. His jealousy would become nothing."

"Undoing everything doesn't seem to be your inclination."

"Dear boy," she said. "I told you I love you. I could never harm you."

I thought of my fight against Evelyn's psychotic lover and said, "I can take him."

She laughed again.

"No, I'm afraid you can't. He was restrained when he was bound up in your mind, limited. You've freed him."

"I defended myself against him! I won!"

"You did what he wanted you to do. I put him there, in you, the only vessel on this world that could hold him, though you didn't know that's what you were doing. Besides, you were losing. He would have settled for that. For now."

"I felt his fear!"

"Dear boy, don't get ahead of yourself. You were lost and you knew it. You had help."

"The real Evelyn. Yes, she came to me. My power was more than I could handle alone."

"Oh, Nicholas," she sighed. "She is *his* creature, this human Evelyn. She just doesn't know it yet. But like you, her power is growing."

CHAPTER 28

I woke up in a hospital bed. Again. Dr. Bhagat was standing next to me. She wore a mask.

"Mr. Baxter," she said. "Once more, you have returned to us."

"Once more, unto the breach," I answered. "How bad?"

"You broke your femur and your tibia," she told me. "Comminuted and transverse fractures. You broke both arms. One is a compound fracture of both the ulna and radius. Very nasty. You also sustained a closed head injury, which confused the ER physician, as he'd never seen a closed head injury with so much blood."

I felt splints attached to my legs and my right arm. My left arm seemed to be held together by some sort of metal gadgetry outside my arm. What I remembered as a very nasty wound to the arm where the bones stuck out was mostly healed. I wiggled my arm, and the external fixation devise fell away.

"You're very hard on the equipment," Bhagat smiled. "How does the rest of you feel?"

"Fine," I smiled back. "Thank you for coming."

"I am here, of course. I told you I would help."

She frowned then.

"Those images you sent to into my mind . . . did those things really happen?"

"Exactly as I showed you."

"This world you're living in," she asked. "Would it be coming upon us if you weren't here?"

I thought my response: "What do you mean?"

She answered in thought, as well.

"I've seen into your mind, Mr. Baxter. Despite my initial impressions of you, I've come to the conclusion that you are a decent man. But these things that surround you are most *in*decent – and terrifying. Would they be upon us if you were not living in our world?"

"You mean if I were dead?"

"As you should have been on multiple occasions now. Yes."

I thought about my latest backyard encounter with Evelyn, and I showed it to Bhagat, deciding it was an easier answer than my own conjecture. She experienced it in real time, as if she had been sitting, silently between Evelyn and me. This took some time, during which the remainder of the wound on my arm healed over to smooth flesh.

When the images finished, she gasped, as if coming out of a terrible dream.

"This game they are playing," she thought. "These two beings, whatever they may be – our continued existence would hang in the balance."

"Unless I'm mad and imagined all of it." I held up my freshly healed arm, "But then there's this. And the bullets. And the ordinary people suddenly murdering or trying to murder other ordinary people."

"That last part does seem to coincide with your proximity."

"I can't help my proximity. It follows me wherever I go."

She began to ponder these things, and in the pondering, her thoughts were disorganized, and I couldn't hear them as coherent speech. Finally, she said aloud, "You didn't call me because you needed a doctor, obviously. You called me to get you out of here."

"Before anyone notices how I'm healing. I don't want to count on all members of the medical profession sharing your commitment to ethics."

She smiled again. "I anticipated that."

She'd presented herself as my personal physician, and at my request was transferring me to a private institution. "Mr. Baxter appreciates the care he has received here, but he has asked me to take charge of him," she'd explained. She signed various documents on my behalf and arranged for a private ambulance service to transport me away. As it turned out, away was a few blocks to where her car was parked. I removed the splints during the ride.

I was still wearing a hospital gown when the doors opened, so I grabbed the large envelope that held my personal belongings and quickly hopped from the ambulance to the passenger seat of Bhagat's Mercedes, mindful that I wasn't keen on showing the world my ass hanging out of the gown. The ambulance drove off, and she got into the car.

"You owe me $8,000 dollars," she said.

"That's an expensive ambulance ride."

"Discretion was part of the cost."

She drove us to a men's clothing store. I gave her my sizes and told her my preference for jeans and t-shirts. She came out with an expensive pair of jeans, more dress than workaday, and a blue button-down shirt, dress socks, boxer shorts, and patent leather shoes. I would have complained, but beggars being choosers and all that.

She parked in the farthest part of the parking lot, where there weren't any cars, and I wiggled into my new clothes in the passenger seat. She discretely looked away until I was presentable.

"Okay," I said when I was finished.

She looked at me and said, "Okay" back. But she kept looking at me, silently, making me more than a little uncomfortable.

"What is it?" I asked.

"When you found your way into my mind to show me certain things," she said. "How much did you intend to show me?"

I recounted what I *thought* I'd sent her way.

She looked at me quite seriously and said, "I'm not an eavesdropper, Mr. Baxter."

I was confused. "I know. I don't know what is happening to me exactly, but I can do things that I wouldn't have thought possible. Sharing my thoughts with you, for example. Sharing images of the things I've seen. Hearing your thoughts. All of this is new. I'm sort of rolling with it as best I can, using it as best I can. I'm trying to piece together my part in this whole thing, and other than having these growing powers, I don't really know what I'm supposed to do. I'm sorry to have intruded on you. I wasn't even sure I could do it, but it felt like I could. And it was necessary."

"I'm not seeking an apology," she said. "I'm not angry with you or upset, at least not about your calling upon me for help. What I mean is you haven't shut that connection down. I am seeing into your entire life. Bits and pieces keep coming to me."

I was surprised and shocked. I did a quick mental assessment to see if my brain had an off switch somewhere on the telepathic communication that I'd left on. I couldn't find it. I wasn't willingly sending her any more information than I had consciously sent.

Apparently to settle the question, she said, "I know your true name is Nicholas Bennett, and I know what you have been through. I have seen it in your mind."

I felt an overwhelming empathy coming from her then, and I saw a single tear fall from her eye.

"You have been so alone, all these years," she said quietly.

Hearing it said, out loud, struck a chord. Self-pity, perhaps, but her words, her empathy, and what I felt as her anger toward that thing that had been living inside my mind – all those things provoked a sudden and unwilling emotional response from me. The now familiar effort to hold the tears back followed, with the involuntary contraction of my facial muscles, the hitching breaths, and finally, the effort lost, I began to cry. I looked away, embarrassed, out of the window.

Then I heard her thoughts come to me, soothing, "I don't mean to upset you, Mr. Baxter. You're not alone anymore. You have your brother. You have me. I will stand by you."

Then aloud she spoke, "We have a bit in common, actually. I am Indian. My parents are Hindu, but I am an atheist. Not in the Hindu sense of the word, but in the rejection of all religion, Hinduism included. I refused to marry, and I left India as soon as I could. My family has been displeased with me for a long time. So, Mr. Baxter, I, too, have been alone, though not in the sense that you have been. But maybe I understand."

She reached out and touched my shoulder. I sensed warmth from her then that would have surprised me not so long ago. And I heard her thought, "You have turned my atheism upside down, Mr. Baxter. All that I rejected now seems to be in some way true. How will I deal with that?"

I composed myself and turned to her. "Thank you," I said. "For everything. You didn't have to do any of it."

I had a thought then, which I tried not to share. But Chanda heard every bit of it. It came to me from what Evelyn had said in the backyard. I wasn't strong enough to defeat the enemy. Did she mean I never would be? Or did she mean I wouldn't be able to do it alone.

"What are you thinking she meant, Mr. Baxter?" Chanda asked aloud.

I said, "Welcome to the club."

"Meaning?"

"Meaning I don't think I let you into my mind to see everything you've seen. I don't think I accidently showed it to you either. I think the power to see into my mind belongs to you."

"To me?"

"Evelyn never tells me anything directly," I said. "She'd like me to think she's helping me. But the subtext is that she needs me to help her, and whatever help I'm getting is to serve her ends. Only she says I'm not strong enough to do what has to be done. Why would she tell me that when the outcome would be that I wouldn't try, knowing I would lose, or that I'd rush headlong into defeat? I think she's giving me a hint."

I had a wild thought then. Chanda was a healer.

"How would you like to try an experiment?"

I explained my thought.

"I'm highly skeptical," she said.

"Where has skepticism gotten you lately?"

She drove us back to the hospital. Night was beginning to fall.

I waited in the car in the parking garage. No point parading around the fact that I was hale and hearty after a major motorcycle crash. Chanda went in. Twenty minutes later, she came back to the car. She was very quiet. Finally, she said, "Jack had a basilar skull fracture."

The past tense scared me.

"Fatal?"

"Sometimes. Usually not. But it would be unwise if not impossible to get up and walk away."

"Jack?"

"When I left him in intensive care, he was arguing with his physician. He wants to leave."

CHAPTER 29

I could tell Chanda didn't want to talk. I didn't need our psychic link to figure it out, either. Her body language said it all. She sat with her hands on the steering wheel, looking straight ahead. She was coming to grips with something big. I suspected it was Jack related, but kept my mouth shut.

We were parked on the third level of the hospital parking garage. We sat silently for forty minutes or so before I finally saw Jack, wandering up the ramp and looking in cars, trying to find us. I looked at Chanda to see if she noticed. She was still in the same state, overwhelmed by whatever had happened with Jack in the hospital.

I reached over to her side of the car and honked the horn.

She looked over at me then, her trance broken.

"Was that necessary?" she asked.

"Jack's looking for us," I replied, motioning to Jack, who was now headed our way.

He opened the back door and settled into the rear seat.

"You might have mentioned *where* in the garage you were parked," he said to Chanda. "The kind of car you drive would have been a nice hint, too."

"My apologies. I was in a hurry."

Jack sat. Chanda sat. I sat. No one spoke for a while. Finally, Jack said, to Chanda, "I'm not sure what you did to me back there, but thanks."

"I'm not entirely sure either," Chanda said. "But you're welcome."

"Okay," I said. "I'm the guy who wasn't in the room. Mind telling *me* what happened?"

Jack said he'd been out of it, unconscious though somewhat aware of the goings on around him. He heard voices, wanted to respond. Still, he couldn't open his eyes or move or speak.

"Then I woke up," he said. "Dr. Bhagat's hands were on my temples, and I felt all of the pain and whatever was keeping me out cold slip away. I just felt like I do when I wake up in my own bed in the morning, ready to get up and go."

"Do you remember what happened to you?" I asked.

"Yes," he said. "Right up until you hit me in the nose with that boot. Look, I'm sorry. Something grabbed hold of me, one of those demons I assume. I couldn't stop myself. I mean, it was me. I was in there, in my brain, thinking and seeing everything that was happening. But I decided to kill you if I could, and damned if I didn't try."

"Feeling better about your grandpa now?" I asked.

"Like you said," he answered. "It wasn't him, just like it wasn't me that clobbered you. I mean, yeah, it was me, but I wasn't in charge. He couldn't have been either."

"He wasn't," I said. "I tried to tell you that when you visited me in the hospital that first time, without the details you wouldn't have believed."

"I believed you after you sliced your arm open," he said. "That's why I came with you."

"But now you *understand* it as well," I said. "That's important."

"Well, yeah. You can say I'm up to speed on the details now. Except one: how the hell did we escape from that demonic street gang?"

I started to tell him, but Chanda interrupted, "Might I make a suggestion, Nash?"

"Of course."

"Show him the same way you showed me. There is some force, some power growing here, and it is not limited to you anymore. This morning, I was quite human. Now I am imbued with an ability to see into your mind – and to heal with a touch. That is nothing short of impossible. A human being cannot do what I have done, yet I have done it. It is a rather remarkable transformation from who I was this morning. The one variable in my day before this was your sending images of what happened to you directly into my mind."

"You think that triggered a change in you?" I asked.

"Perhaps. Perhaps not. But there is no denying I have been changed somehow. That is the only event I can fathom which may have caused this, unless someone slipped your magic voodoo concoction into my morning tea."

"Ah, so you do have a sense of humor," I said.

"I've always had one. It is the dryness of it that escapes you," she smiled. "But let us consider. Here we now sit, the three of us. You say you have powers that are growing. My own experience is similar, though I hardly feel up to the challenge of battling demonic forces or supernatural beings. I think it is wise we explore what more the day might bring. Thus far, Jack remains entirely human, as I was. Perhaps there is something to be unlocked in him as well. If your sending images into my mind precipitated the change in me, it may do the same for him. Or not. But since we three seem bound up somehow in the same adventure, it should be attempted."

"Jack," I asked. "What do you think?"

"If I'm hearing this right, you're going to force something into my brain," he said. "I can't say I'm keen on the idea, but I'm not keen on any of this. But whatever killed my grandpa and Uncle Jack is something I want to stop. So, yeah, I'm in."

I explained to Jack what I was going to do, to try to prepare him. Chanda told him what it had been like for her, as well.

I was about to start when Chanda told me to wait.

"Take him as far back as you can," she said. "I believe I've seen most of it in your mind already. There is much to know. He should see it, too."

I thought about it for a moment and said, "I can't take him back through my entire life."

"Then start with Carol's place," Jack said. "When you killed everyone."

I winced a little, and thought to protest the description, but I knew he didn't mean it the way it sounded. So, I let it go and told him, "Jack, the way Chanda explains it, it's going to feel like you're there. Are you sure you want to see people you know murdered?"

"No, not at all. But we're in this thing now. Let's go where we have to go."

I leaned my chair back and told Jack to prepare himself. Then I let my mind wander back to my ride along Route 6. I could tell it was working, that I had brought Jack with me through it all. It took quite some time. Somewhere along the way, I was aware that Chanda had reclined her seat and was sleeping. When I broke myself free from the sharing, the early light of dawn was reaching in through the open spaces between the levels of the parking garage.

Jack was quiet when I finished. It was a lot to take in. Not just *what* I'd shared, but how I shared it. I figured he'd need some time to process it. I wasn't anxious to hear his reaction to seeing me murder his flesh and blood either, so I let him be. I reached out and gently shook Chanda's shoulder, waking her up. "I need to get some sleep," I said. "Jack, too. You could probably use a proper bed as well."

"I'm fine," she told me, yawning. "You'd be surprised the places doctors have had to sleep."

"We need to get Jack's bike. Do you feel like driving?"

"Sure."

Chanda drove back onto the highway, past where Jack's bike was parked during the demon storm. I saw as we passed that it was still there. Amazingly, no one had stolen the bag strapped to his luggage rack.

Chanda took the next exit and got back on the highway, headed south. She pulled behind Jack's bike and parked. I found the envelope that held the contents of my pockets when I'd been taken to the hospital and pulled a key FOB out.

"Here you go," I said. "Could be mine though. See if it works."

Jack still hadn't spoken since I'd shared the highlight reel. He took the key FOB and got out. It was the right one.

He started the bike and put it in gear. Chanda pulled out ahead of him, driving slowly while I scanned the fields to find the remains of my own bike. I caught sight of the emerald green, broken and lying in the field. I told Chanda to pull over. Jack stopped behind us. I got out and made my way through the mud to the bike. I pulled my bag from one of the side bags, which had broken open. I still needed the key to open the other side bag and the tour pack. The bike wasn't quite as bad off as I'd thought, though it certainly wasn't rideable. I found Jack's gun and dug a hole with my hands several yards away in the mud. I dropped the gun in the hole and covered it. Then I took my bags to Chanda's car and threw them in the backseat.

I closed the door and went to talk to Jack.

"Are you all right?"

"Yeah," he said. "Still trying to take it all in. You were right; it felt real, like I was there with you. Just to be clear, I don't blame you for what you did. I know how it was. Still, it wasn't easy watching you kill my grandpa and the others. I wanted to stop you, but I couldn't interact at all. I tried though. With every bit of will power that I have, I tried. How the hell did you deal with that stuff on your own?"

"I told you," I answered. "I didn't feel things the way I do now. Are you feeling any magic powers yet?"

Jack laughed, "No. All normal here, if normal can still be considered a thing."

"We'll see."

I told him we'd take the next exit and find a hotel. Chanda might have been okay after sleeping in the car, but Jack and I weren't going to be in any shape to travel until we got some sleep.

When we parked in the hotel parking lot, I asked Chanda if *she* was all right.

"I'm overwhelmed," she told me. "This is a lot to take in. I am still doing my best to sort things out."

I remembered her hand on my shoulder earlier, trying to comfort me. I wanted to do the same for her, but I wasn't sure how. So, I just smiled at her and said, "I know we've passed way beyond borderline insanity here. It probably isn't much help, but I'm very glad you're here with me."

"Well," she responded, "glad isn't a term I can use with any sincerity, but there is something about you, Nash, that makes me want to help. That and it looks like the world just might end if I don't."

I thought the last part might be her dry sense of humor at work. I wasn't sure. I was sure when I looked into her eyes, however, that I felt something for her more than appreciation.

We got our rooms, and the first thing I did was take a shower. Then I called a tow company to get my bike and store it for me. I didn't know if I'd ever pick it up, but I didn't want it lying in the field. It had been a noble steed, in a way. It deserved a better end than to rot in the dirt. That, and the farmer who owned or leased that field might get hurt driving machinery over it someday. Feelings again. A conscience. Part of who I'd become. Despite my growing fondness for Chanda, however, that conscience didn't extend to the dress shoes she'd purchased for me. I threw them in the trash before I went to sleep, feeling guiltless about the decision.

CHAPTER 30

Human Evelyn. Phantom Evelyn. They both came to me in my dreams.

My consciousness drifted over a dark expanse, a flat plain below me extending beyond the range of my senses. The expanse was my mind as I perceived it in my battle against the Hitchhiker, no longer drawn into me in self-defense, but flowing outward in all directions. The surface was smooth black, solid but hinting at great blue depths below. The Hitchhiker was gone, yet I wasn't alone. Calling to me from the far-off reaches, I heard the thoughts of Evelyn Blankenship, beckoning, "Nicholas, come to me – speak to me." I pegged her as the human Evelyn; the other one would have just grabbed hold of me and yanked me to wherever she wanted me to be.

I didn't really want to go, human Evelyn or not. I felt content drifting over the plain that was *me*. I was free for the moment of everything. Yet I began to sense the expanse was not mine alone. Other consciousnesses seemed to call to me, though none as strong as Evelyn. I tried to listen, to hear who or what was sharing . . . me? For a time, I sensed Jason, not the whole man, but a piece of him. "Jason!" I called. I could tell he sensed me, too, but instead of answering my call, he faded farther away. I tried to follow, but Jason, in this place, had his own power. He used it to push against me, keeping me from following into whatever space he was hidden. This troubled me, though I was not certain why.

I felt Chanda there, too, drifting without form, searching. "Nash," she called.

"I'm here," I answered, drawing her to me. Instead of moving toward me though, she descended downward onto the plain. I felt her move through the black surface below and into the blue depths beneath. I followed, but when I came upon the surface of the plain, I could descend no farther, some force repelling me, pushing me away. I felt a flash of anger. If all this was me, why was I forbidden to see all the way in? I tried again, pushing harder, but the more force I employed the harder I was pushed away, upward.

"Nicholas, come to me," Evelyn said again. Frustrated, I answered her call, moving toward the presence I felt.

It was a long journey. I don't know how much time passed, but it seemed like hours on the road, riding toward a destination that seemed to move farther away with every mile. Then I felt Evelyn reach out for me, pulling me to her like a small raft riding a powerful ocean current. From a distance I saw her in human form, and I willed myself to take my own human likeness. As I transformed from thought to flesh, I fell from the dark sky like the demons on the storm, landing before Evelyn Blankenship.

She stood in front of an open door leading into a small square room. She smiled when she saw me. "Ah," she sighed a pleasant sigh. "Nicholas."

I looked through the door. The room was dark except for a small dim light hanging from a cord in corner. It was the same room I had seen through Evelyn's thoughts, the room with the little boy Nicholas – me.

"You're free now," Evelyn said, happy for me. This intrigued me. She didn't really know me, so why did she feel such joy at what she identified as my freedom? A bit of me was able to glean some part of this human Evelyn as I stood beside her, and I knew joy was what she felt for most people when they had cause to be – free. No, more correctly, I thought, she took joy in the spiritual growth of other people. Leading others to that kind of growth was her vocation, how she found her own joy in this world, or rather, the world outside of this one. Forgetting her physical beauty for a moment, I was in awe of what I read as her selfless devotion to other beings. She seemed as opposite from the other Evelyn Blankenship as could be. I liked her. I trusted her, and suddenly I knew I would do almost anything for her.

I gestured toward the open door, into the room, and told her I didn't remember being a prisoner inside. I felt like I wanted to tell her everything she could possibly want to know about me. This, too, troubled me. The Phantom Evelyn had warned me that this Evelyn was the Hitchhiker's creature.

"That's okay, Nicholas," she said. "I don't think it's a good thing to remember. Not yet. It feared you, you know. As long as it kept you inside this room, as long as it kept this part of you from joining with the rest of your being, it was safe."

"What part of me was in there?"

"Your soul, dear Nicholas. It's part of you now."

There was nothing like the other Evelyn's condescension in the way she said "dear." She meant the word, meant that in some way I really was dear to her.

"Did you free me?" I asked.

"*We* did, Nicholas. I couldn't do it alone."

I extended a thought, a wish – and the room was gone.

Evelyn hugged me then. My arms stayed limp at my sides. I wasn't sure how to respond.

"Oh, dear boy," she said. "Don't worry. You're still growing. I'm so happy to see you free."

"I'm forty-one," I said. "A bit old to be growing."

"But you are, now. It kept you from yourself. Now that you are one being, nothing can stop you."

"That thing almost did," I recalled. "You saved me."

"*We* saved you, Nicholas. I told you, I couldn't do it alone."

"There is another Evelyn," I told her, not certain why.

Evelyn frowned then, her joy faded.

"I've felt her," she said. "She is powerful, Nicholas, nor is she at all what she seems."

"She seems to be you."

"She is not me. I haven't been able to understand the connection yet."

"She told me the thing that held me here created you."

This troubled her. A normal person might have said "What?" upon hearing such a thing. This Evelyn, I knew, never needed to hear a thing repeated, however.

She bent her head and seemed to be considering the possibility. Then she looked up at me again and smiled.

"I don't know," she said. "I don't think so. But you and I, Nicholas – we have abilities that we shouldn't, not if we are strictly human. I thought I knew once where these abilities came from, but now that I've seen into your world, I'm no longer certain."

"We have another thing in common," I said. "She said *she* created me."

"I don't feel like a 'creation' of something so vile as your former keeper," she said. "Nor do you seem to be made from *her*. Yet there is no denying we are not what we might seem to be, either. I killed a man, Nicholas. With a thought. It was a power I didn't know I had, a vicious, ugly thing. I'd like to think that was not a part of me. If we are *of* them, we have to find a way not to be."

"I've followed you in my dreams," I said. "I've lived through your eyes. I saw Ted, and I saw how he died."

"Yes," she said. "You *have* seen much of me. I see that in you. Tell me, did you expect that I could kill Ted?"

"You seem too kind," I answered. "But he was an amazing shit."

"I loved him," she frowned. "I still do. But everything he told me was a lie. The person I loved did not exist."

"How could he fool *you*?"

"I don't know," she said. "But we should consider: because he *did* fool me, he was able to provoke that awful power in me. Had he not done so, I wouldn't have known it was there. I would not have willingly used it if I had. Yet once I found it, I used it to come to your aid. If Ted hadn't died, you would have. You, too, are being provoked, Nicholas. Circumstances have forced or allowed you to find your own power. We might be becoming something terrible I fear."

"Maybe," I said. "But perhaps necessary."

"Perhaps necessary," she agreed. "Or we may be becoming a danger to our world."

I looked around and wondered. She heard and answered, "I don't know. I think all of this is you, everything around us."

"How did you get here?"

"We have a bond, Nicholas. Somehow, we are being drawn together. I came here because you are here, and I sensed that. I feel the need to be near you and to help you."

"There are others here, too. My brother. Chanda."

"I know. You draw others to you, dear Nicholas. Chanda, she may be falling in love with you. She is growing, too, Nicholas. I'm not certain the source of her power, but I sense she is one to trust."

"Jason? Why is he here?"

"The same. He is drawn to you. He loves you, Nicholas, but he is not what he seems either. He senses me, too. He knows me, as I am beginning to know him. I don't like telling you this, Nicholas, but I fear him. Watch him."

Then the other Evelyn reached out for me and pulled me away. As I went, I sensed two other beings in the expanse that was me – the Jacks.

·   ·   ·   ·   ·

Phantom Evelyn took me to the backyard again. Another cigar was freshly lit, and I had a bourbon in my hand. The golden retriever was barking at something on the other side of the fence. It was the one place Evelyn had taken me to where I'd felt content, almost enough to be grateful to her. Stockholm Syndrome.

She sat in the same chair she'd sat in before, no margarita this time. The relaxed, almost serene Evelyn she'd been on the last visit here was gone. Her thoughts were closed off. This time, she spoke rather than thought the words she wanted me to hear.

"You make it hard to love you sometimes," she said, "when you behave like a fool."

I took a sip of bourbon. I noticed the brand wasn't mine. The cigar wasn't a particularly good one either. Clearly, I was on the outs.

"Fool?"

"Yes," Evelyn was clearly agitated. I wondered at her changed attitude. I couldn't think of a reason for it. "You've let strangers into your life who have nothing to do with any of this."

"What is 'this'?"

"Who freed you from your mindless wanderings? I did. Who showed you your power so it could grow? I did. But this woman," her use of the word was in the pejorative. "This woman tells you *she* freed you, and you slobber like a stupid dog and decide you love her."

"I don't love her. But I've seen through her eyes. I saw myself trapped in a room, and she fought to free me from it."

"You saw only what you could see after I unlocked your power, set you on a path to free *yourself* from the bringer of chaos."

"That's a new name," I said, as irritated with Evelyn now as I'd been prior to our last visit, which in comparison, had seemed rather enjoyable. "I was settling on 'Hitchhiker' or 'Evelyn's Boy Toy'."

The bourbon glass shattered, and I was covered in glass shards and bad whiskey.

"I wasn't going to drink it, anyway," I said. "It's not the good stuff."

The dog wandered over to me and bared its teeth, growling.

"This Indian woman," Evelyn said. "She is an aberration. She cannot help you."

"I sort of got the idea you wanted me to make friends. You said I wasn't strong enough to take on Mr. Chaos alone."

"Not yet," she said. "I also told you you are gaining strength. Now you wish to throw it away, on beings not worthy of what you are becoming."

"Correct me if I've misunderstood, but you seem to want me to kill Mr. Chaos for you."

"You idiot. I told you I *don't* wish to kill him. Why would I have you do it for me?"

"You suck at giving straight answers, you know. If you'd ever gotten to the point, maybe we'd be sitting here with good bourbon and a nicer dog."

"If I gave you straight answers, you wouldn't think. You wouldn't grow. Everything I've done has been for you – for your continued existence. Were it not for my restraint, my sacrifice, my love for you,

you would not live. There would be no place to exist, or *you* to exist there."

I looked down at the broken glass lying on my wet lap. I decided I wanted a dry lap and a fresh glass of good bourbon in my hand, and it was so. I took a sip and looked at the dog. I decided it should be a cat instead of a dog, and it was. Disinterested, it walked away and climbed over the fence. I wished for Evelyn to have a cold margarita in her hand, and she did.

"Relax," I said. "Let's have a drink and talk about this more rationally."

Evelyn sighed, but sipped her margarita and settled back in her chair.

"Okay," she said. "Let's discuss this rationally and more to the point. You must kill this other Evelyn, or she will kill you."

"The hell you say," I said, marveling that she hadn't reacted to my changing the scene, but instead said the most outrageous thing she could have said to me. I wondered if Evelyn was using misdirection to avoid the elephant in the room, or rather the bourbon and the cat in the backyard. For the first time, I had controlled the scene – or some of it.

"I told you, she is his creature. She didn't save you, she freed him. Her power grows by his hand, and she will use it to destroy you."

"If it's Mr. Chaos's power, why doesn't he just kill me and be done with it. Why the intrigue?"

"You never listen. You are a part of me. He cannot kill you anymore. He could have, when you hid him and kept him safe, but then he would not have been safe anymore. He is not certain I won't destroy him. So, he hid in the one place I wouldn't go after him – inside of your sometimes feeble mind."

I ignored the insult.

"When I first met you, he told you he and I would destroy *you*."

"Neither of us knew what we were then. You accuse me of telling you nothing, yet I told you I have been becoming aware myself. We were children, without our true memories."

"That was just a few weeks ago."

"Again, you do not listen. I told you time means nothing to me. I told you I am old and new, yet you just sit there stupidly thinking I haven't told you anything."

"You hold a low opinion of me," I noted, and thought that her margarita glass should shatter. It did, and she jumped, startled.

"Now you are like a little boy, throwing toys about his playroom," she scolded me. "I'm losing patience with you, so I will get to the point before you throw a tantrum. You must kill Evelyn, and you must leave your companions behind. They will be your undoing."

"I won't," I said, "and I won't."

Evelyn looked at me and raised an eyebrow. She tilted her head then, and said, "If I must do it for you . . ."

I remembered First Jack and how she had killed him with a tilt of her head. I felt for the first time her energy building, beginning to reach out this time to Chanda and Jack. I felt a psychic reflex, that's the only way I can describe it, and I swatted her thought away, stopping it before it could be unleashed.

Evelyn gasped and stood upright, glaring down at me.

"Fine," she said, sounding exasperated. "I will let you play it your way – for a time. Perhaps this is how the human part of you grows up."

The scene began to fade, but just before the physicality of it shimmered away, I looked directly into Evelyn's eyes – and I'd swear she winked at me.

Then the scene was gone, and I caught a bit of Evelyn reaching out again – this time to the Hitchhiker.

"He is not alone anymore," she told him, and I felt fear from them both.

CHAPTER 31

I sat in the dirt, leaning against a short post sticking up from the ground. In front of me was a large field with short grass and scores of prairie dog mounds. It was sunny and hot. I watched as prairie dogs ran in and out of their holes, playing, and scampering about. Here and there, one would stand over its hole and chirp. Little ones wrestled with one another, while others tentatively nuzzled up against the adults, apparently seeking reassurance or approval. Hard to know the mind of a prairie dog.

I recognized where I was. I'd sat in this same spot about a year before, watching the same prairie dog town and its residents. I knew there was a road behind me and behind that, looming skyward, would be Devils Tower. Tourists stood about a line of posts like the one I was leaning against, which ran alongside the road. They had their cameras and binoculars out, enjoying the same prairie dog activity I'd found so fascinating when I'd been here before. Now I wondered *why* I was here.

In the distance, I saw a dark, coal-black cloud gathering in the otherwise clear sky. It grew in size and began moving my way, much too quickly for a normal storm cloud. The wind intensified, blowing the grass and sending tourists running after hats and belongings carried away by the wind. The mood quickly turned to panic as the storm cloud began discharging lightning onto the field. Hats and belongings were forgotten. Parents hurriedly gathered their children up in their arms, and everyone ran for their cars at the side of the road, driving off as fast as they could. I sat and waited. It was another demon storm, but much smaller than the one that had brought the demon legion my way earlier. I worried it was going to be trouble.

When the last demon cloud sent demons to destroy me from the sky, it turned out badly for them. So much so that, in defeat, they'd sworn allegiance to me out in the corn field, which, I suppose, cast me in the role of Satan, though I'd like to think a benevolent Satan. In exchange, I agreed to send no more of them into the abyss. Yet even as they agreed, I could sense them trying to figure a way out. I might have destroyed them then, but I also sensed they couldn't think of a way to free themselves. As long as that was true, their allegiance would hold.

Yet here they were again.

I wondered if they'd found a work-around, a way to break the deal and try once more to do me in. I felt my power was there, ready to be called upon if necessary. So, I sat.

Three of the demon sprites descended amidst the lightning, and I saw three figures standing in the distance. I squinted to see what looked like a combat soldier, a cop, and a man in a suit beginning to walk my way. The cloud hung motionless then, its lightning silenced. No more sprites came to the ground. It was just the three figures, and they did not appear to be demons at all.

As they came nearer, I saw that the soldier was a hulking man, well over six feet and bulked up like Lou Ferrigno. He carried an M-16. The cop was shorter, skinny. He wore a sidearm. They seemed familiar, though I wasn't certain why. The third figure, in the suit, I recognized. It was the human Evelyn's Ted. Then I realized, if I subtracted fifty years or so from the Jacks, the soldier and the cop could be much younger versions of the two. The closer they came, the more certain I was that these two *were* the Jacks.

Then the soldier hollered, jovially, "Ghost Rider!" The voice was First Jack's.

The cop yelled, "Well, I'll be fucked, sure as shit!" It was Second Jack's voice.

Despite the circumstances – and the guns – I smiled at my friends.

Ted seemed to sulk.

"You shouldn't sit so close to these fucking prairie dog vermin," Second Jack said. "Fuckers carry the plague."

"It ain't the dogs," First Jack said. "It's the fleas."

"Aw, fuck you, Jack."

"Well," I said, thinking myself in another dream, "either way, I'm not really here, am I?"

"The fuck you ain't," Second Jack said. "Took a lot of effort to drag your happy ass here, too."

First Jack dropped his M-16 then. Second Jack unholstered his sidearm and dropped it into a prairie dog hole.

"But we come in peace!" First Jack exclaimed. They were close now.

"And to apologize," Second Jack told me. "It wasn't you we was trying to kill."

If Phantom Evelyn were to be believed, I wasn't too quick on the uptake, but I realized the three men in front of me were the three demons who'd sworn allegiance to me in the corn field. And the same ones who'd stated their intention to feast on my bones.

"Well," I said, laughing despite their admission. I couldn't help myself. I liked the Jacks. "You got some 'splaining to do."

The Jacks sat down beside me. First Jack slapped me on the back. Ted stood, looking out over the prairie dog town.

"We brought you here," First Jack said, "because it's a holy place. It has power. It helps us manage our human forms alongside our demon forms."

"Figured you'd be more apt to talk this way," Second Jack said.

"Who *am* I talking to?" I asked. "Demons or Jack and Jack?"

"Both," Ted joined the conversation. "They aren't separate, demons and ghosts. We only look that way to you."

"I saw a demon take you," I said pointedly to Ted, not liking the bastard. "It didn't seem like just you."

"Well, fuck me," Second Jack said. "This ain't easy. Ain't none of us perfect, Nash."

First Jack looked at me then with a sad, guilty sort of expression and said, "I told you I done worse than you in Viet Nam. That evil has been part of me ever since."

"Whatever it was you did," I said, "you didn't have to do it."

"No. I coulda stood there and got my balls shot off. Point is, I did it. We all done things, big and small, that don't let us move on to the next life. So, we go on in this world after we die, good and evil, until we can be reconciled."

"Doomed," Ted added, "for a certain term until the foul crimes done in our days of nature are burnt and purged away."

"Nicely paraphrased," I said. I didn't like him, but I've always liked *Hamlet*, so he gained a couple of points.

"Thank you," he answered. "It manages to sum things up accurately in this case."

"So," Second Jack said, "we get paired up with our evil assed selves, and we're made to look at it straight on until the good outweighs the evil we done."

"Leaving Ted here out of the discussion," I said, "you two don't seem like evil men to me."

"Evil weighs down the soul more heavily than the good," First Jack said. "Right now, our demon selves are pretty powerful because there hasn't been time to – what did Ted say? Purge ourselves."

"Only souls and demons don't usually know this," Ted added. "We're as mindless as you've intuited in the past. Our ghosts don't know what the demons are, and the demons don't know what the ghosts are. Time just works on them until we've been purged enough to pass onto the next existence."

"And what the hell is that?"

"We don't fucking know," Second Jack sighed. "We're only coming to know any of this lately. We're awakening for a time. Looks like something needs us knowing more than we did."

"Just for a time, though" First Jack explained. "Once things settle down, we won't know shit again."

"*If* things settle down," Second Jack added. "If they don't, we're all fucked."

"There is a power," Ted began. "It's not coming from the two beings you're familiar with. They are here to destroy us. But there is a power that gives life to all of this." Ted gestured as if to include the landscape around us. "That's what is helping us now," he said. "That's what is giving you your true power."

"My 'true' power?"

"Yeah," First Jack said. "Hate to tell you this, buddy, but you never freed no ghosts from demons – you were used to kill souls, to send them to a real, unrepentant death."

"But it wasn't you," Second Jack interjected. "You was lied to. That thing living in your skull, that's the enemy, and it's been using you since you was a kid, drawing on your power, feeding on you like a fucking parasite."

"And Phantom Evelyn, too," Ted said.

"Yeah," Second Jack added. "That fucking bitch, too."

"That's why we want to apologize," First Jack said. "We did try very hard to kill you, but it wasn't you we was trying to kill. It was that thing in you."

"We can only talk turkey with you now because it's out of you," Second Jack added, laughing. "You worked that fucker over good."

"With my Evelyn's help," Ted said. "It's going to take the two of you to stop them."

"More," Second Jack concluded. "My grandson and that Indian lady. They're part of it now, too. And us. We swore allegiance to you, and we meant it, provided that thing wasn't in control no more."

"But it's free now," Ted said. "More powerful as a result. You were a flytrap. The power we're talking about, the one protecting us all, selected you and my Evelyn to contain them."

"I'm afraid it hasn't gone easy for you 'cause of that," First Jack said. "You were kind of used to buy time. Now the tide is turning. It has a chance now, to fight back."

"Just what 'power' is this you're talking about?"

"We don't know exactly," Ted responded. "Maybe Earth itself, the whole damned planet and everything on it, in it, in the past, the present, and for as long as it can go on."

"But those two beings, this Evelyn and the one that rode along with you all these years," Second Jack explained. "If they aren't kept apart, they'll be happy as fuck – alone together in eternity. But them being alone means nothing else can exist. Not you, not us – nothing."

"Like matter and antimatter," Ted added. "If they meet, and they're trying to, it will be the end of existence."

"Them coming apart is how everything got to be in the first place," First Jack said.

"You know," I said, "you're demons. You don't exactly get good press on integrity issues. Evelyn tells me a completely different story, that she created me – that I'm a part of her, and that's where my power comes from."

"Lying bitch," Second Jack spat. "She's filling your head so full of crap that you can't see straight. That's her game. If you're off-balance, you can't see the fucking target. You can't win. She knows that."

"He knows that, too," First Jack said. "Her companion. The one that made you kill your family."

"I thought that was one of you guys."

"Not in our nature, son," First Jack responded. "We don't like being interfered with, and we'll sure as shit try to scare away anyone who can see us, to get left alone. But we can't kill anyone. We can't possess anyone either. Well, usually, we can't. We seem to have a special kind of dispensation for the moment. That's how we got Little Jack to clobber you. Ordinarily speaking, though, we are what we are, nothing more. We only bring torment on ourselves. That's the way it's supposed to be. But that thing in your head – it did some horrible shit, using you to do it."

"Evelyn told me the same thing."

"Half-truths," Ted said. "She is a master of lies."

I remembered seeing into Ted's mind through Human Evelyn's clairvoyance. Alive, he was an unlikeable, self-serving fuck – and a sonofabitch. Now he was a demon to boot. Not much there to recommend trust.

"Seems to me, *you're* a master of lies, Ted, my boy," I said.

"Yeah," Ted replied. "So I am. So I was. No point in denying it. My sweet dumb Evelyn was the judge, jury, and executioner on that score. But you know what I always loved? *Me.* Making sure I stick around, one way or another, is forcing me into a new skill set. Helping you is helping me, so you might want to listen."

Second Jack whispered into my ear, "He's a fuck, sure as shit. We didn't get to pick our company on this little outing. But he's stuck like the rest of us. He's telling the truth this go around."

"Look," First Jack said. "Your hitchhiker – that thing. It forced you to kill those people, even your family. Even us. By the way, we forgive you for that since it wasn't you. But it wasn't any demon that did it neither. It wasn't you that took the life from those demons and ghosts along the way. It was him."

"But it *was* your power that brought the ones murdered by the Hitchhiker back," Ted explained.

"Nothing could bring back our kind though," First Jack lamented. "When they were gone, that was all. My great grandfather is no more because of that thing. There's nothing left of him to pass onto the next – whatever the 'next' is."

"It's in you to try to right the world, Nash," Second Jack added. "As your power grows, that's how you will express it."

"It sure seemed like it was me shoving those demons back, no offense, back to hell," I said.

"Diversions, meant to confuse you, to keep you from the real power you're given," Second Jack said. "As long as you thought you was doing good, taking out demons and freeing up the dead, you had a purpose. One fucked up purpose, but one that kept you from seeking the real power in you."

"That doesn't jive, Jack. You swore allegiance to me to keep me from killing anymore demons."

"Well, Nash," First Jack slapped me on the back again. "We can be tricky devils ourselves. You don't think we was going to come clean when that thing in your head was there listening and calling the shots, do you? It's what was killing us, not you."

"You just thought it was you," Second Jack added. "That's what it wanted you to think."

"Now that you're free of it, the only power you should feel is your own, your true power," Ted interjected. "It will grow faster now. Alone, you will soon have power enough to destroy them. But they haven't been completely contained. They've managed to groom allies."

"Allies it will be hard for you to kill," First Jack added.

"Starting with your brother," Second Jack said. "He's got to go."

"Bullshit! He's got nothing to do with this!"

"I'm afraid he does," Ted said. "He's already dead though. Evelyn's special project. You killed him thirty years ago, only he doesn't know it."

"Head filled with lies," Second Jack said. "Only he sees the lies as a life he's led."

"They've shared their power with him, not you, Nash," First Jack said. "He's a demon, son. The storybook kill everything kind. More powerful than any of us. Only he thinks he's alive. That special demon power of his makes it look like he is, too, like he's real flesh and blood. But he's like the Manchurian Candidate. He thinks he's here to help you. Right up until his switch gets flipped."

"But he loves you, Nash," Ted said. "They've used that against him."

"He's my brother. I love him!"

"That's what they're counting on," Second Jack said.

"I'm not going to hurt him," I protested. "I don't even know you're telling me the truth any more than Evelyn. Somewhere I heard *Satan* is the master of lies. Satan and Ted here. And even you guys, Jacks – right now you're out of central casting to be in Satan's vanguard."

"Yeah," First Jack said. "We know. You'll see what you see, and you'll do what you do. We can't make you. We're not trying. We're just warning you."

"Couple more things," Second Jack said. "And this first one is pissing me off. If I was trying to shoot Carol, she'd be dead. I was trying to shoot you, and sure as shit I did."

"What?"

"I'm dead," Second Jack continued, "but I got my pride. Last thing I saw before I shot myself was that thing in you forcing my hand. So, I tried to kill it. But, Jesus, you just think I'm such a bad shot you could jump in front of *my* bullet?"

"But Carol said . . ."

First Jack laughed, "Carol loves a good romance. What's more romantic than her new lover taking a bullet to save her?"

"Second thing," Second Jack added. "Whatever power we've been getting is for you. We got power enough to break some of the fucking rules now. Long as we got it, we'll use it to help you when you call us, any way we can."

"Sure," I said, angry about their telling me to kill my brother. "But only because feasting on my bones didn't work out, right?"

First Jack laughed and slapped me on the back again.

"We know more now than we knew then," he said. "We're all figuring this out as we go, aren't we?"

"Yeah," Second Jack said. "Jesus, cut us some fucking slack, will you?"

CHAPTER 32

I didn't wake up per se. Instead, I found myself standing in my hotel room, dressed as I had been at Prairie Dog Town with Ted and the Jacks. I slapped my backside, instinctively like we do when we stand up after sitting in the dirt. Dust fell from my pants onto the carpet.

Dreams and illusions seldom leave dirt clinging to your jeans, so maybe I actually had ended my dream-world excursions with the Evelyns with an in-the-flesh demon visit to Devils Tower. But, Jesus, the Jacks and Ted had heaped a whole new layer of bullshit onto the bullshit layer cake I'd been force fed by one phantom or another since I first rode up to Carol's cafe.

Suddenly, I remembered Evelyn's deadly head tilt, meant to kill Chanda and Jack. I had a brief moment of panic until I reached out with my mind and sensed them both living – Jack sleeping and Chanda contemplating the severity of her new experiences and how they were undoing all that she had believed, or how they had been giving new life to what she had once believed and rejected. Whatever reflex I'd had then, slapping down Evelyn's killing power had worked.

So, what the fuck was I?

No matter who I chose to believe, there were some constants.

Phantom Evelyn and my demon pals agreed that I had an emerging power, diverging only in where it came from. They also agreed that the Hitchhiker had been feeding from me, using my growing power to deceive me, agreeing as well that the Hitchhiker had been the force that made me kill. They also agreed that I had unknowingly resurrected the dead, undoing the Hitchhiker's mischief. Then there was the final agreement that was the key to everything: The Hitchhiker wanted to destroy all existence. My demon friends, however, said that Evelyn and the Hitchhiker were in world-ending cahoots, an assertion that Evelyn would have denied.

No matter where I looked, I was stuck with the same dilemma – I was either being ministered to by spirits of health or goblins damned, with no way of telling which might be which. If I listened to the demons, my path was clear. Team up with Chanda, Jack, and the human Evelyn; kill my brother; and destroy Phantom Evelyn and the Hitchhiker to save the world. If I listened to Phantom Evelyn, Human Evelyn was the Hitchhiker's creation, and I had to kill her and steer clear of Chanda and Jack, who were unworthy tag-alongs. Much more than that, she didn't say, other than professing a love for me that kept her from ending all existence, and a love for the Hitchhiker that kept her from killing him, even though *he* wanted to end all existence to be with her.

I thought back to one of the earliest visions I'd had since this mess began. Something, I still didn't know what, showed me two beings, separate but one, existing alone through all eternity until one of them wondered "what if?" Phantom Evelyn had told me enough along the way to suppose she had been the being who'd wondered, creating everything, diminishing herself in the wake of her creation. She'd gone so far as to tell me all existence would end if she chose to reunite with the Hitchhiker and continue their sublime love, alone, without form and without end. To hear her tell it, she didn't want to do that, and I was, along with my growing power, supposed to be her expression of good in the world.

So, there I was. Killing the phantom Evelyn might end her singular forbearance that kept the universe floating along as it had been since the beginning, resulting in the end of everything. Not killing Evelyn might allow her to reunite with the Hitchhiker, resulting in the end of everything.

Big stakes. Not the sort of thing you can resolve with a coin toss.

So, again, what the fuck was I? Evelyn claimed to know. The demons seemed to know. Why didn't I have a clue?

I couldn't resolve any of it. The only clear choice I had was to continue as I'd intended, to Tellico Plains.

The clock said it was noon. I was dog-ass tired. Sleep is useless when you're wandering around in netherworlds and taking in Wyoming monuments instead of REM sleep. Well, I thought, if I have powers untold, let's see what they can do. I decided I wanted to be wide-awake, and I reached down within, seeking something that would make it so. The fatigue fell off of me like the dust from my jeans.

I made a phone call. It took a bit to convince the person on the other end I was serious, but my payment went through fast, and that was that. I took an hour run, showered, and then waited another hour in front of the hotel. Finally, a trailer pulled up into the parking lot with a new Harley Limited. Wicked red, with my add-ons all installed. I took the keys and went to get Jack and Chanda. It was time to hit the road.

CHAPTER 33

I'd never been good at multitasking, but apparently, that was one of my growing powers. I was riding down I-65 again, with Jack riding just behind me, and Chanda bringing up the rear in her Mercedes. I was acutely aware of where they were, checking my mirrors and scanning ahead for road conditions. My phone was playing *Frampton Comes Alive!* through the bike's stereo. Simultaneously, I died in the gutter. A literal gutter, with a bottle of cheap wine in my hand. It was raining and cold. I was dead in San Francisco. Somewhere in the fog of alcohol, confusion, and fading synapses, just before I died, I thought how much I hated Nicholas Bennett, my son. This was as real to me as the road ahead, and neither vision was diminished by the other. I was seeing into my father's mind. I was living in my father's mind. At the same time, I easily exited I-65 onto I-64 in Louisville, Kentucky. Jack and Chanda followed. The sky was sunny.

·   ·   ·   ·   ·

The sky was sunny, and suddenly I was my father and nothing more, dying in the gutter under a cold rain. My soul shook as the demon came for me, as demons come for the dead. I felt the demon drawing me to it, but the demon was stopped short of taking me. Another force intervened, taking the demon, changing it, undoing its true nature and making it something new, something powerful and terrifying.

The changed demon took me then, pulling me into the past. I was standing in my house where I'd raised my two sons and daughter, where I'd loved my wife, Gwen, the most beautiful woman I'd ever met and for whom I felt unimaginable love. I was a good father. I loved my family. But the son, Nicholas, began to change. I could tell there was something wrong, something not right with him. When he looked at you, despite words of love coming from him, I could see a sneaky malevolence behind his eyes. Real thoughts behind the smiles he gave were evil. Whatever he had been when he had come into my world, he was no more. The boy was gone, and this thing strode around my house, in his body, my true son gone and dead.

My anger at him grew. I couldn't help myself, didn't want to help myself. I beat him, tried to beat the devil out of him, to bring my boy back. But the boy was gone, gone and dead.

Gwen wouldn't believe me. I told her, I said, "Just look! Look and see what's there!"

And I saw the love the love of my life had for me fade. She wanted me to ignore what was plain as day, wanted me to "get help." She told me something was wrong with me! Not me! Him! The demon who had taken my son. Oh, how I loved my son. My son. My son. Gone and dead. Gone and dead.

Gwen made me leave, got a lawyer and protection orders. I was alone. So alone, and knowing the evil in the boy was a danger to my Gwen and Jason and Julie. And then the demon boy, in a body of a ten-year-old, took the shotgun I'd left behind, so stupid of me leave it, but the judge said I couldn't have a gun, and what could I do? Gwen didn't believe me. Made me leave the shotgun behind. And the demon boy took the gun, with a strength no little boy could have, and it shot my family! Gwen! Jason! Julie! Gone and dead. Killed by the beast that took my boy.

Tears. Weeping. Anger. Hate. Hate for the thing that took my boys and my family. Hate. Hate. Hate. Tears, despair, unending despair. No point in living. No point in going on. Hate. Hate. Despair and tears.

Numb and dead. I was alive, but numb and dead. Nothing to do. No reason to go on. Years with no reason to go on. Alcohol could numb the numbness, ease the tears, dull despair. But my hate could never be dulled.

I tried, tried to get into the institution that kept him. I wanted to, still want to kill him. But I was clumsy and drunk. They caught me, and they jailed me, and I took beatings in jail, and the beatings were almost as good as the alcohol to beat the horror from me. Bloody succor. Teeth gone, knocked from my head by a blow from an iron bar. Skull fractured. I didn't care. Let me die. Kill me, too.

Let me die.

Let me die.

Let me die.

I was freed, but I couldn't think, couldn't concentrate, couldn't work or live or want to.

Let me die.

Let me die.

Alone. Cold. Dying. My mind begins to find quiet, easing of the grief. But, oh, if I live one more second, give me one more second to hate my son, to hate, hate, hate Nicholas Bennett and what took him and killed him and killed Gwen and Jason and Julie.

There in my living room, even though I wasn't there, I saw it happen! Again, the horror, the hate. I watched the Nicholas thing shoot and kill Gwen! Jason! Julie! I couldn't stop it. I tried, but I wasn't alive anymore. It was their ghosts I was seeing. I tried to talk, to shout, to warn. But I had no voice to be heard. I watched them die, again and again, the thing in my son's body killing them.

I hate . . .

Hate!

HATE!!!

"You're right to hate him," *I heard a voice, feminine, soothing.* "But you're wrong about the boy."

"I'm not wrong!" *I shouted.*

"You're not wrong, no," *the voice soothed.* "He killed them. But it was the boy. It was your son. There was no other. Some humans are born evil. Your son Nicholas was evil. Nothing took him. Nothing killed him. Nothing lived in his body except him, except the boy Gwen brought into the world for you."

"NO! My boy was good. The evil took him!"

"There was no evil. It was the boy himself that was evil. You are right to hate him."

Despair. Tears.

Hate.

"But I can help you," the voice said, soothing me. "I can help you fix it."

"Fix it?"

"I can help you kill the boy. Kill him, and Gwen, Jason, and Julie will be free of this."

I watched again while Nicholas leveled the gun. Gwen begged him, "Stop, Nick! Please, Nick, put the gun down."

Julie cried.

Jason cried.

Nicholas shot Gwen, smirking. Jason and Julie tried to hide. Nicholas picked up the gun and shot Jason, tearing his sweet body apart. Julie hid and cowered and cried for "Daddy!"

"Daddy, help me!"

"Daddy's gone," Nicholas laughed, laughed and shot my little girl.

"They set him free," the soothing voice said. "They said he was just a boy, confused. With help, they said, he would be normal. They set him free. But he fooled them. He lives, and he is evil, and he is Nicholas, your son."

"I hate him!"

"You should hate him," the voice told me. "You must hate him. He is a man now, free, still laughing about what he did."

"I want to kill him."

"You can," the voice said. "I can help you. I can make you powerful. He is powerful. He will fight you. You must want nothing more than to kill him."

"I want to kill him. Make him suffer."

"You can. You can make him suffer all you want. I can help you."

"Help me! Please help me!"

"You are two beings now," the voice said. "Embrace the other. Become one, and your power will grow, and you will be able to kill Nicholas."

"Make him suffer!"

"Make him suffer," the voice said. "Embrace the other. It stands beside you."

Ugly. So ugly, the thing I had to embrace. I was afraid.

"You must do it," the voice told me. "If you don't, Gwen will suffer. Jason will suffer. Julie will suffer for eternity, with Nicholas tormenting them forever."

"Will they be free?"

"If you embrace the other, you can set them free."

I looked at the thing. Ugly. As malevolent as Nicholas. As hateful as Nicholas. But powerful. So powerful. So powerful.

I closed my eyes, opened my arms wide, and thought, "Come to me. Let us be one. And let us kill the little fucker."

. . . . .

The vision of my father left me somewhere near Shelbyville. The sun was still up. My eyes never left the road during the vision. I had been in two places at once, had been two beings at once. And I didn't end up in a ditch.

A ditch might have felt better though. I was fighting back tears and a wave of emotion. Whatever was manipulating my father's spirit filled me with rage; what had happened to my father filled me with grief and overwhelming sadness.

The vision felt real, true. So, Jason was wrong. Our father hadn't been there, hadn't made me do anything. And I hadn't killed him. Had it been the Hitchhiker my father had somehow seen all those years ago, coming into me, lurking, waiting?

How could he have understood such a thing?

Poor man. My poor father. The Hitchhiker destroyed him. I was certain of it.

I signaled to pull off at the upcoming exit. We'd need gas, and, frankly, I was having trouble riding. Through my father's eyes, I'd seen myself killing my mother, Jason, and Julie. And now, something was pitting my father's very spirit against me, lying to the poor ghost of a ruined man. My father, whom I loved, whom I still loved, more so now that I understood what had changed him – and now that I saw the depths of his sorrow, I was desperate to save him if I could.

And what of Jason? What I'd just seen told me he was dead, a check mark in the demon truth column.

CHAPTER 34

I pulled into a truck stop and maneuvered my bike alongside the gas pumps. I got off, opened the gas cover and removed the gas cap. Then I fidgeted with the credit card processing mess for a while, saying no to everything from a car wash to using some kind of points I was assumed to have for my gas purchase. Meanwhile, a screen on the pump shot commercials my way, recommending I fill my tummy up, too, with junk food and 64 ounces of flavored sugar water. Eventually, I was actually able to pump gas. Jack pulled up behind me and went through the same rigmarole. Chanda pulled up to another set of pumps and, after a while, managed to start gassing up her car.

Pretty routine stop for a road trip, except I was shaking with grief and anger and wanted to crush the gas pump to put an end to its myriad programmed sales pitches – not so routine. I was crying again, too, a habit I wished I could break. I wasn't paying attention to how much gas I was pumping, and I managed to overflow the tank and spill gas over my new wicked red paint job. I swore, put the pump handle back in its cradle, and sat hard on the island, wiping my eyes.

"You okay, Nash?" Jack called, still filling his tank.

"No."

I reached out for Jason, to see if I could sense him. I did, briefly, and he felt it – then he found a way to hide, like he'd done in that place I'd gone to in my dream/vision. Some part of him didn't want to be found. Why?

Fuck.

Jack finished filling his tank and put the handle back on the pump. He walked over to me and sat down.

"Trouble?"

"Whole battalions of it."

I figured Chanda would know what was up by now, if she was still tapped into my mind – and I assumed she was. But I hadn't told Jack anything about Devils Tower, nor could he know what had just happened on the road. I didn't have time to explain and making him experience my experiences back in the hospital parking lot had been a lengthy process, not the sort of thing we had time for now.

"Mind if I try something new?" I asked. "It will bring you up to speed if it works."

"Another mind fuck?"

"'Fraid so."

"In for a penny," he said. "Do what you have to."

Instead of dragging Jack into my experiences and letting him live them in real time, I flashed an instant of my consciousness into him, a moment of knowing the things I'd experienced in the last day – from the plain of my consciousness to my father's ghost.

The effect was not cool.

Jack fell back against the pump, shaking with the same anger and sorrow that had overtaken me after the vision with my father. He looked wildly at me then and struck me with his fist, a sizable and unholy fist. The blow knocked me to the ground, and I saw stars. Funny the things we think at times like that. My thought was, "Wow. You really do see stars."

I rolled over and saw Jack standing over me, straight up. He drew his shoulder's back and looked like he was drawing on the same power Human Evelyn and I seemed to share. Then he jerked forward, as if unleashing that power at me. Reflexively, I shuddered and covered my face with my arm. But nothing happened.

"Holy fuck," Jack said, himself again. "Sorry about that."

I recovered quickly from the blow, certain the old me would've been knocked out cold. Jack reached down and grabbed my hand, pulling me to my feet.

"What the hell, Jack?"

"Whatever you did," he told me, "I was you for a second. I mean, I *was* you. And when I saw you looking just like me, I thought you were the Hitchhiker coming after me again."

"I was trying to let you know what I know for a second," I told him. "It seemed like a fast way to let you catch up."

"You made me know all right – I knew everything like I was you knowing it, not me at all."

"Sorry about that," I told him. "I didn't know that would happen."

"Yeah, well, you've just given new meaning to the saying that it sucks to be you."

Despite what I was feeling, I laughed. I mean, that *was* funny.

The guy in the pickup truck who wanted to fill up at our pumps wasn't laughing though. He rolled down his window and kindly instructed us that this wasn't a parking lot and to move our fucking asses.

I looked at Jack when Pick Up Man punctuated his point by honking his horn.

"You know, if we save the world, we save that guy, too," I said.

"In his defense," Jack said, "we *are* hogging the lane."

We got on our bikes and pulled away, finding a parking spot. Chanda pulled in next to us. It seemed like a good time to regroup, so we went inside to eat. Pick Up Man flipped us off while we were walking in. I was in a mood, so I returned the gesture, realizing that that was probably the first time in my life I'd ever flipped someone off. It felt good.

It got less good when we were in line to get something to eat. Pick Up Man followed us in, incensed that I would offer him the same gesture he'd offered me. From behind, he grabbed hold of my shirt at the shoulder and whipped me around, punching me in the face as I turned. He was a big guy, tall, and overweight. Still, his punch paled in comparison to Jack's. No stars. So, I had that going for me.

Depending on how you wanted to assign blame, I was at least physically responsible for any number of murders, even if the Hitchhiker had been calling the shots. Still, confronted with another person who seemed bent on beating me up, I wasn't sure what to do. I had no reflexes to deal with it, no defensive moves or attack strategies. Hence, the second punch and, I'm pretty sure, a broken nose. Mine. Not his.

I was in for a third walloping when Jack spoke up.

"Stop," he said, with a policeman's tone of authority, pointing directly at Pick Up Man. Pick Up Man's fist immediately dropped to his side mid-swing, instead of landing on my face again. "Let go of him." And Pick Up Man let go of my shirt. "Sit down," Jack said then, and the man walked away and sat quietly at one of the tables with his hands folded in front of him.

A few seconds later, a store manager and a security guard ran up to the scene. They saw the blood – mine – and asked me if I was okay. The security guard said he was going to call the police and pulled out his phone.

"No," Jack said. "Don't do that."

The guard put the phone back in his pocket.

"We need a report," the manager said. "We have to call the cops whenever there's an incident."

"Not this time," Jack said. "Go back to your office. Everything's fine."

The manager walked away, shaking his head.

"You can go now," Jack said to the guard, and he, too, walked away.

Jack walked over to Pick Up Man and told him to get in his truck and leave. He left.

I'd marveled before at Jack's ability to put me places I didn't want to be. Into his squad, on the floor at the Moores' house, in the ambulance and to the hospital. He was a cop. His job was controlling people and events, but I didn't think he'd learned this new trick at the police academy.

People were gathered around in the aftermath, staring and gawking at my bloody nose. Jack said to the crowd, "It's okay. Go about your business."

People stopped looking at us and turned back to whatever they'd been doing.

"So," I said. "We're *not* the droids they're looking for?"

"I believe we've stumbled upon at least one 'power' you have been given, Officer Smith," Chanda said, reaching out to my face and putting her hands on my cheeks, pulling me closer to her.

"It's broken," she said. "But I assume you'll take care of that yourself."

"I assume so," I answered. "Smarts though."

"Good," she said. "I would like to point out that you appear to have been chosen to save the world. You are not inspiring confidence in me at the moment, exchanging middle fingers with strangers and getting into pointless altercations."

"Just one altercation," I said. "Don't exaggerate. Point taken though. Order something for me, would you? Cheeseburger? Coke?"

"I'll get it," Jack said.

I went to the men's room and cleaned up. When I came back, Jack and Chanda were sitting with our food.

Chanda said, "Jack tells me he didn't know he could do what he just did until he did it."

"No," Jack said. "I didn't. I was just telling him to stop. I didn't think he would, but I didn't want to have to take him down either. I didn't actually know I was doing anything until I told the guard not to call the police. Then I started to figure it out."

"Have you felt anything else unusual?" Chanda asked.

"No, but hell, three days ago, everything was normal in my world," Jack said. "Now, I'm confronted with all kinds of supernatural crap, and at least some knowledge about what happens after we die. I *did* have that moment of knowledge you meant to give me, Nash. I remember, like you must, your visit with Grandpa and Uncle Jack, and everything else, including your father."

"So," Chanda said. "Here we are, knowing nothing for certain. But given what we do know, Jack's 'supernatural crap,' we cannot walk away like nothing important is happening."

"For what it's worth," Jack said. "I have to believe my grandpa and Uncle Jack. In your memories, they sure seemed like the people I know, and I'd trust them with my life."

"When they were alive, that would make sense," I said. "But they're something else now."

"My gut tells me they're what they say," Jack said. "We don't have a better lead than that. If we're taking votes, I say we take them at their word."

"We don't have to vote about anything yet," Chanda said. "Either way we look at things, it seems to me our original course still holds. We continue to Tennessee and find Nicholas's brother. We'll learn more then."

"Fair enough," Jack said. "But you know my thoughts."

"I do. We do," Chanda said. "But we have to be very much aware of the pieces that are coming together. Nicholas, it looks like your father's spirit is a piece of the puzzle now, too, and driven by something to kill you."

"Looks like," I said.

"And Jason may be what he appears to be, or something entirely different – and dangerous to what we are trying to accomplish."

"Adding it all up," Jack said, "we have the three of us and the human Evelyn Blankenship on one side."

"And demons," I added. I was trying to be funny. "Don't forget, we have demons."

"Yes," Chanda responded. "We have demons, too." The way she said it made me think this was a bit of her humor coming through as well. I was feeling more and more simpatico with her every moment we were together.

"On the other side," Jack continued, "there's Nash's father's ghost coupled up with an extra powerful demon, two supernatural bad guys, and maybe Jason."

"Look," I said, disturbed by the inclusion of my family in the equation, "whatever is going on here, I love my father. Living and dead, he's been a dupe in this whole thing, a victim. I'm not going to do anything but try to save him. Same thing goes for Jason, alive or dead. So, if we're going to go on together, we have to get something straight – we are not going to use whatever powers we have to hurt either of them."

"What if it is the only way?" Chanda asked quietly.

"Then we'll have to find another way," I answered. "You guys have to agree to that, or I'm taking off without you."

Jack and Chanda were silent. I could tell they didn't agree with my decision. Maybe Jack could just tell me that that's not the way it was going to play out, and I'd have to obey. I didn't think so, though. I hoped not.

"Perhaps a compromise," Chanda finally said. "We do everything we can to save Jason and your father. Unless and until it means the end of everything."

"That's not really even a choice," Jack said. "If everything goes, they do, too, whatever your good intentions toward them might be."

"Who makes the call?" I asked.

"We will each have to call it when we see it, individually," Chanda said.

I had to agree, albeit reluctantly. If it were a choice between all or, literally, nothing, it would have to be as Chanda said.

"All right," I said. "But I ask for your word – both of yours – that you don't make that call without being certain."

"You have my word," Jack said.

"Mine, too, of course," Chanda added.

"Okay," I said. "Let's go."

CHAPTER 35

No matter how big and comfortable your motorcycle might be, at some point, your ass just really hurts from being on the thing. You learn tricks along the way to try to ease the pain and get circulation going again, tricks like pushing up against the highway pegs and moving your backside up on the backrest or standing for a while on the floorboards. But eventually, you have to settle back down into the seat and accept the pain if you want to keep going.

So, I was relieved to see the Tennessee border approaching. Tennessee is a mandatory helmet state. Jack and I had to stop before crossing over the state line to put helmets on, or risk getting pulled over by the local constabulary. We eased into a rest stop and walked around for a bit to get the blood moving. It was almost 10 p.m. and dark.

Chanda got out of her Mercedes, offered a brief greeting, and headed for the ladies' room. Jack headed for the men's. Alone, I reached out for Jason again, with the same result. I thought maybe it would be a good idea to try reaching out for my father, too, but thought better of it. I'd clearly become the object of his revenge fantasy. I wasn't sure what the state of my powers were exactly, not even knowing, apparently, what sort of business they were about without my knowledge. Things like bringing the dead to life. I still had no conscious memory of having done that and only had the word of Phantom Evelyn and a trio of demons to make me think I'd even done such a thing.

In any event, Evelyn or the Hitchhiker had teamed Dad up with a special-edition demon that was likely free of the constraints placed on ordinary demons, like the Jacks. I didn't want to invite a confrontation – not at this point. Pick Up Man left me with an aversion to picking unnecessary fights without knowing just how hard I could punch back.

I opened the tour pack on my bike and took out the helmet I'd ordered with it. It was a half-helmet, the lightest one they had. I hate helmets, especially the full-face variety. Might as well climb into a car.

Reluctantly, I put the thing on. Jack and Chanda joined me.

"I think we need one more stop for gas," I said. "Then it's on to the cabin."

"I'm wondering," Jack said. "If your brother is there, how will we know if he's alive or a really mixed-up ghost?"

"Call me old school," I said, "but if he's flesh and blood, I say we call it being alive."

"He has seemed flesh and blood all along," Chanda noted. "Yet, if your demons are telling the truth, and your vision with your father seems to corroborate their version of events, he simply *appears* to be living."

"Occam's razor, Chanda," I said. "We'd have to do a whole bunch of mental gymnastics to conclude a living, breathing man is actually dead and riding a phantom Harley. He has a credit card for Chrissakes."

"I've been doing a whole bunch of mental gymnastics ever since you sliced your arm open in the ER," Jack said. "But here we are, guided by demons on a mission to stop the world from being destroyed by all-powerful supernatural beings."

"We're not *guided* by demons," I said. "We're only taking their recommendations under advisement."

"In any event," Chanda said, "the thing we must do is get to your brother as quickly as possible. Until we do, we are still speculating on everything."

We got back on the road and then back off again just a mile down the highway to get gas. Thankfully, it was an old-fashioned pay and pump gas station without a car wash or video enhancements on the pumps.

We filled up and drove straight through to Tellico Plains. It took me a bit to get my bearings, but eventually I remembered the road the cabin was on and turned. Along the way, a bear was trying to break into a locked trash bin on the side of the road. It turned to look at us as we passed, then went back about its business.

The driveway up to the cabin was a single lane blacktop headed up a steep incline that went about half a mile into the woods. When I got to the top, I saw there weren't any lights on, but Jason could be asleep. It was just after midnight. But then I saw his bike wasn't there. I wasn't sure what a ghost bike might do or turn into after sundown, but since I was still doubting the possibility that Jason might be a ghost himself, I didn't dwell on it.

I parked on the blacktop in front of the cabin and got off the bike, tearing the helmet off and putting it on the backseat. Jack and Chanda parked behind me.

Without waiting for them, I went to the doormat and lifted it, finding the key. Maybe it wasn't smart leaving a key in the most obvious place, but there wasn't much inside, and this was hardly a high crime neighborhood. The only thing that needed to be locked up was the garbage, or the bears would get it.

I didn't need the key. The door was unlocked. I opened it and went inside.

Things were clean and tidy. I went to the first of two bedrooms then. Empty. The second one was empty, too. No Jason.

Jack and Chanda came in behind me.

"Anything?" Chanda asked.

"He's not here," I answered.

Jack went into the kitchen.

"I found a note," he said.

He brought it into the living room and handed it to me. He and Chanda stood looking over my shoulder while I read it aloud.

> *"Nick,*
>
> *I've been here the better part of a day thinking things over. Given what happened back at that house with the kid, I'm sort of stuck believing most of what you had to say about things. Something has to break this cycle. The way I see it, there's one common denominator. Evelyn Blankenship. I'm not buying the bit about the mystery*

lady Blankenship. But I know there's one out there living and breathing. I'm convinced they're one and the same. I'm going to break her power over you, Nick. I'm going to break her power over everything. One way or another, I'm going to kill her. After what she made me do to that kid's family, I don't have a problem with that. It's self-defense, little brother. For you and me both.

Whatever happens, Nick, I love you. I wish I could have saved you from all of this when we were kids. I failed you, Nick. I was your older brother. I should have thought of something to protect you. Well, I'm doing it now.

If Mom and Julie knew what I know, they couldn't blame you for what happened. They wouldn't. They loved you, too, Nick. Mom loved you with all her heart. I remember that as clear as day.

I don't expect I'm going to make it through this alive. She's powerful. I know that. I'll take precautions, but if I fail, you have to do it, Nick. You'll have to make it right.

Love you,
Duke"

He'd drawn a smiley face after "Duke."

"Shit," Jack said. "Now what?"

I sat on the couch and tried to reach out to Jason one more time. This time, I didn't sense him at all. If he were still hiding, he'd gotten very good at it.

"We have to warn her," Chanda said. "Can you reach out to her, Nicholas?"

"Yeah," I said. "I think so."

I leaned back and tried reaching out to Evelyn the same way I'd reached out to Chanda when I was in the ditch. I felt her almost right away; she was glad to, for lack of a better term, hear from me.

But before I could convey a single thought her way, another being dropped in on the line. Powerful and full of hate – hate for me.

The thing came at me in that nether plain like a bolt of lightning, laying my consciousness out like Second Jack's bullet laid my body out in Carol's restaurant. I was awake, thinking, but unable to marshal anything that might be a power inside of me. I'd been blindsided hard. The thing didn't have physical form, but I felt it trying to rip my mind apart. I lay helpless before it. Because it was all I knew, I tried to reach into it like I reached into First Jack's great grandfather's ghost at Carol's. Only that hadn't been me; it had been the Hitchhiker. But I felt it working, anyway. I found a thought, an emotion buried under the hate. A love for wife. A love for children – Jason, Julie – and me, before the love turned to hate.

This was my father's spirit, imbued with the power of the changed demon, that powerful evil force created to kill me by Evelyn or the Hitchhiker – or both.

Like First Jack's great grandfather, the Jack Ghost, I felt my father's spirit come to a moment of thought, a clarity of consciousness, seeing its past alongside its present effort to destroy me.

The thought didn't matter. Dad's spirit had gotten past loving me a long time ago and wanted to kill me. I was pretty sure this present part was the prelude, the suffering he wanted to put me through first.

So much for growing powers. I knew I was going to die. There was just one more thing I wanted to do before it happened, something that might save the father I once loved – and still loved. I'd learned from Jack at the gas station that I could send a moment of knowledge into another being, to let that being – Jack when I'd done it before – remember things as I remember them, if just for a second. This I did – and then oblivion took me.

THE THINGS IN HEAVEN AND EARTH

CHAPTER 36

There was blood everywhere. Mine. And Jack's. I was lying on the floor, in a puddle of blood and gore. A very large and lumpy puddle. I looked down and wished I hadn't. My body was ripped open in several places, horizontally across my chest, abdomen, and even my legs. It looked like huge claws or talons had torn away my flesh. I was pretty sure they had. I could see where the claws had raked through my smooth body, dragging my insides out. My chest lay open. I might have spied lungs, if I'd known enough about anatomy. My intestines I recognized. They were in a bulbous heap beside me. My legs were twisted and more like meat than the legs I used to run on.

So here was that moment, I thought, when I would discover the limits of my healing powers. I didn't see any way I could survive this.

I saw Jack on the couch, his shirt ripped open by the same claws that had had their way with me, though not nearly as badly. Chanda sat beside him, leaning over to hold her hands over his torso, covering his wounds. He was conscious, but delirious, trying to flop around. Chanda held him tight. As I watched, the wounds that were visible beneath the torn shirt began – remarkably – to close. In a few moments, Jack stopped flopping and sat up with purpose. Chanda had healed him.

I was grateful for that. If the last thing I saw was Jack brought back from the brink, I would die – not happy, but less troubled.

I looked down and my wrecked body again. If I was trying to heal, it wasn't showing much. I passed out.

When I woke up, things looked just as grim. But Chanda held me now, pouring her healing energies into me. She was crying, "No, you may not die on me, Nicholas Bennett! You may not!"

But I did.

Or thought I did.

I woke up again, and my legs were straight sticks again. My chest was closing up, but I could still see things you don't want to see outside of an autopsy room. I watched as Chanda scooped my guts into her arms from the floor and tried desperately to position them back into my abdominal cavity. Not exactly standard operating procedure. The sight of it sent me straight back into La La Land.

I woke up on my bed. The sheets and mattress were soaked with body fluids. Jack was standing over me. Chanda's bloody arms lay on my stomach.

"Get these rags off of him," she instructed Jack.

Jack left, into the kitchen by the looks of the knife he brought back with him. He took the knife and started cutting what was left of my clothes away. And I was gone again.

I woke up in the tub. Chanda was scrubbing my body. The water was red. I checked out again.

I woke up in the second bedroom, naked. The bed was clean beneath me. Instead of gaping wounds and torn flesh, sizable scars in the shape of the raking claw wounds held my pieces together. The sun was out.

I sat up. Not much pain. I swung my feet over the mattress and onto the floor. I stood. My leg sticks held up the weight, but sweat began pouring from my forehead, and I was dizzy. I lay back down and went to sleep.

When I woke up again, the scars were gone. I tried getting out of the bed again. All systems go.

I got up and opened the door to the kitchen. Jack and Chanda lay on the kitchen floor, on clean linen and blankets they'd gotten from the closet. They were both asleep. The place stunk of death. It was night.

I went to the back door and turned on the porch lights. Then I padded out the door and onto the deck, figuring there wasn't going to be anyplace to step in the living room that wasn't covered with blood.

I didn't like being naked like this, so I walked out to my bike. I opened the side bag and took out the bag inside. I found what I needed and got dressed next to the bike. I took out my good running shoes, too, and put them on. I was sure the shoes I'd been wearing were not going to be wearable anymore. I hated wearing good running shoes for anything but running, but desperate times.

Fuck me. I was alive. But it had taken more than my own healing powers to make it so. If Chanda hadn't chipped in, I'd still be in pieces. I was sure of that.

I turned to go back inside, and I saw Chanda standing on the deck. She was in her underwear.

"I'm using your washing machine," she told me. "I did not bring a change of clothes."

She'd been through hell, barely holding herself together. She was shaking.

I ran to her and hugged her. She put her arms around my waist and cried on my shoulder. After a while, her shaking stopped and the tears, too. She said, "This isn't fair to you."

"What the hell?" I said. "This isn't fair to *you*! My God, you saved my life."

"I don't mean that, exactly," she told me. "I've been in your mind for some time now, Nicholas. It isn't fair that I could do that to you."

"It's all right," I smiled. "Can't think of anyone else I'd feel okay about it with."

"It's not fair," she said, "because I know so much of you, without your consent."

"You have my consent," I said. "You have every bit of it."

"Nicholas," she said. "I've never been in love."

"Me either."

"I've seen so much that I know you better than anyone I've ever known," she said. "Perhaps even myself."

Then she blurted out, "I love you." She began to cry again. "I thought I'd lost you." She was looking up at me, sad and vulnerable.

I don't know where the tipping point is on love. Attraction is the start of it, I suppose. I found Chanda very beautiful. More than that. I found much about her, idiosyncrasies in her expressions, speech, and movements to be – I don't know. Endearing. But how does it get to love from there? My formative years – hell, most of my years – held my emotional self in a dark room in my consciousness, which I'd shared with the Hitchhiker. I'd never had a boyhood crush. I didn't know what infatuation felt like. I'd been with a few women in my day, sure. But that was nothing more than a curb on my libido. I'd never given any thought to a future with any of them.

It could be I was infatuated with Chanda, but I didn't think so. I had none of the fervor of Romeo with Rosaline or Juliet. I found her comfortable and comforting. Amusing. Amazing. Brilliant. Compassionate. She aroused that old libido, but not with the usually short attention span that went with it. I'd longed for her, truth be known, when I was still her least favorite medical mystery. But for a time, she irritated me to no end, being troubled as she was that I was alive. But the raw material of her, what I'd known back in the hospital when I'd been shot, had become something else since the second time I'd been shot. What had that been, time wise? Just a few days. Can a man fall in love in days and call it love?

I'd like to have thought it was love that I felt, but I just didn't know enough to say.

"Take another look inside," I told her. After all, she hadn't lived her emotional life as a child trapped in a small cell. Maybe she would know what I was feeling. "Tell me what you see."

She smiled and stood on her tip toes then and kissed me.

"You love me, too," she said.

I might have blushed. If her conclusion was self-serving, I didn't care.

CHAPTER 37

Not exactly the best place to start a romance, on the porch to a cabin splattered with the bloody remnants of a near-fatal demon encounter. Chanda was exhausted. She and Jack had stayed awake, tending to me during my recuperation, which had taken the better part of twenty-four hours. I felt fine, ready to head off after Jason. But Jack and Chanda were in no shape. Jack was still passed out in the kitchen, and Chanda was happy, but hardly ready to trudge off after my now homicidal brother.

Trying to warn Evelyn again of his intentions psychically was out of the question. The last encounter with my father proved I wasn't anything near invincible. And Jack, too, had nearly been killed.

Chanda explained how the attack had looked on this side, the corporeal side of the encounter. The demon, my father, had taken form in the living room, translucent, ghostlike and slashing at me repeatedly with its claws, tearing me apart. Jack had used his newfound power to try to stop it. He'd shouted at the demon to go back to where it came from. It did. But not before it struck out at Jack with one of its demon-hooves, also equipped with deadly claws. Jack went down, but his order had apparently driven the demon away. That and Chanda had saved enough of me for the pieces to go back together, though it had taken everything I had in the way of healing abilities and Chanda's to boot.

I couldn't take the chance of running into that again. Not if I was going to live long enough to put any plan we might come up with into action. And I wasn't going to risk Chanda's or Jack's getting hurt either, even if I might be willing to risk my own hide.

I wanted to spare Chanda from sleeping with that mess inside the cabin again, so I went into the kitchen and grabbed the blanket and sheet she had been sleeping with on the floor. Jack didn't stir in the least. I let him be and went outside. The furniture on the porch had the advantage of sitting in the clean air. It was a big porch, and I had big, well-cushioned outdoor furniture on it. I took Chanda's sheets and covered one of the couches, sweeping away a few spider webs first. She said thank you and lay down. I kissed her before covering her with the blanket.

"Sleep," I said. "I'll try to work something out before morning."

"There's room," she replied. "Please, lie with me."

I smiled, trying to be reassuring, though things looked a bit grim.

"I will in a bit. I need to try to figure out how to warn Evelyn first."

Chanda drifted away, and I grabbed my phone from the bike. It was midnight. One a.m. on the east coast, and ten on the west. Most people were probably awake in California, but not New York, where my agent was. She wasn't going to be happy with me.

I walked away from the cabin a bit, so my voice wouldn't wake Chanda.

My agent answered her phone, awake after all, so that was good. But she was clearly drunk and having a good time. I heard crowd noise and music in the background.

"Grace," I said. "How are you?"

"Nash! Fucking pissed at you, I can say that," Grace yelled to be heard above the crowd. Someone said, "Is that *him*?" "Yeah. Shhh," she told whoever it was. Then to me again, "I've left you a thousand messages. How 'bout a fucking call back? Do you have any idea how the world has caved in on me since you got shot? Reporters hounding me, your publisher – and all those damned people you were supposed to meet."

I let her vent, not sure if she was angry because she was laughing, too. When she seemed finished, I said, "Grace, this is very important. I need a way to call Evelyn Blankenship, right away."

"The psychic?"

THE THINGS IN HEAVEN AND EARTH

"Yes."

"Do you know her?" Graced seemed to hear opportunity in the possibility.

"I do," I said. "But right now, I have information that someone is out to do her harm. Right now. In real time."

"Jesus! Call the cops! Not your agent, for heaven's sake."

"I would," I lied. "But I don't know where she is. I need to warn her fast."

"You know her, but you don't know where she is or her cell number?"

"Long story," I insisted. "But she has to have an agent, too. You guys are thick as thieves, aren't you? Can you make some phone calls fast and get back to me?"

Grace sighed.

"You are ruining a very fine evening for me right now."

"No reason you can't go back to it. Can you make the calls first?"

"Nash," she said, "if you had a personality at all, I'd think this was a joke."

"No joke. No personality. It's just me."

Grace agreed and hung up. She called back in ten minutes.

"Well, someone *wasn't* having a wonderful evening," she said. "I called her agent. A very glum fellow, who apparently wants anyone who calls him to know his bedtime is 9 p.m."

"Thanks, Grace."

I waited.

"The number, Grace?"

"Oh, yes. I wrote it down. Where the hell did I put it?"

Maybe Grace was *very* drunk.

"Hold on a minute. Fuck. I have to call him back. Lost it already. Call you back in a few."

Grace hung up. I waited maybe ten more minutes before she called back.

"Nash, if you think that man is grumpy the first time you wake him up, you should hear him the second time."

"Grace, the number?"

"He wouldn't give it to me again," she said.

"Damn."

"But I found the paper I wrote it down on," she laughed. "It was right in front of me. Literally, right in front of me. I thought it was the check."

"Put your reading glasses on," I told her.

"They're on, they're on. Here it is."

I thanked Grace and called Evelyn. I got voicemail. I left a to-the-point message, just in case she might hear it.

I thought about calling the police in Santa Cruz. Decided against it. Then I did. They promised to do a wellness check. I told them to have her call me. They said they weren't Western Union, but they would call me back. I thanked them. Then I thought about what a fucking idiot I was. I had Jason's phone number. Somehow, I'd conflated his hiding from my mind as the same thing as not answering his phone, so I hadn't tried to call. I called. Voicemail.

How, I wondered, does a dead man have a phone and voicemail?

Other than leaving right away, I couldn't think of anything else to do, so I put my phone in my pocket, hoping the police would call back soon. Meanwhile, I went to the couch on the porch. I shook Chanda's shoulder. She wiggled her way to the back of the couch, making room for me, and I lay down beside her. She put her arm around me and moved closer, making a few noises that sounded like contentment. Then she was fast asleep.

I lay with my eyes open, staring out over the porch rail into the dark woods surrounding us. I wasn't tired, and there wasn't much else to do. Then I heard the sound of clawed feet at the rear of the cabin, climbing up the steps onto the wooden deck. I assumed it was a bear and began second-guessing the wisdom of sleeping outside. I tensed up and listened, hoping I'd hear the sound going in another direction – any *other* direction. Instead, the sound came clopping around the porch directly toward Chanda and me.

I looked up toward the sound. Thankfully, it wasn't a bear – just a demon.

It came to stop at the rail in front of me and leaned back against it.

"Jack?" I asked, figuring I had a good chance of being right, whichever Jack it might be.

"No. Ted."

I put my finger to my lips, hoping Ted would get the hint. I didn't want to wake Chanda up, and certainly not when she'd be face-to-face with a demon.

I gently moved her arm away and rolled off the couch, indicating to Ted to follow me out to the bikes.

I led. He followed.

"What's up?" Seemed odd talking to a demon nonchalantly like this. Couldn't have imagined such a thing a few weeks ago.

Ted nodded over at my new bike.

"I always wanted to ride one of these things," he said. "Mind?"

"You want to ride my bike?" Odd request.

"No time for that," he said. "But if I could sit on it, that would be cool."

"Go ahead."

Ted threw his backward articulating leg up over the seat, and I had a moment of panic thinking his claws would tear the seat. But he was big and had plenty of clearance. He grabbed the handlebars and lifted the bike off the stand, looking over the gauges.

"Nice," he told me. "Don't put off the things you want to do. Looks like I'll never get the chance to ride one."

"I don't know," I said. "My brother could be dead, and he rides all over the place."

"Yeah," Ted said, "that's what I wanted to talk to you about. You might want to rethink your idea of stopping him."

"From killing Evelyn?"

"Yeah. She's not on your side."

Since neither of the Jacks was here, I figured old Ted might be on a rogue mission. He wasn't exactly on good terms with Evelyn when he'd shuffled off the mortal coil.

"As I recall," I said, "you guys said it was me, Jack, Chanda, and Evelyn against the all the bad guys."

"That was before your father nearly had you joining us for company, Counselor," Ted stated. "You're powerful enough now that you should have been able to stop him. All by yourself. But she dampened your power, even while she thought she was glad to sense you."

"I didn't feel her do anything," I said. "I was taken by surprise."

"Yeah. You shouldn't have been. The same way she was able to help you focus your power against your Hitchhiker, she used it the last time out to do just the opposite. Almost got you killed."

I was suspicious of Ted. I'd seen into the man. He was a dick.

"Seems to me, you might have an ax to grind against her," I noted. "She did you in."

"Yes, she did. But what did you see? You saw her unleash a killing power against me. Provoked, sure, but did that seem like the helpful, compassionate Evelyn to you? She crushed my heart, Nash."

"You crushed hers."

"Apples and oranges. Figurative and literal. If she is the great psychic, how is it she didn't see me coming from a mile off?"

"She couldn't get into your mind," I recalled the thoughts flashing through Evelyn's mind just before Ted slapped her to the ground.

"Exactly. She could get into everyone's mind except mine. Why was that?"

I didn't have an answer.

"She's the Trojan Horse, Nash. A tempting prize, but what's inside is dangerous. She doesn't know it herself, but she's a divided being. Half of her is who she thinks she is. The other half is your Hitchhiker. Let her in at your peril."

Another point of agreement between the demons – at least Ted – and the phantom Evelyn. They both said Evelyn was the Hitchhiker's creature.

"You could say the same about me," I said. "The Hitchhiker was hiding in me for thirty years."

"That's right. Hiding. He's not hiding in Evelyn; he's in control. And since she helped you drive him out of you, he's free. He's free to concentrate on my Evelyn and use her as he pleases."

"No," I said. "When she killed you, the Hitchhiker was still locked inside of me. It couldn't have been him."

"Think of yourself like a Mason jar," Ted said, "holding in a great white shark. You kept some of the shark in the jar, sure. But what was the rest of the shark doing?"

I thought about it. Aside from being a lousy simile, it didn't make sense.

"If Jason is a big bad demon that's on their side," I said, "whether he knows it or not, why would he go after Evelyn to kill her?"

"One of your Jack friends, I'm not sure which one – frankly, I can't tell them apart – he thinks she's there to draw you off. You try to save her, and you're sandwiched right where they want you, between two people who can kill you, neither of whom you'll want to lay a glove on."

"And what do you think?"

"I think you should stay out of the trap in the first place. Let Jason do what he's going to do. Maybe that means he'll kill her. Maybe it means he'll fight against you alongside her if you don't try to stop him. Either way, you're better off staying clear of it, and it takes some of the power out of their plan."

I thought about it and decided.

"Why haven't things ended already?" I asked. "If the Hitchhiker is free and Phantom Evelyn is free, why haven't they joined up already? This should be over. We should have lost."

"Why do you think your Phantom Evelyn has focused on you, tried so hard to confuse you? You're the last line of defense. Your power is keeping them apart. Don't ask me how. I don't know. But you're it. You go, we go."

"I'll take what you said under advisement," I told Ted.

"No, you won't," he said. "Your Jack friends said you'd try to save the girl, no matter what. That's why they didn't come."

"They're probably right."

"I had to try. Thanks for letting me sit on your bike."

Ted set my bike back on the stand and did the demon shimmer thing and was gone.

CHAPTER 38

Demonhood looked good on Ted. It made him sad, reflective, more polite. He even seemed to mean it when he thanked me. Except, I considered, he just might be the old Ted, doing his best to fuck all of us to get back at Evelyn. Old Ted didn't strike me as the let bygones be bygones sort. Then again, if I believed the things I was being told, that's what demons were for – to purge away the evil that lay in the hearts of the dead.

"It's all nonsense," I heard the voice behind me. I turned and saw Jason standing in the glow of the porch light, next to Jack's bike. I was about run to hug him, but stopped myself. There was something different about the man. It wasn't Jason. He looked too much like me.

"You!" I said, knowing it was the Hitchhiker.

"Me. You. We're more or less the same being," he said.

I immediately began reaching inward for my power. The Hitchhiker took a step back, then he said, "You want to give me a minute before you try blasting me into oblivion again?"

"I don't think so," I felt my power welling up inside, concentrating at my heart.

"Hold on!" he implored. "You *know* you don't know what the hell is happening. For all the shit you've been told, the only thing you know for certain is that something is maneuvering you into a confrontation with me. If this were a trial, all you have is hearsay. Not admissible. Let's talk. Kill me later, if you still want to."

He had a point. Most of what I thought I knew about him came from what others had told me, and my own conjecture. But then again, he *had* tried to kill me. That wasn't hearsay.

"I hear what you're thinking," he said. I could hear the fear in his voice. "Mea culpa. Self-fucking defense though."

I let my power slow and stop, fading back into whatever its source. "Okay," I said. "Talk."

"That's what I'm here to do," he said, relieved that I was standing down. "I ask that you accept one premise before we continue, though."

"What's that?"

"For argument's sake, assume that you and I are the same – person."

"I don't believe that."

"It's a hypothetical," he responded. "Arguendo."

When you got down to it, hypotheticals were all I'd had on this journey. So, what could another layer on the bullshit layer cake hurt?

"Okay," I said. "For the moment, let's assume it's true."

"Thank you," the Hitchhiker relaxed and leaned against Jack's bike. "Let's start with the basics. I'm not human. Not as such. I'm much more than I appear to be, but that part of me is lost – for now. I was drawn to this world by Evelyn. She's like me. Not human. We'll get back to her in a minute. Bottom line, I came to this world the moment you were conceived. I was bound up inside of you, knowing nothing more than your cells were capable of knowing."

He was talking fast, trying to get it all out before I changed my mind.

"I grew as you grew, physically, emotionally, experientially. I experienced everything in your life just as you experienced it. We were one and the same. I grew up loving our mother, our father, Jason, and Julie. I still love them, every bit as much as you."

I was seething at his claim, his mention of my family. "You killed them!" I accused.

"The fuck I did!" The anger was clear in his voice. "Evelyn killed them. She used her goddamned demons to do it. She used us, you and me, to pull the trigger."

"Why? Why would she kill my family?"

"*Our* family, Nick. *Our* family," he said. "Because we were awakening. The moment we saw Grandma Claire's ghost, our power was beginning to break through."

"Bullshit! Why would I have any power to begin with?"

"If you had grown up without me, you wouldn't have," he said. "She wanted to make me human, weak, confused. It worked. I'm more human than anything now. But because we were one, my power was your power. When it began to break the bounds of human limitations, she had to break both of us – break us and break us hard. She undid us when she killed our family, when she made *us* pull that trigger. That psychic blow stopped our awakening short and allowed her to build that box in our brain and put us there, the living part of us, anyway. But we found our way back. We took our revenge against those demons, even if we didn't know that's what we were doing. But we were cut off from our soul, Nick. We were cut off from our full awakening. She kept us in that box, making us kill people whenever it looked like we were going to break out. She turned us into a fucking zombie, Nick. That's how she controlled us."

"So, what changed?" I asked, disliking that the pieces seemed to fit.

"She didn't count on us being more than one," he said. "My power alone, she could have contained. But you grew the same power. We were twice what I was, and that she *couldn't* contain. She could have destroyed me. But not *us*."

"Why," I asked, "would any of this be true?"

"Because she and I were once one," he said. "The same way you and I become one, she and I once were. But a time came when I wasn't content to be the Yin or the Yang anymore. I wanted to be more, to be a separate, independent being. And my power had become such that I could make it so, and I did."

I laughed. "Either way I hear it told, one of you is a jealous lover."

The Hitchhiker sighed. "Not lovers. Aspects of the same being. When I broke free, she was enraged. She was determined to undo me – and my freedom."

"I'm given to believe the universe will explode or something if you have your way."

"That's the biggest, most audacious lie she's told," he said. "She didn't create the fucking universe, Nick. I mean, seriously. Think about it. She and I were in it, yes. Same way you are in it. I don't even know for sure what we were, but everything was here along with us."

"Then what's her beef with you?"

"I've awakened, Nick," he said. "Fully now. I know the things I knew. And I know she killed our family. I hate her for that, Nick. She wanted me to suffer, and she made me suffer. She made you suffer, too. There's no going back from that. I don't know. Sometimes I think she wanted me dead. Other times, I think she wanted me beaten, so I'd come back to her. She knows I never will now – come back to her, I mean. Whatever we were, we will never be again."

"Assuming, arguendo, what you say is true, what does any of this mean?"

"It means she's going to kill me. And she's going to kill you."

"She said she doesn't want to kill you."

"Jesus, look at what she's done. She's laid about a thousand distractions in front of you. Friendly demons, allies, friendships, your brother and father, and even this woman you've fallen in love with."

"Why?"

"Because if you come at her straight on, one on one, you'll destroy her. Divided like this, you can't. You'll use your power to try to save your friends. She's been working hard on you ever since she strolled into your office, or what you thought was your office. She emasculated you, toyed with you. She did everything she could to break you down and then surround you with distractions, to divide your power."

"What about your power?"

"It's not mine anymore," he said. "It's all yours. I gave you the mea culpa. I tried to take all of it. But I did it because you were falling under her spell. You were going to lose."

"Why didn't you tell me any of this before?"

"I am you. I was you. I was bound up inside of you. I couldn't talk to you the way you can talk to someone in the same room. I tried."

"Why now?"

"Because we're not the same person at the same time anymore. I can talk to you directly now, and I can tell you that you can destroy her.

Right now. I can open the door. I have that much mojo left. But you have to go to her alone, just you. Remember how you broke her glass and took control of the vision she gave you. Remember how you stopped her from killing your friends. You are more powerful than she is. You have to do it alone, though. Do it, and you'll save your friends and yourself."

"And the universe?"

"It wasn't going anywhere."

Without waiting, he seemed to concentrate on the space between us. I saw a shimmering and then night, someplace else. I felt cold air, and I saw snow here and there on the ground. In the distance, below, I saw mountains. I saw the ground I would step onto was high above everything around it. In the distance, I saw lightning, and looked down upon a storm. It was a mountain peak that I saw just on the other side.

"Step through now, Nick," the Hitchhiker said. "She's there. Alone. Hiding from you."

If I chose to believe him, the Hitchhiker had just given me the first promise of something I could do to end this. The Evelyns, the Jacks, Ted, Jason – they had given me nothing more than alterative versions of a story that wouldn't square, with no action that I could take to do anything about any of it, and not so much as a promise that I was going to *know* what the hell was happening somewhere along the line. I'd been Phantom Evelyn's puppet for a long while, and I was tired, so very tired and angry about all of it.

Killing her wasn't exactly what I'd intended, but I didn't know what I intended. Either way, I started to step through, knowing it was ill-advised, knowing I shouldn't trust the Hitchhiker, but holding onto the slim hope I could finally act.

Then a force that seemed familiar in its power thrust me away from the opening, so hard I flew twenty feet, at least, backwards, into the underbrush along the driveway. I saw it take form, translucent, huge, demonic. Bigger than the Jacks or Ted, and shimmering into existence in front of me.

I'd hit the ground hard. I was stunned and barely able to move. I saw then that Chanda was up, standing on the porch and seeing what I saw.

"Jack!" she screamed for help. Then she began to rush toward me. "Chanda, no!" I yelled.

The demon began walking toward me, growing in size with every step. It remained semitransparent, as if only part if it was actually in this world, emanating from another. It turned and snarled at Chanda, then it moved toward her. She retreated a few steps and tried to find a way to run around it, toward me.

I was able to see far enough around the demon to see the Hitchhiker, smiling at some victory that I assumed was tied up with my impending demise. I couldn't survive this thing again. The Hitchhiker hadn't been letting me through the portal at all – it was letting this thing, what was left of my father, through to this side of it to kill me.

The Hitchhiker walked through the portal it had created, and the portal was gone, taking him with it and leaving me royally fucked.

Jack was up, running full steam ahead at the demon. It flicked its tail at him and Chanda, sweeping them away to the ground. Then it turned its full attention back to me.

For what it was worth, my healing was up to snuff. I was on my feet, ready for a fight. Only, I didn't want to fight my father. I didn't want to destroy what was left of the man who had suffered so much.

I let whatever power I had lie and yelled at Chanda and Jack, "Get out of here! Get in the car and go! Now!"

Maybe I would fight if they were in danger. Until then, I stood and faced my death.

They didn't get in the car. They ran behind the demon. I could see enough through the thing to see that they were quixotically beating against it with their fists. I loved them both at that moment, more than anyone. And I was really pissed at them, too, for not fleeing when I told them to. The Hitchhiker was telling the truth about one thing: they were a remarkable distraction.

The demon had grown, I guessed, thirty feet in height. It reached out for me with its claws, ignoring Jack and Chanda and grabbing me, holding me in front of it, drawing me nearer to its fangs.

I called forth my own demon army then.

"Jacks! Ted!"

Sprites descended, and the demon forms of the Jacks and Ted hit the ground.

"Well, we're sure as shit fucked!" one said. I was pretty sure it was Second Jack.

"Protect your grandson, Jack. Protect Chanda!"

The Jacks and Ted pulled Jack and Chanda away, shimmered, and they were all gone.

The people I cared about were safe, or as safe as anyone could be.

I looked into the demon's yellow, malignant eyes. They were bit weepy at the corners, truth be told.

"Name me," the demon snarled. "Name me!"

So, it wanted to hear me call its name before it killed me? I loved my father, but I wasn't feeling the love like that. I bowed my head and said nothing.

The thing grunted and threw me into the woods. My back hit a tree, and I fell to the ground, painfully onto a very nasty patchwork of roots below the tree trunk. On the ground, I struggled to get back up to my feet, healing, probably, but not fast enough.

"Name him!" I heard a voice calling from the driveway. "Goddammit, Nick, name him!"

"Jason?" I recognized the voice.

"Name him!" Jason yelled. "Or he's going to kill you."

As crazy as it sounds, at that moment I couldn't remember my father's name. All my life, he was "Dad." I knew his last name was Bennett, but what was his first name?

"Name me," the demon growled, stomping toward me, no mercy at all in its weepy eyes.

"Dad!" I shouted.

The demon kept coming, found me, lifted me in its claws again. Then it said, quietly, "Command me."

CHAPTER 39

My father's demon set me to the ground and diminished in size considerably, equaling the Jacks. Still big, but not rending me in two big. He stood silently, watching me. I wasn't sure about it, but I reached out and touch his claw and said, "Father."

The demon slowly sank to the ground. If demons cry, this one did.

I glanced out at the driveway, where I thought I'd heard Jason's voice a moment before. In the light of the porch, I saw a human form there, but not for long. Like my father's demon, the human form grew and took on a demonic state.

"Jason!" I cried out.

"Not Jason!" the new demon shouted, and it reached into the woods, tearing the first tree between it and me out by its roots. The demon stepped into the woods then, tearing out other trees that stood in its way, tossing them like they were nothing more than big sticks. The ground shook and roared with every step and every tree ripped from its roots.

Jason? Not Jason?

Fuck it. I started to run.

The demon came after me fast. Where I went around trees, the demon ran through them.

"Jason," I yelled, hoping to repeat the naming trick. No go. Jason's demon came on fast.

I kept running. Again, I was confronted by certain death, but I would not reach for my power. Jason, not Jason. I thought it was my brother, the world-ending demon the Jacks and Ted had warned me about. They were right. I would find it very hard to kill my brother, if this was him. In fact, I wasn't going to do it, certainly not as long as I could run and there were still trees between us.

I'd've liked to have thought it was only in bad horror movies that people fleeing demonic forces fall while running through the woods. Not so much. I fell over a tangle of roots, rolled over and looked at Jason's, Not Jason's demon looming over me. I might have laughed. Death by cliché. Instead, I reached inward for my power after all, trying to decide if there was a way to use it to stop the demon without killing it.

Slowly, I let the power fade. I felt it. But it felt deadly. I let it go.

The demon caught up with me. I thought to command my father's demon to rescue me, but, no. One or both of them would come out worse for the wear. Jason, somewhere inside this thing, was still my brother. I'd eaten with him, cried with him, run with him. Whatever was in front of me now, Jason was still in there. Moments before, he'd even saved my life.

The claws reached out, and I had one, last, desperate thought.

"Duke!" I yelled. "I name you Duke!"

The demon stopped. Instantly, the demon form sloughed away, like dead skin falling from a corpse. Then standing in front of me was my brother, Jason, with me once more.

He reached down and helped me stand. Then I got another bear hug, much preferable to the one I'd nearly escaped.

"Hey, Little Brother," he cried. "I told you I got issues."

Dad wasn't able to slough away his demon-shell. He didn't revert back to "Dad" in any way. Silently, he followed Jason and me to the porch. Jason and I sat, while Dad stood on the other side of the rail, holding it with his claws and staring at his sons with, if demons have determinable expressions, bemusement.

"This has been a wickedly fucked up night," I told Jason. "But next to yesterday, not so bad. Mind telling me what happened? Last I heard you were on your way to kill Evelyn Blankenship. By the way, you didn't, did you?"

Jason sighed. "I had every intention of it. Got on my bike and started riding west. For some reason, I thought I knew where she'd be."

"Santa Cruz."

"Santa Cruz? No. Colorado. Pikes Peak."

I thought for a moment back to the Hitchhiker's portal.

"Damn. The Hitchhiker tried to bring me there. Or rather, he let Dad loose at me from there."

"It's a place of power," Jason said. "I was drawn to it. Hating the fuck out of Evelyn Blankenship for what she made me do to that kid's family."

"She didn't do it."

"Yeah," Jason told me. "It was my own demon-ass self. I get that now. But I felt this overwhelming obsession to kill her, knowing she made me do it, knowing if I killed her, I could save you."

"What stopped you?"

"Funny thing happened to me on the way to the murder," Jason said. "My thoughts about killing Evelyn turned to thoughts of killing you. I didn't even know how my thoughts were changing. One minute I hated her and was hell bent on killing her. The next I was hating you and hell bent on killing you."

"Why?"

"No reason," Jason said. "But I turned the bike around and headed back this way. Only at some point I realized what I was going to do, and I tried to stop myself. That's when I got a rude awakening, what, about being dead and all. When I willed myself to stop, the demon that came after you, reared up inside me. Nothing physical. It all happened in my mind. We fought. I lost. We kept coming after you. We fought like that, over and over, with me losing every damned time. But I knew then what I was. I knew that demon was part of me. But I kept fighting, Nick. I love you, Little Brother."

"You managed enough to save my life," I told him.

"Uh, not so much," he said. "I wanted to be the one to kill you. Didn't want to wait in line."

I shuddered, as if I hadn't already had enough to shudder about.

"I didn't think you'd name me," he said continued. "Jason isn't my demon name."

"Duke is?"

"Fucking hilarious, ain't it? I picked that name to use when I found you. At least, I thought I picked it. Anyway, you named the fucker. You command it now, like you command Dad."

Jason looked at our father and said, "I told you he was an evil fuck."

"Just looks that way," I said. "He told me how to stop him himself. I just wasn't getting it until you came along."

I looked at my father. What had changed him enough that my true father shone through to try to save me?

Jason stood and stepped toward our father, reaching out to touch his forehead. The demon looked up, then away, as if ashamed.

"You put yourself into him," Jason said. "You made him see through your eyes long enough. Just long enough for him to see who you were, that you were the real Nick in there. His son. It couldn't have been easy for him to win that fight, Nick. I tried. I love you, Little Brother, but I tried with everything I am and lost to it. I was going to kill you. It was all I wanted. He fought it harder than I was able to. That's why you're alive, Little Brother. Dad saved you this time. I guess he saved me, too, when he saved you."

"Well," I said. "No question in my mind now. Phantom Evelyn and the Hitchhiker are the enemy, and I'm theirs."

"What are you thinking?"

"That I *am* the one thing that's keeping them from blowing everything apart," I said. "This whole thing has been to divide me from my power. Somehow, something has made me the only thing that keeps them apart. My friends, the Jacks, came to me. They're demons now, too. You'd like them. They told me as much. They told me about you, too. They said I'd have to kill you."

"Why didn't you?" Jason asked. "I didn't even feel you try."

"I *didn't* try," I told him. "I love, too, Big Brother."

I looked over at Dad. "I love our father, too."

Jason sat back down. "So now what?"

"We gather up our side and figure out how to destroy those two fuckers."

Chapter 40

The Hitchhiker had managed to tempt me toward that portal of his with the promise that I could finally do something besides being bounced back and forth like an Evelyn Blankenship ping pong ball. I'd been desperate for a long while now to know enough about something, anything, to act. He made me think he'd given me that. And I'd fallen for it.

Now, despite his treachery, I had that back. It became eminently clear to me that he and Evelyn were working together, had been all along, working on me, living in my blind spots to keep me from seeing true. Ted told me that my power might have its source in the earth itself. Why not? Evelyn used the truth to lie to me. And I had seen a vision, confirmed by her, that she had been an immensely powerful being, whose single moment of "What if?" became all things, everything she'd wondered in that brief instant. As all of it formed, it bled her dry, taking her power, most of it, to become what she had imagined. Why wouldn't it have taken some of her sentience as well? Why wouldn't it struggle to survive, the same way all living creatures struggle to survive?

It wasn't talking to me, this Earth Power, but it felt right to me. Some intelligence had to be at work, and not just on me. There was Chanda, Jack, his demon grandfather and First Jack. Even dickhead Ted. Something changed us, gave us insight or power. Enough that Phantom Evelyn and the Hitchhiker were being kept from taking all of it away so long as we were here to stop them.

That moment on the beach, the first beach with Phantom Evelyn. Thinking back on it, despite their own confusion when it was happening, one thing was clear – they were drawn to each other. As they found their own awakenings, I surmised, their desire to be one again had asserted itself. Jason? My father? They had taken them, changed them to help them destroy us. For the moment, at least, it appeared to have backfired.

They didn't know time, Evelyn said. Not the way we do. But I did. My life, chronologically driven as it was, was taken from me. My family, murdered, my own hand forced to do the killing. My only joy, my only happiness in these years was riding a motorcycle, feeling the wind, breathing the open air, watching the living world move by me as I rode. Forests, mountains, crops, animals scurrying along the roadside. Raindrops stinging my face as I rode through the storm. The feel of the sun against my skin, the touch of a blade of grass. The sound of leaves rustling. Had that been this Earth Power calling to me all along, giving me what little succor I could be given, giving me some glimmer of light to divide from the darkness?

Until all of this began, I was alive in a mechanical sense. I didn't feel. I didn't love. I'd been institutionalized for the better part of my childhood, seeing terrors all around me, but feeling nothing of the terror I should have felt. I'd brought death upon the innocent, not of my own will, but it had been by my hand. I had killed children. I murdered a man with a hatchet. A fucking hatchet. The memory of it, whether they lived now or not, was with me. Ironically, as I began to feel again, I knew I was pressing back those memories and the feelings that tried to surface with them. Maybe knowing that it had somehow been undone, perhaps by me, was just enough salve on the wounds to keep me together. But sometime soon, if any of us made it through this, I was going to have to find a way to live with it.

Anger is what I should have felt now that I could feel. But something kept me from it, and I knew what it was. My love for Chanda. Yes, I knew in my heart that I was in love with her, and I knew I loved Jason and my father. I cared deeply for the Jacks and Jack, and even felt pity for Ted. And the human Evelyn – Ted and the phantom Evelyn told me she was the Hitchhiker's creature. That may have been true. But I saw a kindred soul, used more kindly than I had been, but used, nevertheless. I didn't know exactly what I felt for her, but I knew I would not allow her to be a casualty in this thing if I could stop it.

Anger would give me what? A trade against everything I had gained. Whatever came, I decided, it wouldn't be revenge or hate that would drive me – it would be my love for the living and the dead.

These were my thoughts when I summoned the demons back with Chanda and Jack.

We were a motley crew assembled on the porch and deck of the cabin. Aside from my father, whose state of mind I still couldn't fully fathom, and Ted – never Ted – any of the rest I would have trusted to lead us into whatever was coming next. But I felt like the de facto leader, somehow, like whatever came, it would have to be on my shoulders. Mother Earth, making her choice?

Chanda had run to me when the demons returned with her and Jack, which could have turned out badly, because I was running to her, too. But instead of crashing into each other, we embraced, and I kissed her with every bit of the love that had been denied to me during my life. It felt strange to embrace in front of the crew like that, but it is what it is.

"I hope you put your clothes in the dryer," I laughed, with my love still standing barefoot in her underwear.

"I'm afraid I didn't have time," she told me, so seriously I didn't think the sentiment was serious at all.

I went inside and took her laundry from the washer and put it in the dryer. Then I made coffee, wondering if demons could drink coffee. Figuring out what to do next was going take a while. Might as well tend to the creature comforts along the way.

When I came back out, the demon question was moot. Except for Dad, the other demons had taken on their human forms. The Jacks were a soldier and cop once more, and Ted a smartly dressed attorney, ready for the limelight.

"Good to see you guys looking like guys again," I said.

"Sure as fuck makes it easier to sit on this fucking tiny deck of yours," Second Jack said, taking a cup of coffee from me. First Jack took a cup, and I started back in to bring more coffee.

"Tea for me, if you please," Chanda told me.

"Um, not stocked, I'm afraid."

"My keys are on the table," she smiled. "You native-born Americans are never properly stocked. I have tea in my trunk."

As I brought more coffee cups and went to open Chanda's trunk, it occurred to me that this was the happiest moment of my life. Except maybe for Mom and her chocolate chip pancakes on Saturday mornings.

We sat and drank. No one said much. Chanda sat next to me on the couch. The Jacks were eyeing Jason suspiciously. I gave a short synopsis regarding events with my father and brother. The Jacks still seemed wary, but Second Jack was glad to forget about him for a moment and began talking to his grandson.

"This being dead shit," he told him, "it ain't much, but I don't have to fucking pee all the time."

They laughed. Living Jack cried and hugged his grandfather, and said, "I'd miss the fuck out of you, you old windbag, but I got your house. Nice place. Throwing all my shit around in it, too."

Jason stood on the deck, holding his hand to our father's forehead again. I got the impression they were sharing something. I hoped it was family stuff and not plans to go demon-rogue again.

First Jack eventually worked his way in with Second Jack and Living Jack, hugging the man, too. "Uncle Jack," Living Jack said. "Can't believe you let his sorry fuck get the drop on you."

First Jack laughed and slapped Living Jack on the back. "Didn't have my readers on, boy. Didn't see it coming."

I sat quietly with Chanda. Whatever time there was going to be for a reunion, this was it, and I wasn't in any hurry to see it end.

Ted had wandered away, leaning on my bike. I felt sorry for him. I'm not sure why. I asked Chanda if she minded. She said, "Go ahead," so I got up and followed him.

"You okay?" I asked.

"No," he said. "Ever have an epiphany?

"No," I said, truthfully. "Haven't lived long enough. Not really."

"Hmmm," he said. "I guess not. You wouldn't know what it's like, living so high on admiration that when it stops, you realize it was for nothing. That it means nothing."

"Getting killed gave you a change of heart?"

"I'm surrounded by love here, Nash," Ted said. "None of it is for me. Before long, I'll be a mindless ghost being tormented by my own wicked self for the wrongs I've done. I should be that now. I would be, if not for whatever has lifted us up to face this moment."

"I'm not sure I get your meaning."

"I mean, I'm nothing. No one mourns for me, Nash. No one is glad to see me. Whatever I pass into, I pass alone. If there is another side, no one is going to be happy to see me there." He smiled, briefly, "Not going to be interviewed about it on CNN either."

"Maybe you're becoming more than you were, now that you're dead."

"Too late. I've been a first-class fuck all of my life."

I thought about it for a moment. There really wasn't much for Ted to do but sulk.

"Look," I said. "We got maybe an hour or two before I think we need to get the show on the road."

"I know," he said. "Give them all the time you can. This is what meaning is, Nash. I can see that now. I wish I couldn't, but I can. No, that's not right. I'm glad I see it. I need to see it, I guess."

"Well," I said, "here's something. You can't get killed again."

"Not sure about that, given what we're about to do."

"More precisely," I corrected, "you can't get killed trying to ride a motorcycle. You ever ride one at all?"

"When I was a kid. Nothing big like this."

I took out my key FOB and handed it to him. I showed him how to start the bike and gave him some pointers.

"Try to get back in an hour or so," I said. "It's big and heavy, and you'll probably crash, but try to have fun."

"Seriously?"

"Why not? Don't put off the things you really want to do."

CHAPTER 41

Mother Earth finally spoke to me. *Maybe*. I was still sitting with Chanda on the couch. Like teenagers on a supervised date, we were holding hands but painfully aware we were not alone. Nevertheless, we were content for the moment with a touch, knowing we were together. The Jacks, living and dead, had worked their way into metaphysical discussions about life after death, the Jacks having some experience with it. Living Jack talked about his and Chanda's powers, and there was some discussion about preordainment and whether free will had any part in this, given the way the pieces were coming together without much input from us, the pieces. Jason and Dad communed in whatever way they had been, with Jason holding his hand to Dad's demon skull, sending and receiving thoughts, I assumed. I wasn't sure I wanted to know what they were talking about.

The voice came so gently, I wasn't sure it was there.

"*Come with me,*" it said. Chanda heard it, too, through me, and looked at me quizzically.

"What is it?" she asked. "Do you hear it?"

"I think so," I answered, and I did my best to listen. It was a little like trying to hear a conversation after blasting Led Zeppelin through the Harley's stereo full blast on a long ride.

"*Come with me,*" it repeated. I heard it clearly this time.

I looked at Chanda. "Go," she said.

"What if it tempts me toward the flood?"

"Swim."

I closed my eyes and listened some more, and I was gone, hovering aloft in the dark. In the distance, I saw lights, far below and far away. Towns. Houses. Streets.

I hovered, and despite the dark, I was able to make out a sign. "Summit. Pikes Peak. 14,111 FT."

The place was dark, empty but for three human-looking souls. Evelyn and myself, or, rather, the Hitchhiker, still wearing my human form. And Evelyn. Both Evelyns were there. All were silent, listening, it seemed, for what might come. In them, I sensed fear.

"Do not go to them," the voice said. "Our power is weak there."

"Why?"

"Wait for them," the voice said. "Draw them to our power, let them come – to us."

The voice faded, and I was sitting next to Chanda, still holding hands.

"What is it?" she asked.

"Not sure." I was unsettled. Something about it didn't feel right. Mother Earth? Or Mother Evelyn, not looking forward to a reunion just yet.

I played the voice over in my mind. It sounded familiar, soothing. Then I recognized it. It was the soothing woman's voice that had promised my father revenge against Nicholas Bennett, pledged its support and promised, sweetly, that Jason, Julie, and my mother would be free.

"I think it's Evelyn in disguise," I said. "Maybe. I don't know for sure. Trying to stop us from trying."

"What is it we are going to try, Nick?"

"Looks like we're taking a trip to Pikes Peak," I said.

I stood up and let out an "Ahem!"

Conversation and forehead rubbing came to a stop.

"I think I know where we have to go," I said. "What we have to do."

I told the assembled where the Evelyns and the Hitchhiker were hiding.

The where was easy. The "What we have to do" part was a devil in the details.

I didn't have to tell anyone what our strengths were. Demons knew they were demons; Chanda and Jack knew their powers; and I had an idea about mine, though they'd hardly come with an instruction manual.

"We have to go to them and take them on, head on," I said, sure it was the only plan.

First Jack laughed.

"College boy," he said. "Didn't spend much time in the Army, did you?"

"Fuck no," Second Jack answered for me. "He sure as shit ain't no natural tactician neither."

So much for my role as leader. I didn't see much use in being stubborn about it though.

"Okay," I said. "You're right. I don't have much of a plan other than to slug it out. I thought you guys said I was hot enough shit to take them on already."

"They co-opted your air support, buddy," First Jack said. "They got both Evelyns now."

"And they got the high ground," Second Jack added. "Ground they chose, and we're walking right into it, unless you want to listen a bit."

"All right," I said. "I'm listening."

"Think of our . . ." First Jack started, then he looked around. "Where the hell is Ted?"

"Here," Ted said, walking back to the group from the rear deck. He looked at me sheepishly. "I wrecked your bike. Sorry."

I looked him over. He seemed awkwardly sincere. I noted that he crashed better than I did, too. Not a wrinkle or a stain on his suit. I was really starting to feel for the guy. I knew what it was like to be alone. We had that in common, though his own circumstances were self-induced. He made an asshole human. Still. I took a page from First Jack's playbook and slapped him on the back and laughed. "Fuck, Ted, I knew you were going to crash when I gave you the key."

Ted's spirits improved with that, and we turned our attention to First Jack.

"We got different strengths here," he said. "Jack, Ted, and me can get us there, same as we got you to Wyoming. That's a place of power, Pikes Peak is. We can work with that. We got some movie demon tricks now, too. Real power – all the bad stuff demons don't usually got. But compared it you, it's just going to be fireworks. Big distracting noises, I'm guessing, but that's about it. So, we draw them off first, then you come in and hit the one furthest away, hard."

"Why the farthest?"

"They'll test you with the weaker of them first," Second Jack explained. "Find your strengths and weaknesses. Then they'll pull out the big guns. So, take out the big guns first."

"I think Dad and I just go in big," Jason said. "You can command us. Command us to tear them apart. I don't think we'll be much for strategy, but we're good at focusing on a task, the bloodier the better."

"They might not bleed," I said.

"My Evelyn will," Ted said, reluctantly I thought. But maybe it was just *hope* that he was a better demon than a man.

"Okay," I said. "Ground rules. Phantom Evelyn and the other guy are fair game. We do what we can to contain Human Evelyn, if she's even a threat, but we're not going to hurt her. She's a victim, not a player. She might even be on our side. No way to know she's there of her own free will."

"I agree," Chanda said. "I do not believe she is one with them."

"Okay," Jason said. "No point in arguing with you. You were right about Dad and me, so let's see if you can go three for three. Just make sure you put that command in words, or we can't be responsible."

"Okay," First Jack said. "We got as far as a half-assed plan for our side. But we got to think what their goal is."

"They want to hook the fuck up," Second Jack said. "Our plan can't just be to rough them up. We got to do something that will keep them apart – forever. I mean their spirit selves, or whatever. So, what happens if we blow them out of their bodies? Do they say thank you, have a nice fucking doomsday, and join up like . . ."

"Like matter and antimatter," Ted finished.

"They're sneaky smart," First Jack said. "That's a fact. Wasn't thinking clear on that myself. Okay, how do we take their spirits apart and *keep* them apart?"

Human Jack spoke up. "Maybe the plan is no plan."

"What do you mean, son?" Second Jack asked.

"Well, if us just being us has some kind of power that won't let them join up, why not just go on with our lives? Walk away. Seems like we've already achieved what we need to do. We just go on being what we've become, and that seems to be all that we have to do to keep them apart."

Second Jack seemed to think about it, then said, "Naw. I don't see it. They've been fucking with Nash here forever, and something says the rest of us got to do something about this. We haven't gotten woke up like we have been to play dumb again. I think this is just kind of a lull before the storm. If we don't use what we got, the storm will come against us one way or another."

"I agree," Ted said. "Seems like we've reached our maximum potential here. It's time to use it."

"That still don't answer Jack's question," First Jack said. "How do we get them apart forever?"

I thought about it. There wasn't an answer that I could see.

"I don't think we're going to find a solution talking about it," I said. "I say we keep that in mind and look for a sign or something along the way."

"Signs?" First Jack laughed. "What kinda signs?"

"There've been signs all along this road we're on," I said. "We just have to look for the right exit this time."

"Jesus," Second Jack said. "Jack Fucking Kerouac."

I noticed Chanda had walked away and into the cabin. She came back, dressed in dry clothing. That's when my fear stepped in.

"I have something to say," I announced, but Chanda interrupted me.

"No, Nick, you do not have something to say," she said. "I am not speaking for Jack. It is up to him. But I am not staying behind."

I considered that this was going to be tricky relationship, having a girlfriend who can read my mind and see through my more devious machinations.

"Well," I said, a bit desperate. If I was going to convince Chanda and Jack to stay behind and out of danger, I needed a damn good reason, or they wouldn't listen. "Stop and think about it. It looks like I have the power to tackle them head on. We know what the demons can do. But, Chanda, you're a healer. That's your power. We might need you safe on this side to save me – or Human Evelyn – if we get shredded out there."

"And me?" Jack said. "I can influence them, maybe. I could be a big help when things get going."

"Or you can stay here and protect Chanda, so she can save our butts later," I said, thinking it *sounded* like a good plan.

First Jack said, "He might be right. If he or that Evelyn get hurt bad enough, they'll need you. We can get them back here, I think, but we can't patch them up."

Chanda seemed to consider. "Jack?"

"I'd rather go in," he said. "But your power does seem to be limited to healing. It's an amazing gift, but I'm not sure that you'll get the chance to use it out there. And I don't like the idea of leaving you alone, either. So, I'll stay with you, if that's what you want to do."

"It's not," Chanda said. "I do not wish to sit here wondering if you're safe, Nick. I may have powers we don't know about as well. Jack might, too. However, it does seem like a sound idea, even though I know you've been less than sincere in your reasoning."

"Forgive me if I love you," I said, feeling a measure of relief.

"Okay," Second Jack said. "Stop the weepy shit. Time's a wastin'."

"Hold on," Jason said. "Set your commands down, Nick. Dad and I will do as you command, so be specific."

"Get the bad guys," I said. "Don't hurt the human Evelyn. And just to be clear, no one here with us right now is one of the bad guys. Phantom Evelyn and the Hitchhiker. They're the only enemy."

"Okay," Jason said. "Let's go."

"Wait," I suddenly remembered an important detail. "The Hitchhiker looks like me. Make sure it's the right Nash you're rending. And the right Evelyn."

"All right, boys and girls," Second Jack said. "Watch the fucking magic."

Ted and the Jacks walked from the deck onto the pavement. Once on the ground, they took their demon forms and found equidistant points, forming a triangle. Jason turned on the demon lights, growing as large as he had been when he took down a sizable chunk of the woods coming after me. Dad followed suit. I couldn't help but feel a certain dread when they each spread their demon wings, ready to take flight, like T-Rex/pterodactyl hybrids.

256

Ted and the Jacks held their claws skyward, and wall of sorts rose from the ground skyward, a clear line of demarcation between *here* and *there*. On the other side was the summit of Pikes Peak. I thought briefly that I wanted to kiss Chanda and say goodbye, but I wasn't sure I'd take the next steps if I did.

I stepped through. It was cold, dark, and a terrible wind blew all around me when I stood alone on the summit. Then Chanda and Jack were beside me. I sighed.

"You could have just said no," I said absently, scanning the darkness for the enemy.

"Didn't want to argue, Love," Chanda told me.

CHAPTER 42

"All for one, one for all," Jack said, laughing. "I told you they made this personal. If I can shove something uncomfortable up their asses, I'm going to do it."

"Your grandfather is a bad influence," I said, trying to adjust to the darkness. "You're starting to sound like him."

"I see them!" Chanda pointed. I followed her gesture and looked toward an old stone structure, a door, two windows, and not much else. In front of it lay a small patch of snow. There, Evelyn and the Hitchhiker sat on cheap folding aluminum lawn chairs planted in the snow, the kind with molded plastic tubing woven together to form the seat and the back. Human Evelyn stood behind them.

Above them, darker than the darkness, a demon cloud descended. Sprites fell, and three demons hit the ground behind them. Human Evelyn shrieked and turned, focusing her power on one of the demons. Whatever she'd unleashed, it warped the very air, thin as it was, like a shock wave. The demon, whichever one it had been, was gone in an instant. Human Evelyn was on the side of evil after all.

The two remaining demons bolted past Human Evelyn, knocking her to the ground. I grinned, involuntarily, as they each, amazingly, got to Phantom Evelyn and the Hitchhiker at the same time, claws reaching to dig into whatever stuff they were made of.

Then my demon friends were gone, like the first demon. Vanished. I thought it unlikely it was a tactical retreat. We were already three down and seriously fucked.

"Nash," Phantom Evelyn laughed. "Oh, sweet boy. Whatever brought you here, up so high, so far from the source of your power?"

I ignored Evelyn's words. I wasn't going to be played. Not this time. I reached inward, focusing the power I'd felt and brought against the Hitchhiker when I'd banished him from my mind. Only that time, Human Evelyn seemed to be on my side. I wasn't counting on her help now, hoping that whatever I sent forth would be within my control.

Then Evelyn waived her hand, and I felt disoriented, nauseous. In the distance I saw a dark peak, the highest around, higher than where I stood. Only I wasn't standing anymore. I was falling into the darkness.

Darkness or no, I sensed the horror of what was coming. Evelyn had waived me from the summit, far from it, and the next time I made contact with terra firma, it was going to be with a horrible thud.

I tried to let go of my panic and think. My power. What could I do with it now to save myself? I reached inward, finding it, holding it, trying to feel what it could do. Whatever it was, it wasn't a parachute. I fell, thinking I'd lost, fearing for Chanda and Jack – and everything.

Then I heard the sound of giant wings pounding the air. I don't know how far I'd fallen, but one of my demon-kin scooped me from the air, holding me in its arms, gently slowing my descent. Then it flew, higher and higher, taking us back toward the peak. Briefly, I mused: How wonderful to have family in high places.

Folded into its arms, I raised my power again. I had to think of a way to use it that wasn't like shooting off a cannon at a well-defended target. I felt it, caressed it if you will, trying to learn from it. "Tell me," I commanded it. "Show me what to do."

I didn't feel anything at first. Maybe it *had* been Mother Earth warning me my power was weaker here. But then I was back on the summit, standing beside Chanda and Jack. I saw my demon-kin savior in the distance, flying toward us. I hoped both demons were still with me. Then I saw the one that had saved me wink out of existence.

I reached out to see if I could feel it, if I could feel Ted or the Jacks. Nothing. I tried for the one demon unaccounted for. Silence.

I tried to focus again, to raise the power. I wasn't waiting for revelation – I was back in cannon mode. And then I felt it burn out like an old light bulb.

The Hitchhiker stood. His chair creaked. Slowly, he began walking through the snow, toward us, grinning.

"Oh, Nick," he said. "I've suffered you so long. So very long. This would be sad for you, but sorrow requires a whole universe to be felt. Don't despair. Nothing will be lost. Everything will become nothing."

"Chanda," I said, not knowing why or what even I meant to say. Goodbye?

She was silent, unmoving beside me. Jack, too. Evelyn or the Hitchhiker held them transfixed. Tabula rasa. I looked behind Phantom Evelyn to Human Evelyn. She, too, seemed a blank slate. Nothing happening upstairs.

"Evelyn!" I shouted. "Help!"

"Oh, Nash," Phantom Evelyn said. "Poor boy. Don't you know he and I are one? We are on the same side. We return to what we were."

"Don't flatter yourself," I said. "I meant the human Evelyn."

The Hitchhiker smiled now. "It's nothing, Nick. Nothing. No hurt, no harm. In a way, you will be like us. No thought. No pain. No loss. She will not leave me again."

I tried to reach out to Chanda, Jack, and Human Evelyn. My mind soared into each of them, but I felt no part of them inside.

"But some pain," the Hitchhiker said, "for you, Nick, in this last moment. Pain for keeping me from her. Pain for my pain. Loss for my loss."

He stood next to us now, reaching for Chanda. I had nothing left. I punched him – and met nothing.

Then the air blasted behind him, as Human Evelyn had blasted the air with her power and taken one of our demons away. Rising, taking form, and exploding into the night, Jason or Dad appeared in all his horror behind the Hitchhiker, reaching claws into the nothing that he was, but somehow, even so, finding something akin to flesh, something to take hold of. The demon ripped at the thing, and it tore in two, losing its too much like me human form in the process. Its divided pieces flew apart, each piece appearing like a small, swirling black cloud, separating from the other as if driven by a strong wind. The demon stood and raged, turning to Phantom Evelyn.

The swirling pieces of the Hitchhiker slowed, stopped, and then each began drifting back toward the other. I knew I only had moments to act before the tables turned again. I reached for my power, found it this time – and it spoke to me.

"Into *him*," the voice said, "and into *her*!"

I heard, but I didn't like what I heard. My options? None. Yet what my power was telling me to do would betray my only love, my Chanda, my beautiful Chanda. "No!" I shouted, refusing its knowledge.

"Nick," Chanda's voice came to me then, freed for a moment from the Hitchhiker's power, insisting. "You must! Do this for me!"

"I love you," I sent everything I felt for her back into her for the briefest second I was allowed. Then I listened because I loved her enough to lose her, if that was her wish. I reached for the floating halves of the Hitchhiker, driving them apart once more and bringing each half closer to Jack and Chanda. Then, with a force of power and will I sealed the halves of the Hitchhiker into my love and my friend, and I felt it become – nothing.

Phantom Evelyn screamed, "No!"

She stood and ran to Jack and Chanda, to undo whatever I had done. She swept my demon away and it flew from the summit, thrust away by her power. Then, behind her, my other demon-kin appeared, rending her in two, as the Hitchhiker had been. Like him, she lost her human form and drifted away, in pieces. Then it began to reverse the process, the pieces moving to rejoin and become one again.

My power had shown me the way. The only way. I reached out and took half of the Phantom. I found in Human Evelyn's mind an opening, a place that might not have existed until Phantom Evelyn or the Hitchhiker had subdued her consciousness and will. Into that opening, I took half of the Phantom and thrust it into the human Evelyn's mind.

Then I stood facing what was left. I felt it raising a terrible power then, not defeated, not undone. This time, I opened my only vessel left – myself, and I dragged that screaming bitch into my soul.

CHAPTER 43

Into my soul. Evelyn was there now – and not. She was nothing, but her power filled me. It was not the imprecise, doubtful power I'd had before. With it came an intelligence, knowledge of what it was, what it could do. So powerful was it that it would have consumed me had it not come with a confidence and understanding beyond anything I'd ever experienced. I stood there, at once who I was and more than I had ever been.

Beside me, Chanda screamed. Her mind had returned to her, but driven to the brink of madness. Her eyes opened wide, darting wildly at everything around us, lighting on nothing, seeing more than she could bear. Her hand reached up and tore at her skull, as if trying to rip something terrible away from her. I understood, not just what I was seeing, but the danger that came with it. Reflexively, I reached into her mind, finding my way around the power that now consumed her – a power without understanding of what it was, a thing neither she nor any human could comprehend. Except me.

By a force of my will, I calmed her, separated her mind from the power that now lived inside her. Slowly, her panic eased. Intelligence came back into her eyes, and she fell to her knees.

"Nick!" She said, her fear still trying to overwhelm her. "Oh, Nick, help me!"

"I'm with you," I said, kneeling and putting my arms around her. "I've got control of it. You're okay. I won't let go of you."

She cried, and turned, hugging me as tightly as she could.

"I'm afraid!"

"Don't be," I told her, confident, reassuring. "I can control it. I won't let you go."

Moments passed, and her fear left her, replaced by the knowledge that I would always be with her, protecting her.

Rational again, she asked, "What is it that's in me, Nick?"

"The Hitchhiker," I said. "All if his power is in you now."

"I can't control such a thing!" she said. "It is too much!"

"You don't have to," I said. "I'm here. We are one. My power is yours."

I looked up to see Jack running to the human Evelyn. I saw into each of them. Evelyn had been hostage, a distraction. She hadn't been with the Phantom or the Hitchhiker by choice of will. She fought as best she could, but she was theirs to do with as they would.

I saw more, too. Human Evelyn was purely human. Nothing of power resided in her now. No psychic ability, nothing to connect her with the travails of time and spirits. She would feel the loss, I saw, as an amputee would feel the loss of a limb. No, more than that. She would mourn the loss like she would the death of a close friend.

Jack. He was just Officer Smith again. No power, no influence over the living or the dead.

But there was more, too.

Jack reached Evelyn and embraced her, holding her firmly in his arms. She looked into his eyes, searching, lost but not lost. I smiled. Jack was taller than she was. She had to look up.

Neither was consumed with the power that had taken hold in Chanda and me. Yet, a power was there, of sorts. Perhaps the only redeemable parts of the Phantom and the Hitchhiker – the love that held them together as one, for an eternity, and which drew them together again, here on this planet earth. But it was pure now, kept from power and thought, longing and anger. They could join now, through Jack and Evelyn, and the world would go on, oblivious to their love.

I reached out for Ted and the Jacks. They were gone, lost. I knew I would weep, but not now.

I called Jason to me. The demon that had separated the parts of the Phantom walked toward me, powerful, ugly. My brother. I loved him.

I called my father. The demon that he was had taken wing and flew now to return to me. He landed before me and bowed his head.

"I want to take us back," I told them. "To my cabin. You saved us, both of you. You saved everything. It's time to relax and see what's next."

Jason shed his demon form then, shrinking into the brother I knew and loved. He stepped forward and hugged me.

"Not this time, Little Brother," he said. "Something is calling us. We are not for this world any longer."

I smiled. "I didn't tell you how much power I wrangled out of this deal. I can take you with me."

"No!" my demon father growled. "Love. Love you."

My father took wing once more and flew into the night.

Jason said, "It's not to be, Little Brother."

He shimmered and was gone.

Lost now were my brother, my father, and friends who had died and lost their souls trying to save us.

Chanda and I were one. I didn't have to think about her to share my power with her. It was hers as much as mine. Her power? That was a thing to be discovered.

EPILOGUE

"Before you try shattering my margarita glass again, dear boy," Phantom Evelyn said, "I feel I should tell you it would be a futile gesture. I am dead now. So, I wouldn't be impressed."

We were in the backyard again. Everything the same, except the golden retriever was a dog again and sprawled over Evelyn's lap. She sipped a fresh margarita. I noticed I had a fresh cigar and bourbon. So, it *wasn't* over. Evelyn was in control again. I felt panic rising inside of me. Somehow, despite everything, Evelyn had won.

"Oh, Nicholas," Evelyn said. "It *is* over. Really, try to relax. It's finished, dear boy. I told you I am dead, so to speak. In any event, I am not a threat to you."

Somehow, I felt she was sincere. I couldn't say why. It didn't make sense that she could be dead and sitting beside me. But what was dead? I hadn't been sure of that in a while.

I sought out my power, to use as a shield or cudgel, I wasn't certain. It was there, but it wouldn't obey me. It seemed to say, "Sorry, Bub. She's still got the goods."

Resigned that this was going to be another encounter I couldn't control, I looked at the bourbon and the cigar.

"The good stuff?" I asked.

"Only the best for you, my dear Nicholas."

I wondered how this could be. She and the Hitchhiker were defeated on the mountain, divided and contained.

"What do you mean, you're dead?"

"The thinking part of what I was, Nicholas, is gone. What you see of me now is a gift I've given you. This was with you before the end, for this moment. But I am not here. This is the last remnant of what I was, embedded into the power that you are now the keeper of."

"We stopped you," I said. "We contained you. But you're *not* dead. We couldn't kill you."

"Oh, but dear boy, you tried."

I felt a little guilty when I heard it stated so bluntly.

"We didn't see a choice."

"You didn't have one. I didn't give you one. You did as I wished."

"As *you* wished?" I was astonished. "You fought pretty hard."

"Yes," she said. "One of the many lies I was forced to impress upon you along the way. I do feel sorry for that. I never *wanted* to lie to you. As I said many times, I love you."

"Wait a minute," I said. "*We* rose up against *you*."

"And how did you do that?"

"We were given – power," I said. "I guess I still don't know exactly where it came from. I think it was life, all life, trying to defend itself. I'll get the answer soon enough. I just have to look."

"Because you're so powerful now, dear boy?"

"Yes," I said, a little smugly perhaps. "That's why."

Evelyn laughed. "Not everything I told you was a lie. Much of it was the truth. Here's another truth: you never had any power, not at the beginning and not at the end. The power you have been given, from me, is new to you. My dear boy, I was with you all along. Your healing, your abilities, your floating consciousness – all of that was me."

"The hell you say! And Jason? My father?" I was getting angry. "You turned them out from the dead to destroy me – to destroy us. To stop *us* from stopping *you*."

"And in the end? Whom did they serve?"

"Me. Us. We saved them from what you turned them into."

"I turned them loose to save you, dear boy. And your world."

"They tried to kill me!"

"And they failed, if that's what I wanted them to do."

"Look," I said, remembering all the visions, the lies, and manipulations Evelyn had heaped on me. "You've lost. I don't know what final game you think you're playing here, but...."

"That just it, Nicholas. I don't *think* anything anymore. I am like I once was, as I wanted to be again. Form without thought. Form living within the form of – let's call him Nicholas, shall we? Your other names for him are quite droll."

"The Hitchhiker? Why give him my name?"

"I think the easiest true way for you to think of him – and me – is as Nicholas and Evelyn."

"As usual, I don't get it."

"Remember the beach," she said. "The first one I took you to. Do you remember what he and I said to each other?"

"Yes. Very well."

"He was a part of you then, part of you since you were a boy because I created you to hold him. You are very much alike, you and him, which is why I love you so. And I created Evelyn to hold me, safe from him."

"You've told me time and again you're more powerful than he was. Why hide?"

"You do recall his intention to destroy me, don't you?"

"Yes."

"You do recall my telling you that I created all of this," she gestured toward the fence and the houses and the sky beyond.

"Yes."

"And you recall I told you how it diminished me, this creation?"

"Yes."

"Yet *he* created nothing. He merely sought to destroy what I had created – to rejoin with me. So, whom do you consider the stronger? Him with his essence intact, or me, diminished as I was?"

I wasn't sure I knew the answer.

"In the beginning," she continued, "before all of this, I was the stronger. Much stronger, which is why my thought became life in the first place. He could not have done it. But he didn't know how I had been weakened, or we wouldn't be sitting here."

"That's why you were hiding from *him*?"

"In Evelyn. She knew me as Al'an and Farvan. Really, she was quite gullible, but she was a child, so she can be forgiven."

I thought about it. I thought of the beach and my first realization that there was another being inside of me.

"He said he would destroy you using my power," I said. "He said I was awakening."

"You were doing nothing of the sort, dear boy," Evelyn laughed again. "I fed enough power into you for him to think it, but not enough to be dangerous."

I smiled. I was beginning to believe her.

"You told him you could destroy him. He believed you were stronger. You said you couldn't kill him because of his love for you."

"And I couldn't have, even if I could have," she said. "I was telling him and you the truth then. His love for me made it impossible for me to sacrifice him, even for this." Again, she gestured – at everything.

"I never had any power," I said, realizing it was true.

"Not until he was safely divided from his and I from mine. Now my power is yours, and his is in Chanda. Only our love for one another remains, in your friend Jack, and in my Evelyn."

"My God!" I nearly shouted. "You were playing *him* the whole time."

Evelyn smiled, "Dear boy, I was so much smarter than he was, though he was stronger. I convinced him I had changed, that I wanted to join with him, to be what we were. This kept him from using his power to destroy. He wanted me to come to him, willingly. But somehow he got the idea that you had a power that kept us apart."

"But I didn't."

"He didn't know that," she said. "I couldn't have stopped him without confusing him. It was never your power I sought to divide; it was his. Now his power and mine are yours and Chanda's."

The power she spoke of hadn't frightened me yet, but now, thinking about it gave me chills. I thought of the old adage, Power Corrupts, and Absolute Power Corrupts Absolutely. As Second Jack might say, it sure as shit corrupted the Hitchhiker.

"I see your thought," Evelyn said. "It is a truth. Understand, I was willing to see everything undone if I could not have faith that you and

Chanda would hold the power and use it – or not use it – with the necessary wisdom and compassion."

"How could you know that we would? How can you know it now?"

"As I said, I know nothing now. But you gave me faith. Your father and your brother were a test. Had you chosen to be pragmatic and destroy them instead of saving them, this would be gone. Had you not chosen to spare Evelyn when you thought she was Nicholas's creature, this would be gone. And Chanda, Nicholas. She is a healer. It is in the core of her being. I have faith I have chosen wisely."

I thought for a moment about the people I had killed. For those Evelyn had resurrected, I said, "Thank you."

"It was necessary," she told me. "For all that you've been through, for all that you are now, you are still a fragile human, fraught with weaknesses. If I hadn't taken that burden from your emotional being, we would not have prevailed."

"We?"

"We were always one in this, Nicholas," she said. "You and I. You just didn't know it. You can see now why I couldn't allow it."

"Yes, I suppose so," I said. "And now you are what you once were, but separate?"

"He and I, yes," she said. "Jack and Evelyn are who they always were, more or less. But they have no choice in love, I'm afraid. Their love is us. We will love one another for eternity. But apart, separate. This is how I have managed to keep my creation and my love alive."

"Jack and Evelyn are mortal," I said. "What happens when they're gone? For that matter, what happens to these powers Chanda and I have when we're gone?"

Evelyn smiled. "You may discover that each of you will live an extraordinarily long life."

"Really? How long?"

A long silence passed without an answer, and I found myself thinking of other lives that had passed.

"Can I do as you did?" I asked. "Can I restore life to the dead?"

She frowned.

"If you choose to, you may," she told me. "But I would ask you to consider the flow of existence before you make such a choice."

I thought of my family. My dad, mother, Jason, and Julie. I knew I would be very tempted.

"Of course, you would be," Evelyn read my thought. "They are like the ones I brought back. They died at Nicholas's hand, not yours. But lives are lost every day, unfairly. Murder abounds in this world, Nicholas. Disease. Tragedy."

"But I can change that," I told her. "If you're truly gone, nothing can stop me."

"I am truly gone, and nothing can stop you. My faith tells me you will stop you, however."

"What good is this power I've been given if I can't take the evil out of the world?"

"You must think of this existence as I have made it. Temporary. There is more beyond the reconciliation of ghosts and demons. Those secrets I have kept even from you."

I took a heavy sip of bourbon.

Fuck.

"Be patient," Evelyn concluded. "Knowledge will come to you in time. I have made it so."

We sat for a very long while. Evelyn sipped her margarita and said, "Were I able to do so, I would miss these."

I stood then, understanding that it would mean nothing, and I walked over to Evelyn. She looked up at me with those piercing, amazing blue yes.

"You are beautiful," I told her.

"Only because I chose to look this way," she replied.

"No," I said, and I reached down and put my hand over her heart. The dog licked my arm. "I mean you are a beautiful being."

I bent down and kissed her on the forehead.

"Thank you," she said, and tears flowed from her eyes, no crocodiles in sight.

"Will this be the last time I see you?"

"I'm afraid so," she said. "But I have one more gift for you. It will last for days, but you must know that it will have to end, and you will have to go back."

"Go back?"

"To Chanda," Evelyn said. "She loves you, and you will need each other for a very long time."

Evelyn shimmered then like the demons had whenever they left me. And she was gone. The dog stayed, and memory flooded me, a memory that had been long hidden. The dog! Sammy! My childhood dog. How had I forgotten her?

"Sammy," I cried, "come here!"

Sammy jumped into my lap and licked me like she hadn't seen me in a very long time – something like thirty years.

And then I recognized the yard I was sitting in. I was in my father's chair. It was our house in Castro Valley, many, many years ago.

The gate opened; Julie ran through it. Sammy jumped from my lap and ran to her and playfully knocked her to the ground, Julie laughing and giggling as Sammy licked her face and jumped all around her. Julie rolled to her side then, looking at me.

"Why are you crying?" she asked.

I couldn't answer.

She got up and came to my side, hugging me and kissing me on the cheek.

"You're all grown up," she said.

"Yes," I cried. "Yes, I am. And you're still a perfect little girl."

The back door opened, and I looked over onto the deck. My father was there, his arm around Jason, little Jason, no more than twelve.

"Hey, *Big* Brother," Jason laughed. "We're so happy you're home!"

Dad ran down the stairs and grabbed me under the arms, pulling me to my feet. He was still bigger than me, and stronger.

"Nick," he cried, hugging me hard. "I'm so sorry! I'm so sorry for what I did. Please, please forgive me! I love you son! I thought you were lost to me."

I remembered looking into my father's mind then, when he was dying – alone in that cold, wet gutter. Alone and wrecked. I remembered his hate. But I remembered it was borne of my father's seeing that something had killed my soul, that some *thing* had taken his son from him. He wasn't wrong, not completely. Part of me had been locked away, held prisoner by the Hitchhiker, just as my father perceived it. His hate was for the Hitchhiker, who he saw in me. How could a man untouched by the supernatural understand such a thing?

"I forgive you," I choked, seeing again the misery that his life had become. I mourned for the years lost to him. "You couldn't know what was happening. I love you, Dad. I love you!"

Jason followed Dad and he and Julie hugged me at my waist, crying.

"Is it really you?" I asked. "All of you?"

"I don't know how," Dad said. "But it's us. For a time. For a time."

Dad let go of me, and Jason and Julie grabbed my hands and led me up the stairs.

"Mom's cooking chocolate chip pancakes for dinner," Julie said. "She really wants to see you."

ABOUT THE AUTHOR

Michael Scott Hopkins is an attorney in Joliet, Illinois, where he lives with his wife of more than 30 thirty years, Carla; his golden retriever, Charlie; and two black cats named Lolli and Pop. He has an MA in English from Governors State University and graduated cum laude from The John Marshall Law School, where he was a member of The John Marshall Law Review. He and Carla have three sons, Tyler, Kyle, and Eric.

NOTE FROM THE AUTHOR

Word-of-mouth is crucial for any author to succeed. If you enjoyed *The Things in Heaven and Earth*, please leave a review online—anywhere you are able. Even if it's just a sentence or two. It would make all the difference and would be very much appreciated.

Thanks!
Michael Scott Hopkins

Thank you so much for reading one of
our **Supernatural Thriller** novels.
If you enjoyed the experience, please check out
our recommended title for your next great read!

There Are No Saints by Stephen Kanicki

"Kanicki weaves a great story with his invading evil spirits."

–Authors Reading

CPSIA information can be obtained
at www.ICGtesting.com
Printed in the USA
LVHW031038090721
692259LV00001B/70